DRAGON FIRE

Dina von Lowenkraft

Twilight Times Books
Kingsport Tennessee

Dragon Fire

Paladin Timeless Books, an imprint of
Twilight Times Books
P O Box 3340
Kingsport TN 37664
http://twilighttimesbooks.com/

First Edition, December 2013

Library of Congress Control Number: 2013920304

ISBN: 978-1-60619-291-7

Cover art © 2013 Renu Sharma

Printed in the United States of America.

To all who fight against prejudice and
strive to make our world a better place.

Acknowledgments

The path to becoming a published writer is long, and I would never have gotten here without the support of many people.

First of all, thank you to my mom, for loving everything I have ever written and for discussing my characters and their problems with me as if they were real. Thank you to my husband, for understanding my need for time and space to write – and giving me the opportunity to do so. Thank you to my son, for your eagerness to read the next chapter and making my science-based fantasy more realistic. Thank you to my daughter, for being proud of me long before anything was ever in print. Thank you to my family for understanding and making dinner or cleaning the house on all those occasions when 'I just need to finish this' took a bit longer than I expected.

Thank you to all my friends, family and acquaintances I have ever pestered with questions as I researched different aspects of this book - your help has been invaluable.

And to everyone who ever asked 'how's your writing going?' thank you! You'll never know how much that simple question means to an aspiring author.

But even with the support of my family and friends, my writing would never have improved enough to be published without the help of my writers groups. Thank you to everyone I have met along the way and in particular to my crit partners Jeannine, Karen, Mayra, Michelle, Natalie, Olivia and Sabrina. You have all helped make this manuscript better, and I am immensely grateful to each and every one of you.

In addition to my crit partners, I know I wouldn't be where I am today as a writer without the help and support of SCBWI. Through SCBWI I have met hundreds of other writers, illustrators and industry professionals – all inspiring people who work hard to make creative dreams come true. I am honored to be the Regional Advisor for Belgium and truly enjoy being able to give back to others some of what was given to me, even if I may never quite catch up on the debt that I owe.

But even with the help and support of my fellow writers, *Dragon Fire* wouldn't be published today without the enthusiasm and support of Lida Quillen and Twilight Times Books. Thank you for believing in my world of Draak and Elythia and giving me the opportunity to see my book in print – a dream come true for every writer.

And last, but not least, thank you to all who read *Dragon Fire*. I fell in love with Rakan and Anna as I was writing this, and hope you will too.

Dina
Bruxelles, 2013

In the Arctic winter, the sun never rises.
In the Arctic summer, the sun never sets.
In the Arctic, the world is at your feet.

Chapter 1

The Circle Tightens

THE CANDLE FLICKERED IN THE SUBZERO WIND BUT ANNA MADE NO MOVE TO protect it. She stopped on the hill in front of Tromso's three-year high school and watched the water of the fjord shimmer below. Even though it was mid-afternoon there was no sun, just the luminous reflection of the moon. The procession of students continued on without her, leaving only the fading sound of crunching snow in their wake.

"You seem as eager to go to Fritjof's memorial vigil as I am," June said, startling Anna with her sudden appearance.

Anna fingered the oval piece of bright orange coral that she had carried around like a talisman since she was a child. She usually kept it in her pocket, but today she wanted to feel its soothing energy closer and had it in her glove. She had never liked Fritjof, and even though she wasn't glad he had died, she wouldn't miss him.

She turned to face June whose cobalt blue eyes were at odds with her otherwise Asian features. June and her boyfriend had also been out on the mountain when the avalanche claimed Fritjof. "I'm glad it's not yours too," Anna said. "I'd really miss you."

"It would take more than an avalanche to kill me," June said, trying to smile. But Anna could feel her friend's pain lurking under the surface.

"Hey." She wrapped an arm around June to comfort her. But as soon as her hand touched June's shoulder, a burst of energy exploded from her stone. Anna ripped off her glove and the piece of coral went flying. "What the—"

June spun around, pushing Anna behind her as if to protect her from an attack. She scanned the area, her body tensed for a fight.

"Who are you looking for?" Anna pressed her palm to dull the pain as she glanced around the deserted hilltop. "Whatever it was, it came from my stone."

June relaxed her stance. "Are you okay?"

"I think so." Anna gestured towards the coral-colored sparks that crackled in the darkness of the Norwegian winter. "What do you think it's doing?"

"Don't know." June crouched down to get a better look. Her hand hovered as a bright green light flashed around the stone.

"Don't touch it," Anna said sharply. Her stone had always had a special energy, but never coral-colored sparks. Or green flashes of light.

"It's okay now." June pulled her hand back. "Look for yourself."

Anna knelt next to June. The stone was dark and lifeless and she felt a sudden pang of loss. She prodded it gingerly with her good hand, but felt nothing. She picked it up. It was just a pretty bit of coral. The gentle pulsing energy that she had liked so much was gone.

"Can I see it?" June asked.

Anna nodded, her throat constricted. The stone had always reminded her of her father. Its energy was something he would have been able to feel too. The only other person she had met so far who was open to that kind of thing was June. Everyone else got freaked out, or thought she was crazy. So she had learned not to talk about it.

June closed her fist around the stone. "Where did you get this?" Her voice wavered.

Anna's attention flicked back to June. She never wavered. "I found it in the mountains. Years ago. Why? What is it?"

"A trigger."

"A trigger for what?"

June returned Anna's searching look. "I have no idea." She handed the stone back.

"So how do you know it's a trigger?"

"I just feel it." June picked up the candles that lay forgotten in the snow. "If you're okay, we should go."

Anna picked up her discarded glove and froze. In the middle of her left palm was a star-shaped scar. She stretched her hand to get a better look. It was about the size of a dime. She touched it. Like an echo under the fading pain, she could feel the energy of her stone pulsing faintly in her palm.

"Here," June said, offering Anna a candle. She stopped mid-motion. "What is it?"

"I don't know. The stone…" She held out her palm. "Look."

June dropped the candles and took Anna's hand in hers. Gently, she ran her fingers over the slightly raised ridges of the scar. "A Firemark," June said as if talking to herself. "But how…?"

"What's a Firemark?" Anna examined the scar. It was almost silvery in the moonlight.

June looked up, her fingers still on Anna's palm. "It's like a living connection between two people. But… there was only the stone."

"It always felt alive," Anna said. She touched the Firemark one last time before putting her glove back on. It was warm and smooth.

June shook her head. "But even if it felt alive, it shouldn't have left a Firemark."

Anna shrugged. "Maybe. But I like it." Anna closed her hand around the Firemark. It felt like she was holding her stone. She smiled. She'd never lose it now.

June re-lit the candles again and handed one to Anna. "Ready?"

Anna hooked her arm through June's. "I think so." They walked silently through town and across the bridge that straddled the green-black fjord.

"Do you think it's over?" Anna eyed the Arctic Cathedral that sprawled like slabs of a fallen glacier on the other side of the fjord. It was lit up like a temple of light.

June shook her head. "It's only just begun."

"That's enough." Khotan's voice snapped like a whip across the barren land of Ngari in western Tibet. "You're not going to kill her. I will."

The wind howled in agreement. Rakan bit back the urge to argue with his father whose shaved head and barrel chest marked him as an Old Dragon. But Khotan's massive physique belied his diminishing power, and Rakan knew that his father wouldn't survive a fight with the female dragon they had finally located. He had felt her power when she had set off his trigger just a few hours before. And she was more powerful than any other dragon he had ever met. Rakan clenched his fists. Blood for blood. It was the Dragon Code. And he would be the one to honor it.

"You need to start a new life here," Khotan said, his hand like a claw of ice on Rakan's bare shoulder. "I will end the old."

His tone of voice, more than his touch, sent shivers down Rakan's spine. But before he could question his father, a flicker of red caught his attention and his older half-sister, Dvara, materialized on the sparring field. Except she wasn't dressed to fight. She was wearing a shimmering red gown that matched the color of her eyes and her black hair was arranged in an intricate mass of twisted strands.

"It's too late to teach Rakan anything." She made an unhurried motion towards the targets at the other end of the field. One by one, they exploded with her passing hand.

"We weren't practicing," Rakan said calmly. "Although if we had been, you'd need to start again. You used a trigger. You didn't manipulate their structure on a molecular level."

"Who cares?" Her Maii-a, the pear-shaped stone that every dragon wore to practice manipulating matter with, sparkled like an angry flame at her throat. "They've been demolished. And that's all that counts in a fight."

Rakan slid his long black braid over his shoulder. "How you fight is just as important as how you win."

"I'd rather stay alive," Dvara said. "But you can die honorably if you want."

"Neither one of you will fight anyone," Khotan said. "Remember that."

Rakan bowed his head. There was no point arguing about it now. But Dvara lifted her chin defiantly. "Kraal was my father. I will avenge his death."

Khotan growled and stepped towards Dvara, dwarfing her with his size. He held her gaze until she dropped her eyes. Rakan shook his head, wondering why Dvara always tried to challenge Khotan's authority in an open confrontation that she was sure to lose. Khotan was the guardian of her rök, her dragon heart and the seat of her power, and she had no choice but to abide by his will.

Their mother, Yarlung, appeared without warning. "I will speak with Rakan'dzor." She crossed her arms over her white gown that sparkled with flashes of turquoise. "Alone."

She waited, immobile, until Khotan and Dvara bowed and dematerialized, shifting elsewhere. As soon as they were gone, her face relaxed and she turned to Rakan, her nearly blind eyes not quite finding his. "I always knew you would be the one to find her," she purred. "You have the strength and the will of my bloodline. And the time has come for you to use it." Yarlung tilted her face to the wind. "Kraal gifted me his poison before he died. Neutralized, of course."

"But no one can neutralize dragon poison."

"Kairök Kraal was a great Master. His death is a loss for us all."

Rakan struck his chest with his fist. "Paaliaq will pay for his death with her own."

"Yes. She will. And you will help me." A faint smile played on her usually austere face. "I will mark you with his poison so that we can communicate when necessary."

"Khotan and Dvara have a full link, isn't that enough?"

"You don't expect me to rely on secondhand information, do you?" snapped Yarlung. She paused and spoke more gently. "Or are you scared to carry Kraal's poison?"

Rakan knelt down in front of Yarlung. "I will do whatever it takes to kill Paaliaq." His voice cut through the arid cold of the Tibetan plateau.

Yarlung's eyes flashed momentarily turquoise and Rakan stepped back as she morphed into her dragon form. She was a long, undulating water dragon and the scales around her head and down her throat glistened like wet opals. Without warning, a bluish-white fire crackled around him like an electric storm. His mother's turquoise claws sank into his arms and pain sizzled through his flesh. The fire disappeared and Rakan collapsed to the ground, grinding his teeth to keep from screaming in agony.

He would not dishonor his family.

"No, you won't," Yarlung said in his mind.

Rakan's head jerked up in surprise.

"You have just become my most precious tool." Her voice hummed with pleasure. *"You will not fail me."*

As suddenly as the contact had come, it was gone. And so was his mother. Rakan didn't like it. Not her disappearance. That was normal. Yarlung had always been abrupt. But he didn't like hearing her in his mind. It was something only dragons who were joined under a Kairök, a Master Dragon, could do. Few dragons were able to survive the rush of power that happened when their röks awakened without the help of a Kairök. But Rakan had.

He gritted his teeth and stood up. If sharing a mind-link with Yarlung was necessary to kill Paaliaq, then he would learn to accept it.

He held his arms out to examine the dragons that had appeared where his mother's claws had dug into his biceps. They were long, sinuous water dragons like Yarlung. But they were black, the color of purity, the color of Kraal. Rakan watched the miniature turquoise-eyed dragons dance on his arms until they penetrated under his skin. He felt a cold metallic shiver deep inside as they faded from view.

A rush of pride exploded in Rakan and he raised his arms to the frozen winter sky, the pain like a blood pact marking his words. "I will avenge your death, Kairök Kraal. Earth will become our new home and your Cairn will once again prosper."

"You can drop me here." Anna glared at her mother's boyfriend who reminded her of his namesake: a wolf.

Ulf turned the car into Siri's driveway and flashed his all too perfect smile. "Not unless you want me to carry you in. Your shoes aren't practical for walking in the snow."

Anna snorted. "You're one to talk. You're the one driving a sports car in the winter." And she didn't feel like having her teammates from the handball team see it.

Ulf threw his head back and laughed. "I only take it out for special occasions. Like New Year's." He leaned towards her. "Especially when I have the honor of accompanying a lovely lady."

"You're not accompanying me. You're dropping me off."

"Precisely." He pulled up in front of the house that pulsed with music, revving his engine one last time. He jumped out of the car and got to her side just as she was opening her door. He offered her his arm. "And since I'm a gentleman, I'll accompany you to the door."

Anna ignored Ulf and struggled to get up while the dress she had decided to wear did its best to slide all the way up her thighs. Ulf moved to steady her as she wobbled in the high heels she wasn't used to wearing but she pushed him away. Her shoes slipped on the icy snow and she grabbed the railing, wondering why she had decided to wear them.

"It would be easier if you'd accept my help."

"I don't need your help," she said, walking up the stairs. When he followed anyway, she turned to face him. "Don't you have anything better to do?"

"As a matter of fact… no," said Ulf. He straightened his white silk scarf that didn't need straightening. "Ingrid won't be off work until eleven."

The evening was cold and Anna regretted wearing a dress. "You're not coming in."

"We can stand out here, if that's what you prefer," said Ulf, looking up at the sky.

Randi opened the door. "Anna! Finally," she squealed. She threw herself at Anna. "I didn't know you were bringing someone."

"I'm not," Anna said. "He's leaving. Now."

Randi glanced at Ulf who was leaning elegantly against the railing in what could have passed for a golden boy fashion shot. "Is that your boyfriend?" Randi asked hanging onto Anna. She looked Ulf up and down. "Is that why you didn't come earlier?"

"Let's go in," Anna said, trying to get Randi back in the house.

Ulf slid an arm around Randi's waist. "Perhaps I can help."

"Oh sure," Randi said. She giggled as she leaned into Ulf. "You have a nice… car."

"Leave her alone." Anna pried Ulf's wandering hands away from Randi who was happily wrapping her arms around Ulf's neck. "Randi, knock it off."

"Oh, I'm sorry." Randi pushed away from Ulf. "He's yours. I forgot."

"I'll take her," said Siri, steadying Randi. "That way you guys can come in and take your coats off."

"Ulf has a date," Anna said. She blocked the door after Siri and Randi disappeared inside. "With my mom. Or have you forgotten?"

"Sweet little Anna." Ulf reached out to touch her cheek with his leather gloved hand.

Anna slapped it away. "Get away from me."

"You're so adorable when you're angry," he said with a laugh. "Call me when you want me to come for you."

Anna resisted the impulse to slam the door and closed it calmly instead. The living room was packed with people dancing. She rubbed her forehead and walked over to the dining room table that was laden with food and drinks instead. She'd never understand her mom's taste in men.

Siri came and nudged her shoulder. "Where's the guy you came with?"

"Gone," she answered, rolling her eyes. "Finally."

"He didn't look your type," Siri said with a shrug. "But you never know."

"He's not. He's my *mom's* boyfriend. And he's a jerk."

Siri's hand hovered over the massacred chocolate cake. "That's a mess."

"Tell me about it." Ulf was by far the worst of her mom's recent boyfriends. He was a liar and a manipulator. But her mom never saw beyond a pretty face.

Siri dropped her voice. "Have you seen June? Is she coming?"

"No. She went away with her boyfriend and his family for the vacation." Anna noticed Siri's look of relief. "Why?" she asked sharply.

"I was worried that maybe she didn't feel welcome. And I felt guilty. I mean... I'm really sorry about Fritjof." Siri paused. "But I'm starting to wonder why I thought some of his ideas were good. I know you never liked him. But... I thought he was right. About June being different and the need to keep our race pure and all that." Siri looked away. "I'm embarrassed I let myself believe any of it."

"He was persuasive, I guess." Anna tried not to rub it in, but she was happy that at least one friend was coming back around.

"Maybe. But I really am sorry."

"Tell June after the break." Anna put her glass up to Siri's. "She'll understand."

"Why are you girls being so serious?" boomed Anna's cousin, Red. He put an arm around each of them. "There's music. You should be dancing. Or aren't there any nice guys?"

"Anna never thinks there are any nice guys. But I see a few." Siri raised her glass and headed across the room that had started to get crowded now that a slow song was playing.

"What are you doing here?" Anna playfully punched her cousin who was built like a rugby player. "You graduated last year. You're not part of the team anymore."

"We told the guys that we'd be back," said Red, nodding to where his best friend, Haakon, was surrounded by half the boys' team. "But we can't stay — we promised the girls we'd go to a dinner party. And they'll kill us if we're late." Red and Haakon had dominated the court with their size and skill for the past three years, but neither of their girlfriends played.

"I'm surprised they even let you out of their sight." Anna waved a finger at her cousin who had the same ultra blond hair and pale blue eyes as she did. "I've hardly seen you at all this vacation."

"I know. We've been busy. But I'm here now." The music picked up again. "Dance?" He took her hand and then dropped it as if he had been stung. He grabbed her wrist and turned her palm up, revealing the star-shaped Firemark. "Who did this?" he growled, his face turning the telltale shade of red that had earned him his nickname.

Anna pulled her hand out of his and closed her fist. "No one."

"A mark like that can't just appear."

"Why do you care what did it?"

"What do you mean *what* did it?" Red gripped her shoulders. "You were the one…?" Red's voice trailed off, but his eyes bore into hers as if he was trying to peer into her mind.

Anna pulled back, breaking the contact. "What are you talking about?" She hadn't said anything about what had happened on the hill and June had left town right after the vigil.

Red laughed, but Anna could still feel his anger like a tightly coiled snake. "Nothing," he said. "Let's dance."

Dvara paced around the massive table that filled the stone hall of Khotan's lair. "Why are we waiting? Paaliaq has had more than enough time to hide again."

"That is for Kairök Yarlung to decide," Khotan said, using Yarlung's official title as the head of their Cairn. As Kraal's mate, she had taken over after his death.

"She's too busy with her political games to think about it." Dvara snorted. "She's never had time for us anyhow."

Rakan looked up from the intricate wire sculpture he was making. "Maybe she just wants to make sure you won't throw yourself at Paaliaq in a hotheaded rage."

"I'm no fool." Dvara leaned over the table towards her half-brother. "I won't attack until I'm certain to win. But I will attack. Unlike some I know."

Rakan stood, towering over her. "What's that supposed to mean?"

"Sit," Khotan said from his high-backed burgundy chair at the head of the table. "Both of you." He waited until they complied. "The only reason you're going instead of one of us is because Paaliaq won't recognize you. Unfortunately, neither one of you is experienced enough to trap Paaliaq on your own." Khotan looked from one to the other. "You'll have to work together. Remember that."

"But why did she set off one of Rakan's old triggers?" Dvara hit the table with her fist. "It makes no sense. Even a newborn whelp would have felt what it was before touching it."

Khotan created a burgundy colored fireball that floated in front of him. "Either she isn't Paaliaq, or she's luring you into a trap." The stone walls reflected the warm glow of the fireball. "This isn't a game. And I wish we didn't have to send you." Khotan's face went blank for a split second as it always did when he spoke mentally with another dragon. "Yarlung bids us come to Lhang-tso," he said, standing up. "Now." Khotan disappeared without a sound, the fireball still suspended in midair.

Dvara followed in her stepfather's trail, leaving Rakan to arrive last on the silver shores of the intensely blue lake that was Kairök Yarlung's home. They faced the lake in their dragon forms. Khotan, an air dragon, rose on his burgundy hind legs and bellowed their arrival.

The blue-white coils of Yarlung's water dragon form undulated majestically in the center of the crescent shaped lake. Rakan had always felt a sense of awe in front of his mother's abode. Something about its starkness, the pungent salty flavor of the wind that rolled off the lake, the beauty of the contrasting red hills that surrounded it in the thin air of its 4,500 meter high perch had always made him feel like he was in the presence of something profound. He smiled and rocked back onto his own hind legs, stretched his majestic coral wings and added his greetings to his father's. Neither animal nor plant life ventured near the lake. They were refreshingly alone. And free.

Dvara, a compact fire dragon with only the shortest of wings, dug her claws into the ground. She raised her jewel-like vermillion head and joined her voice to the others'.

Yarlung approached the edge of the lake and morphed into her human form. She signaled for them to do the same. Flashes of turquoise glinted off her metallic white dress. Rakan knelt next to his father and Dvara, his right fist on the center of his chest where his rök pounded in excitement.

"Rise. It is time," Yarlung said, her voice snapping like thunder. "If the dragon who set off Rakan's trigger is Paaliaq, I will savor her death." Yarlung paused and then spoke again, more quietly. "If not, I will bind her to me by taking her rök whether she wills it or not. But I believe she is Paaliaq. Too many things confirm it. Including the presence of a male dragon who can only be her mate, Haakaramanoth."

The wind howled across the lake.

"From what our scouts have been able to gather these past three weeks," Khotan said, "she has created the illusion of being an untrained whelp and goes by the name Jing Mei. But don't be fooled by her innocent appearance."

Yarlung's nostrils flared. "If she even begins to suspect who you are, she'll kill you. Pretend you're untrained. Take your time and get close to her. But not too close. Only one member of her Cairn is left and she will want to possess you both. Starting with Rakan'dzor. She has always preferred males."

"But the Code forbids blood relatives to have the same Kairök," Rakan said.

Yarlung snorted. "Paaliaq has no honor. Never forget that." She turned to Khotan. "Give Dvara back her rök. Paaliaq will be suspicious if she doesn't have it."

"But the risk…" stammered Khotan.

"Is of no consequence. Do it. Now. And then bind her to you as Kraal taught you."

"No," said Khotan. "It's too dangerous."

"Have you become so frail that you can no longer master even that?"

Khotan bowed his head. "May your will be done," he said, saying the traditional formula of submission to a Kairök. But Rakan could feel his father's anger.

Dvara tilted her chin and gave Rakan a look of triumph. She had wanted her rök back ever since Yarlung had declared that he would keep his and remain independent. But learning to control his rök had been harder than he had let on. Starting with when he had morphed for the first time not knowing which of the three dragon forms he would take. But even after he knew he was an air dragon, his rök's wild power had nearly overwhelmed him. It wasn't until Khotan had taught him to control his emotions that he could morph without fear of involuntarily killing himself or his family.

Khotan walked over to Dvara, his fluid black pants snapping in the wind. They stood still, facing each other as equals even though Khotan loomed over Dvara's delicate figure. Khotan began a low chant in Draagsil, the ancient language of the dragon race. He lifted his arms to the sky, his bare chest glistening like armor. Energy crackled and began to circle him. It spun faster and faster until Khotan was nothing more than a shimmering mirage in front of Dvara. A faint drum-like beat began, steadily increasing in tempo as it grew louder. Suddenly, the wind died and the beating stopped. A mass of pure vermillion energy licked Khotan's hands like the flames of a fire. The energy condensed in a flash of vermillion light, leaving a bright red stone in Khotan's palm. Dvara's dragon heart.

Khotan held the egg-shaped rök to the sky before releasing it to hover above Dvara's head. It glittered like a crown jewel. "My will has been done. You are now your own master. May your will be one with your rök."

A red flame moved up Dvara's gown, circling her body until it reached her rök. The rök ignited in a ball of wild energy. It spun around her in an uncontrolled frenzy. It was going to kill her. Rakan sprang forward, desperate to catch Dvara's rök before it was too late, but Khotan stopped him. "No. Their reunion can't be interfered with. It must run its course. For better or for worse."

The rök lurched. Rakan stood ready to intervene if things got worse. Whether he was supposed to or not, he wouldn't stand by and watch her die. A brilliant flash of intense vermillion encompassed Dvara, knocking her to the ground.

Yarlung snorted in contempt. "Tend to her."

Khotan knelt next to Dvara and touched a hand to her forehead, healing her with his energy. She latched onto Khotan, her red eyes echoing the wildness of her rök.

"Come," Khotan said, helping her to stand. "Do you accept of your own free will that I mark you with Kraal's neutralized poison and bind you to me in a partial link?"

"I do."

"And do you understand the consequences of this act?"

Yarlung growled her impatience, but Dvara didn't take her eyes from Khotan's.

"I do," Dvara said solemnly.

"What consequences?" thought Rakan, glancing at his mother. But she ignored him.

Khotan morphed and sank his claws into Dvara's bare arms. Rakan watched, horrified, as Dvara writhed by the edge of the lake in a mixture of rapture and agony. A black winged air dragon with burgundy eyes danced on each arm before fading under her skin.

"Go now," Yarlung said, her words lingering for just a moment after she disappeared.

"Rakan…"

"Yes, Father?"

"If you need to contact us, send a message through Dvara."

Rakan nodded, confused. Didn't his father know that Yarlung had marked him too?

Khotan disappeared. It was time.

Chapter 2

Back to School

ANNA SAT IN THE KITCHEN WINDOW RUBBING THE STAR ON HER PALM. IT WAS a perfect morning. The mountains across the fjord gleamed in the moonlight and the snow reflected the peaceful radiance of the never setting moon. Plus, Ulf hadn't come back after going out last night. It was the kind of morning Anna wished she had had more of over the vacation.

"Why are you sitting in the dark?" Ingrid flipped on the light that bounced off the window, turning it into a black mirror that blocked the view of the outdoors.

"Because I didn't think you'd be getting up." Anna scowled. The bright kitchen suddenly felt like a cage that was closing in on her.

"And you can't turn the lights on without me?"

"I just—"

"—like to see outside," her mother finished for her. "Just like your father."

Anna looked at her mom, surprised. The subject of her father was taboo.

"I'm glad you're up early," continued Ingrid. "I think we need to have a little chat."

Anna braced herself. Having a 'little chat' had never been a good thing.

"I think I'm finally ready to have a real relationship with someone again." Ingrid twisted her wedding band around her finger. "I gave Ulf keys to the apartment last night."

Anna glared at her mom. She was lying. The spare pair had been missing for at least a week.

"I know it might seem a bit fast to you," Ingrid said, misinterpreting Anna's silence. "But it really is different with Ulf." Ingrid waited for a response, but none came. "He suggested we keep both apartments for now, to give you some time to adjust. He said that it might be hard for you to accept him since he's so much younger than me. He really wants you to feel comfortable with this. He even suggested that maybe you could spend some time together – he loves being outdoors as much as you do. And I don't. Not since your father…"

"…died," said Anna, finishing the sentence her mother never could.

"Didn't come home," snapped Ingrid.

Anna shrugged and looked back out the window, even though she couldn't see anything. "Whatever." Her father hadn't come home from his solo expedition to the North Pole ten years ago. And her mother still couldn't face the facts. About that or anything else.

Ingrid took a deep breath. "I'm sorry, honey. I didn't mean to react that way. What I'm trying to say is that maybe you and Ulf could go skiing one afternoon."

"No."

"Can't you give him a chance? It means a lot to me."

Anna glowered at her mother's reflection.

Ingrid sighed. "Ulf said you'd probably refuse and I shouldn't worry about it. He says it's normal for a seventeen-year-old to be jealous of her mother's boyfriend, especially when he's young enough that he could've been yours. But I didn't think you were like that."

"Mom. Believe me, I'm not jealous. I just don't like him. He's a total jerk."

Ingrid's pale skin flushed bright red. "There isn't a more honest or hard working man than Ulf. In spite of being only twenty-six, he's a brilliant cultural anthropologist. And part of his work is observing how people interact in nightclubs."

"Yes, I know. He keeps telling us that."

Ingrid blinked. "So what's the problem?"

"He's a liar and his idea of research is running around," Anna said, unable to control her anger any longer. "He doesn't even care about you."

"Is that what this is all about? You're worried he doesn't love me? I know I've had a lot of men in and out of my life since… in the past ten years… but this time it's different. You'll see. It'll be okay." Her mother came and gave her a hug. "I love you, too, honey."

Even though it was early, Anna got up and pulled on her outdoor clothes. With a little luck, her mother's new toy boy wouldn't last any longer than any of the others anyway. And her mom wouldn't be hurt, yet again.

The arctic air nipped Anna's cheeks. She stopped on the slope to look up, expecting to see the bright green Northern Lights. But they weren't there. And yet she had felt something. The star on her palm throbbed and Anna closed her eyes. She felt the power of the mountains that jutted up around the island town. If only she could somehow slip into them and away from the city that was just beginning to wake up.

Rakan sank onto the couch of the rooms that Khotan had arranged for them at the Tibetan House in Tromso, run by one of the few Tibetan nuns in Northern Norway. They were enrolled at the local high school under their Tibetan names: Dawa and Pemba Ngari. Rakan snorted. At least Dawa sounded like Dvara. But Pemba didn't even come close to his name and he hated it. It made him sound like a puppy. He closed his eyes for a moment. The shift from Tibet to the arctic town where Jing Mei had set off his trigger had been complicated. He had followed Dvara through the deeper rock that she preferred, being a fire dragon, instead of shifting through the surface layer that was easier for him as an air dragon. He had wanted to make sure she would be okay. It was her first time shifting on her own and he knew how tricky it could be.

Slowly, his breathing became more regular and he opened his senses to what was going on around him. Dvara, whose special skill was in triggers, was checking for detecting devices that the local dragons could have planted. And he could feel the nun, Ani-la, meditating in the room below.

Rakan focused on the multi-colored prayer flags that hung in the windows. His specialty was tracking and the bits of cloth were the easiest source from which to identify the scent of everyone who had been in the apartment in the past six months. He ran through them quickly, but there had only been humans. He mentally catalogued them in case he came across one again. Humans were no threat in and of themselves, but they were easy to manipulate and Paaliaq and Haakaramanoth would probably use them to set traps or gather information. Dragons considered humans as nothing more than animals. Or worse, as targets to practice on. But Rakan didn't agree. Humans were too similar to dragons in their humanoid form.

Dvara finished her scan and turned to Rakan. "No alarms or other triggering devices. The house is as sparse and clean as it looks. Any interesting trails?"

Rakan shook his head. "Only humans for as far back as I can trace."

"They weren't expecting us," Dvara said. "Although they know we're here now, since we didn't even try to hide our arrival." Dvara opened the doors to the two small bedrooms. The only decorations were a couple of hanging scrolls. "We should put up a shield. But it can't be too sophisticated or our cover of being untrained will be blown."

"Go ahead." Neither one of them was a shielder. "I trust your judgment." And he still needed to scan the trails outside.

"Thanks, *Pemba*."

Rakan let it slide and looked out the window at the street below. It was covered with trails. He let his mind roam, following the different trails as they meandered across town. He caught a trace of Jing Mei and the thrill of the hunt hit him. He reached out with his rök and connected with Dvara. Although they couldn't have a true link and mind-speak, the blood bond of having the same mother, even though they had different fathers, meant they could have a partial link. It was limited to impressions and emotions, but since they had been trained together, they usually knew what the other would have said. It was an invaluable tool for tracking and hunting together.

"Ready to play?" He snatched his sister's bright red scarf, the one touch of color in her otherwise all-black outfit.

"Idiot." She mentally maneuvered the scarf out of Rakan's hands.

Rakan smiled. He could feel her excitement even if she didn't want to show it.

"We'll go see Ani-la later," she said. She narrowed her eyes. "This is our hunt. We decide what needs to be done. Okay?"

"We're only supposed to find out if Jing Mei is Paaliaq. And trap her if she is."

Dvara scoffed. "Scared of Mommy and Daddy? Or do you think Yarlung had Khotan give me back my rök but didn't expect us to act independently and kill Paaliaq?"

Rakan didn't answer. Dvara was impulsive and headstrong. She didn't have the self-control it would take to set up a successful attack against a dragon as powerful, and experienced, as Paaliaq. Especially since they'd have to neutralize Haakaramanoth first.

"They've trained us to kill. And you know it," Dvara continued. "Khotan is too old, and even when he was young he was no match for Paaliaq. He's a strategist, not a warrior. He'd be dead before the fight started."

Rakan agreed. And he wasn't about to let his father fight Paaliaq. But what Dvara didn't realize was that she wouldn't last any longer than Khotan. She had no training in controlling her rök by herself and it would be easy for a more experienced dragon to take it if they morphed into their dragon forms. And they'd have to morph to kill Paaliaq. "Let's go," he said, impatient with the whole situation. He could feel the other two shapeshifting dragons nearby. And one was radiating so much energy it felt like a gong pounding across an open plain. He had never felt anything like it. Pure raw energy. It could only be the elusive Paaliaq.

"I'm ready, but you're not," Dvara said. "You forgot your colored contact lenses."

Anna wasn't surprised to see the schoolyard nearly empty. Most people went into one of the student lounges when it was below zero out. But June was outside, as usual. Anna smiled. June often acted more Norwegian than many of the students who had grown up in Tromso, and it was easy to forget that she was an exchange student from California. They were the same age and had quickly become friends even though June was in the third year and Anna in the second.

"I'm glad you're back." Anna gave her friend a hug. "Did you see the e-mail about the extra handball practice tonight?"

June turned and showed Anna her sport bag. "Wouldn't miss it for the world." She laughed and then paused. "I just wish Lysa was feeling better."

Anna felt a pang of guilt and looked away. She hadn't even tried to contact Lysa and probably should have. Because even though they'd had a falling out before the avalanche, Anna was sure that Lysa needed all the support she could get. Fritjof had been her boyfriend. "I'll try to call her later."

"She won't answer. Her family thought she needed some more time. They won't be back for another week or two." June didn't sound too happy about it, but then again, June was dating Lysa's brother, Erling.

"I'll leave a message." Anna looked at her watch. "We should go – the bell's about to ring."

She turned to walk toward the main building, but pulled up short when she felt something touch her, as if the wind had grown hands. She backed up, but still felt it. Her palm tingled. "What...?"

June was staring across the schoolyard towards the entrance but snapped back to look at Anna. "You felt that?"

The feeling disappeared. "What was it?"

June didn't answer. She was leaning against the wall, just as she had been before. Except that she was staring at the gate as if she expected someone to walk in. A little later two students Anna didn't recognize walked into the schoolyard. They were lithe and graceful, even with their biker boots. They reminded her of black panthers. One male, one female.

Anna watched as they walked nonchalantly towards the main building and disappeared inside. She tried to put her finger on what made them look different. "They didn't look cold," she said, suddenly realizing that they hadn't been wearing hats or gloves. Although the girl had a red scarf.

June laughed and hooked her arm through Anna's. "No, I'm sure they weren't." They walked into the school and merged with the crowd. "See you later," June said as they were about to separate on the second floor landing. "Oh, wait. I forgot to give you your Christmas present. It's a Chinese good luck charm. Sorry I didn't wrap it." June dropped a small jade medallion in Anna's hands and ran up to the third floor where the third year students had class.

Anna stopped to look at the delicate green medallion as the stairwell emptied. It was beautiful, and so detailed that the dragon looked like it should come alive. It looked a little like a serpent, except that it had four feet – each with five claws. Anna smiled, the emerald dragon's ferocious face made it look like a protective guardian. She wrapped her hand around it. It felt alive, just like her stone used to feel. She sat on the stair and put it on her necklace with the golden heart that her father had given her when she was little. He had said it would keep her safe. And she had always wished she had given it to him when he had gone on his expedition. He had needed it more than she did.

"Oh, Anna – are you alright?" Mrs. Johansen, the school's librarian-like secretary, came up the stairs followed by the two new kids. "You're going to be late for class."

Anna tucked her necklace back under her turtleneck and scrambled to her feet. "I'm on my way." But she just stood there, watching.

The secretary turned to the dark-haired girl. "Dawa, this is Anna Strom. She's also in the second year, but in the other homeroom. She plays on the Tromso handball team."

Anna smiled and held out her hand, but Dawa averted her eyes.

"Anna, this is Dawa's brother, Pemba Ngari," continued Mrs. Johansen. "He'll be in the third year."

When Anna met Pemba's gaze, she felt a tingle around her. As if invisible hands were trying to touch her. She looked around wondering where it was coming from and then focused back on Pemba. There was something familiar about him, but she was certain she had never seen him before. She would have remembered him with his dark-toned skin and pitch black hair that was pulled back from his face, showing off his high cheek bones and broad forehead. He had an animal-like quality that made him seem pulsingly alive. And she liked it.

"Can you take Dawa to her homeroom while I bring Pemba up to the third floor?" asked Mrs. Johansen. "And maybe you can show Dawa around during lunchtime – she was asking about handball. Alright, shall we?"

"What? Yes, of course," Anna said, still staring into Pemba's eyes. They were brown, like all Asians she had ever seen, but somehow on Pemba it looked wrong. She watched as Mrs. Johansen escorted Pemba upstairs, mesmerized by the slow movement of his long black braid that twitched like a tail. Finally she turned to Dawa, who was waiting patiently next to her.

"When did you arrive?" Anna asked as they walked down the second floor hall. She glanced at Dawa who had some of the same look as Pemba. But whereas Pemba felt like he was ready to fly into action, Dawa felt like a delicate flower.

"This morning," said Dawa, her voice neutral.

"From Tibet?"

Dawa gave a faint nod that Anna couldn't decipher.

"Did you play handball there?"

"Yes."

"Well, we have practice this afternoon." Anna wondered how Dawa could play handball if she was so shy. "You can come watch."

"Can I play?"

"I don't know," Anna said, eyeing Dawa again. She knocked on the door to Dawa's new homeroom and introduced her. "I'll come pick you up for lunch," she said and went across the hall to her own homeroom.

"Sorry I'm late," she said to her teacher, Berit Knudsen, who was also the local team's handball coach. "I was with the new girl who wants to join the team."

"I didn't know we were expecting any new students," said Coach Knudsen. "Where was she playing before?"

"In Tibet. Somewhere."

A couple of the other students laughed. Coach Knudsen raised her hand. "That's enough. Anyone who wants to play is welcome. Remember that. Anna, take a seat."

Anna took out her books, trying to imagine Dawa playing handball. But couldn't. Gymnastics maybe. But not handball. Pemba, on the other hand, looked like he should play. He was as tall as her cousin Red, but not as massive. His movements had been fluid and powerful. Effortless, even. Like he could hang in the air as he was about to throw the ball... but there was something disconcerting about his eyes. They hadn't seemed natural. Or maybe it was their hypnotic effect that made her want to run her hands up his chest and rip off his shirt... Anna's heart raced as her thoughts caught her by surprise.

Anna wrapped her hand around the jade pendant and forced herself to focus, blocking everything – especially Pemba – out of her mind.

Rakan sat on the bleachers of the local sports hall with a group of boys from the high school, wondering just how far he could play with Jing Mei – or June as they called her here. Better to err on the safe side and keep his powers leashed. She had reacted immediately that morning when he let his mind wander over the school as clumsily as he could manage, pretending to be an untrained acolyte. But he still couldn't understand her reaction. She had shielded the human next to her – who had actually reacted to his touch. But Paaliaq was ruthless. She didn't even care about other dragons, so why would she care about a human? And even more puzzling, how could a human have felt him?

Rakan waved cheerfully to Dvara as she walked onto the court with Anna. He looked seriously at the human girl for the first time. The only thing he remembered about her was her hair that was so pale it looked almost white. And that she was taller than most humans. She had square shoulders and an open face that reflected all her emotions – which she didn't even try to hide. And right now she was confused. Rakan watched her as she introduced his sister to the others and then started to warm up. She was agile and athletic and he found himself absorbed by her movements. Finally, she turned and returned his stare. He looked away, only to meet June's eyes. He felt a heady rush of her power and wondered how he had let himself be caught off guard. He hadn't even felt her come out of the locker room. At least it would help confirm the disguise that they were putting up of being untrained. He pushed his curiosity about Anna out of his mind. All they needed to know was why she was important to June. Nothing else.

The girls began a game and Rakan let his mind roam around the gym. He had already identified most of the people there from school, but there were a few others, including the couple that had brought June. He let his mind wander back to them. The guy had the bulky mass of an Old Dragon and Rakan had already checked him several times, but he didn't have a rök or a Maii-a and his trail was typically human. Rakan turned away – they were involved in each other and totally unaware of his presence. Just like all the other humans. He let his mind wander even farther. He hadn't felt the other dragon since they had arrived. It was as if he had vanished, leaving Jing Mei inexplicably alone.

Confused and frustrated by the male dragon's disappearance, Rakan focused back on the handball practice. He could feel Dvara's thrill as she played. Jing Mei – June, he reminded himself – was goalie and Dvara was attacking. Rakan smiled as his sister played, gently increasing the pressure of her attacks that June blocked easily. But then June began to let some balls slip by on purpose. She had backed off. Rakan sat up. If Jing Mei was Paaliaq she would never have allowed an apparent novice to think she could get by her defenses. Or was it part of her disguise?

Chapter 3

Questions

OBLIVIOUS TO THE COLD, RAKAN SAT PERCHED IN THE OPEN WINDOW OF THEIR apartment, watching the street below. He liked picking out each person's scent from the many interwoven trails spread out everywhere. Tracing where they had been and where they went. It was a huge three dimensional maze that was in constant flux. And being so close to the center of it made the small arctic town seem like a living animal of pulsing threads.

"It doesn't make sense," Dvara said, interrupting his tracking. "Did you see her eyes? They're blue. Cobalt blue. But Paaliaq is green."

"Maybe she isn't Paaliaq." The thought had been nagging him all day.

"Don't be stupid, Rakan."

"Then she's wearing contacts, like we do."

"No. I checked when we were playing."

"Then she's changed color. Yarlung has."

Dvara snorted. "Yarlung lost her color after Kraal died. It's not the same thing. And Yarlung's eyes haven't really changed; they've just become cloudy with her blindness."

"The only other possibility, if Jing Mei is Paaliaq, is that she's found a way to change them while she was hiding. Just like she's managed to make herself feel like a whelp."

Dvara stared out the other window. Her frustration echoed his.

"If she is Paaliaq she'll eventually let something slip," Dvara said after a long pause. "Or we'll have to find a way to make her slip up and give herself away."

"Normally whelps love to play," Rakan said. "So maybe we need to play in front of her and see how she reacts. We can do things like place triggers all over town for each other to set off or disarm."

"And she'll have to respond eventually since no whelp would ever resist playing for very long." Dvara smiled. "And then I can hide a double layer of triggers that no whelp could disarm by herself – and if she doesn't disarm them, they'll explode."

"Exactly." Rakan felt the thrill of closing in. And then it disappeared. They looked at each other, and knew what they were both thinking, but didn't want to admit. They had no idea where the other dragon was. Or if there really was only one dragon of her Cairn left. And any dragon linked to Paaliaq would come the moment she was in danger since she was a Kairök and the dragons whose röks she held would die with her unless she had time to release them. It was in their interest to protect her whether she commanded them to or not.

"She could be a New Dragon," Rakan said. Maybe he and Dvara weren't the only dragons who had been born on Earth and not on the now defunct Red Planet.

Dvara snorted. "You know that Yarlung won't let the other dragons breed on Earth until Paaliaq has been killed – unless they agree to give her their offspring. And no one accepted that." Dvara paused. "Even if two dragons had managed to come to Earth to breed without Yarlung knowing it, they'd never have been able to hide their whelp for so long. Especially not when she radiates so much energy. Exactly the way Paaliaq is said to have done."

"What about the human?" asked Rakan. More curious than he wanted to admit.

Dvara smiled. "Pretty looking thing, isn't she? Her ultra blonde hair would contrast nicely with your dragon black."

"It's not for me that I'm asking," Rakan said coldly.

"As you wish. But playing with her might be a good idea. Especially since she seems to be Jing Mei's pet."

"No."

"Why not? She wouldn't mind. I felt it rolling off of her."

Rakan growled a warning. "I don't play with humans. You know that."

"But you want to with this one."

Rakan realized he should have ignored her comment from the start. But he had taken her bait like a fool. He switched tactics. "How could she feel me run my mind over the school, even if it was heavy handed? She's human."

"Yes. She is." Dvara looked thoughtful. "Or just appears to be?"

"She doesn't have a rök. I would've seen it in her trail."

"Maybe she's… a variant."

"What do you mean?" Rakan turned to look at his sister. "You think there are other kinds of humans that we've never come across?"

Dvara hesitated and then looked away. "No. Humans are all the same."

"What if they weren't," Rakan said, getting excited. "She reacted to the ball as if she could feel it, without seeing it, just like we do—"

"—humans aren't like us, Rakan," interrupted Dvara. "None of them. Don't forget that." She stormed out of the living room and slammed her bedroom door.

Rakan stared at his sister's door, more worried about their mission than he had been before. Dvara would never be able to control her rök if she couldn't even control her emotions. And if she morphed when her rök was out of control there was no telling what would happen.

His thoughts turned back to Anna, and Rakan remembered something his father had once told him. He had said that pre-shapeshifting Beings of Matter had existed long ago on the Red Planet. They didn't have a rök and couldn't morph into dragons or shift to other places, but could still manipulate matter with their minds. Rakan had dismissed it as a legend, but if it wasn't… could a human somehow develop those same skills?

Anna stood, irritated and cold, in the schoolyard. Her mother had worked the nightshift at the hospital, and Ulf had come home after his nightly 'research.' Although Anna didn't really think Ulf was the kind of guy to attack her, she had still locked her door. And then, in the morning, she had gotten dressed and left the house without breakfast. Just in case he got up early.

But worse than that, she had actually run to school, hoping to see Pemba again. And now that she was here, and he wasn't, she felt stupid. And hungry. She should have realized that he wouldn't be running to school to see her. They hadn't even spoken. Not even after handball when he had been waiting for his sister. She had just said goodbye to Dawa and continued walking.

Anna half-listened to the conversation that June and her classmate Kristin were having, but they were talking about a project they had to do together. Anna wandered away and joined Siri and Randi, hoping to get her mind off Pemba. But they were discussing what they should do for Lysa and it made her feel even worse. She hadn't left her a message. Or sent a text. Anna groaned inwardly. Why had she wanted to come to school so badly?

Pemba and Dawa walked through the high metal gate and Anna caught her breath. He looked even more like a panther as he padded languidly across the schoolyard. Anna watched, captivated by his fluidity. She imagined him pouncing like a panther and smiled. As if he could feel her staring at him, Pemba turned, his eyes honing in on hers. Anna turned away abruptly, her cheeks flaming. She closed her eyes, shame filling her as she felt his presence pressing against her. She was an idiot. The only thing she had been hoping for, all through her sleepless night, was that she would see Pemba again and that he'd come talk to her. And then when he finally did show up and actually looked at her, she turned away.

Rakan lingered after the bell rang, placing a few touch-triggers in the schoolyard. He and Dvara had decided to start by planting simple detectors that any dragon would detect – and almost instinctively know how to neutralize – just to see if June would react at all. And even if he had been careful not to mention it to Dvara, he was more than a little curious to see if Anna would feel them. He tried to quell the eagerness he felt at the prospect. He had barely been able to control his reaction when Anna had turned her back to him that morning, like a female dragon inviting him to chase her.

When Rakan walked into the classroom, he was surprised to see June run her hands through her long black hair and re-adjust the sunglasses she wore to keep it back. Rakan frowned and walked over to his desk on the opposite side of the room. Only pre-adolescent whelps let their hair down in public. Rakan looked back at June and she smiled at him. She looked so open and welcoming. He looked away. She wasn't how he had expected. She really seemed like a clueless puppy. With enormous untapped power just waiting to explode.

Rakan pretended to listen to the teacher, and then wadded up some paper. He took his time to manipulate its inner structure and turn each little ball into a crude touch-trigger – a trigger that would give off a small jolt of energy to any other dragon who touched it and send a signal back to the maker. He could feel June's attention on him even though she was looking at the teacher. He ignored her and put them into his bag to place around the school as if he was doing it to bother his sister. He kept a few out that really were just wads of paper and aimed them at some of the guys he had identified as practical jokers while the teacher's back was turned. A few of the girls scowled at him, but June smiled to herself and Rakan wondered how long she'd resist before playing with them.

Dawa whacked another ball in past June's defense and Anna shook her head. She was sure June wasn't trying to block them. Dawa had turned out to be a great player, probably better than any of the rest of them. Funny how wrong she had been about that. Dawa seemed so timid and self-effacing at school. And the old-fashioned way she wore her black hair in a huge bun at the nape of her neck reinforced that image. Coach Knudsen blew her whistle marking the end of practice and the other girls flocked around Dawa. But Anna went over to June who stayed in her goal, tossing the ball up and down.

"You okay?" Anna asked.

"Yeah, of course. Why?"

"I don't know. You don't seem to be trying to block Dawa."

"She's good."

Anna gave June a look. "So are you."

June broke the eye contact for a second. "You're right. I'm not. To be honest, I don't know what to think," she said, tilting her head towards Dawa.

"I know what you mean," Anna said with a sigh of relief. She could feel that June was telling the truth. "It reminds me of how the team got messed up by Lysa last semester."

"She knows she was wrong now," June said, defending her boyfriend's sister.

Anna shrugged. Lysa had been a close friend until she had followed
Fritjof's racist preaching and manipulated the team against June. Even if
June had gotten over it, Anna would never trust Lysa again. And Dawa's
aggressive playing reminded her of Lysa.

"It'll be okay." June put an arm around Anna's shoulders and they followed the other girls into the locker room. "At least she's a good player."

"Why can't you just get close enough to read her mind?" asked Dvara
impatiently as they walked home from school later that week.

"We've been through this before. Humans are sentient beings. I'm not
going to pretend I'm attracted to her just to get close enough physically to
penetrate her mind without her consent."

"But you are attracted to her. And even if you think humans are sentient when they can't manipulate matter without their hands, they don't
know you're reading their mind when you're—"

"—I'll never use a human like that," Rakan said coldly. "It's unethical."

"Your principles are ridiculous," Dvara said. "Humans are clueless. Why
does doing something that they aren't aware of bother you? She'll never
know."

"But I will."

"Then ask her if you can read her mind."

"No." Rakan glowered at his half-sister. All his attempts to be honest
with humans had ended in disaster. And he had promised himself never to
take that risk again. Better to leave the humans alone than to have to alter
their minds or kill them in self-defense when they freaked out.

Dvara threw her arms up in frustration. "You drive me crazy. We need
proof that Jing Mei is Paaliaq. We need to attack her before she's had time
to analyze our strengths and weaknesses. Don't you understand that? We
need to attack her now."

"No we don't," Rakan said as they went into the Tibetan House. "Not if
she isn't Paaliaq."

Dvara stopped abruptly on the first floor landing. "Who else can she
be?"

"I don't know yet."

"Then read Anna's mind. She's sure to have seen something that Jing Mei did that will prove she's Paaliaq. Humans always block out what they can't understand." Dvara yanked open the door to their rooms and froze.

Rakan nearly tripped over himself trying not to run into her.

"T'eng Sten," Dvara said. "What are you doing here?"

"Ah," came T'eng Sten's rumbling voice from their living room, "the question is more why you are here. Alone and unprotected." T'eng Sten sniffed the air. "When you are so desirable."

"She's not alone," Rakan said, pushed forward by his sister's fear and his own pent up frustration. "Or unprotected." He lunged at T'eng Sten who was stretched out on their couch like a pasha, his spiked black hair and long sideburns a signature departure from all the other Old Dragons' shaved heads. But he never made it that far. Another dragon in human form collided with him in midair in a flash of violet. They hit the table with a thundering crash, bits of wood splintering under them.

Rakan growled and lashed out at Kakivak, T'eng Sten's male bodyguard. He should have remembered that a Kairök never travelled alone. Rakan stood up, flipping Kakivak over his back, but the other dragon twisted in the air and landed lightly on his feet with a smile before spinning into a flying roundhouse kick. Rakan ducked and blocked the follow-up punch, twisting his full weight into Kakivak's gut with an uppercut.

Kakivak crumpled on his fist and Rakan took a step back, quickly hitting his chest with his right fist and holding up his left hand in the symbol of truce before Angalaan, T'eng Sten's female bodyguard, jumped in. His fight wasn't with them.

"Well, that was entertaining," said T'eng Sten, clapping. "I see that Yarlung and Khotan have at least trained you to fight. Unfortunately, it would appear that they have neglected the rest of your upbringing. Your manners are appalling."

"Why are you here?" growled Dvara from the doorway where she stood, her fists clenched.

"Greetings Kairök T'eng Sten," Rakan said, gathering his wits and placing himself between Dvara and T'eng Sten. "Accept my apologies. I was surprised to see another dragon in our home. May I ask why you honor us

with your presence?" Rakan didn't bow as he should have done according
to dragon Code. He faced T'eng Sten as if they were equals.

T'eng Sten jumped up from the couch as nimbly as a gymnast in spite
of his massive build. His long indigo overcoat flowed around him like a
cloak and his bare chest gleamed like armor underneath. It was another
one of T'eng Sten's new traditions. No male dragon from any of the other
Cairns wore anything but the fluid black pants that were perfect for fighting. "You'd be an interesting addition to my Cairn," he said, standing only
inches away from Rakan who didn't flinch, "if I hadn't already placed my
claim on your sister." T'eng Sten went around Rakan and walked towards
Dvara. "For obvious reasons."

"That doesn't answer my question."

"Ah, but it does." T'eng Sten fixed the broken table with a wave of his
hand. "Ask your sister."

"Dvara?" asked Rakan, wondering if there was something he didn't
know about. He had never liked T'eng Sten's flamboyant disrespect for
the traditional ways of the Red Planet but he could understand that Dvara
might prefer him to any of the others. He was the youngest of the Kairöks.
And one of the youngest dragons to have survived the destruction of the
Red Planet after the war started by Paaliaq when she attacked Kraal.

"Greetings, Kairök T'eng Sten." Dvara bowed her head, ignoring Rakan's
question. "We did not expect you. To what do we owe the honor of your
visit?"

"You know why I'm here. You once promised me something that I can
now claim."

Dvara tilted her chin defiantly. "That promise was extracted from me."

"That's not my memory of it," said T'eng Sten. He touched her cheek
gently.

Dvara growled and threw a strike to his solar plexus. T'eng Sten grabbed
her hand and twisted it behind her, pulling her against him.

Rakan moved to help his sister, but Kakivak and Angalaan stopped him.

"So much fire," T'eng Sten crooned. "I like that in a dragon. Especially
one I intend to mate with."

"I'm not free to be claimed," hissed Dvara, turning her face away from
his.

"Ah, but you are," T'eng Sten said. He released her but kept her hand in his. He passed his other hand above it, revealing her vermillion dragon form, her white claws flashing like diamonds. "This, my desirable mate, is all I need to know. Your white claws show that you are free. You no longer wear Khotan's burgundy. You have been given back your rök."

"I'm not free," she said, yanking her hand back.

"Why not? Who else's fire have you stood in?" He grabbed her around the waist and pulled her to his chest, his indigo Maii-a glowing. "I can take you right now, if I want to." He leaned forward and bit her neck. "You're so ripe. So ready for me."

Dvara groaned and leaned into him, her black school clothes transforming into a long vermillion dress as she melted into his embrace.

"Give me your rök," said T'eng Sten softly. His hands slid down to her hips.

"I can't," Dvara said, her respiration coming in short breaths.

T'eng Sten growled and flung her onto the couch. "I hate games, Dvara. I want you. Now." He towered over her. "I've already waited too long."

"I have no choice," Dvara answered, without looking at T'eng Sten. "I won't be free until my father's death is avenged."

T'eng Sten laughed. "Is that was this is all about? You think you can find Paaliaq and kill her? You barely even protected your lair and you didn't feel us arrive. Anyone could have come in here. How can you two puppies be a match for Paaliaq, even if she were alive?"

"What we do, or intend to do, is none of your concern," Rakan said, his voice flat and emotionless. "And if your intentions are honorable I see no reason to have your bodyguards flanking me. I am, as far as I know, still in my own home."

"Release him," said T'eng Sten with a dismissive wave of his hand. "He's harmless until he can unleash the power of his rök."

Rakan suppressed the boiling rage that flamed inside. He wouldn't give T'eng Sten the satisfaction of rising to his bait. "My sister does not appear to accept your claim. Your business here is finished."

"I am not so sure," said T'eng Sten with a mocking smile before turning his attention back to Dvara. He walked slowly around her, appreciating the backless dress that clung to her body and revealed her curves.

"I don't know what the two of you think you're up to," said T'eng Sten once he had finished examining Dvara, "but, you, my desirable mate, are proof that the ten cycles we granted Yarlung to find and kill Paaliaq are over. You are ready to breed." He stood behind Dvara and unfastened her hair, letting it tumble down her back. "And you want to," he whispered in her ear.

Dvara inhaled sharply and closed her eyes.

"What do you mean the ten cycles are over?" asked Rakan.

"Didn't Yarlung tell you? She was granted ten cycles to find and kill Paaliaq. After which time Paaliaq would be assumed dead. And Earth free to be colonized."

"Only four cycles have passed on the Fragments," countered Rakan. "Everyone is aware of the time differential."

"You are your mother's son," said T'eng Sten with a curt laugh. "She claims that the ten cycles of her sovereignty should be in Fragment time, not Earth time. But no one knew that we wouldn't be able to breed on the Fragments." T'eng Sten ran his hands through Dvara's black hair and smelled it. "Although I have to admit I am pleased with the time differential."

Dvara extracted herself from T'eng Sten's arms. "Yarlung has every right to kill Paaliaq. She's only honoring the Code." She redid her hair with trembling hands.

"Yarlung is a fool," said T'eng Sten vehemently. "Paaliaq isn't alive. And even if she were, Kraal was the traitor who started the war, not Paaliaq."

Dvara flung herself at T'eng Sten, wavering in and out of a partial morph. T'eng Sten raised his hands and stopped her in midair. "Learn to control your rök or it'll kill you," he said quietly. Once she had stabilized in her human form, he released her. "But to do so you must know who you are and claim your dragon name."

"I already have," Dvara said with a growl. "I am Dvara Azuraal, daughter of Kraal and bearer of the Line of Aal."

T'eng Sten smiled. "Are you? I'm not so sure." He walked over to join his guards who still hovered near Rakan. "And you, young Rakan'dzor, when are you going to cut your hair and become a real acolyte instead of harnessing your rök in a prison? You do know that you won't come into your full power until your rök is free, don't you? Or did they forget to tell you that? Control is only half the equation."

Rakan glared at T'eng Sten, too angry to respond without exploding.

T'eng Sten faced them both. "A Meet of Kairöks has been called to discuss the matter. And unless Yarlung can somehow get the majority, Earth will be ours. And her right to hunt Paaliaq will be over." T'eng Sten bowed formally to Dvara. "I'll be back to claim you after the Meet. And since I guard what is rightfully mine, I have protected your lair for you. No other dragon can enter without my approval. Until then, my fiery mate."

Dvara flung herself once again at T'eng Sten's throat, but he just laughed and shifted out of the room in a swirl of indigo rimmed with the violet and fuchsia of his bodyguards.

Dvara howled and punched the air where T'eng Sten had been.

Rakan let his mind-touch run over T'eng Sten's shields. "How many shields did he place?" Their rooms had been turned into a sound-proofed fortress.

"He'll know every time we go in or out," Dvara said, exploring the shields with her mind-touch. "And no other dragon can enter. Not Yarlung, not Khotan, not Jing Mei. No one. Just us. And T'eng Sten. Whenever he wants." Dvara sank to the couch. "I can't undo it. If I do, the house will explode. And so will we."

Chapter 4

Pressure

A SLOW SHADOW SLIPPED ACROSS LAKE LHANG-TSO AS YARLUNG CIRCLED around Dvara, taking in her crisp scent of a mineral spring. "Perhaps the time differential and the fact that you have come of age to breed can be used to our advantage." The corner of Yarlung's mouth twitched up. "Yes. I'm sure that several of the male Kairöks would give me their vote in exchange for the chance to breed with you. And I only need one more vote to have the majority."

"That won't be necessary," Khotan said. "Kairök T'eng Sten—"

"—can't be trusted," interrupted Yarlung with a snarl. "Dvara, however," Yarlung said, tilting Dvara's chin up, "will bring several of them to me groveling." Yarlung smoothed back her daughter's pitch black hair. "The Dwarf Jewel. Your name suits you, Dvara Azura." Yarlung smiled. "Perhaps you will be useful to me after all."

Dvara stood stiffly, trying not to show any reaction, but Rakan felt her rage.

"That still doesn't excuse your incompetence," continued Yarlung, her voice scathing. "How can you not know where Haakaramanoth is? He would never leave Paaliaq alone with two unknown dragons even if they are New Dragons. Especially not after T'eng Sten showed up in your rooms and turned them into a real dragon lair."

"But T'eng Sten is on their side. He said Kraal was the traitor not—" Dvara began.

"—enough," Yarlung said, cutting her off. "T'eng Sten would change the color of his hide if he thought it would gain him more power. Everyone knows that." Yarlung turned to Rakan. "You're a trailer. I trained you myself. Where is Haakaramanoth?"

"I don't know. He disappeared when we arrived."

Yarlung hissed and sent a shock wave through the lake. "That makes no difference. All you have to do is follow the trails to his lair. And then you'd know."

"I tried. But he's brushed out most of his trails – except for a few in public places and up in the mountains. There's no house or place where the trail is stronger."

"That's not possible. No one can erase their tracks. I said tread carefully, not do nothing. The trails will fade. Or have you forgotten even that?"

Rakan didn't answer. He hadn't been doing much else, but he still couldn't find anything distinct enough to know where the male dragon's lair was. And there were some faint trails of... void. He had never come across anything like it and had no idea what else to call it. The energy of the void trails vibrated in a weird way. Like it was there and not there at the same time. So he had come to the inexplicable conclusion that the dragon had somehow learned to erase his tracks.

"And you haven't found a single trigger, trap or any other detecting device in spite of being Khotan's apprentice?" Yarlung snarled at Dvara.

"No. Nothing."

"You're both useless. How can you find nothing? No dragon would live unprotected. Not even Paaliaq and Haakaramanoth would be so foolish."

Dvara didn't answer. They both knew that when Yarlung was angry it was best to say as little as possible. And especially not to try to explain a failure.

"Are they using any of the humans?"

"No," Rakan said.

"Yes," Dvara said at the same time.

The howling wind stopped abruptly, leaving behind the painful void of silence.

"Show me," Yarlung commanded.

Rakan stopped Dvara from coming forward and bent his head down for Yarlung to put her hands on so that she could see some of his memories of Anna. Better to be the one to choose the images their mother would see.

Yarlung smiled. "A female. So you must seduce her and find out what she knows. That will be easy, the females never resist very long."

Rakan stared at his mother, forcing his anger to remain bolted in place. He couldn't play with Anna, but he couldn't defy a direct order from Yarlung either.

"Nima'kor and Yuli will arrive shortly so that we can prepare for the Meet," Yarlung said, naming the two dragons who were in charge of her Cairn on the Fragments. "I would have preferred to have confirmed Paaliaq's identity before their arrival. Your further presence is unnecessary."

Yarlung spun on her heel and walked back to her lake. "Make sure you bring me more satisfying news next time." She morphed back into her water dragon form and disappeared into the lake.

Dismissed, Rakan and Dvara shifted back to Tromso.

"Don't disappoint me with the human, Rakan'dzor," Yarlung said in his mind as he and Dvara collapsed onto the couch in their rooms. *"Make her believe you care and she'll give you everything you desire."* The sun lurked below the horizon, creating a cobalt blue twilight that lingered for hours. *"And then she'll show you everything I need to know."*

"But Mom, I don't want to," Anna said for the third time.

"Why not?" asked Ingrid, exasperated. "You love being outdoors."

"Because I don't want to be alone with Ulf, okay?"

Ingrid took a deep breath. "I really don't understand your reaction."

Anna hesitated. "He's always... touching me. And I don't like it."

"Ulf's a friendly and affectionate person. That's all." Ingrid sat next to her on the couch. "You're being over-sensitive."

Anna rolled her eyes. She hated it when her mom went into denial. "Ulf isn't being 'friendly', he's hitting on me. There's a difference."

Ingrid didn't say anything for a long time. "Are you attracted to him?"

"Mom!" Anna said, jumping up. "Don't be ridiculous."

"Why not? He's not too old for you. And he is a handsome man."

"Stop," Anna said, shaking with revulsion. "I don't like Ulf. That's all there is to it."

Ingrid pushed back an imaginary strand of pale blonde hair. "Okay. So then we need to figure out why you don't like him. Is it because he goes out all the time? I mean, I know you don't like going out very much yourself, but that doesn't mean that people who do can't have a stable relationship."

Anna didn't answer. When her mom put on her reasonable tone of voice, there was no possibility of discussing anything.

"Well, maybe I should talk to Ulf about it. We can start having regular at-home evenings. Yes, that would be a good idea. That way we can have more of a family feeling and then you'll understand how kind and caring he is. Or maybe we can find a way for you to train with him sometimes? He is one of Tromso's best handball players, after all. Maybe that's something the two of you can do together without you feeling uncomfortable?"

Ingrid stopped and waited for an answer.

"No."

"Anna, you're going to have to make an effort to at least accept him into our life. I know that I've dated a lot of men since your father... had some difficulties... but Ulf is different. We really care about each other." Ingrid twisted her wedding band. "I know you feel like he's taking me away from you, but he isn't. You just need to give him a chance."

"Mom, that's enough," Anna exploded. "I don't like Ulf and I never will. He's a freak. I don't want to go on the glacier with him, I don't want to play handball with him, and to be honest, I hope you guys break up."

There was an uncomfortable silence in the room as Ulf walked in with his gym bag. "Hello darling," he said to Ingrid, giving her a kiss. "Good afternoon, Anna. Any plans for the evening, or would you like to join us?" he asked as if he hadn't overheard the end of their argument. "I have three VIP passes for the music festival."

"Oh, that's wonderful," Ingrid said. "What a nice idea. Don't you think, Anna?"

"No. I don't. And I'm not going."

"Anna, what did we just agree—"

Ulf put a hand on Ingrid's shoulder. "It's okay. If she has other plans, she doesn't need to come with us. It was just an offer."

Ingrid looked up adoringly at Ulf. "You're so understanding."

Anna snorted and stomped out of the room, blocking out their murmurings while she flipped open her computer in the little office space that no one else ever used. She scanned her e-mails, hoping that June had changed her mind and was staying in town for the weekend. But deep down Anna knew her friend was desperate to see her boyfriend even if she tried not to talk about it too much. Being apart from him was killing her.

"Here," Ulf said, catching Anna off guard. He dropped a VIP pass on the keyboard. "You can come join me after Ingrid goes to work at 11:00. The party won't really start until then, anyhow." He leaned against the desk, nearly sitting on her laptop. "And then I can begin your introduction to the wonderful world of nightlife. I have so much to teach you, my sweet little Anna. And it will be such a pleasure to do so." He reached out to touch her cheek.

Anna flew back, knocking the chair over. "Get away from me," she hissed.

"So much passion," Ulf said with an appraising glance up and down her body. "I can't wait to show you a better use for it." He flashed his wolf-like smile. "See you tonight."

Rakan paced back and forth in their living room. "No."

"You don't have much choice, unless you want to go against Yarlung's orders."

Rakan stopped pacing and growled. Dvara was enjoying the situation a little too much.

"You read the minds of our herds all the time," Dvara said. "What's the difference?"

Rakan exploded. "She's a human. The herds are animals." He took a deep breath. "When we read their minds it's to help the herd as a whole. But if I were to read Anna's mind it wouldn't be to help her. It would just be to get information. And I'd have to pretend to have a relationship with her to get close enough to do it. It's not like the herds whose minds I can read from far away. They project everything to each other. I just listen in. Humans aren't like that. I'd need to…" *get close enough to smell her skin, to taste her lips and to feel her energy pulse under my hands…* Rakan turned and pummeled the punching bag that they had hung for training. The real problem was that he wanted to get closer to Anna. But humans couldn't mind-speak. All they could do was be close physically. And that wasn't what he wanted. It wasn't enough.

"Why are you so uptight?" interrupted Dvara. "She'd be willing."

"I'm not uptight." He trembled with the effort it took to keep from yelling. "Using humans like that is wrong. It's a violation of their being. It's demeaning. And I won't do it."

"Rakan," Dvara said gently, "what if you could do it without sleeping with her? I mean... maybe if you just start talking to her and see if you can lead her to answer your questions, see if you can read the images she's remembering while you're holding her hand or something? Would that still seem like something unethical to you?"

"I don't know." Rakan sank to the couch. "Do you really think it could work?"

Dvara shrugged. "We'll never know unless you try. But she seems more sensitive than most humans, so it might. Especially if the memory was a strong one — and seeing June manipulating matter or shifting would be for a human. If she's seen her."

"What if she wants more? What if..." Rakan trailed off. *What if I want more?* His desire to take Anna in his arms was so intense that he'd probably lose control of his rök and explode in an involuntary morph if he did. And he didn't want to imagine what would happen then.

"Where is she, can you tell?" asked Dvara, softly interrupting his thoughts.

Rakan shut his eyes and ran his mind over the maze of trails he knew by heart. His mind-touch ran up the hill behind the school, to where Anna lived on the top two floors of a three story building. She was running down the front stairs, agitated and angry. Something had happened. His eyes flew open as he jumped up, ready to fight.

"Okay," he said, unclenching his fists. "I'm going."

Dvara was silent for a moment. "Good luck, Rakan. You're doing the right thing."

Rakan nodded and hoped he was.

Anna hadn't planned on where she was going, she just knew she needed out when Ulf had gone up and joined her mother in the shower. She sat at the counter in the window of Helmersen's café and flipped through her contact list, wondering which of her friends wouldn't already have plans for a Saturday night. If June had been in town, it would have been so much easier. June's boyfriend played in a band and Anna was always welcome to come with.

"May I join you?" asked Pemba.

Anna almost knocked her coffee over before she realized it wasn't Ulf hunting her down. "You surprised me."

"I'm sorry." He hesitated. "Do you want to be alone? You seem upset."

"Yes. No. It's okay," she said. "Do you come here often?" she asked as he slid onto the stool next to hers.

"It's on the way to school." He pointed at her phone. "Were you waiting for someone who's late?"

"No." She tucked her phone away, hoping he hadn't seen her searching her contacts. "You can take your coat off," she added, noticing that he was still bundled up.

"You're letting me stay?"

"No, I'm chasing you away," she said, laughing.

"Are you?" Pemba unzipped his coat, revealing a body hugging black tee-shirt that molded to his chest. Anna hadn't realized that he was in such good physical condition since she had always seen him wearing baggy sweatshirts.

"No, I guess not." Anna forced her eyes back up to his face. But she got stuck on the pear-drop piece of coral that he wore on a black chain. "Where's your necklace from?" she asked before realizing that it was a bit direct. "I mean, it's pretty. I like it." But more than that, it was the same color as the stone that had marked her hand.

"You're curious."

"Sorry," she said, looking away.

"It's okay. It was a gift from my parents. Dawa has one, too. It's called a Maii-a."

"It's beautiful," she said. She wanted to touch it. To know if it felt like her stone.

He took it off and handed it to her. "Here."

She hesitated, wondering if it would react like her stone had. But when she saw that he was looking at her questioningly she braced herself and took it. It throbbed wildly in her hand. It was her stone. Only stronger. "It's the same." She smiled and closed her eyes. She had missed being able to hold onto it, even if she still felt its trace in her palm.

"The same as what?" asked Pemba, eyeing her with curiosity.

"As the ones that June and her boyfriend wear," she said quickly. She didn't want to reveal what had happened with her stone. "It feels alive."

Pemba sat perfectly still, his eyes riveted to hers.

She handed back the Maii-a with her unmarked hand. "Did I say something weird?"

"No," he said, looking away.

"Maybe it's not the same. It just looks similar." She hadn't actually ever touched June's necklace. Anna glanced at his again. "Is it from Tibet?"

"The Maii-a?" asked Pemba looking at her sharply. "No. Why?"

"I don't know. Just wondering." Anna squeezed her left fist over the star. How could it feel the same as the stone she had found in the mountains? "Are they common?"

Pemba faced her. "How many have you seen?"

"Not many." Anna fiddled with her empty cup. "How do you like it here?" she asked, trying to break the uncomfortable silence that had settled between them.

"In the café?" he said with a smile. "Not bad."

"You know what I mean," she said, returning the smile. "Here. In Tromso."

The smile slipped from his face. "I don't know yet."

"Why did you come in the middle of the year?" she asked before realizing that it might sound rude.

Pemba didn't answer right away. "My parents have a research project here."

"Oh." That didn't sound too permanent. "How long are you staying?"

"Don't know," he said, examining his cup.

Anna just sat there, watching him.

"What?" he said, finally looking up.

"Is that why you act the way you do at school?"

"What do you mean?"

"You pretend to be… I don't know, different. You hide behind the image of someone who doesn't care about what's happening. When you do."

Pemba looked away and Anna rubbed her Firemark, worried that she had offended him. "Pemba?"

He didn't answer. He just sat there, frozen in place.

"Are you okay?" Anna asked, leaning closer. A faint smell of incense clung to him. She closed her eyes and breathed the smell in, letting it wrap around her. She felt a sudden urge to bite him and pulled back, shocked by her reaction.

"Anna," he said without looking at her. "I need to go outside."

Anna felt her heart beat wildly in desperation. "I'm sorry," she said, wishing she had never said anything. Wishing she could control her bad habit of just blurting things out.

"Come with me." He stood up abruptly without looking at her. He grabbed his coat and walked out the door.

Anna scrambled to her feet and put her coat on. She hurried to catch up with Pemba as he walked across the street and headed towards the fjord, his coat still in his hand.

Chapter 5

Getting Closer

Rakan walked as fast as he thought Anna could go, wanting to get away from the town that pressed in on him. He needed to find a little more self-control. He could feel the shield that Jing Mei had placed on Anna. And it annoyed him. When they got to a relatively isolated spot on the fjord he stopped. He let his mind-touch wander out, breathing in the calm of the ocean as it rippled against the mountains.

"Aren't you cold?" asked Anna after a while, looking at him with concern.

"No."

"But it's ten below. You should be cold."

"Haven't you heard of the Tibetan monks who can control their body temperature?"

"No. But you're not a monk."

Rakan laughed and put on his coat. "No, I'm not. But it is also a lot colder up on the Tibetan Plateau than it is here." Although even there he didn't need a coat. No dragon did.

"Oh," Anna said, sounding surprised. "So how do you do it?"

"It's a question of mind over matter."

"Can you teach me?"

Rakan searched her eyes. How much did she already know? "Maybe. But I've never taught anyone before." She had reacted so strongly to his Maii-a that he had felt a connection to her in spite of the shield that Jing Mei had placed around her. And he had been surprised by the strength of her energy. "Let me think about what to start with, okay?" He needed time to figure out how to do it without triggering Jing Mei's shield.

Anna smiled and his blood thickened. He felt the throbbing need to morph. But he'd never be able to show her his true shape. Humans just couldn't deal with it.

"Are you hungry?" Rakan asked, harnessing his desires.

"Um, sure." She turned away abruptly, sending a thrill along his spine that already ached to expand and flesh out. He clenched his jaw and braced himself against the urge to morph.

"Aunegarden is nice..." she said, her face still turned to the fjord.

"Okay." He'd stay human. They'd just talk and he'd see if he could read anything through the shield.

As they walked back into town, anger replaced the need to morph. No matter what happened or who Jing Mei really was, he'd free Anna from the shield. No dragon would be allowed to keep her in a cage. Whether she knew it was there or not was irrelevant. It wasn't right.

The waitress at Aunegarden smiled and led them to an isolated table upstairs. They were seated on a balcony overlooking the indoor alley of the restaurant that sprawled chaotically through several attached houses. It reminded Rakan of some of the human dwellings that the Old Dragons had carved in the Fragments, the moon-sized clumps that orbited the gaseous mammoth that was once the Red Planet.

Anna settled into her chair and Rakan watched as she redid her pony-tail. Her fine blonde hair slipped through her fingers and sent his blood racing. Even though he knew humans didn't attach any significance to letting their hair down, the sight of hers, even briefly, flowing around her face and down her back was so provocative that he didn't dare do anything for fear of losing control and taking her then and there. Whether she wanted him to or not.

She looked up and smiled nervously. "What?"

"Nothing." He couldn't take his eyes off her. She had on a black turtle-neck and no makeup. Her eyes were pale – typical of all humans – but the color was pretty. Like a pale blue spring sky.

"What do you want to eat?" she asked, propping her menu up like a wall.

Rakan frowned and picked up his menu. "I don't know." He tried not to breathe in the spicy odor of her skin that reminded him of wild chrysan-themums and beckoned him in closer. Instead he focused on the source of the shield. It was connected to a pendant Anna was wearing under her turtleneck. But the shape seemed wrong. To his mind-touch it felt like a sinuous water dragon, but Paaliaq was a winged air dragon, just like he was.

The waitress came over a few times before they finally managed to decide, Anna for salmon linguini and Rakan for wild reindeer steak.

Rakan leaned forward. "Can I ask you something?"

Anna's pale skin flushed. "What?"

Rakan sketched a water dragon. "Do you know what this is?"

Anna looked at it and her hand went up to her neck. "Oh. It's a dragon. It's beautiful."

"But do you know what kind?"

"What kind?" Anna looked at him blankly. "No. Chinese?"

Rakan laughed so loudly the other tables looked over. "Why does it look Chinese?"

Anna removed her necklace and held it out to him. "Because it looks like this. And it's Chinese."

Rakan flew out of his seat. "What are you doing?" His touch would probably trigger an explosion.

"Showing you my good luck charm. It's not going to bite you, you know."

Rakan picked up his chair and sat down again, wondering if she really didn't know what the necklace was. He let his mind reach out and touch it, checking to see if it was more than a normal shield. But there was nothing else. No triggers, no energy deviators, no spying mechanisms. It was only a shield. Rakan snorted. It wasn't even a sophisticated shield.

"What's wrong with it?" asked Anna.

A wash of emotions hit him and Rakan looked up at Anna, surprised. He hadn't realized that the shield had been working both ways. "Nothing, I…" *What?* "It feels funny."

"You haven't even touched it."

Rakan reached for the pendant, but paused when the jade water dragon twitched. He made a counter shield for his hands and picked it up. It was warm to the touch and the dragon itself was exquisitely detailed. But every fiber of his being wanted to destroy it. It was green. Bright green. The exact same shade that his father had shown him as being Paaliaq's. But it was a very clearly a water dragon and not an air dragon. So the maker couldn't be Paaliaq. It didn't add up. A dragon couldn't take more than one shape. It was impossible. But it was just as impossible to have two different dragons be the same color. Even if one was an air dragon and the other a water dragon.

Frustrated by the lack of answers, Rakan wondered if he could tweak the shield to allow him to touch Anna. Maybe she had seen something more, and she would project it so that he could see it. And even if she hadn't, he wouldn't mind getting closer to her. No. He was doing this for his Cairn, not for himself. She was human. He wrapped his mind around the shield and gently altered its structure. Why had Jing Mei made it so simple? Paaliaq had been a golden crested shielder. But this shield was so elementary that no shielder, even if they were still a puppy, would have made it that way. Every time one thing confirmed that Jing Mei was Paaliaq, another confirmed that she wasn't.

The waitress brought them their food and Rakan handed the pendant back to Anna.

"You don't like it?" Anna asked, taking it back gingerly.

Rakan looked sadly at the over-cooked reindeer steak. "No."

"Why not?"

"I don't like green. It's the color of death and destruction."

"Death? How can green be like death?"

Rakan shrugged. He wished he could have destroyed the pendant. Or at least taken the shield completely off, but he didn't want Jing Mei to realize that he had access to Anna.

Anna looked at it again before putting it back on. "It's beautiful, though. It looks so real I almost expect it to come alive. I wonder what it would do if it did?"

Rakan knew exactly what it should have done: the miniature dragon should have flown at him and exploded, stunning him long enough for Jing Mei to appear and finish him off. But it was as if Jing Mei had opted for a pure shield. Unless the triggers were so sophisticated that he hadn't felt them. He was a trailer, not a triggerer. What little taste the reindeer had had, suddenly disappeared. He hadn't felt anything, but that didn't mean he hadn't just set off a trigger and set some other trap in motion that he wasn't aware of.

Anna pushed the linguini around on her plate. "Why don't you like it?" she asked again. "Did you feel something on it?"

Rakan looked carefully at Anna. Somehow she knew it wasn't the color that bothered him. "Often that kind of thing has... a spell on it."

"Does it?" Anna put her fork and knife down and looked him square in the eyes with a look that said *tell me the truth.*

"Yes." Rakan looked away. He couldn't lie.

"So why didn't you tell me that instead of handing it back to me?"

"It can't hurt you." The anger in her voice surprised him. "It's just a shield."

"A shield?" Anna took it off and looked at it. "Against what?"

"Dragons."

Anna stared at him, obviously confused. "Dragons? But dragons don't exist. Why would anyone make a shield against something that doesn't exist?"

"And what if they did?" Rakan leaned towards her. His desire to touch her now that the pendant was no longer blocking him was driving him crazy. His mind-touch slipped forward.

Anna tilted her cheek into his touch and smiled. "It was you the other day in the schoolyard."

Rakan pulled his mind-touch back. He had just made an unpardonable mistake.

"Do it again," she said, leaning across the table towards him.

Rakan's rök whirled in excitement as he reached out with his mind and touched her cheek, cradling it as if he was touching her physically.

"How do you do that?" She touched her face where he had touched her.

"By allowing my mind to go beyond my body." Rakan put his hand on hers. "It's called a mind-touch. Try." If he could prove that humans could develop certain skills, maybe he could convince the other dragons to stop playing with them. "Focus on where we're touching, and then let your mind slip from your hand to mine."

Anna closed her eyes and Rakan felt her focus on their hands. But she got stuck.

"Feel me with your mind the way your hand feels me physically." He squeezed her hand gently, mentally creating a path that would pull her in.

"Don't do that." Her eyes flew open and she pulled her hand away. "I want to do it on my own."

Rakan laughed.

"What?" she asked.

"You reacted just like a puppy," Rakan said. He remembered how annoyed he'd get when the Old Dragons had tried to help him that way. But Anna stared at him, confused.

"Okay, okay," he said, holding up a hand. "Next time I won't help."

"Better not," she teased. "Or how can I learn?"

"By accepting my help," Rakan said, smiling. "You'd make a good dragon."

"So would you," Anna said with a smile that caught him off guard.

Rakan's smile faded. *Did she know?*

The waitress cleared their plates and took their dessert orders.

"You have a thing for dragons, don't you?" asked Anna, picking up the sketch he had done earlier of a water dragon.

Rakan took it back and crumpled it up.

"Why did you do that? It was beautiful," Anna said. "I would've kept it."

"I'll draw you a better one," he said. He sketched himself answering the Call to Rise. "Here," he said, handing it to her.

The waitress came with their desserts while Anna was still staring at the drawing. It was of a dragon flying in the sky, wings outstretched and flames curling from its mouth as it faced the rising sun. It looked completely different from the dragon on her pendant. More like what she had always thought of a dragon looking like. "Can I keep this one?"

"If you want," answered Pemba. "But it'd be better in color."

"No. It's perfect." Anna looked at it more closely. "Where'd you learn to draw?"

"I've always drawn. But I prefer sculpting."

"You should sign up at the Art Center — they have studios you can use."

"I don't think I could work with people around," Pemba answered. "I'll wait until I'm back home."

"Oh," Anna said, feeling hurt. "Is that what you miss the most?"

"No," Pemba said without further explanation. He played with his glass, spinning it around as they both sat in an uncomfortable silence. "What do your parents do?" he asked out of the blue.

Anna looked away, surprised by the pain that the question brought up. "My mother is a nurse at the hospital. My father…" she shut her eyes. "My father died ten years ago when he was coming back from a solo expedition to the North Pole. He was with a dog team. Sledding. And he was only a few kilometers away from base camp when a freak storm came up. Nothing was ever found. No dogs. No sled. No radio. Nothing."

Pemba was silent. "I'm sorry," he said. "I didn't mean to cause you pain."

Anna looked up into his eyes and saw a flash of orange, the same color as his Maii-a. "Your eyes…" she started to say.

Pemba looked away and Anna once again felt like she just couldn't get it right.

"I'm sorry," she mumbled into her lemon tart.

"No," Pemba said. "It's not you. I… I'm not used to this."

Anna nodded but didn't look up. "Me neither."

"You know what I miss the most about home?"

Suddenly, Anna didn't want to eat anymore. *His girlfriend. He misses his girlfriend.* She put her hands in her lap and shook her head. *I'm such a fool.*

"I miss our yaks. I miss taking care of the herds." Pemba's voice dropped so low she had to strain to hear him. "I miss the high altitude where the air is thin and the only sound is the wind," he said. "I miss being free."

Anna looked at Pemba. She could feel his longing for the open space. Suddenly she felt like the restaurant was closing in on them and she panicked. And then it all disappeared. The restaurant felt normal again. But she couldn't feel Pemba anymore. She looked at her hands, feeling abandoned. His mind-touch cradled her face. She looked up.

"I've never met anyone like you before," he said.

Anna smiled, relieved to feel him again. "Neither have I."

They lingered over their desserts until they were the last ones in the restaurant.

"It's dark out," Pemba said after they had paid their bill and stepped out into the cold. "I'll walk you home."

"It's been dark for a couple of months," Anna said, still feeling the rush of independence she had felt in the restaurant. "I'm used to it."

"I know. But I want to walk you home."

"Okay," Anna said. She wanted to link her arm through his as they walked up the hill, but she didn't dare. The snow crunched under their feet and echoed through the night. And for once, she wished the walk was longer.

"Oh, look," she said, stopping Pemba on the edge of the wooded area near her home at the top of the hill. She felt him looking at her and smiled. "Not at me. Up there." She pointed to the sky. "The Northern Lights. We don't usually see them this late at night."

Rakan looked up and saw clouds of bright green light undulating across the sky. His first reaction was to morph, ready to fight. But then he realized that whatever they were, they weren't aware of him or anyone else. But the color, the color of Paaliaq, terrified him. "What are they?"

"I don't really know," Anna said, still looking up. "Something about solar storms and the earth's magnetic field. I just like to watch them. They're so peaceful. And this year they've been particularly active."

Rakan wrapped his arms protectively around Anna, pulling her back against his chest. His initial reaction to morph and fight had been protective. She was so vulnerable. They stayed like that, watching the clouds of green light as they undulated across the sky. Anna's head rested gently against his shoulder. Her wool hat against his cheek.

She turned around to face him when the lights had finally disappeared. "What do you think?"

"About the lights?" he asked, holding her against him. "Or this?" His voice sounded strange even to his own ears. He breathed in her enticing scent and held her close, knowing he shouldn't. But he didn't want to let her go.

She stiffened when a car drove up the street, and then relaxed when she saw it. "I should go in," she said. "Before... it gets too late."

Anna hesitated, and Rakan wondered what was wrong.

"Thank you for tonight." She ran up the stairs and disappeared inside.

Rakan melted back into the forest and waited until a car drove up about an hour later. He recognized one of the trails that was often in Anna's apartment. It was a man, probably in his mid-twenties, and more than a little drunk. Rakan let his mind follow the man up and into the apartment. Rakan felt Anna wake up, tense. He growled. He'd kill the man if he touched her. But the man just stumbled into another room and passed out.

Rakan waited until Anna fell back asleep, but even then he couldn't shift home. He lay back in the snow and watched the moon follow its arc in the sky. His family had entrusted him with a mission and getting distracted by Anna wasn't part of it. Worse, it made him vulnerable. And careless. He hadn't checked even once while they were at the restaurant to see where Jing Mei was. And now he couldn't feel her anywhere.

She had disappeared.

Chapter 6

The Void-Trails

On Monday morning, Rakan paced back and forth. The strange void-feeling trails had intensified on Sunday, not long after June had reappeared. Since then, she had been crooning with pleasure at being reunited with her mate. And yet he still hadn't felt the other dragon come back. Or figured out how June could have shifted somewhere else Saturday night without leaving a trail. All he had found was a trace of emptiness. As if she, too, could erase her trail at will. Which would mean she wasn't a puppy. And she might be Paaliaq.

"Stop pacing," Dvara said from the couch. "We need to see how he reacts to our trails and triggers at school first."

"If he can erase his trails, he can avoid our triggers."

Dvara smiled. "Yours, yes. But I made some that can only be triggered when they're together. And when they're together, I don't think they're looking for triggers."

Rakan stood still. "You're a genius. But I still think we should go." He could feel June's throbbing energy at school. And she was projecting as loudly as a thunderstorm that she was with her mate. And yet, Rakan couldn't pick up any trace of another dragon's energy.

"You're useless when you're in puppy love. Jump her and get over it. We probably won't stay here much longer anyway, now that the other dragon is back." Dvara stood. "Alright, let's go."

Rakan ignored her comments about Anna and took off down the stairs until he realized that Dvara had shifted to school. The upper hallways always remained empty until the bell rang. He cursed and followed her trail to the third floor corridor, surprised to see her sprawled on the floor. And to find himself face-to-face with two identical men.

Every cell in Rakan's body braced for combat. They were the source of the void-feeling trails, but they weren't dragons. They didn't have a rök. Or a smell. They were dressed in the fluid black pants that all male dragons wore and their heads were shaved like Old Dragons even though they had the lean build of a younger dragon. Their chests and arms were covered in runic like tattoos that made the hair on Rakan's neck bristle. As did their identical purple eyes. "What are you?" Rakan mind-touched his sister, relieved to find she was only stunned. "Why did you attack Dvara?"

"Quiet," said one of the men, silencing Rakan with a unidirectional sound wave that knocked him to the floor. "Verje will ask the questions."

Immobilized by the high pitched whine in his left ear, Rakan watched as Verje cupped his hands. Two spheres of white light emanated from his palms. They grew as they moved forward. Dvara struggled to her feet and lurched to the side, but the light surrounded her anyway. Rakan stood slowly, still dizzy, and reached out with his mind-touch to analyze the sphere as it circled him, but all he felt was the chill of emptiness. He reached out farther and hit a thin layer of void that his mind couldn't pass through. He slid his mind-touch along the void. It surrounded them both. He tried to shift out of it, but couldn't. They were trapped. Rakan growled. "What do you want with us?"

"The rules are simple," said the one called Verje. "If you answer the truth, or at least what you believe to be the truth, nothing will happen. If you answer in any other way, the pressure of the sphere will increase. Which should prove to be rather unpleasant. Sverd tends to be heavy handed."

As Verje spoke, thousands of scintillating points filled their spheres. Rakan tried to touch them with his mind to determine what kind of parti-cles they were, but couldn't. They were unlike anything he had ever come across. He quickly rescanned the sphere. If their spheres were surrounded by a thin layer of void, how could new particles have entered? Matter can't travel through void. Neither can sound. Yet he could hear Verje. There had to be a passage he could exploit. If he could find it.

"Why should we answer you?" Dvara moved as if to attack, but instead fell to her knees with a gasp of pain.

"We have no quarrel with you." As Rakan spoke, a weight squeezed his chest like a huge pair of hands on a child's toy. His knees wobbled. The pressure made it nearly impossible to breathe.

"As I said," repeated Verje in a detached voice that matched his expressionless face. "Say anything other than a truthful answer to my questions and Sverd will increase the pressure around you. A truthful answer will decrease the pressure, thus allowing you to control your own level of comfort. We will begin."

"Go to hell," Dvara said. She dropped to the floor with a groan.

"Why are you here?" Verje asked, unmoved by Dvara's pain.

"That's none of your business," Rakan said. The sphere of pressure lightened. Rakan looked around, surprised. It had been a truthful answer but he hadn't expected the pressure to lift. He hadn't given them any information. Released from pain, his mind cleared. He'd only have seconds to figure out what kind of shield he needed to build before the increased pressure from the next answer would incapacitate him again. Rakan's mind sharpened and he entered the emotionless state of combat.

Verje nodded. "Do you seek someone?"

"Don't answer." Dvara twitched in pain on the floor.

Rakan scanned the sphere again, trying to tame some of the wildly spinning particles into a shield, but he couldn't manipulate them. They were more like flashing specks of light than anything else. "No more than we already have elsewhere," answered Rakan slowly, watching to see how the pressure of the sphere was being increased since the particles weren't actually closing in on him or getting denser. The pressure hesitated – his answer had been a partial truth. Finally, the pressure increased slightly.

"And is this someone a threat to you?" asked Verje.

The pressure had increased proportionately to the increased charge of the particles. To stop it, he'd need to make an electromagnetic shield. Except that he couldn't access any matter outside of their spheres. He hesitated, knowing that it was risky to use matter from his own being, but he couldn't see any other possibility. He wasn't wearing any metal. He meshed as much of his own trace elements into a continuous conductive layer as he thought he could manage. "No," answered Rakan, hoping that the microscopic shield he had been able to create would be enough to turn his skin into an ideal hollow conductor. As if he himself had become a Faraday cage. The weight throbbed around his chest, but nothing more. It worked. For now.

"Are your intentions honorable?" continued Verje, narrowing his eyes.

"Yes." The particles of light faded and Rakan relaxed. But he didn't drop his shield, even though the strain of maintaining it was draining him.

"Have you found the one you are looking for?"

"It's none of your business," snarled Dvara from the floor. She groaned as the pressure in her sphere increased. "If you have a problem with us then at least face us honorably."

Rakan bit back his desire to lash out at them. He needed to keep his shield from their notice. And maintain it as long as possible.

"We seek only to know your intentions in coming here unbidden," Verje said.

"We didn't even know you were here." Dvara's voice was so distorted by pain that her words sounded more like a growl than anything else.

Verje raised his eyebrows. "The rules are simple and yet you continually go against them. Why?"

"Because this is no way to fight." Dvara jumped to her feet when the pressure in her sphere of light lifted.

Sverd laughed. His voice was just a fraction deeper than Verje's. "No, it isn't, little fireball. But we aren't here to fight. Although I wouldn't mind going a few rounds."

Dvara threw herself at Sverd and hit the barrier of void. She jerked back as if burnt.

Verje turned to Rakan. "I ask again, have you found the one you are looking for?"

"No." Rakan forced himself to maintain the eye contact even though Verje's eyes repulsed him. They were swirling orbs of dark purple light. With no pupils.

Verje looked at Rakan for a long time without saying anything.

Rakan stood his ground, trying not to let his indescribable aversion for both of the void-trails show. Everything about them was wrong.

"Then it would behoove you to look elsewhere," said Verje. "You are not welcome here."

The spheres lifted in a flash of purple and they were alone. Sverd and Verje had shifted elsewhere.

"They're not dragons," Rakan said after a long silence.

"They're bastards," Dvara said, spitting on the ground.

Anna couldn't relax. Pemba hadn't arrived yet and everyone else she usually hung out with was busy. June was wrapped around Erling, now that he was back. And her other friends were huddled around his sister, Lysa. Anna grumbled to herself.

She had only realized on Sunday that she didn't have Pemba's phone number or know where he lived. All she had was the drawing she had put in her room. The bell rang and he still hadn't come, but she couldn't bring herself to go in. She lingered in the empty schoolyard until she realized she couldn't just wait there for him to show up. She walked up the stairs and stuffed the things she wouldn't need in her locker. She was late.

"I thought I'd missed you," Pemba said, appearing next to her.

"Pemba." Anna threw her arms around him impulsively. He didn't respond. She pulled back.

"Meet me for lunch?" he asked.

"Okay." She watched as he walked down the hall. Something was bothering him — she had felt it when she hugged him — but she didn't know what.

At lunchtime, Rakan walked slowly down the stairs. He stopped when he felt Dvara running up. He'd rather talk to her alone. Even if none of the humans would understand if they spoke in Draagsil, Jing Mei would. Out of the second floor window Rakan saw a shimmering mass of Jing Mei's blue. He stopped to look. She was wrapped around a tall medium-built guy with blond dreadlocks pulled back in a ponytail. Jing Mei's energy was flashing sporadically as she crooned over him. She was claiming him as her mate, but he didn't appear to be a dragon. Rakan let his mind-touch move forward. But the guy's energy was so controlled that Rakan couldn't get any reading on him at all. Maybe he was a dragon who had transformed his hair blond. And was hiding his rök. Rakan snorted. A rök couldn't be hidden. The guy was another void-trail. Which didn't make sense either. Jing Mei wouldn't be mating with him if he wasn't a dragon. Would she?

Dvara joined him at the window. "Weird, isn't it?" she asked in Draagsil.

Rakan glanced at his half-sister and saw a second haze of bright blue energy out of the corner of his eye. His attention snapped back out the window. "Did you see that?"

"What?"

"His energy," Rakan said with an involuntary shudder. "It's the same color as hers."

Rakan felt Dvara focus her dragon vision on June and her boyfriend. "I don't see energy, I feel it. But his eyes are the same color as June's."

"Which is impossible," Rakan said. "Unless he isn't a dragon."

"No. They've just altered their appearance. Like those two creeps this morning." She pointed to the other side of the schoolyard. "There's one more. Her name is Lysa. She's in Anna's class. Apparently she plays hand-ball too."

Rakan looked at the fourth void-trail. She felt younger than the others. She was standing in the middle of a group of girls, her blonde hair flowing down her back. "She doesn't look so bad," he said, eying her yellow-green shroud of energy. He could see it best when he looked slightly away from her. It reminded him of spring leaves.

Dvara snorted. "I don't know. All the girls feel sorry for her because her boyfriend was killed in some freak accident in December. But given what we saw this morning, I doubt it was an accident."

"What are they?"

"Repulsive, twisted creeps who don't have any sense of honor."

"Yes, I know that. But they aren't dragons. They don't have a rök. And they're too powerful to be humans."

Dvara shrugged. "It's as you said before. They've learned how to hide their trails."

"No," Rakan said, shaking his head. "They aren't hiding them. They just don't have trails like we do. It's as if they aren't even made of matter."

"Maybe they hide their trails by making negative projections of them-selves. Which would also explain why they're blond."

"No."

"You drive me crazy, Rakan. Look at them. They aren't human," insisted Dvara. "What else can they be?"

"I don't know, but they aren't dragons. Dragons don't have shrouds of energy that pulse around them like some kind of halo."

"I don't know. I can't see it. But maybe the shrouds you see are what's blocking their röks," Dvara said. "Like shields of some kind."

"No. They must be some other kind of humanoid species. Didn't you feel them this morning? They were manipulating particles we can't even touch. And they knocked us to our knees with sound waves. No dragon can do that without manipulating matter first." Rakan growled. "We should talk to Khotan about it. He might know how they're doing it. Or at least have an idea what those particles were."

"Why are you so stubborn?" exploded Dvara. "We don't need Khotan's help. Leave him out of this. Humans don't have that kind of power. Dragons do. And there aren't any other humanoid species. Which means that they are dragons. They're just hiding. Work on figuring out how they make their shrouds, okay?" Dvara turned and stalked down the stairs.

"What does Draak mean in Tibetan?" asked Anna.

Rakan spun around to face her. "What?" He had been so preoccupied with Dvara that he hadn't even felt Anna come up.

"You kept saying Draak or nak Draak or something like that. What were you arguing about?"

Rakan took Anna in his arms. If only he could be sure of being able to protect her. Because whatever they were, the void-trails would have no scruples in eliminating whatever was in their way. "I wish we were somewhere else right now," he whispered. "Far, far away from here." Away from the void-trails. His face touched the soft skin of Anna's neck and his fingers wandered down her back, feeling the ridges of her spine that he wished could morph into a spiked crest. His blood thickened and pounded in his ears. He could almost see Anna as a pale blue air dragon with the golden crest of a shielder. Anna's natural smell of wild chrysanthemums increased as the temperature of her skin began to rise. He wished she was a dragon and that he could wrap his neck around hers and plummet through the clouds in a series of wild arabesques.

Anna let herself be pressed into him, her breath catching almost imperceptibly. Rakan leaned into her, bending her slightly backwards. He opened his mouth to bite her. To mark her as his. And then closed it again. "Maybe we should go have lunch?" he managed to say, painfully forcing himself to stop in spite of the way Anna was arching into him.

Anna nodded, her uneven breathing echoing his. Rakan felt himself being drawn towards Anna's mouth. Her lips were the color of the sunrise. He tore his eyes away and guided her downstairs to the packed lunchroom.

Anna nudged Rakan. "Over there, with June," she said. She pointed towards June who was waving to them.

"No," Rakan said, pulling back. "She's not alone."

"I'll introduce you. It's just her boyfriend, Erling, his brothers and his sister."

"No." Rakan didn't need anymore of an introduction than he had already had. "Over here." He maneuvered through the crowded room to where two people were just getting up from one of the couches.

"What's wrong?" asked Anna following him to the other side of the room. "You don't like the look of the twins or something?"

"No."

Anna laughed. "To be honest, I don't either. But they aren't that bad. Even if they look like mafia bodyguards." Anna placed her tray next to Rakan's on the low table in front of the couch. "Sverd is the worst. He looks like he could kill someone without giving it a second thought. And I wouldn't want to be there if he did."

Rakan laced his fingers through hers. "No, I wouldn't want you to be there then either." He let his mind-touch wrap around her. She was so fragile, so vulnerable.

Anna squeezed his fingers and smiled at him.

Rakan's rök lurched. She was so trusting.

When she shouldn't be.

Chapter 7

The Sun Rises

T HE NEXT DAY, THE HALLWAY WAS FILLED WITH EXCITEMENT AS THE STUDENTS flowed outside just before noon to watch the sun rise for the first time in two months.

"You're not going," Rakan said in Draagsil. "You've never resisted the Call to Rise without a Kairök."

Dvara scoffed. "And so? It can't be that different. We need to see how Jing Mei reacts. No untrained whelp who has already awakened could resist it."

"I'll go," Rakan said. "You stay inside."

"Don't tell me what to do," Dvara said, her hands on her hips. "I'm older than you, remember? We need to observe all of them. It'll be easier if we're both there."

"You're not going outside," said Rakan, raising his voice in the now empty corridor.

"Yes, I am." Dvara marched towards the stairwell.

Rakan tackled her and they tumbled to the ground. She growled as she twisted out from under him. They circled each other, waiting for the other to attack.

"Well, well," T'eng Sten said. His long coat swirled behind him as he strode towards them. "This is hardly the time or place for that."

Rakan twirled to face T'eng Sten just as Kakivak and Angalaan appeared, walking as they materialized two steps behind their Kairök. But Angalaan wasn't wearing her dragon dress. Instead she was dressed in fuchsia body armor that covered her chest like a leotard and her black fighting pants.

"The Meet hasn't even started," snarled Dvara. "Why are you here?"

"I told you. I protect what's mine and the sun is about to rise. You'll answer the Call with me."

"I'm not going anywhere with you," Dvara said.

Steps echoed up the stairs and they all turned to see Anna appear behind T'eng Sten.

"No," Rakan said. He shifted between Anna and T'eng Sten without thinking.

"Pemba." Anna pulled up short. "How did you get here? You were just…"

T'eng Sten laughed. "You'll have to erase her mind now. Humans can't deal with it."

"Go back out," Rakan said to Anna. He put his hands on her shoulders to block her view of the others. "I'll be right there."

Anna shook her head. "How did you move so fast?" She tried to get around Rakan. "What's going on? Who are they?"

Rakan felt T'eng Sten run his mind over Anna. She backed up, shaking her head and trying to block the Kairök's mind-touch. Rakan threw up a shield, but he was too late. Anna stood perfectly still, frozen in time.

"Well, at least I understand your interest in her," said T'eng Sten, raising an eyebrow.

"Let her go," growled Rakan. He tried to undo whatever it was that T'eng Sten had done. But he couldn't, not without a risk of harming her. "Free her," he snarled. He threw himself at T'eng Sten's throat.

"Your manners truly are appalling," said T'eng Sten, flipping Rakan over his shoulder and immobilizing him on the floor. "You should say thank you – I erased her mind. She'll snap out of it as soon as I leave and she'll have no memory of my time here. Or of you shifting so foolishly right in front of her." He got off Rakan and turned to Dvara. "Will you honor me by answering the Call to Rise by my side?" His voice was firm.

Dvara tilted her chin up. "Leave now and I'll join you."

T'eng Sten came and stood directly in front of Dvara, but without touching her. "If you're playing with me, I'll have your hide. Is that clear? This isn't a game, Dvara."

"Then you should leave," she said coldly. "Now."

T'eng Sten gave her a terse bow and disappeared with his bodyguards in tow.

Anna felt a sudden wrenching pain in her head and put a hand out to steady herself. The tension around Pemba and Dawa was electric. Pemba spun around as if she had just appeared. He flung his arms around her and squeezed her so hard she coughed. "Anna, Anna," he repeated. He put his hands on her face and searched her eyes. "Are you okay?"

"I'm fine," she said, pulling away from his touch that vibrated anxiety. "Why are you acting so worried?" Anna took a step back. "Don't you guys want to see the sunrise?"

"No." Dawa spun around and went the other way.

"Wait…" Pemba said, letting go of Anna. She wobbled on her feet and he steadied her before running after his sister. He grabbed Dvara's arm and pulled her to a stop just as she reached the stairwell. "Don't go," he said.

"I'm doing this for you," she snapped. Then added more gently, "Just let me go. Okay? I'll be fine."

Pemba watched as Dawa ran up the stairs and disappeared around the bend. He turned to Anna, but he wouldn't meet her eyes. "Let's go."

They walked down the stairs and outside in silence.

"Uh, Pemba, what's wrong?" asked Anna as they crossed the schoolyard to join the rest of the students on the hill overlooking the fjord. But Pemba didn't answer.

Anna jumped in surprise as a small jolt of electricity ran up her leg. "Hey." She turned to see what she had stepped on, but there was only a piece of paper.

Pemba grabbed her by the shoulders, grinning. "You felt it."

"For a minute I thought it was another trigger," she said. "But it's nothing."

"What do you know about triggers?" he asked, his voice dropping.

"Nothing. I mean… we should join the others."

"Anna, tell me."

Her Firemark throbbed, as it often did when she was near Pemba. She closed her fist. Pemba saw the movement and slid his hand down her arm. He took her hand in his and opened it gently. "How did you get this?"

"I don't know. I was with June and my stone…"

Pemba placed his other hand over the Firemark and searched her eyes. Anna stared back, mesmerized. She had never noticed that his eyes had orange and copper flecks. "Your eyes… are beautiful."

Pemba turned away. "We'll miss the sunrise if we don't hurry up."

Anna scurried after Pemba, wishing she didn't always blurt things out. They stopped at the top of the hill, slightly apart from the crowd. Anna stood awkwardly next to Pemba whose immobility made her feel even worse. She didn't want to watch the first sunrise with anyone else. But she wasn't sure Pemba wanted to be with her.

Little by little the sky ignited until finally the edge of the sun managed to pull itself up above the horizon. The darkness slipped from the town into the fjord and a cheer rose from the crowd, unified by a primordial response to the return of the sun. The teachers walked around, distributing the traditional custard rolls called sun buns that marked the occasion. Anna felt an incredible warmth spread through her as the sun's rays caressed her cheek for the first time in two months. She closed her eyes and raised her face to the sun, basking in its gentle touch that she had almost forgotten. The sun tried valiantly to inch its way up into the sky, but after about ten minutes it sank back down again. As if the effort had been too much, leaving behind a pale gray sky in its wake.

Pemba stood behind Anna and pulled her against his chest. "I'm sorry." His voice choked as his heart pounded against her back. "I really am."

Anna put her hands on his arms and didn't say anything.

Rakan sat in class wishing he could shift elsewhere. His trigger shouldn't have left a Firemark on Anna's hand. It hadn't been set up that way. And yet he had been filled with inexplicable joy when he had seen it. It marked her as his. When she couldn't be. She was a human. Rakan writhed silently as his rök twisted in agony, desperately trying to get free. Resisting the Call to Rise with Anna next to him, and knowing she wore his Firemark, had been an act of sheer will power. He hadn't even been able to observe Jing Mei or the void-trails. He had failed Dvara. She had left with T'eng Sten to free Anna and all he had to do was observe Jing Mei. And he hadn't. His rök lurched wildly in his chest. The room closed in on Rakan. There was no way he'd make it to the end of class without exploding. He eyed the door. Could he even make it that far? A wave of peace rolled over him. Another dragon was nuzzling him. He looked up in surprise. June watched him from across the room, her cobalt blue eyes open and friendly.

Rakan was flooded with an aching desire to respond, to nuzzle her back. A different ache flared up inside him, an ache he had always refused to acknowledge but which he could no longer deny: the ache of loneliness. Wave after wave of pain came back up, choking him with years of unacknowledged suffering. June wrapped him in warmth, easing his pain. Little by little, Rakan's rök calmed down until he was once again in control. The wailing of his rök turned into a whimper, but he knew it wouldn't last. He needed to join a Cairn.

The rest of the afternoon Rakan sat, watching June. Unable to even pretend he was doing anything else. He ached to merge with her, to know what she was thinking, to become part of her Cairn and share in a way that only dragons linked through the same Kairök could share. Rakan struggled to maintain control of his rök. Dragons didn't heal each other unless they were members of the same Cairn or shared a blood tie. Jing Mei had no reason to touch him, and he couldn't figure out why she had. But his rök didn't care. It just wanted her to do it again.

The bell rang and Rakan hung back, letting everyone else run out of class. He lingered at his locker, confused, until the hall was empty. According to Code, he should have acknowledged Jing Mei's help. But how could he thank a dragon he might need to kill? Especially when all he really wanted was to throw himself at her in a desperate attempt to merge with her — either by giving her his rök or taking hers. He flung his backpack over his shoulder and headed for the stairs. He felt June coming back up and froze. His body tingled in apprehension.

"I forgot something," June said when she arrived at the top of the stairs. "Well, no, not really. Are you okay now?"

"Yes, thank you," Rakan said, bowing to her before realizing what he was doing and jerking himself back up. He had bowed as if she was a Kairök.

She smiled. "You were in too much pain for me to leave you like that." She got the blank look his parents had when they spoke to each other mentally. "Erling's worried," she said, rolling her eyes. "See you tomorrow." She turned and ran downstairs.

Rakan dropped his bag and slumped on a stair, watching the empty stairwell. Only dragons linked through their röks could mind-speak. But the void-trails weren't dragons. He was sure of it now that he had felt the twins in action. And June still had her rök. Yet June and Erling could mind-speak.

Rakan was still sitting on the stairs when Dvara shifted next to him. She radiated peacefulness.

"You okay?" She sat down next to him and sent him a wave of warmth.

"Thanks," he said, leaning against her shoulder. "I'm fine."

Dvara gave him a look. "No you're not. What's wrong?"

Rakan groaned. What was he supposed to say? That Jing Mei had helped him? And that he had wanted to respond? That Anna wore his Firemark? Rakan put his head in his hands and dug his nails into his scalp. The pain was coming back. He couldn't even tell Dvara that June and Erling could mind-speak since she'd just take it as proof that the void-trails were dragons and that Jing Mei was Paaliaq, their Kairök. When she couldn't be, or she wouldn't have helped him.

"Hey," Dvara said, wrapping him in another wave of warmth. "Was resisting the Call to Rise that bad?"

"Have you ever noticed that you can see when a dragon still has their rök?" asked Rakan, changing the subject to something he could deal with.

"What are you talking about? You can feel it. But you can't see it."

"In our trails. Look. The three of us all have a thin stripe that glows."

Dvara focused on the trails. "I don't see anything different from usual. Nothing is glowing in any of them."

"Look at yours, it might be easier," Rakan said, pointing to the center of her trail. "It's like a fine thread of vermillion silk that runs straight through your trail. See?"

"No."

"Mine was the only one I could see before. I thought it was because it was my own."

"Didn't Yarlung explain it to you? Surely she would have seen it before since she was a Master Trailer before she started to go blind."

"No. I asked her when she first started training me." Rakan's voice sank lower. "But she thought I was making it up." She had locked him in solitary confinement as punishment.

Dvara snorted. "She never thinks anyone can do something she can't. Ready to shift?"

"No. Let's walk." He wanted to follow the trail of June's rök that he had finally been able to see. It was more complex than theirs. It had three strands instead of one. And it didn't glow her cobalt blue, it shimmered like an opal with a multitude of colors. It was hard to see unless the trail was fresh.

"Alright, then. Let's go," Dvara said, sounding annoyed.

Rakan looked carefully at his half-sister. "Are you okay?"

"Why wouldn't I be?"

He stood up slowly. "How did things go with T'eng Sten?"

"Fine," said Dvara. She took off down the stairs. "But we have work to do. They haven't tripped a single trigger, even though they've been totally wrapped up in each other. I don't understand it."

Rakan ran after her. "Dvara…"

"What?"

"Nothing," he said, pulling back. She'd never tell him what had happened and he couldn't read her at all. "Thank you."

She looked at him questioningly.

"For Anna," he said, unable to meet her eyes.

Dvara pushed him in the shoulder. "You're welcome. And don't worry, it wasn't so bad." A smile played on her lips and she turned away, blocking him off again.

They walked in silence until they neared the Tibetan House. "What do you think about the twins?" Dvara asked. "How can they can be identical like that? It can't be natural."

"They aren't actually identical," Rakan said, his eyes on the void-feeling trails that led to their home. "Sverd's trail is sharper, like the edge of a blade, and Verje's is harder. Or denser. His trail is more like a barrier or a shield." Rakan stopped in front of the Tibetan House. "Look, they must have stood here. The trails are clearer."

Dvara looked around. "I don't see them. Have you tried to erase yours yet? Maybe that would help you figure it out. But they have to be dragons: Erling is wearing a Maii-a. I felt it on him this afternoon."

Rakan shrugged. "Anyone can wear one." An image of Anna wearing his and nothing else floated into his mind.

"Except that they can't be made on Earth. The only Maii-as left are those that the Old Dragons were wearing when the Red Planet exploded. And both June and Erling have one. How could they have gotten them if they aren't Old Dragons?"

"Maybe two Old Dragons gave them their Maii-as, like Yarlung and Khotan gave us theirs. Because otherwise they'd all have Maii-as." Rakan tried to push the image of Anna wearing his away. But he couldn't. It had felt too good when she had held his Maii-a at the café. Intimate and warm. And soft. So soft.

"You think they're all New Dragons?" Dvara paused on the porch. "It's true that they look like New Dragons if you forget about their coloring that they've transformed. But five of them? That Yarlung and Khotan never detected before?"

Rakan didn't answer. He was struggling to control his desire to morph.

"I can't do this on my own, Rakan. Okay?" Dvara said sharply, dousing him with a wave of cold energy. "Maybe you should stop with the human girl if it's going to mess you up like this. You need to figure out how they're blocking their trails so that we can figure out who they are. Now. The longer we stay here, the easier it'll be for them to kill us first. Our only hope is to move fast and attack them before they attack us."

"The void-trails aren't hiding their trails," Rakan said, flickering out of control. "For the very simple reason that they aren't dragons. Only the Old Dragon is hiding his trail. And he's not one of them."

"Well what else can they be?" growled Dvara. Her eyes flashed vermillion.

"I don't know," Rakan growled back, ready to fight. "But we can't attack anyone until you learn to control your rök."

Dvara snorted. "Speak for yourself, playboy." And slammed the door in his face.

Chapter 8

Frustrations

ANNA WALKED HOME SLOWLY AFTER HANDBALL PRACTICE ON THURSDAY.
Pemba still hadn't talked about getting together this weekend, and
she wasn't going to ask him. Not after he had refused to tell her what he
and Dawa had been arguing about all week. Whatever it was, it made him
impossible to be around. And didn't help her like Dawa any better. How
could she trust someone who behaved like two different people? Quiet
and withdrawn at school and then so aggressive, even violent, on the court.
And the coach seemed to have forgotten that handball was supposed to
be a team sport. Even if one player was clearly a star. By the time Anna
reached her apartment, she wasn't sure if she was angrier with Pemba or
Dawa.

"Hi, honey," said her mom as Anna dumped her stuff in the hallway.
"How was school?"

"Okay."

"I know this is hard on you, Anna. And I'm sorry." Her mom paused.
"But can't we make an effort? Maybe we can go see a movie together
tomorrow, just the two of us…?"

Anna stared angrily at her mom. Why did she always think everything
was about her? But her mom looked so hopeful, and so unsure, that Anna
felt trapped. "Okay," she mumbled. "Are you sure Ulf won't mind?" She
wanted her mom to be happy, but being at the movies with them both was
more than she could handle.

Her mother laughed. "You're so sweet. No, he won't. He has to work.
But even if he didn't, he understands that girl time is important."

Anna rolled her eyes and went up to her room. Girl time, not family
time. Her mother never understood.

"Can I walk you home?" Rakan asked Anna after school the next day.

Anna looked at him, shrugged her shoulders and headed out of the schoolyard.

Rakan jogged after her. "I'll take that as a yes?"

"Take it any way you want."

Rakan grabbed her arm and spun her around to face him. "What's wrong?"

"Maybe you should tell me." She pulled her arm away. "You've been fighting with your sister all week and you won't even tell me what it's about. You never even told me what Draak meant."

Rakan stared at her. Surprised that her anger stoked his desire to possess her. His rök lurched in frustration and Rakan struggled to force it back into submission. He couldn't just throw her on the snow and take her. But he wanted to.

Anna turned and walked away. "Forget it, Pemba."

Why did she always turn her back to him? He could barely control himself as it was. He ran after her and stopped her again. "Draak means dragon," he blurted out, so close to losing control that he didn't even realize he was breaking an unspoken code. Draagsil was a secret language.

Anna didn't say anything. She just crossed her arms and waited.

Rakan looked away, not wanting her to see his raging desire to chase her. "What else do you want to know?"

"Why you and Dawa are fighting since it's all you think about," she snapped. "Just tell me what's wrong, Pemba," she added more softly, taking a step toward him. "Let me in. Please."

Anna's closeness threw him off balance. He didn't want to lie to her, but he didn't know what to say either. "We don't always agree. She…" she what? Wants to kill June and her boyfriend? And the other void-trails, too? Rakan looked at Anna, wishing she would turn and run so that he could chase her. "She doesn't want to stay here very long," he said, his voice rougher than he expected.

Anna dropped her eyes and turned away. "Do you?"

Rakan inched closer, pulled forward by the intoxicating scent of her skin. "Maybe." Even if he shouldn't.

Rakan felt Anna relax. She took his arm, and they walked slowly up the hill. He was relieved that her anger was gone, even if he didn't know why.

ഇ൦ൠ

Pemba and Anna sat on her apartment steps, shoulders touching every once in a while as they talked. Anna didn't even notice Ulf coming up until he was in front of them.

"I thought you were working tonight," Anna said, scrambling to her feet.

"I am. But I thought we could have dinner together first." Ulf's eyes narrowed on Pemba who had remained seated. "Who's he?"

"It's none of your business."

Pemba stood slowly and placed himself between Ulf and Anna. "Stay away from her."

"My, my. Aren't you possessive," Ulf said with a lift of his eyebrows. He walked around Pemba and up the stairs. "It just shows you're unsure of her feelings for you. Because if you knew she cared, you wouldn't feel threatened by me. Don't be late for dinner," he said to Anna and disappeared inside.

Anna reached for Pemba. "I hate him," she said, curling up into his neck.

Pemba put his arms protectively around her. "Who is he?"

"My mother's boyfriend."

Pemba rubbed his cheek against hers. "And she doesn't keep him in control?"

Anna laughed at the image of her mother being in control of anything. "No."

"Then I will," said Pemba solemnly.

Anna closed her eyes and leaned into him. Pemba's energy wrapped around her and she relaxed. For the first time since her father died, she let herself be comforted by someone else.

Later, Anna sat next to her mom at the movie theatre wishing Pemba had asked her out earlier. Her mother's incessant chatter was getting on her nerves. She handed her mom the popcorn. "Can you hold this while I go to the bathroom?" Her mom was in gossip mode and there was no point in trying for a real conversation.

"Oh sure, honey. Hurry up though, the movie will start soon."

"Don't worry." She walked out with a sigh of relief. She'd make sure the movie had started before going back in. Anna wandered around the lobby.

She stopped in front of the poster displays for the upcoming movies, her mind on Pemba.

"I knew you'd come looking for me," said Ulf in her ear, making her jump. "You just can't stay away. I feel you watching me all the time, even if you like to pretend you're avoiding me."

"I'm not pretending," she snapped. "I don't want to have anything to do with you." She turned and walked away.

"Not so fast, my sweet little Anna." He grabbed her by the wrist and pulled her back. "So far I'm enjoying our little game of hide and seek, but at some point the foreplay will have to end." His hand squeezed so hard it hurt. "And there are two things you should know. One, I always get what I want. And two, I hate being second."

Anna yanked her arm away from his grip and pushed him away. "Get away from me."

A security guard came over. "Everything okay?"

"My girlfriend's daughter is going through a rebellious phase." Ulf adjusted his silk scarf and buttoned his three-quarter length wool coat. "I said I'd try to help out, but it's not easy."

"That's not true," Anna yelled. "She never asked you to help with anything." She balled her fists. If only she could wipe the wolfish smirk off his face. "You're not even supposed to be here."

"Keep your voice down, young lady, or I'll have to ask you to leave," said the guard to Anna. "Good luck," he said with a nod to Ulf and walked on.

Ulf lifted his eyebrows with a self-satisfied nod and strolled leisurely out of the movie theater. He disappeared into the night as Anna stood, fists still clenched, glaring at his back. She hated herself for letting him get to her. But she hated him even more.

Rakan followed Ulf down the street, wondering if the Old Dragons were right about certain humans. It wouldn't be a loss to humankind if Ulf were to disappear. Rakan hesitated. It would be so easy.

Rakan trailed Ulf until he went into a bar, and then he shifted home. He ripped off his shirt and flung himself at their punching bag, pounding it with a volley of hooks and punches. He had once promised himself never to kill another human. But if Ulf ever attacked Anna, he would.

It wouldn't be killing an innocent human. And that was a distinction he could live with. He threw in a few kicks and knees for good measure. He'd rip Ulf apart, bone by bone, molecule by molecule, until there was nothing left. And he'd enjoy doing it.

It wasn't until he eased off the bag that he realized Dvara wasn't home. He reached out and she responded. She was on a glacier on the other side of the fjord. Alone. Rakan shifted next to her and into a long, sinuous crevasse that was nearly ten feet wide. The majestic blue glacier radiated a quiet warmth that made the space feel sacred. Dvara was perched on a narrow ledge, staring at the opposite side.

"What are you..." but the rest of the question died in his throat when he saw the intricate rendering of a dragon cove.

Never had he seen such a perfect vision of the coves of the Red Planet. Rakan stood in awe, amazed at the prowess of the Master Craftsman who had made each and every surface of the sculpture within the ice seem alive. The aquamarine cove was surrounded by a towering red mountain whose majestic spires reached proudly up to the sky.

Rakan let his mind-touch slip forward and move around the brilliant masterpiece of minute carving done in the inner reaches of the glacier itself. But something was missing. Rakan looked around, trying to figure out what. And then it hit him. The cove was empty. There were no dragons even though the sand floor of the sleeping arena still bore the marks of the Cairn that had slept there. The imprints even felt warm to his mind-touch. But an eerie silence encompassed the whole thing, broken only by the sound of the aquamarine ripples that lapped gently against the sand in a pathetic attempt to ease the pain of the mountain that cried for its inhabitants.

"Beautiful, isn't it?" Dvara said, calling him back out of the glacier.

"No," Rakan said, shaking his head. "It's empty." His rök twisted in pain, clamoring for attention, but Rakan quickly stifled it back into control. He'd deal with his rök later. After all this was over. He couldn't join a Cairn before Paaliaq was found. And dead.

"They were here for the sunrise. At least a hundred of them, just as the sun touched the ice wall."

Rakan stared at his sister in surprise. "T'eng Sten made the sculpture for you?"

"No," Dvara said, laughing. "He found it on a previous visit to Earth."

Rakan nodded. "I didn't think he'd have the patience to carve something like this."

"Idiot," Dvara said, throwing an ice ball. "You barely even know him."

Rakan stopped the clump of ice midair and let it float to the ground. "So who made it?"

"It's beautiful. Isn't that enough?"

Rakan groaned. Why didn't Dvara ever pay attention to details? "Well, whose cove was it then?" Rakan ran his mind-touch over it again, trying to find the Master's imprint. But he couldn't find anything. He tried to alter different parts of the sculpture, but it was protected. Even the time release triggers had been protected – he couldn't feel any of them.

"T'eng Sten said the cove could be one of dozens that were on the southern shores of Ka. He said it was a typical structure for breeding grounds." Her voice softened.

Rakan looked back at Dvara. "I thought you didn't want to join his Cairn?"

"Rakan, sometimes you're just such a puppy. How can I avenge my father's death if I give my rök to a Kairök? I'd have to do what he or she wanted. Not what I want." Dvara jumped gracefully from the ledge. Her vermillion dress transformed into fighting pants and red chest armor. "But soon, very soon, Paaliaq will pay for having destroyed the Red Planet. And I will be free."

"There's no proof that Jing Mei is Paaliaq."

"I found the other dragon," she said, tilting her chin up. "I caught his scent. Once."

"Why didn't you tell me that before? When? Where?"

"Here." She held out a glistening metal ball. "And you were right, it's not Erling."

Rakan took the small, but extremely heavy, ball of iridium. He penetrated it with his mind. He eased some of the atoms apart, creating a porous opening in the dense silvery-white metal. He inhaled once and resealed the ball. It was a mixture of musk and something metallic. Clearly a male dragon. And an Old Dragon. He handed the vial back to Dvara. "It corresponds to the faded trails."

"Of course it does," snapped Dvara. "It's Haakaramanoth."

"It isn't the smell of any of the 1337 male dragons that Khotan has catalogued on the Fragments. So, whoever he is, he must have been one of Paaliaq's Cairn. But whether it's Haakaramanoth or not is another question."

"Why do you get that way? It has to be Haakaramanoth. How much more proof do you need?"

"You should bring it to Yarlung so that she can confirm it."

"No."

"Khotan then. It'll fade soon. And he can make a facsimile to add to his library."

"Leave Khotan out of this. We don't need their help, okay? Let's go, so you can figure out which trail is his." Dvara got ready to shift.

"Wait. Tell me how you caught his scent first."

Dvara growled, but answered. "I made triggers for their Maii-as all over town. And after the first one was triggered earlier this evening, all the others were disarmed. But not by someone wearing a Maii-a. I had made them to react to being disarmed differently, depending on whether the person was wearing a Maii-a or not. Can we go now?"

"If it is Haakaramanoth, then it proves that Jing Mei isn't Paaliaq," Rakan said. "Since he was Paaliaq's mate and Jing Mei's mate is Erling."

"Except that Paaliaq wasn't monogamous."

"But Jing Mei is."

"Yeah, well, Jing Mei appears to be a lot of things that Paaliaq wasn't. She's made herself a perfect disguise, that's all."

"No," Rakan said. "It's not a disguise. Or they wouldn't—" *be able to mind-speak.*

"What?"

"Nothing." If Dvara knew that June and Erling could mind-speak she'd take it as proof that the void-trails were dragons. But in his gut he knew that they weren't.

Rakan felt a tingling on his arms and watched ruefully as the black dragons appeared on his biceps. *"Any news, Rakan'dzor?"* asked Yarlung. *"You feel agitated."*

"Yarlung," Rakan answered out loud so that Dvara could hear his part of the conversation. "Dvara captured the other dragon's scent. He's here, but hiding."

"Ah, that is good news. Have you identified his trail?"

"Not yet. We're going there now."

"And the girl? Has she proved useful?"

"No, she doesn't seem to know anything."

"Humans always know more than they think they do. The problem is finding a way to get it out of them. If seducing her doesn't open her mind enough for you to sift through her memories, then you can always force your way in."

"No."

"You're too soft with the humans, Rakan'dzor. And you don't need to be. Most of them survive that kind of thing."

"I'll get the information without that."

"Do what is necessary to get the information that we need – that is important, not the human," said Yarlung. *"If you can't do it, Dvara will. Just like she's playing into T'eng Sten's desire to believe that he can claim her."*

Yarlung disappeared, leaving Rakan to contemplate her last sentence.

"You okay?" asked Dvara, sending him a mental nudge.

"No." He pulled away. His was fairly sure his mother was wrong about Dvara and T'eng Sten. But she was probably right about Dvara's willingness to get the information from Anna if they needed it to confirm June was Paaliaq.

"Life isn't always easy, Rakan. But it helps when you remember the big picture. We need to kill Paaliaq so that we can be free. Once she's dead, we can start a new life here. It's the only way that the other dragons can come and breed before they get too old." Dvara walked over to the image of the cove. "And then we'll be able to be part of a Cairn."

The longing in her voice resonated with Rakan's rök and deep down he knew she was right. They both needed to join a Cairn. And even if he did have a relationship with Anna, she'd die long before he did anyhow. A human's life was measured in years. But a dragon's life was measured in cycles of geomagnetic reversal. There was no future for them together.

"I need your help with his trail while it's still fresh," Dvara said. "Can we shift now?"

"I guess so." He followed her to the Botanical Gardens on the northern side of the island. But his heart wasn't in the hunt.

"It was here." Dvara stood next to a large boulder, looking around. "Why are there so many trails? They look like... ours. But we weren't just here."

Rakan stifled the urge to jump off the path and into the trails that criss-crossed over the entire park. They floated above the pristine snow that showed no footprints.

Dvara took a step towards the trails.

"Don't touch them," he said, putting out his hand to block her. "The other dragon must have made them. There must be triggers here some-where." He had never seen anything like it. Part of a trailer's training was learning to create static images of trails which looked like abstract sculptures made of wire. But this was something entirely different. It was a vibrant, pulsing trail. It looked real.

"I'll check." Dvara reached out with her mind-touch. Suddenly, her trail shimmered and a second Dvara came to life. The perfect double screamed hysterically and ran over the snow, following the fake trail that disap-peared behind her. The double morphed into Dvara's fire dragon form in an eruption of vermillion sparks. The dragon thrashed wildly as blood and guts spewed in volcanic profusion.

Dvara stifled a scream as the image of her dragon self disappeared into nothingness, leaving behind the terrifying void of emptiness.

"That's the answer," Rakan said calmly.

"What are you talking about?"

"He's the one who made the sculpture in the glacier."

"You just watched me explode and that's all you can think of? The sculpture? He knows our dragon forms even though we've never morphed here. And we know next to nothing about him. How are we going to fight him?" Dvara growled in frustration and shifted home.

Rakan studied his fake trail. It was almost his. But not quite. The stripe of his rök didn't glow. Rakan smiled. *You're good, but so am I.* If the Old Dragon had figured out how to hide his trail without seeing everything that Rakan could, then he should be able to figure it out too. He was curi-ous to see the animation of his trail that the Old Dragon had left them as a warning, but he knew it would be more important to see if the trail evolved over time. If the Old Dragon had managed to make it into a four dimensional sculpture and not just a normal trigger, fighting him would be a whole different challenge. Manipulating matter over time was a sign of the High Masters.

And there weren't many of them.

Chapter 9

Games

A NNA SAT IN THE LOCKER ROOM AND FIDDLED WITH HER NECKLACE. EVER since dinner with Pemba, she had felt uncomfortable wearing it. She didn't like the idea of it being an amulet with special powers.

"What's up?" asked June, coming back into the locker room. "It's not like you to be the last one out. Especially when we have a game to play."

Anna hid her necklace in her backpack. "I'm coming."

"Is it the pendant?"

"No. Yes. I mean…" Anna hesitated. "How would you know if something had a charm or something on it if you couldn't feel it?"

"You wouldn't, I guess."

"What is the pendant supposed to do?" Anna asked quietly.

June paused. "Protect you from dragons."

"But what if I don't want to be protected?"

"Then you take it off," June said. "Or you undo the protection."

"How?"

"Give me the pendant."

Anna handed it to June and watched as she held it. Nothing happened.

"Did Pemba touch it?" asked June with a smile.

"Yes… you can feel that?"

"Here," June said. "Just make sure you don't run into any unwanted dragons."

Anna laughed. "I'll let you know if I do. But I haven't seen any yet."

The pendant looked the same, but it no longer felt like it could come alive. Anna wrapped her hand around it. "How did you do that?"

"I don't really know, I just feel it," June said. "I mean, how do you feel it's different?"

"I don't know."

"Me neither."

"I guess some things can't be explained." Anna put the necklace back on. She was relieved to know that it wasn't an amulet anymore, but a part of her missed feeling that it could somehow turn into a miniature dragon. "We'd better go, or Coach Knudsen will yell at us for being late."

June laughed. "You forget that Dawa's here. Coach doesn't even see us anymore."

Anna shook her head as they walked out to join the rest of the team.

Rakan sat in the crowd on the bleachers, waiting for the game to start. He could feel the other dragon's hidden presence. But he couldn't find him. His gaze went back to Erling and his sister Lysa. They were sitting a couple of rows in front of him, unconcerned by his proximity.

Rakan's attention snapped to Anna and June as they came onto the court from the direction of the locker rooms. They had taken a longer than usual. Anna was always one of the first ones out. And he had liked that, it reminded him of a puppy eager to play. Rakan let his mind-touch reach out to Anna to see if she could still feel him. She turned and smiled. He waved, happy that June hadn't discovered the change in the shield.

He watched as she laughed with June. They tapped hands and joined the others. Rakan felt jealous, but he wasn't sure if it was of Anna or June. Both, he decided as he watched, wishing he could play with them. His eyes lingered on Anna and an image of her as a beautiful, pale blue air dragon danced in front of him. He closed his eyes and imagined flying high up in the sky and then plunging down into the ocean with her...

A mental thud on his head snapped his attention back to Dvara. She was warming up, tossing the ball back and forth with the other girls, apparently oblivious to him, but he could tell she was pissed. *I know we're supposed to play*, he growled mentally as if they could mind-speak. He tweaked the ball just enough so that she missed it. She spun around and picked it up, furious, but then laughed and tossed it to another girl. She sent Rakan a whack at the same time. But this time, he put up a shield and it bounced off. June frowned at Dvara and then glared at Rakan with a look that clearly said 'Stop.' Rakan glanced at Erling, who was ignoring it all. But Lysa looked up, more curious than worried.

The game started and Rakan watched Dvara dominate the others. After she had scored a few times, he tripped her up. She went sprawling to the floor as if she had tripped over her own feet. Rakan felt someone place him in a body freeze. But it wasn't coming from Dvara. It was June. Jing Mei had responded.

The body freeze disappeared and Rakan smiled. It was time to play. He set up triggers and tweaked the ball whenever it came to Dvara or June. Not so much as to make them miss all the time, but enough to make them fumble. But June never responded. Finally, she put up a shield and his nudges bounced off. Rakan tried to get beyond her shield, but couldn't. He continued playing with Dvara, hoping June would join back in. But she didn't. During the break, June and Dvara argued. June flung her arms out but Dvara just shrugged and turned away.

Anna dropped onto the bench next to Siri, who handed her a bottle of water.

"Weird game, huh?" said Randi, joining them. "What's up with Dawa? She's never dropped the ball before."

"Don't know," said Siri. "But in a way, it's better. At least we can score too."

"That's true," said Randi. "I guess we should enjoy it while we can."

Anna nodded, but June caught her eye. She was arguing with Erling. She hadn't seen them argue in about two months – when they had been the worst on-again off-again couple. Anna felt bad for her friend. She hoped it wouldn't start again. June had been a mess.

A tingle ran over her, like a body wrap of static electricity. She looked over at Pemba, wondering if it was a different kind of mind-touch. But he was staring out over the crowd. Her cousin's best friend, Haakon, was sitting behind Pemba, and he waved. She waved back, wishing she knew how to nudge Pemba mentally and wondering who he was looking for.

Rakan scanned the crowd for the fifth time. He couldn't shake the feeling that something was wrong, but he couldn't figure out what. The game had started again before he realized that halftime was over. He let his mind run over the game and smiled when Anna turned to him. Dvara blocked him with a ball of her own energy and June… had disappeared. Cold seeped into him. He was staring at her and she was playing. But he couldn't feel her. He closed his eyes and concentrated on where June was in the goal. There was only the faintest trace of Jing Mei. In her place was something that felt almost like a void-trail. Controlling his urge to run down and fight her until she turned back into a dragon, Rakan began different mental attacks. Nothing went through. He increased the intensity of his mental jabs, trying to feel how her shield was working. But there was no reaction.

Dvara whacked him hard and his concentration slipped. The ball that he had been angling towards June deviated and headed for the crowd like a ballistic missile. Coach Knudsen jumped to intercept it and slammed into one of the girls. They both fell to the ground, but the coach didn't get back up. She moaned in pain on the floor.

Cursing Dvara, he let his mind-touch scan the coach. Her ankle was broken. He wished he could fix it for her, but knew that humans freaked out even more when they couldn't understand something. So he just watched, like everyone else, as she was transported out of the sport hall on a stretcher.

The junior coach took over for the final ten minutes, but no one was into the game anymore and only a few goals were scored. The teams went to their locker rooms and the crowd dispersed.

Dvara came back out and joined Rakan where he was sitting alone on the bleacher. "What were you doing?" she hissed.

"You're the one who made the attack go wrong," Rakan threw back.

"But why were you bombarding Jing Mei like that? What got into you?"

"You didn't feel it?" Rakan gestured at the court.

"Feel what?"

"She turned into a void-trail. Or half of one."

Dvara stared at Rakan, her face a mix of hope and disbelief. "Are you sure?"

"Come feel for yourself," he said and strode down to the court. Rakan paced angrily in the first goal as he waited for Dvara. "You can feel her trail here, right?"

"Duh. It wasn't that long ago."

Rakan glared at her. "And now tell me what you feel over here." He headed to the other goal that June had been in for the second half of the game.

Dvara didn't answer, but the surprise he could feel rolling off of her confirmed what he knew. It was as if June hadn't been there. And yet they both knew she had.

"Next time you should pay more attention," Rakan said.

"You're one to talk," snapped Dvara. Her eyes flicked behind him and Rakan turned to face Ulf.

"Well, I must say I agree with Pemba. For once," said Ulf. "My name is Ulf, and you are…?"

"What are you doing here?" growled Rakan.

"Ah, yes, the aggressive male hormones of adolescence. It passes and then one can get on with the more pleasant things in life. Ingrid and I came to watch Anna play – I thought it would be nice to observe her game." Ulf flashed his perfect teeth and ran his eyes over Dvara. "You played very well, young lady, even if you weren't always paying as much attention to the ball as you should have."

"Thank you," Dvara said in her sweetest voice. She offered her hand to Ulf. "My name is Dawa. Do you play too?"

"Do I play?" Ulf tilted his head back and laughed. "Tell you what," he said, still holding on to Dvara's hand. "I'll get you a ticket for our next home game in a couple of weeks and then you can tell me if you think I can play or not."

"Really?" Dvara said with a squeal. "Oh, that would be wonderful. Thank you."

Rakan hit his sister with a cold wave. *Knock it off.*

Anna walked out of the locker room with her mom, eager to escape somewhere – anywhere – with Pemba. She slowed down when she saw that he was speaking with Ulf and Dawa.

"Oh," said her mom, squinting in his direction. "Is that Pemba? He doesn't seem very happy to be waiting for you. That's not a good sign, you know."

Anna rolled her eyes and walked over to Pemba. "She's being impossible," she whispered and then turned to her mom. "Mom, this is Pemba and his sister Dawa. Where are you and Ulf going out tonight?"

Ingrid stared at Anna, taken aback by her abruptness.

"Oh, we thought a little family time at home with you would be nice," said Ulf, draping an arm around Ingrid's shoulders. "Your friends can join us, if you wish."

"Why don't you come have some coffee," Ingrid said, eyeing Pemba.

"Oh, how kind of you to offer," said Dawa. "That would be lovely. Right, Pemba?" Dawa nudged Pemba out of his eye-lock with Anna.

Anna sat with Pemba on the couch under the picture window that faced the fjord. She'd rather be looking out than at the living room that was lined with books that hadn't been read in years. But Ingrid had squatted the couch that was backed against one of the ceiling high bookshelves so that she could get her scrapbooks out. Anna thought it was on purpose so that she and Pemba would have to hold their coffee cups – the square coffee table was overflowing with picture albums and souvenirs.

Ulf had an arm casually spread out across the back of the other couch behind Dawa. But she had turned her back to him and was plying Ingrid with a never ending supply of questions. And her mom was thrilled to answer them all. Anna put her empty cup on the carpet and leaned against Pemba's shoulder. "What do you want to do later?"

Ingrid's head jerked up. "Look, Anna – do you remember my friend Kjersti?" Ingrid plopped the album on Anna's lap. "Look at how pretty she was in her traditional Norwegian costume. It's a shame her boyfriend didn't want to stay in Norway after they got married. I'm sure that they'd have been happier here than in Kenya."

Anna rolled her eyes and bit back a sarcastic reply.

Ulf looked at his watch and stood up. "Well, I think I should get changed. Sure you don't want to come, darling?" Ulf asked Ingrid.

"No, I'd rather stay here for once – it's so nice to have some time at home with Anna." Ingrid smiled at Ulf. "You don't mind, do you?"

"As you wish. If you change your mind you can find me at the Driv later." Ulf's gaze lingered on Dawa.

"It's okay, Mom. You can go," Anna said, wishing she would. "Pemba and I were planning on having dinner somewhere anyhow."

"Oh, I think it'd be much nicer if we all had dinner together." Ingrid forced a smile. "Why don't you both stay?"

"We don't want to be any trouble," Dawa said.

"Not at all, it'll be nice to get to know you. Don't you agree Anna?" asked Ingrid. "I'll go get dinner started. Can you put the albums away, please?"

"Okay," mumbled Anna as her mom left the room.

After Anna had put all the scrapbooks away, Ulf came back in.

"I was just coming to help," he said, leaning against the doorway. "But I guess you have it all under control. So, tell me," he said to Dawa, "how are you enjoying Tromso? Have you had a chance to get out on the town yet?"

"No, not really. I mean…" she looked up at Ulf. "I wouldn't know where to go."

"Then you've come to the right man."

Anna glared at Ulf. "I thought you needed to go."

Ulf threw back his head and laughed. "Anna, Anna. Don't worry, my dear. I'm on my way. Here," he said, handing Dawa his card. "Call me so I can get you tickets to a game. And maybe we can go for a drink after." He looked over at Anna. "No need to be jealous, you can come too." He turned and walked out.

Anna stared at the empty doorway, to angry to say anything. Pemba took her hand and rubbed her Firemark. A slow wave of warmth filled her, soothing her raw nerves. "Sorry," she said, looking at Pemba's naturally tanned hands. Even his skin tone was warm. And tempting. She ran her eyes up his chest and wished they were alone.

Dawa stood up. "I'll go help Ingrid, okay?"

Anna watched Dawa walk into the kitchen. "She's leaving us alone?"

"She's not always a monster, you know." Pemba pulled her against his chest. "But she is a pain, sometimes."

"Pesky little sister?"

"Bossy older sister."

"Older? What do you mean, older?"

Pemba shifted his position. "I mean, she acts that way."

Anna gave him a quizzical look before settling back down against his chest and breathing in the faint smell of incense that always lingered around him.

"Anna?" he asked after awhile. "Did June do something to your pendant? It feels different."

"You can feel it?"

Pemba nodded without meeting her eyes.

"She took the charm off for me. Why?"

Pemba smiled at her, but he looked confused. "She did?"

"Here. Feel for yourself." Anna took it off and handed it to him.

Pemba examined at it and then handed it back. "It's just a pendant."

"I kind of miss how it felt alive before, though."

"I can try to teach you to change that."

"How?"

"With this." Pemba handed her his Maii-a. "It's the easiest thing to practice with. What do you feel when you hold it?"

Anna closed her hand around the Maii-a. "You, but…" she looked at her Firemark and then up at Pemba.

"It also feels like the Firemark," he finished for her. "I know. But I don't know why. The stone shouldn't have left a mark."

"How do you know about my stone?"

He looked away. "I felt it in the Firemark."

Anna eyed him carefully. She was sure he knew more than he was saying.

"It'll be easier if I change it," Pemba said, taking the Maii-a back. He held it in his palm and closed his eyes. When he opened his hand again it had changed color. It was a pale cornflower blue laced with large swirls of gold and burnt umber.

"Oh, that's pretty," Anna said, taking it. But it was lifeless. "What happened to it?"

"You don't like it?"

"No. It doesn't pulse anymore."

Pemba took it and changed it again. This time it was an intense pale blue, and the swirls of gold and burnt umber were barely visible.

Anna smiled when she held it. "That's better."

"Why do you like it like that? The other way feels more like you."

"Because this way it feels alive." Anna turned it around in her hands. "It feels like you could shape it into anything you wanted."

Pemba smiled. "You can."

Anna squeezed it, but it didn't budge. "How?"

"With your mind," Pemba said, stifling a laugh. "Not your hands."

Anna poked him in the ribs. "It's not nice to laugh at people."

Pemba pushed her back with his shoulder, and she resisted. He pushed harder and then pulled back when she pushed into him – guiding her deftly onto his lap with a twisting motion.

A pot clanged in the kitchen and Anna jumped up. "I thought you were going to show me how to shape the Maii-a." She glanced towards the kitchen where she could hear her mother and Dawa chatting away. She sat down next to Pemba, too embarrassed to meet his eyes.

"I am. I was showing you how matter reacts. When I pushed you, and you resisted, we were both stuck. But when you pushed back, and I moved out of the way, you were propelled in the direction of the force you were exerting upon me. All I had to do was direct you for you to change positions."

Anna nodded, her cheeks burning. Sitting on his lap hadn't meant anything.

"The molecules in the Maii-a have been simplified," continued Pemba, his face and voice neutral. "So that they can be manipulated easily." He held the Maii-a out in his hand for her to see. "The first thing you need to be able to feel is how to roll the molecules over each other. Once you've felt it, then you can try to move them around to make basic shapes, like a ball."

The Maii-a morphed slowly in Pemba's hand.

"Wait. How do you do that?" Her eyes snapped to the Maii-a. She took the ball shaped Maii-a from Pemba's palm and examined it. It felt the same as before. "How can you feel molecules?"

"I can show you," Pemba said quietly. "If you'll let me."

Anna nodded and offered the Maii-a back to him. But instead of taking it, he wrapped his hand around hers. Anna's whole body tingled again with the contact and she breathed in sharply. She ached to throw herself into his arms, to give herself up to him, to feel his body against hers...

"Focus your mind on the Maii-a. Feel its energy, how it pulses. Follow that pulsing inside, deeper and deeper until you feel it beat all around you, as if you were inside it."

Anna tried to focus on the Maii-a, but when she looked at it all she could see was his hand on hers. She closed her eyes and tried to feel it instead. Little by little, everything faded away except for the Maii-a. It was there, humming with its energy that rang like a golden bell. Or bells. Each one a perfect sphere that vibrated as it rubbed against the others, clinging together like thousands of tiny magnets.

Pemba's grip tightened around her hand, bringing her back out. "You felt it."

Anna nodded, hypnotized by the feeling of the Maii-a and the intensity of the look in Pemba's eyes. Something opened inside her mind, like a wing unfurling, and her mind slipped forward until she could no longer tell where her hand ended and his began.

"You can feel me." His voice was husky.

"Your eyes never look like they should be brown."

Pemba let go and looked away. And Anna wished she hadn't said anything.

"That's probably because I wear contacts," he said, his voice once again neutral.

"Anna?" called Ingrid from the kitchen. "Can you and Pemba set the table, please?"

After Pemba and Dawa left later that evening, Ingrid said, "Dawa is such a nice girl. I'm sure she'll be the kind of friend you can really count on."

Anna shrugged her shoulders in a non-committal way and pushed up her sleeves to do the dishes. Her mother hadn't been as annoying during dinner as she had expected. But Anna was sorry that she hadn't had another chance to be alone with Pemba. She wanted to hold the Maii-a again. And to feel his hand on hers.

"But I'm not so sure about Pemba," continued Ingrid. "I know you're not going to like my saying this, but I hope you'll take your time getting to know him. I just don't think he's trustworthy."

"What?" The soapy water splashed. "You just met him, how can you say that?"

"Maybe it's a mother's intuition." Ingrid twisted her wedding band. "And you've only just met him, too. Dawa told me they arrived during the Christmas vacation."

"Don't worry, Mom." Anna rolled her eyes at the pot she was cleaning. "We'll go slow."

"I care about you, honey. And I don't want you to get hurt. That's all."

Anna didn't answer. She continued doing the dishes until her mother walked out of the kitchen. And then she slumped over the warm suds, wishing she was in Pemba's arms.

"That was an evening from hell," Dvara said once they had shifted home from the park near Anna's. "What do you see in her? At least Ulf has something to offer."

"Shut up, Dvara. You didn't have to stay, you know."

"Yes, I did. You weren't supposed to fall in love with her. You were just supposed to read her memories of Jing Mei. And if I need to do it myself, it would be better if she trusted me. But she doesn't, so I'll have to go through someone else. Like Ingrid or Ulf."

"You won't touch her." His rök was ready to explode in an involuntary morph.

"Snap out of it. We have a problem to deal with. And your feelings for Anna are blinding you completely. You're not even trying to figure out how Haakaramanoth duplicated our trails."

"I have been working on it."

"Like when you stare out the window all afternoon?" Dvara snorted. "Right now they know more about us than we do about them. You felt Jing Mei hide her trail. What further proof do you need? Wake up. The void-trails are dragons. That means that there are at least four more than—"

"—they aren't dragons," Rakan said coldly.

"Well, dragon or not, they're protecting Paaliaq. So, unless we can figure out how to kill only Paaliaq, we'll have to kill them too."

"Even if she is Paaliaq, we can't kill the others without reason. It's against the Code."

"If they block our right to kill Paaliaq, then we can."

"There are too many of them."

"There are ways of killing them. If we choose to use them."

"What ways?" Rakan didn't like the cold look of intent on Dvara's face.

"With a trigger."

"No trigger is strong enough to do that."

"Khotan has been working on a trigger to explode a Maii-a."

Rakan examined his sister. "Khotan wouldn't develop that kind of bomb." Each gram would release enough energy to explode a city. And a Maia-a weighed about twenty grams.

Dvara raised an eyebrow. "Ask him."

"Even if he has, it would be against the Code to use it."

"We're allowed to use triggers."

"Only while in hand-to-hand combat. Not to destroy everything within a hundred kilometer radius, including ourselves."

"The Draak will die if we can't use Earth as a breeding ground. And Yarlung will never agree to anyone settling on Earth until Paaliaq is dead. Why does it matter how we kill her?"

"Because there's such a thing as honor and being able to live with yourself. I couldn't live with knowing that we had killed everyone in Tromso." Including Anna. Rakan's vision of Dvara shimmered as a thermal image of her overlaid the normal one. "I think I need to morph." His vision only included the infrared range when his pupils spread into the cat-like slits of his dragon form. He was losing control.

Dvara put a hand on his shoulder. "Khotan said I should come home for my first morph on my own. I can tell him I want his help now."

Rakan shook his head. "I just need some time."

"We don't have time."

"I'll be fine."

"I told him we were coming."

"Why did you do that?"

"For you, you idiot." Dvara flung her arms up in the air. "Why can't you ever accept anyone's help?"

Rakan watched Dvara disappear into her room. His rök lurched violently. He needed to morph, but he didn't want to leave Tromso. Not when Dvara might have already planted one of the triggers she was talking about.

He'd never forgive himself if something happened to Anna.

Chapter 10

On Edge

MONDAY MORNING ANNA WOKE UP EARLY. SOMETHING WAS WRONG, BUT SHE didn't know what. Her cheekbones burned, the way they had when her father disappeared ten years ago. She got up and went to her mom's room. She listened at the door, wondering if Ulf was there and if she could somehow check that her mom was okay. But she was too repulsed by the thought of seeing Ulf to look. She made coffee and sat in the window seat instead. *It's okay, everything's fine. Or as fine as it can be with Ulf still around. Right?* But even the mountain across the fjord had abandoned her. Instead of shimmering in the arctic twilight, it sat hunched over like an old man, looking cold and lonely. Anna leaned against the window and stared at the parked cars below. Why hadn't Pemba returned her calls?

Anna walked slowly to school. Half of her wanted to run and the other half knew Pemba wouldn't be there. She stopped on the hill and tried his phone once more. She hung up when the voice mail answered on the first ring. Again. And then she couldn't take it anymore. She panicked and ran to school.

She stood at the top of the hill, anxiously waiting as people arrived. But not Pemba. Anna even started hoping Dawa would arrive. At least she could ask her what was wrong with Pemba.

"Hey, Anna," June said, coming up the hill with Erling. "What's up?"

"Nothing." Her voice snagged.

June let go of Erling and came closer. "What kind of nothing?"

Anna shrugged her shoulders.

"You want to talk about it?" June hooked her arm through Anna's and walked with her towards the schoolyard.

"Do you ever get the feeling that something has happened, but you don't know what?" Anna stopped June so that they were alone.

June looked at her for a long time without saying anything. "Yes.

Although I usually have a gut feeling about what happened, even if I don't want to believe it."

"Me too," Anna said quietly. It wasn't really what she had wanted to hear.

June put her arm around Anna's shoulders and they walked across the schoolyard. "Join us for lunch?" asked June as the bell rang.

"Okay." Anna gave her friend a hug when they split on the stairs. She walked reluctantly to class. If she knew where Pemba lived, she'd skip school and go to his house.

He was in pain. She could feel it.

Rakan twisted in agony on the couch. "Don't morph until Khotan can talk you through it," he croaked. "I can't help you right now. I..." His body shook violently, flashing hot and cold as his rök veered out of control. "I'm losing it."

"Stop talking, Rakan," Dvara said, steadying him as he stood up. "You should have agreed to go earlier. Just shift."

"Dvara?"

"What now?"

"Thanks."

"Idiot," she said, punching him gently in the arm. "Let's go."

Rakan didn't even need to nod. They shifted simultaneously. But he nearly got stuck in some of the transitional layers between the different tectonic plates and came out a fraction of second after Dvara. The thin air of the Ngari plateau filled his lungs. He dropped to his knees, trembling with pain and exhaustion. Even though the actual shift was nearly instantaneous, the effort was excruciating. And for the first time it had scared him. He had felt himself on the verge of an uncontrolled morph, which would have meant instant death. It wasn't possible to morph and shift at the same time. He shivered at the thought and sank his hands into the arid earth. Home. His pulse quickened as his flesh became denser, thickening and hardening as he morphed into his true form. He bellowed in pleasure and stretched his wings. Free at last. The sun had long since risen, but he launched himself into the sky to greet it anyway. He pumped the air with his wings, feeling the rush of flight that he loved so much. He flew through a series of arabesques until his rök responded, purifying his flame. He shot higher into the sky. His coral-colored flame burst out from within. Pure and powerful, like the sun itself. After days of repressing it, he had finally been able to answer the primordial Call to Rise in a magnificent display of orange flames.

Satisfied for the first time in weeks, he stretched his wings and circled above the plateau, angling down slowly. But then he remembered that Dvara was about to try her first morph alone. He folded his wings and plummeted. A writhing mass of vermillion and burgundy showed him he was too late. Khotan was struggling to restrain Dvara. She howled in rage and frustration at her captivity. She thrashed wildly, trying to kill Khotan just to get free. Rakan knocked his father to the side and flattened Dvara. If he could restrain her long enough for Khotan to reach her mentally, she'd be alright. But she wouldn't calm down. Rakan had no choice but to claw into her to keep her from disappearing into the earth's mantle and tunneling down to the molten rock that she craved with suicidal wrath.

She went limp. Rakan loosened his grip on her bloodied hide. She scrambled to her feet and slithered into the ground. Rakan morphed back to his human form and turned to his father, who was panting on his knees.

"She'll be okay now," Rakan said. "Are you alright?"

"I think so." He pushed himself up. "But she'll need some time alone for her pride to adjust." Khotan stood still, majestic in his flowing dragon pants and shaved head in spite of the dust and blood spattered on him. "Just thank her for having brought you. I wouldn't have been able to help you both, had you waited any longer."

Rakan stared at his father. Dvara had only asked for Khotan's help because Rakan needed to morph. She'd never have asked otherwise. Even if, given how her morph had gone, it was obvious that she had needed the help. He wished he had realized how bad a state she had been in, but he had been in too much pain. "You knew she asked because I needed to morph?"

"Rakan," said Khotan gently. "I know Dvara even better than I know you. I've held her rök. She has no secrets – good or bad – for me. I just pretend not to know, for her sake. She needs time to learn that she has nothing to prove. Until then, it will be difficult for her to control her rök." Khotan put a hand on Rakan's shoulder and guided him towards the mineral hot spring that they always soaked in after sparring. "Let her be for now. She'll come back when she's ready."

Rakan threw off his black pants and sank into the water, blissfully free until the thought of Anna soaking in the spring with him aroused something he didn't want to feel. He groaned and leaned stiffly against the rock, wondering if he should morph again to let off some steam.

"I think you need some time alone too," Khotan said. He hoisted himself out of the pool. "Do you remember what I told you when you came of age, and Yarlung decided that you would stay here and keep your rök instead of joining one of the other Cairns?"

"That I needed to learn to control my rök or it would kill me?"

Khotan smiled. "Yes. But that was only part of what I said, and I think you've taken it too literally. What's even more important is that you need to be true to yourself. If you aren't, a breach with your rök will appear. And as that breach increases, so will your difficulty in controlling your rök when you morph." Khotan's outline was visible against the pale evening sky. "There are only two possible outcomes. Either you learn to accept who you really are and you become one with your rök, or you don't and your rök kills you."

His father's outline faded into the night. Rakan groaned and sank under the water until his lungs were on fire and he was forced to come up, gasping for air. He morphed out of the water in a bellowing rage. He wanted to fight. At least when he was fighting, he knew what to do.

Anna paced back and forth in the living room. She had a ton of homework, but couldn't sit still to do it. Pemba hadn't been at school for more than a week. Her phone rang, and she lunged for it. But it was only June.

"Hey – we're going to watch the film on the snow screen, want to come?" June asked.

"Uh, I don't know. It's kind of late."

"It's only 8:00 – and Haakon says they can drop you off, it's on their way back to campus. You coming?" June paused, waiting for an answer. "It'll be fun. See you in ten?" she said when Anna didn't respond.

"I guess so," Anna said. Going out would be better than staying at home and checking her phone every few minutes. "Are you guys already there?"

"Almost. We'll save you a place. Bye."

Anna scrawled a note for her mom, even though she was working the nightshift. She didn't like the idea of her mom worrying if she came home early for some reason. Anna jumped off the porch and embraced the winter air that wrapped her in its heavy mantle. She paused for a moment to enjoy the pristine beauty of the snow that scintillated in the moonlight and breathed in deeply, coughing once as the cold air hit her lungs.

By the time Anna reached the town's main square and the huge outdoor movie screen made of snow, there were couples and families and groups of friends sprawled along the gentle slope that eased into the shimmering fjord. But she didn't see June. Or Haakon, who was as massive as a bodybuilder and hard to miss. Her happiness at being outside disappeared. Being the only single person with two couples wasn't going to be much fun either. The aching void that Anna had tried to push aside came back full force.

"Anna, we're over here," someone called. Anna turned around to see Erling, June and Lysa waving from makeshift seats carved out of a snowdrift. Haakon was spreading out some blankets for his girlfriend, Liv, to sit on. Anna made her way through the crowd to join them. Even the twins were there.

"Hey. Glad you could come," June said. She gave Anna a quick hug and patted the snow bank next to her. "I saved you a seat."

"You haven't missed much," Haakon said as Anna squeezed in between him and June.

"Want some coffee?" asked Liv. She leaned over Haakon and offered Anna a plastic cup.

"Ah, sure." She felt the twins lurking behind them and looked their way. They were standing perfectly still, their faces like masks. As always, they reminded her of bodyguards and made her feel uncomfortable. She felt Haakon take her cup. "Oh, thanks," she said, turning back to him as he poured her some coffee from a thermos.

"You're welcome," said Liv and Haakon together.

Anna smiled and shook her head. They were the only couple she knew who were always in synch. Maybe it was because they complemented each other – there was something aerial about Liv with her undulating blonde hair, blue eyes and pale skin. Haakon, on the other hand, looked like a rock with his square jaw and high cheekbones. Solid and stable. Or maybe it was because they had been dating for as long as she could remember.

Anna sipped her coffee and watched the movie. It was about two friends who couldn't manage to communicate. The movie had been shot in the high mountains and the rugged beauty of the land underscored their estrangement, making the movie painfully difficult to watch. Especially when she would've loved to be in the high mountains with Pemba. But he wasn't even in Tromso anymore. She wished she hadn't come.

"You're not alone," June said, nudging her shoulder. "Remember that."

Anna felt a wave of warmth surround her and she looked at June in surprise. "How do you do that?" It was just like something Pemba would do.

June laughed. "Ask Haakon. He's much better at it than I am."

"Later," Anna said, looking back at the snow screen after a quick glance at Haakon and Liv confirmed that they were cuddled up in a ball.

But she couldn't get back into the film, in spite of the majestic images of the mountains. Or maybe because of them. She ached to be there with Pemba, high above the treeline where the mountains were alive. She felt a ripple in the air and something tingled at the nape of her neck. A void was being filled. Her heart raced. Pemba. He was back. She could feel his whirling energy pulsing nearby. She jumped up and ran towards the feeling, blindly following it to the empty street that ran along the top of the square. "Pemba?" she called out, looking around. He wasn't there. Confused, she closed her eyes and concentrated on the whirling energy that was throbbing nearby. She reached out to touch him, to let him know that she was there. A wave of warmth enveloped her. She floated in his touch. He was here. She smiled and opened her eyes, eager to throw herself into his arms, only to see a man who looked like a Mongolian prince striding towards her. His heavily brocaded overcoat flowed around him. Despite the biting cold he hadn't even bothered to close it. Anna's heart pounded. The feeling was his, and he wasn't Pemba.

Petrified by her mistake, Anna stood still as the man approach. He had spiked black hair and long sideburns. Something flickered deep in her memory, as if she should recognize him but didn't. And it terrified her even more.

He strode up to Anna. "You really know how to be in the wrong place at the wrong time, don't you?" he hissed, his breath hot on her face.

Anna felt a wave of his anger rush over her. She wanted to turn and run away. But her legs wouldn't respond. "I thought you were someone else," she said, trying to keep her voice monotonous.

"Don't ever reach out to touch someone unless you know who they are. There are those who would kill you for less. Is that clear?"

"Torsten, my old friend," said Haakon, pushing Anna gently to the side. "We weren't expecting you back so soon. Why don't you go join the others, Anna? Torsten and I have a few things to discuss."

Anna nodded. Torsten frightened her so much it made her bones hurt. But the tension that clung to the two men like a haze made her hesitate. She backed up a few steps before walking to the edge of the crowd. She'd get help if they started fighting.

Anna tried to listen to their argument, but they were too far away. All she could make out were harsh guttural sounds that reminded her of when Pemba and Dawa spoke together. Anna moved closer. It couldn't be the same language. Haakon was her cousin's best friend. She had known him all her life. Haakon was half Sámi and half Norwegian. He had always lived in Tromso.

But when Torsten raised his voice, she heard him say something that sounded like 'Draak'. Her curiosity got the better of her and she took a few more steps towards them. She didn't speak Sámi, but she had heard it. And whatever they were speaking, it wasn't Sámi.

Another pulsing energy moved behind her. Anna spun around, ready to flee. But it was only June, running through the crowd. Why hadn't she ever realized that June felt like that too? Anna watched as June jumped into Torsten's arms as if he was her favorite uncle. But even more surprising, the tension between the two men dissolved as if it had never been there.

"When did you get back? Haakon didn't tell me you were here," June said with an accusing glance at Haakon.

Torsten laughed and twirled her around playfully. "It's not his fault, little sister. He didn't know that my plans had changed." Torsten put her back down.

"I'm glad they did," June said. She linked her arm through his. "Come join us." She directed him towards the square and straight to Anna.

She backed up, but it was too late. June and Torsten were nearly upon her.

"Oh, let me introduce you to my friend, Anna. Anna, this is Torsten, an old friend of Haakon's." June cast a glare at Haakon as she linked her other arm through Anna's. "You could've introduced them yourself."

"I thought you'd prefer to do it," said Haakon.

Anna didn't say anything. She had no desire to ever speak to Torsten again. And June obviously hadn't picked up on the tension between the two 'friends' that had dissipated upon her arrival. Relieved that Torsten took no further notice of her as they walked back to the others, she slid into her place on the snowbank and pretended to watch the movie.

When June finally sat back down she gave Anna a quick hug. "Torsten's great," she said. "I wish he was staying longer."

"He doesn't live here?" Anna asked, trying to sound casual.

"No. I wish he did. But his fiancée moved here recently, so he'll probably be coming more often."

"Great," Anna said, thinking it was anything but. "Is he part Sámi?"

"I don't know. I don't think so. Why?"

"He looks like he could be Haakon's brother."

June laughed. "It's true. And they're a lot more alike than most siblings."

Erling whispered something in June's ear and she disappeared back into their bubble.

Anna sat numbly. She shouldn't have come. And having thought Pemba was back when he wasn't had made her feel even worse.

Liv reached over and touched her arm. "Are you okay?"

Anna nodded and fought against the tears that were stinging her eyes.

"You look cold. Come share my blanket. Haakon won't be back for a while anyhow. And being cold is no fun."

Anna accepted Liv's offer silently, sliding over to join her.

Liv wrapped her electric blue blanket around Anna's shoulders. It was light and warm, like the softest down. It felt like being in a cocoon.

"Life can be complicated," Liv said quietly. "Or it can be quite simple. It all depends on you."

"I can't decide what will happen," Anna said. "No one can."

"But you can decide how you will react." Liv's eyes had an intensity that made them glow. "And how much you want to see." The air around Liv shimmered and the sounds of the film and the crowd faded first into a humming background noise, and then into nothingness.

"How do you do that?" Anna sat up straight and took a deep breath. "It feels like being in the high mountains."

Liv laughed. "I've never thought of it that way. But yes, it is."

Anna floated in the feeling of freedom that surrounded her. She had never realized how oppressive the town was with its multitude of people and emotions and energies all crammed on top of each and clamoring for attention.

"Anna," said Liv, gently calling her back to Earth. "I can make it so that you always feel this way, if you want."

"What? Why would I want that?"

Liv studied Anna for a long time. "Only you can know the answer to that."

"Can you teach me to do it instead?"

Anna felt Liv's mind-touch probe her gently, as if she was looking for the answer. "I don't know. You need to learn to control your mind-touch first."

Anna felt her cheeks burn. Did Liv know what had happened between her and Torsten? "Pemba should be back soon," Anna said, looking away. "He's already started teaching me."

When Liv didn't say anything, Anna looked back up. "What?"

"If he doesn't come back within the coming week, or if he no longer wishes to teach you, will you accept my help?"

Anna felt her glow of peacefulness fade away as Liv's intense eyes bore into her. Why wouldn't he come back? Or want to help her?

Slowly, Anna nodded. "I will," Anna said. It felt like signing a binding contract.

"Good," said Liv with a curt nod. "The film's over and Haakon's coming back. I'll undo the shield. Ready?"

Anna nodded, but was still surprised by the rush of sound and energy that flooded her senses. "Ouch." She put a hand to her temple.

"You okay?" asked Haakon.

"I'm fine. My head hurts, that's all." Anna looked at Haakon. His energy was flat. It didn't have the three-dimensional quality that Liv's or June's did. Anna stood up and looked at the others. Erling, Lysa, the twins. They all had that feeling of pulsing energy around them, now that she was looking for it. But not Haakon. Or the other people in the crowd. Anna did a double take. There had to be other people who had it. She scanned the crowd again. No one.

Anna wondered why they were different as she helped pack up and get ready to go. She noticed Lysa, sitting on the snowbank, staring at the air in front of her. Anna hesitated, but then went and joined her. "You should come play handball again. We're supposed to have a new coach tomorrow."

Lysa looked up, her eyes blank orbs of pale green. "Erling says I should play again. That it'd help me feel better. But I don't know."

"You should try," Anna said. "You can always stop if it doesn't work."

"Thanks," said Lysa, looking away. "And I'm really sorry about... everything."

"Me too."

They sat in silence until Anna realized that Haakon and Liv were probably waiting for her. "Uh, I better go." Anna stood and paused for a second. She wanted to reach out and help Lysa who felt so broken. "It might help to be part of the team again."

"I don't know if anything will help."

"You won't know until you try." Anna gave her a quick hug. "See you tomorrow." Anna walked to where Haakon and Liv were waiting. She groaned when she saw Torsten.

"Ready to go?" asked Haakon. "We'll drop you off first."

"I guess so," Anna said. She avoided Torsten's gaze that tried to latch onto hers. It felt like he wanted to dissect her with his eyes.

"You still live by the observatory, right?" asked Liv, as she climbed into the driver's seat of her red beater.

"Yes." Reluctantly, Anna got in the back next to Torsten. "But you can drop me off at the bottom of the street." She'd rather walk home than be in the car next to Torsten for too long. He was worse than the twins any day.

"I promised June we'd drop you off in front of your door. And if I don't, she'll yell at me," said Haakon with a smile.

"You're on a short leash," said Torsten, punching Haakon's shoulder playfully.

Torsten's brocaded overcoat touched her thigh and sent a jolt of electricity through her body. She jerked to the side. "Watch out," she said and glared at his coat. It was teeming with dragons of all different colors.

Haakon snapped something at Torsten. And this time Anna was certain. It was the same guttural language that Pemba and Dawa spoke together.

"Why are you speaking Tibetan?" Anna asked. "You've never been in Tibet."

The silence that followed was so excruciating that Anna couldn't even breathe.

"I told you that this was going to turn into a problem," said Torsten calmly. "She's a wild card and we can't afford one right now."

Chapter 11

Challenges

R AKAN TORE INTO THE NGARI PLATEAU WITH HIS DIAMOND-LIKE WHITE CLAWS.
Thrashing at it as if it was his desire for Anna. He was a dragon. He
needed to mate with a dragon. But he didn't want a dragon. He wanted
Anna. Would he be able to forget her if he joined a Cairn? Or would
everyone know that he craved the company of a human and reject him?
Rakan writhed in agony. No matter what he did, it would be wrong. He
flung himself into the sky, but even the sensation of the air currents along
the membranes of his wings didn't bring any pleasure.

He wanted to go back to Tromso. To see Anna. To watch her hair slide
through his fingers. To feel her gentle energy respond to his and grow in
intensity. To feel her lips...

Without warning, the bright yellow Nima'kor slammed into him and
they plummeted, tearing at each other. They morphed and shifted as they
hit the ground, popping back out in human form. "What was that for?"
growled Rakan as they circled each other.

"To knock some sense into you. You didn't feel my attack until my
claws were in your hide because you can't think about anything but that
worthless human." Nima'kor spat on the ground. "Take her if you want,
but don't ever forget that you're a dragon. And not just any dragon. You're
Kairök Yarlung's son. Your desire to claim the human is demeaning."

Rakan lunged in fury at Nima'kor only to find himself on his face in the
dirt. Nima'kor twisted his arm and pressed a knee into his back.

"If you can't control yourself, you'll never be able to join a Cairn. No
Kairök will accept you." Nima'kor jerked his arm until it was about to
break. "And if that happens, I'll kill you to avenge your mother's shame."

When Liv pulled up in front of her house, Anna jumped out, barely
saying goodbye. She had no idea what Torsten had meant about her being
a wild card. And she didn't want to know. *Where are you Pemba?* If only he

would come back and things could go back to being normal.

Anna sat on her bed in the dark, fully dressed. Her phone rang and she jumped. It wasn't someone in her contact list. The phone trembled in her hand. What if it was Torsten? She answered on the fourth ring, just before it went to voicemail. Better to face him than to hide. "Hello?"

"Anna, it's Liv. Are you okay?"

Anna heaved a sigh of relief. "Yeah, I'm okay. I guess."

"You're worried about Torsten."

Anna didn't answer. She had never had a reason to distrust Liv, but her instincts were screaming at her to keep some distance.

"Do you want me to shield you?" asked Liv.

"No. I'll be fine."

"Call me if you change your mind."

"Okay. Uh, thanks."

"If Pemba doesn't come back by next week, I'll work with you on your mind-touch. Okay?"

"Okay." Anna hung up and stared at the phone. She couldn't figure out whether Haakon and Liv were really friends with Torsten or not. Either way, it was weird that he and Haakon dropped their argument and pretended everything was fine in front of June. Anna groaned. How was she going to explain the situation to June who thought he was great?

Anna walked over to the window to watch the lights play on the fjord. But a thick fog had rolled in and smothered everything. Anna pressed her forehead against the window, cut off and alone.

"You have no choice," Khotan said. His dark burgundy eyes glowed in the delicate light that came through the intricate lattice work of the living rock of his lair. "You will wait."

Rakan growled. Normally, he loved his father's study. It felt like being inside a three-dimensional fractal. But today it was a prison. Nima'kor's attack had made him anxious for Anna. He'd protect her, even if they couldn't be together. He had never liked Nima'kor. But now he hated him. He knew what the right thing to do was. And that was why he hadn't mated with her. He hadn't even touched her... that way. Rakan slammed a fireball into the fireplace. "I've waited long enough."

"Still an impatient puppy, Rakan?" sneered Dvara, shifting into the room wearing her vermillion gown that shimmered like molten metal. She held her head high and challenged him with a look of disdain.

Rakan jumped up to hug his sister. She was okay. And he knew her aggression was just a façade. But he stopped as soon as he touched her. "You smell like T'eng Sten. You've been with him while I've been going crazy waiting, thinking you—"

"Enough," Yarlung said, appearing next to Dvara. "At least he's a dragon and not a human."

Rakan stiffened, expecting an onslaught. But Yarlung turned to Khotan. "Dvara knows what I expect of her now. She'll accept the advances of the next Kairök of her own accord." She cupped Dvara's chin in her hand. "Since you're so eager to mate."

Rakan felt Dvara's energy flicker in anger, but she stood still.

Yarlung turned back to Khotan, her nostrils flaring. "Why did you hide this from me?"

"I didn't."

"Then why was T'eng Sten's Firemark camouflaged?" Yarlung pointed accusingly at the star on Dvara's chest, just below her Maii-a. It hadn't been there before. "You expect me to believe that she stood in T'eng Sten's fire without you knowing?" Yarlung lifted her hand and Khotan groaned in pain. He dropped to his knees. "You lie," she said.

"I've never lied to you. I can't. And you know that," said Khotan. He struggled to his feet. "T'eng Sten chose to transform it, not me. As far as I'm concerned, it makes no difference whether it's visible or not. When I die, she'll have to join a Cairn. You can't claim her. She's your daughter. T'eng Sten is no worse than any of the others. His claim was irrelevant as long as she was my kai. There was no reason to mention it."

Yarlung hissed. "Fool. T'eng Sten is a weak political alliance." Yarlung faced Dvara again. "But we can turn this situation to our advantage. If the choice of your heart is stronger than your new suitor, he'll win and take control of the other Cairn, which will make him a better match. And if he's weaker, it won't matter anymore. He'll be dead."

"I'll play my part," Dvara said. "But I won't allow two Kairöks to duel over me."

"You'll have no choice. Not once Khotan asks it of you. Even you, with your unbridled passion can hardly desire a long, painful demise." Yarlung turned her back to Dvara. "You're too ambitious to die for someone else." She faced Rakan. "You're a dragon. Act like one."

Yarlung disappeared, her words hanging like poisonous darts in the air.

"We'll kill Paaliaq before it gets to that," Khotan said. "And then you'll both be free."

Rakan's rök seared his insides in a flame of blind rage. He wanted to lash out and destroy the world and everything that was wrong in it.

Khotan placed a large hand on Rakan's shoulder, draining him of his pent up tension. "Trust yourself," said Khotan. He turned to Dvara. "Bring him back before he explodes."

"May your will be done," she answered, bowing her head.

Rakan looked at his half-sister. Why was she acting like Khotan was her Kairök?

"I thought you were in a hurry," Dvara said, ignoring his look. She walked over to Khotan's worktable. It was cluttered with bits of rock that looked more innocent than they were. "Or we can stay a few more days." She picked up a small stone. "Oh, that's interesting. How did—"

"I'm ready," Rakan said, interrupting her. If she and Khotan began to talk shop about triggers and other exploding devices they'd never get back to Tromso. He jumped up and transformed his black pants to jeans and a sweatshirt. He buckled on the belt he had crafted out of a strip of leather and as many different metals as he could find. He wouldn't be caught off guard by the twins again. "Let's go." He needed to see Anna. Just to make sure she was okay. But he wouldn't touch her.

When Rakan and Dvara walked into the schoolyard, Anna ran over and threw her arms around him. "Where have you been? Why didn't you call me?"

"Anna." Rakan wrapped his arms around her before he realized what he was doing. But by then the pure sweet smell of wild chrysanthemums had beckoned him in and he nuzzled her neck, wanting to bite her even if he knew he shouldn't. He forced himself to release her.

"No," she said, gripping him tighter. "Don't let go."

Her panic hit him like a cold shower. "Anna," he said, holding her face in his hands. He searched her eyes, his inner turmoil forgotten. She was scared. "What happened?"

"Nothing." Her eyes filled with unshed tears.

"Did Ulf touch you?" Rakan's blood rushed in anger. "I'll kill him."

Anna shook her head.

"Did the twins hurt you?"

"Pemba, stop. Please."

Rakan stiffened at the use of his code name.

"You're here. That's all that counts," she continued as if he was the one who needed reassuring. "I'm fine."

"I won't let anyone hurt you," he said. He wrapped his arms around her. She had no idea how defenseless she was. Or how much danger he was exposing her to.

"I know. Just don't disappear again. Please."

Her fear ate into him. Rakan wrapped her with his mind-touch, wishing he knew what had happened. She relaxed. And responded with her own gentle mind-touch, sending a jolt of energy through him. He crushed her against his chest, choking on his desire to morph and possess her. No matter what the consequences. "Anna," he said, because he couldn't say anything else.

"Meet for lunch?" Her warm breath teased him, making him want to stretch and thicken... "Pemba?" Her lips were warm and soft against his neck.

"What?" he asked, trying to understand what she was saying as he stifled his desires.

"The bell rang," Anna said, pulling herself together. "We have to go in. See you at lunchtime?"

Rakan nodded. When they reached the second floor, he watched her walk down the hallway to her classroom. She had undeniable courage. His rök ached to claim her. To meld with her. To feel their minds merge until they became one. But she was human, he reminded himself. She'd never be able to do that. Even if he mated with her.

She waved goodbye as she entered her classroom. He ran up the stairs four at a time. He needed to find the strength to stay away from her. It was bad enough that T'eng Sten had erased her memory once. But it would be so much worse if his mother or Nima'kor decided to intervene.

Rakan slid into his seat, forcing his rök to calm down. They needed to leave Tromso and then Anna would be safe. But to do so, they'd need to figure out who Jing Mei was. If she was Paaliaq, they'd kill her. And if she wasn't... The idea of his mother taking June's rök was unbearable. As was the idea of one of his mother's cronies taking Dvara's. Rakan's rök vibrated frantically. He blocked everything out and focused on June's trail. It was normal. Or as normal as it could be with a triple twisted strand running through it. His mind ran over her and she pushed him back immediately. He smiled. At least that was normal dragon behavior. He poked at the shield she had put up, trying to get her to react again. June's energy crackled in annoyance. As much as he had hated it when she changed her trail, he wanted her to do it again. He needed to analyze it to prove to Dvara that it wasn't the same as the void-trails' trails. She was a dragon and they weren't.

When the bell rang for lunch, June slammed her book closed and stomped over to his desk. "What's wrong with you?" she said, leaning forward.

"I was just playing," he answered. "What's wrong with that?"

"You send the coach to the hospital with your idiotic games and you ask me what's wrong with that? Are you kidding me?" June kept her voice low even though she was shaking with anger.

"The ball wasn't supposed to hit her. Dawa—"

"—it doesn't matter who did what. How can you play with people like that? Don't you realize how much those girls care about their game? Haakon's right, you're both just unruly puppies."

"Haakon? Who's Haakon?" asked Rakan exasperated.

"The guy who was sitting right behind you during the game." June waved her arms in disbelief. "Don't you even pay attention to who's around you? Didn't anyone teach you anything?"

Rakan remembered everyone who had been in the sport hall and even what they had been wearing. And no one had been sitting behind him. The place had been empty.

June leaned forward over his desk, her cobalt eyes flashing. "I'm sorry I tried to help you the other day," she hissed. Her energy snapped at him like sparks of electricity.

Stung to the core, Rakan watched June stalk out of the room. "June, wait." Rakan ran after her, unable to control himself any longer.

"Go away and grow up, Pemba. I don't want to have anything to do with you." She pushed him away. "And you had better not be playing with Anna. Because if you are, I'll have your hide. Stop messing with people. Life isn't a game."

Rakan watched Jing Mei stomp down the stairs. A tremor of excitement pulsed through him. She cared about the humans. Her emotions had been thick and clear. She wasn't Paaliaq. She was a New Dragon like they were.

Anna warmed up with the rest of the team. They hadn't played since the coach had broken her ankle, and Anna was itching to get back into gear. But she stopped in her tracks when she saw Ulf come out of the men's locker room with a whistle around his neck.

No. Not that. Not this. Not. Anna stared in disbelief.

"Oh my God, is he our new coach?" asked Randi as all the girls watched Ulf strut across the court.

"Look at his legs."

"Look at his butt."

Anna clenched her fists. "I hate him."

"How can you hate a guy who looks like that?" asked Dawa.

"Isn't that your mom's boyfriend?" asked Siri.

"Yes, and I wish he wasn't," Anna answered.

Randi laughed. "You're just jealous."

"What are you girls waiting for?" said Ulf. "I only said I'd help out because I thought you were serious about your game." Ulf strutted over to where they were standing. "You should be warmed up and ready to go by the time I get here," he said, tapping Dawa playfully on the butt. "Let's go."

Ulf took them through an intense workout, focusing on their offensive game and drilling them through wave after wave of fast break attacks.

Anna sullenly followed the giggling girls into the locker room after practice. As much as she wanted to hate everything about Ulf, she had to admit that he was a good coach. Except that he touched the girls whenever possible. Which was bad enough, but what really got to her was that the girls responded like kittens wanting more.

"He's good," Siri said to Anna. "And you have to admit he's hot."

"He's too hot," said Randi, fanning herself. "Have you ever tried to see him in the shower? Like you just walk in — 'oops didn't know you were here'? I would…"

"I wouldn't," said Lysa flatly. "He doesn't seem real."

Anna smiled at Lysa. *Thanks.*

"Who cares?" said Randi. "His body is real. That's enough for me."

"Looks don't mean anything," June said.

"That's easy for you to say," replied Randi. "You're dating a guy who models."

Anna blocked the rest out, hoping that Ulf wouldn't be waiting to drive her home.

"We seem to be enjoying each other's company, Pemba," said Ulf, coming out of the men's locker room. "We keep running into each other."

As Rakan hesitated between answering him, punching him or ignoring him, Dvara appeared by his side.

"I'm sorry, I must've made a mistake," Dvara said, glancing at Ulf. "I didn't think it was my brother's company you wanted to enjoy."

Ulf laughed. "You are most decidedly more… enjoyable," he said in a half whisper before switching to a matter-of-fact tone of voice as Anna and some of the other girls came out. "You have talent. It'll be a pleasure to teach you a few things."

Rakan turned away in disgust. "I'll walk you home," he said to Anna when she joined them.

"There's no need," said Ulf. "I'm driving there anyway."

"I'd rather walk," Anna said coldly.

"I'll accept the ride," Dvara said, glancing at Ulf. "That is, if you don't mind?"

Rakan glared at his sister, but she ignored him and smiled sweetly at Ulf.

Ulf's eyes slid down Dvara's chest. "My pleasure." He looked back at Anna. "See you at home." He flashed his perfect teeth. "For dinner."

"I'm not your daughter," Anna shot back.

"Don't worry, I never thought you were."

Rakan shifted back to their rooms as soon as he had walked Anna to her door. "Why did you ask Ulf to drive you home?" he asked Dvara who was reclining on the couch.

"Because every time you see Anna, you forget why we're here," Dvara snapped. "This way, I knew you'd come home."

"I know why we're here. I just don't think that Jing Mei is Paaliaq," Rakan said. He sat in his favorite window perch and watched the trails below. "She's a New Dragon."

"Rakan," Dvara said, taking a deep breath. "We've been through this before. Yarlung said that both Yuli and Nima'kor are certain that none of the Old Dragons left the Fragments long enough to have had a child. Even with the time differential taken into account."

"What if her parents have never been on the Fragments?"

Dvara stared at him like he had grown two heads. "You think Paaliaq and Haakaramanoth are her parents?"

"It would explain why Jing Mei has blue eyes instead of Paaliaq's green."

Dvara shook her head. "I don't know. It just doesn't feel right to me. I think Paaliaq found a way to change her eyes and is pretending to be a whelp."

"So why does she care about humans? She's not using them. She's trying to help them. Remember how she took the shield off Anna after I had manipulated it?" he said, not wanting to talk about the argument with June that had convinced him she wasn't Paaliaq.

"She could take the shield off so that you would start to trust her, or believe that she really was clueless. And she hasn't morphed once since we've been here, has she? How could a puppy who seems as young as Jing

Mei not morph for that long? It's not possible. She can't be as young as she seems. And besides, if she really was Paaliaq's whelp, her mother wouldn't let her roam Earth pretending to be a human. Even with the protection of four other dragons."

"They aren't dragons. Why can't you accept that?" insisted Rakan, facing Dvara.

"You're the one who can't accept the facts. You felt June hide her trail like the others do. Why do you need more proof than that?" Dvara held up her hand to stop him from answering. "Whatever. Dragons or not, they're protecting her."

"Maybe Paaliaq is already dead," Rakan said. "We've only ever come across one Old Dragon's trail. Not two."

"It doesn't matter what either one of us thinks, Rakan. We need proof. One way or the other. And we need it now. Yarlung is starting to manipulate the other Kairöks to determine which one she'll promise me to." Dvara paced around the living room. "I'll have to accept him. And then T'eng Sten will kill him and..."

Rakan slammed into the punching bag. "But Jing Mei isn't Paaliaq. We can't kill her."

"We can if she's Paaliaq's daughter."

"It would be killing an innocent dragon."

"No, it wouldn't. It would avenge Kraal's death. Blood for blood. You know the Code as well as I do."

Rakan glared at his sister. "The Code doesn't say we have to kill her. Only that we can. There doesn't have to be blood for blood."

"You drive me crazy, Rakan. You know Yarlung won't let the other dragons settle on Earth until she has revenge." Dvara took a deep breath and let it out slowly. "It's the only way to be free. Her death or the death of the Draak. Can't you understand that?"

Rakan sank to the couch. He wouldn't let them kill June.

Dvara took his silence as acceptance. "If Jing Mei is Haakaramanoth's daughter we can lure him out by getting her to trust us and then trapping her. If Paaliaq is dead, he'll do anything to get her back. And if she isn't... we'll finally meet her."

Rakan stared at his hands, wondering how he could protect June. "Okay," he said slowly. "I can work on getting closer to her." And then he could warn her. Against his own family.

"That's probably best. I'll figure out how to trap her."

Rakan nodded. Sick about his duplicity.

Dvara sat next to Rakan and nudged him in the shoulder. She sent him a wave of warmth. "I know you hate the idea of manipulating someone, but it's the right thing to do."

Rakan returned the wave of energy, but he didn't dare look at his half-sister. He stood abruptly and walked back to the window. He watched the trails undulate across the street and around the town, weaving back and forth in an intricate dance. If Dvara found out that he was protecting June, she'd never forgive him. And he'd lose the only friend he'd ever had.

Rakan stared blankly out the window.

It was a risk he'd have to take.

"Why do you always ask me out at the last minute?" asked Anna. She stood stiffly on the porch in front of her house. "My mother cornered me yesterday and made me accept a babysitting job for one of the other nurses."

Pemba looked confused. "We don't make plans, at home. We just... do things."

"Well, here we make plans." Anna looked down. "Maybe we can get together tomorrow?" Tomorrow was Valentine's Day.

Pemba leaned back against the wooden railing on Anna's porch and crossed his legs. "I guess so," he said. He picked at the hard snow. He shaped the ice-like snow into a smooth ball with his bare hands and threw it effortlessly into the trees on the other side of the parking lot. "So what do we plan for tomorrow? I can teach you how to keep warm." He took her hand and slid off the glove that hid her Firemark. "I said I would."

Pemba's hands were warm and soft against hers. Even after playing with the ice. Her Firemark tingled with the contact, as it always did when Pemba touched it. Warmth rushed through her body. "Why do you wear a coat if you don't need one?" she asked.

Pemba dropped her hand and stared across the fjord, like a panther observing his prey. "I'll call you tomorrow." He jumped off the porch and landed silently. His long black braid flicked behind him like a tail.

Anna watched him disappear into the woods. Why did she always blurt out something stupid every time he touched her?

Rakan shifted from the park behind Anna's house to the Botanical Gardens. He jumped lightly onto the big rock in the middle of the clearing where the Old Dragon had long since removed the fake trail, much to Rakan's frustration. But the rock had quickly become a favorite perch. It had a different vibration to it than other rocks on Earth. It felt like the Fragments, and it made him feel less alone.

But right now he was mostly interested in the vantage point he could get from it. He stood on the rock and looked across the fjord at the mountains behind the Arctic Cathedral. He had glimpsed a shimmering light from Anna's porch that didn't correspond to any of the habitations he had catalogued. And he hoped it might be the void-trails' lair.

But there was nothing. Rakan growled at the emptiness, trying to visualize what he had seen from the corner of his eye as he played with the ice on Anna's porch, wishing he could make an animated sculpture for her. But he couldn't. She'd freak out. Rakan picked up a fistful of snow and squeezed it angrily into a clump of ice and then opened his hand. He could make it for her now. Even if she'd never see it. He molded the packed snow into a miniature air dragon and held up his hands. *For you, Anna.* It stretched its wings and flew down the hill towards the fjord.

"What are you doing?" asked Dvara, appearing suddenly.

Rakan jumped off the rock. "Nothing."

"I can see that," she answered. "How are you ever going to get Jing Mei to trust you if you don't spend any time with her?" Dvara looked around the empty gardens and shivered. "Why do you keep coming back? This place gives me the creeps."

"I like the rock."

"What?"

"Never mind." He picked up more snow. "You wouldn't understand."

"What's that supposed to mean?"

Rakan glared at his sister, but didn't say anything. The tension between them had increased over the past few days. His duplicity weighed on him, and he felt increasingly isolated.

"You know Rakan, neither one of us has a normal life."

Rakan snorted. "I've never been a kai or shared a bond. I've never stood in anyone's fire. At least you've had that." Rakan threw the snowball into the fjord.

Dvara's face flushed with anger. "I'd rather be alone than forced to be a kai to someone I don't like." Her voice sliced through the evening stillness. "My life has never been my own. And it still isn't. There are only two things I have ever wanted: to revenge my father and to join T'eng Sten. And if I do one, I can't do the other. Have you ever even thought about that?" Dvara morphed and shifted deep into the earth's core, to a place where he'd have to be a fire dragon to follow her. And he wasn't.

Rakan sank to the ground and leaned against the rock, wrapping his mind around it as if it were alive. He didn't want to be alone anymore. He wanted to be part of a Cairn. And he wanted to be with Anna. And like Dvara, he couldn't do both.

When the snow began to fall, Rakan let it cover him where he lay.

Chapter 12

Valentine's Day

"CAN YOU COME OVER?" RAKAN ASKED ANNA WHEN SHE ANSWERED HER PHONE the next afternoon.

"Uh, hi Pemba," Anna said. "I can ask." She paused. "Are you okay?"

Rakan cringed at the name Pemba. He hated lying to her. "I guess so." Dvara had come home around noon. And still wasn't talking to him. "But Dawa isn't feeling so great," he said, forcing himself to use her human name.

"Okay. I can ask. Hold on."

Anna picked up the phone again. "She says she'd rather you come here." Anna's voice so clearly said she was rolling her eyes that Rakan laughed.

"What's so funny?"

"You are." Rakan glanced at his sister who was curled up on the couch. "I'll come. But if Dawa gets worse I'll have to leave."

"Aren't your parents at home?"

"No. I'll be right there," he said and hung up.

Rakan sat on the low table in front of Dvara. "I can stay if you want."

Dvara didn't answer.

"You shouldn't have morphed last night. It would've been easy for some-one to take your rök." He had stayed all night by the rock, waiting for Dvara to come back.

Dvara snorted. "You're so naïve. Go play. No one can take my rök."

"I'm not the one being naïve." Rakan pulled on his coat. "I hate these clothes."

"You can always ask Anna to help you take them off—"

Rakan cut her off with a guttural growl.

"I really don't understand the problem. How can dating her be wrong? Even Khotan has been with humans—"

"—I don't want to talk about it." He shifted into the park near Anna's house. Talking about Anna – or his father – like that with Dvara wasn't something he could do. He stalked over to Anna's porch and jabbed her doorbell.

Anna opened the door a few moments later. "How'd you get here so fast?" She looked into the parking lot. "Did you drive? I didn't know you had a car."

"What? No," he said, following her up. He felt the faint buzz of Ulf and Ingrid's energy in the apartment.

"Do you want some coffee?" asked Anna as they walked through the kitchen and into the living room.

"No."

Anna stopped abruptly and faced him. "First of all, you're supposed to say yes. Saying no isn't polite. And secondly, if you're in such a bad mood why did you come over?"

"Because we planned it." Her fierceness quickened his pulse. "And because I want to see you," he added, unable to keep from closing the distance between them. He took her in his arms. Her spicy smell wrapped around him, stirring a desire he knew he couldn't act on. He'd just hold her. Smell her. A little longer.

"Then act like it," Anna said, twisting playfully out of his arms. She turned her back to him and his desire flared to new heights. "Mom and Ulf will be down again soon. Go sit. I'll make coffee," she said over her shoulder as she disappeared into the kitchen.

Rakan followed her. "I'd rather watch you make coffee."

"Hello, Pemba," Ingrid said, coming into the kitchen. "Dawa didn't come with you?"

"Mom," Anna said, before Rakan could answer. "They aren't Siamese twins, you know."

"Speaking of twins," said Ulf, buttoning his shirt as he appeared behind Ingrid, "X-Saturnia is playing tonight. Have you heard them play?" Ulf asked Rakan. "No? Ah, then you should bring him, Anna. We're going."

Anna put four cups on a tray. "We'll see."

Ulf laughed. "Rather celebrate Valentine's Day in the apartment alone, eh?"

Ingrid spun around. "I'm sure Pemba would love to see them play." She smiled brightly at Rakan. "After all, you already know Erling Engelmann, don't you?"

"Erling? June's boyfriend?" asked Rakan.

Anna nodded. "Yes. With the twins and Lysa. They're actually really good."

Rakan looked at Anna, trying to get a better reading of what she wanted. She felt conflicted. "I'd like to go," he said slowly. "If you want to."

Anna responded by wrapping her arms around his waist. "As long as we're together," she whispered.

"Let's have some coffee, shall we?" Ingrid picked up the tray and ushered them into the living room.

Ingrid had assigned them the task of making dinner so she and Ulf could shower. "Where did you learn to cook?" asked Anna, watching Pemba.

He looked up, surprised. "Everyone knows how to cook."

Anna laughed. "No, they don't."

Pemba shrugged and turned back to deboning the chicken. "What's Erling like?"

"Open. Friendly. But he didn't use to be. He's changed a lot since June came this summer. He never spoke to anyone except his brothers or Lysa last year."

Pemba looked up. "He was here before June?"

"Well, yeah. She's an exchange student for the year. She's living with Liv's family."

"Who?"

"Haakon's girlfriend," Anna said. "You probably haven't met him yet. They started University this year. But he's almost always at handball practice these days. You've probably seen him. His sister, Kristin, is in your class."

"Kristin? The little one who sits with June and talks all the time?"

Anna smiled at the description. "That's her. They live next door to each other. But Kristin doesn't look anything like her brother. He's huge – he looks like a bodybuilder even though he isn't. There's a picture of him over there." Anna pointed to the wall of photos. "It was taken last summer, with my cousin Red. Haakon is the one with black hair." Anna looked at the picture again. Red and Haakon looked alike with their massive build and close cropped hair except that Red had the same shade of ultra blond as she did.

Pemba looked at the picture of Anna holding hands with her cousin and Haakon as they jumped off a boulder into the ocean. For a moment Anna thought he was going to rip it off the wall.

"What?" she asked. "They're nice guys. They've been friends forever."

"Are Haakon and June close?"

"The four of them are pretty inseparable, actually."

"Which four?" He turned back to the chicken with a decisive whack of the de-boning knife.

"Erling and June and Liv and Haakon."

"Haakon will be there tonight?"

"Probably." Anna watched him dissect the chicken in swift, precise strokes.

"Good. I'd like to meet him."

"Why?" She didn't really want to see Haakon. Or Liv. And she definitely didn't want to see Torsten if he was with them.

"Because you just said he was a nice guy." Pemba turned to examine Anna. "Why don't you want me to meet him?"

"I didn't say that." Anna turned away. "We can go. I just... I don't know who else will be there." She didn't want to imagine Torsten and Pemba meeting. It could only end in a fight.

Pemba came and stood in front of Anna, the knife gripped in his hand. "I'll be there," he said quietly. "You'll be safe."

Anna nodded, but didn't meet his eyes.

"Well," Ingrid said as they were cleaning up after dinner. "I have to admit your cooking surprised me, Pemba."

"Thank you, Ingrid," Rakan answered. He felt the compliment she hadn't voiced.

Ingrid smiled and waved a finger at him. "Doesn't mean I trust you."

"Oh, Mom," Anna said. "I'm seventeen, you know."

"Precisely. That's exactly how old I was when I got pregnant with you. Mistakes can happen when you're that young."

"Mom!"

"Don't worry, Ingrid," Rakan said. "We haven't planned that yet."

"Pemba!" Anna said.

"What?" Rakan watched Anna stomp out of the room. "What did I say wrong?"

"Sorry," Ingrid said, trying not to laugh. "I thought she only did that to me. Oh, go ahead, run after her and tell her you're sorry."

Rakan handed Ingrid the dish towel and followed Anna into the darkened living room.

"Anna..."

She didn't answer.

"I'm sorry," he said, not quite sure what he was apologizing for.

Anna didn't look at him. "It's not you," she said. "It's my mom. She always makes it sound like I ruined her life. She thinks I'm a mistake."

Rakan stood behind her and hesitantly put his hands on her shoulders. She didn't push him away, so he wrapped his arms around her and pulled her against his chest. She turned and cuddled into his neck. "She never wanted me. It was my father who insisted...."

"Anna," Rakan said, gently running his hands over her face. "It's okay. Why you were born doesn't matter. You're here. That's what counts."

"But she doesn't love me."

He held her face in his hands. "Do you really think that?"

"She didn't want me."

"But she does love you."

Anna shrugged and pulled away.

"My parents have never been a couple," he said. "They don't even live together."

"But I thought you said they have a research project here."

"They do. They work together. But they don't... love each other."

"Do they love you?"

Rakan looked into Anna's pale eyes that he could barely see in the dim light of the evening. But he could feel them searching his. "I don't know. I guess so." Rakan wasn't even sure if dragons ever really loved each other. "We don't talk about love. But I know that—" Rakan cut himself off, surprised that he had been about to say, '-*if we were to fly into battle, I could trust them.*'

"What?" asked Anna.

"I can trust them with my life," Rakan said. "They'd never abandon me. And I'll never abandon them."

Rakan looked at Anna's upturned face, her lips so close to his. They were so ripe, so tempting. Her breath so sweet. He ached to lean forward, to take what was on offer, to forget about fighting and revenge and...

"Anna," he said, hugging her instead. For the first time he realized that he wanted something else than what his family wanted.

The Blue Rock was already crowded by the time they arrived. Ulf was greeted by nearly everyone, and Ingrid hung to his arm, beaming with pride.

"Let's go upstairs," Anna said. She took Rakan's hand and pulled him away from Ulf and Ingrid. "They'll probably start playing soon."

Rakan followed, mentally checking to see who was there and if anyone had weapons. He hated the feeling of so many people in a small space, even if the crowd seemed in a good mood. He knew from experience that humans could turn aggressive quickly.

Anna stopped nervously at the top of the stairs and looked around. Rakan wondered who she was looking for, but she relaxed and led him across the dance floor. It was packed with people waiting for the band to start. They made their way over to June who was perched on a bar stool. Kristin was next to her, looking almost like a child in the arms of a lumberjack sized guy. Rakan scanned him, but he was human. Clueless and weaponless. Rakan scanned him again. He looked like an Old Dragon if you ignored the pale skin and short brown hair.

"Hey, Anna," June said. "I'm glad you changed your mind."

"We decided at the last minute," Anna said. "I should've called."

June smiled. "Don't worry about it. I'm glad you're here. And just in time," she said, nodding towards the stage. Erling, Lysa and the twins were coming out.

"Hey everyone, how're you doing?" said Erling. He waved to the crowd and their round of applause. He was dressed in jeans and a white tee-shirt that revealed his athletic build and cobalt blue Maii-a. His blond dreads were pulled back in his usual ponytail. "Tonight is a special night," continued Erling, adjusting his microphone. "Know why?"

Rakan focused his sight as the crowd yelled back "It's Valentine's Day," and zoomed in on Erling's eyes. They were identical to June's. Except that they had hardly any pupils. Rakan controlled a shiver of revulsion.

"Yes it is," said Erling, answering the crowd with a few strums on his guitar. "But it's also my true love's birthday. Happy Birthday, June." The crowd cheered. "Hope there are a lot of happy couples out there, because tonight is our night."

Rakan glanced over at June, wanting to ask her how old she was in dragon terms. But she was connected with Erling mentally and oblivious to everyone else.

The music started and Rakan jumped, wondering who to fight first, but no one was attacking. He tried to relax, but couldn't. The twins were dressed in black jeans, their tattoo-covered torsos a mass of indecipherable symbols. Rakan shuddered as he felt power roll off them and spill around the people in the club. Rakan ran his mind over the crowd. Something had changed. They felt different, like they had been transported to a state of ecstasy. He growled. What were the void-trails doing to the humans? Even Anna. He took her in his arms and felt a flood of happiness flow through him. Rakan immediately blocked it with a shield. His mind-touch hovered over her. Not wanting to shield her without her consent. Anna leaned into him, exuding bliss. He clenched his jaw in frustration. If he shielded her now, she'd feel it. But if the void-trails changed what they were doing, he'd shield her anyhow. He wouldn't let her get hurt.

Anna's energy began to vibrate in pleasure, like a kitten purring for the first time. Rakan nuzzled her cheek. Why was she so trusting? He held her closer, trying to understand how the void-trails were manipulating the humans. It was clear they could control the crowd in any way they wanted. Rakan tried to stay calm enough to let go of his normal senses and focus on seeing what the void-trails were doing. But he couldn't. He needed someone to shield him. He cursed to himself. He'd have to ask Dvara. But he hated asking her for help when he wasn't being honest with her.

Eventually, he reached out. *Dvara, I need you.*

Rakan stood stiffly, all his senses tensed to feel if Dvara responded or not.

"You okay?" asked Anna, looking up at him.

"What? Yeah, sure."

Rakan felt Dvara appear in the empty stairwell. "She came," he said, relieved.

"Who?"

Rakan pointed to Dvara who was dressed in a slinky vermillion top that plunged into her cleavage. Rakan groaned – she looked like an exotic flower waiting to be plucked.

"I guess she's feeling better," Anna said, without much enthusiasm.

"I'll be right back." He let go of Anna and walked over to his half-sister who was letting herself be cornered by a drunk guy. He separated her from the man's groping hands and then snarled at her. "Why do you let them do that?"

"How else am I supposed to get you alone?"

"Anna doesn't understand when we speak in Draagsil."

"Yeah, well, Jing Mei would. And in case you've forgotten in your zeal to get closer to her, she's not really supposed to know what we're doing."

Dvara's rebuke hit him square on. June wasn't the one he needed to hide anything from. "Thanks for coming," he said, feeling like a hypocrite.

Dvara scanned the crowd. "Why did you call me?" she asked moodily. "Nothing's wrong."

"That's exactly what is wrong. The void-trails are doing something to make everyone happy."

"I don't feel anything."

"No, neither do I. But when I touch Anna I do. I need you to shield me while I try to see what they're doing."

Dvara shook her head in annoyance. "You can't see what they're doing. You have to feel it. And there isn't anything to feel except their energy pulsing around us."

"They're not dragons, Dvara. They don't manipulate matter. That's why we can't feel what they're doing even if we can feel their energy."

Dvara looked at him strangely. "So what do they manipulate?"

"I don't know yet," he said quietly. "That's why I need you to shield me."

Dvara looked skeptical. "Okay. I can shield you."

"Behave," he said to Dvara as they came back to where Anna was standing near June.

Dvara rolled her eyes. "Relax and have some fun," she snapped. But he felt her shield him, even as she turned to flirt with a guy who was standing nearby.

Rakan stood behind Anna and wrapped her in his arms. "Dvara looks for trouble sometimes," he mumbled.

"I noticed," Anna said, placing her hands on his.

He opened himself to her emotions, trying to see how the void-trails were affecting them. He let go, knowing that Dvara was there. Out of the corner of his eyes he saw bits of light, like shimmering reflections on a lake. But they kept disappearing when he would look at them directly. And then Lysa started to sing. Her voice had the soft vibration of gold and it drew him in. He stared at her, transfixed by her pale green eyes that had the intensity of a dragon's. But they had no pupils. They were just hypnotic orbs of color.

When the song ended, Dvara nudged him. "Pretty good, don't you think?" she asked, dowsing him in a freezing wave of energy.

"Hey," Rakan said, retaliating for a split second before he realized that she was trying to help him. He pulled himself back from the void-trails' net of sound and light. "Uh, thanks."

"My pleasure," she said, smiling. "But you'll have to explain it to me, because I have no idea where you went." Dvara turned to the guy who was standing next to her. "Let me introduce you to my brother and his girlfriend. Pemba, Anna, this is Haakon. I'll be right back," she said and took off towards the bar. Rakan stared at Haakon. He looked exactly like an Old Dragon should, even with his close-cropped black hair. But he felt flat. Like a human.

"Oh, Haakon. I didn't see you arrive," Anna said, looking around anxiously. "Was Dvara hitting on you while Liv was at the bar?"

Haakon laughed. "No, she's just talkative, look – she's chatting with Liv now."

"Pemba, this is the Haakon I was telling you about," Anna said. "Kristin's brother."

Rakan nodded and scanned Haakon, but felt nothing. Haakon wasn't wearing the three-pronged knives that all dragons always wore. He wasn't even wearing a Maii-a. Rakan reached out warily, but there was no resistance. He was as open as any other human. Rakan pulled back. There was a blandness about Haakon's energy that he didn't like. Rakan glanced at Kristin. Anna was right. They didn't look like brother and sister.

Liv and Dvara came back, and Rakan had to stifle a growl when he realized that Liv was yet another void-trail. How many of them were there? Liv handed Haakon a glass of beer and settled herself against his side. She lifted her glass. "Cheers." Her electric blue eyes almost glowed.

All the stories about the now-extinct Beings of Light, the so-called Elythia, who were the antithesis of the Draak, came tumbling back at him. They were said to have had no pupils and no rök of their own since they weren't made of matter. "I'm Pemba," he said to Liv, challenging her to take his hand. He'd know if she was made of matter or just a complex illusion if he touched her.

She smiled and shook his hand. "I'm Liv, June's host sister."

Rakan felt her hand solidly in his and relaxed. It was made of flesh and blood. And she had pupils. Small ones, but they were there. She wasn't an empty shell of light. Her hand had been slightly warmer than most humans, but other than that, it had been no different.

Ingrid came up with Ulf to find Anna. "I have to go to work now," she said, "but Ulf is staying, so he can drive you home."

"But—"

"No buts, Anna, or you come home with me now – oh, hello Dawa. You look lovely. Are you enjoying the show?" Ingrid turned to Ulf. "Maybe you can drop Dawa and Pemba off on your way home?"

"As you wish, darling," Ulf said, smiling. "I'm easy."

Ingrid kissed Ulf and waved goodbye to everyone else.

"Can I buy you a drink?" Ulf asked Dvara, before Ingrid had even disappeared down the stairs.

"After this one," Dvara said, nodding to the guy who was next to her.

"No, I think I'd rather not be after," said Ulf, slipping a hand around Dvara's waist. "Not when firsts look like this."

Dvara giggled and twisted out of his grasp.

Anna pushed herself between Dvara and Ulf. "Knock it off."

"Why?" Ulf leaned towards her. "Are you jealous?"

Rakan pulled Anna back and faced Ulf. "Leave her alone."

"Tsk, tsk. Such a quick temper, Pemba," said Ulf casually. "Hope he doesn't always blow his fuse so quickly – for your sake, Anna." Ulf offered Dvara his arm. "Come, we can speak more freely downstairs."

Dvara giggled and wobbled downstairs with Ulf.

Rakan cursed under his breath. Haakon and Liv were gone. He tried to follow Liv's trail, but it was fainter than the other void-trails and he lost it. And Haakon's was so generic it blended in with all the others'. June was still sitting on her stool, in a trance-like state, watching Erling. Rakan wished he could send her a cold wave and knock her back to her senses. Her rapture wasn't normal.

"How can my mom be so blind?" asked Anna.

"What?" Rakan said, looking at Anna. "About Ulf you mean? I don't know. But I wish Dawa wouldn't do things like that." He took Anna back into his arms. "We'll find them on the way out. Right now I'd rather not think about it." Dvara was still shielding him, and pretending to be a little drunk probably made it easier for her to do it without being noticed.

Anna sighed. "I'd rather never see him again."

"I could arrange that, if it's what you really want," Rakan said quietly.

Anna looked at him inquisitively. "And how would you do that? People can't just disappear into thin air."

Rakan shrugged. Maybe not thin air, but something close enough. "Do you really want to know?" There were hundreds of ways he could kill a human without leaving a trace visible to the human eye. Many of which he and Dvara had tested as part of their training. Before he had decided it wasn't right to use people as target practice.

He felt a tremor of doubt go through her, but he didn't look away or try to make it seem like a joke. It was who he was.

"Sometimes I feel like we're from different worlds," she said. "I can't even tell if you're joking or not."

"What do you want, Anna?" Rakan unleashed his power and let it roll over her as the band played another love song. If his power scared her away, it would be better for her anyway. Rakan braced himself for the movement of fear or revulsion that humans always had when they felt his dragon nature.

Anna smiled and hugged him closer. "You. Without your contacts. They give your eyes a funny color."

Rakan pulled her in and held her tightly. She hadn't run away. He closed his eyes and it felt like they were standing on a bed of wild chrysanthemums. His hand found her ponytail and he groaned in frustration at not being able to undo her hair and let it flow through his fingers. But he wouldn't be able to control himself if he did.

Anna held on to Pemba and floated in the magic of the moment. She had never felt more comfortable with someone than she did with Pemba. The band played their final encore and people started to leave.

"Why does it have to end?" she asked.

"I'll walk you home."

Anna smiled and hugged him closer. "Okay."

They went down and found Ulf, his hand on Dawa's thigh.

"Time to go," Pemba said to Dawa.

"Do I have to?" asked Dawa, clinging to Ulf.

"I can drive you home," answered Ulf, standing up. "Unless Pemba would rather walk you home instead of accompanying Anna," said Ulf with a smirk. They walked out of the Blue Rock and into the frozen night. "Younger man's choice," he said with a flourish. "Your sister or Anna. I'll take the other."

Pemba spoke sharply to Dawa in Tibetan, ignoring Ulf's taunts. He took Anna's arm and they walked up the hill. Anna fumed in silence. Ulf was such a jerk. And Dawa no better.

Pemba touched her cheek when they arrived at her house. "You'll be safe."

Anna leaned into his hand. "Are you worried about Dawa?"

"No," Pemba said, his voice hard. "I'm angry with her."

"You should go home," Anna said, sorry that the mood from the club had gone.

Pemba nodded. "I'll see you on Monday."

"Okay." She watched him fade into the night. She wished that the evening had ended differently. That Ulf had gone to another party, that Dawa had stayed away, and that Pemba had kissed her once they were alone.

Chapter 13

Manipulations

R AKAN STOPPED PACING WHEN HE FINALLY FELT DVARA COME HOME IN THE early hours of the morning. He glared at her but didn't say anything. At least she hadn't brought Ulf to the apartment.

"Are you going to be pissed off all weekend?" she asked. "Or are you going to tell me what was going on at the club?"

"How can you let yourself be touched by someone like Ulf?" exploded Rakan, no longer able to contain his feelings.

"He's no worse than any of the others. And if you really want to know, I didn't let him do anything more than kiss me," Dvara said, taking off her coat. "And I won't. He just likes the excitement of the hunt. Especially if he thinks he's the first."

"He's repulsive," growled Rakan.

"Because he likes sex? Grow up, Rakan. He's no different than T'eng Sten."

"Ulf shouldn't be running after other women when he already has one."

Dvara laughed. "You've been brought up so sheltered, you don't even know what natural behavior is anymore. Most humans like to think they're monogamous. But they never are. And dragons don't even try to pretend."

"Kraal never mated with anyone other than Yarlung," said Rakan. He sat down on the couch with a thump. "Some dragons partner for life."

"Kraal was different," Dvara said quietly as she sat next to Rakan. "But even Kraal took all the females of his Cairn when they gave him their röks." Dvara was silent for a moment. "Giving your rök to your Kairök is much more intimate than sleeping together. They know everything you've ever felt, and everything you feel. You give up your individual identity. But at least you're never alone."

Rakan watched as a variety of different emotions played across Dvara's face. She felt his eyes on her and looked up. "Khotan was a good Kairök," she said. "He gave me as much independence as he could. And he never abused the power had over me. But most Kairöks aren't like that. You're bound to their will and have no choice."

"How can you know how they'll treat you before giving up your rök?" He had never considered the importance of which Kairök one had.

"You can't, really." Dvara looked down. "Although I know who I don't want. But right now I'm not sure I'll have a choice. The rest of my life could be hell."

"I won't let them take your rök."

"Don't be stupid." Dvara nudged him gently and wrapped him in a warm wave of energy. "You'll just get yourself killed. And what good would that do?"

"I won't get killed."

"Just promise me not to challenge a Kairök on my behalf. Okay?" Dvara's voice had an edge of pain. "Please. I couldn't live with losing you."

Rakan gave a low growl. He couldn't promise something like that.

"Idiot," Dvara said, punching him in the shoulder. She stood and began to pace around the room. "There's something I want to tell you. Even though I promised Khotan not to."

"What?" Rakan didn't like learning that his father had been keeping secrets from him.

"It has to do with the void-trails. Maybe you're right. Maybe they aren't dragons."

"They aren't," Rakan said slowly, wondering what she knew that he didn't. "They don't have röks."

"No. But they have something — they were mind-speaking tonight. And they have power. Especially Erling." Dvara stopped pacing. "Khotan didn't think you would understand, but I think you need to know. After the Old Dragons tried unsuccessfully to mate with the humans, Khotan conducted a series of experiments. Eventually he was able to modify a few females and have children with them. None of the offspring had röks, even though they looked like dragons in human form."

Rakan sat in shock. "But..."

"Khotan refused to continue the experiments after the children... died. And that's when Yarlung and Khotan decided to have you." Dvara struggled to contain the pain that the memory had unleashed. "The only reason I'm telling you this is because it's not impossible that Haakaramanoth modified something to be able to mate with the humans, and the void-trails are his offspring."

"How did they die?" Rakan asked.

Dvara looked away but Rakan caught an image of fire and terror before she closed herself off.

"Tell me," Rakan said, inching forward.

"Other humans killed them. Because they were different. And had powers that humans couldn't understand." Dvara's voice became distant, as if she was reciting a lesson she had learned long ago. "The last one died by the hands of his own people. The people he went back to help. But humans are weak. They don't have the courage to face the truth. When Qadan revealed what he really was, the humans feared him. They killed him…" Dvara's voice was choked with pain. "They poisoned him like the cowards they were."

Rakan felt Dvara's blind rage and he saw the Steppes covered with blazing fires, people screaming in terror and fleeing in front of Dvara in her dragon form as she sought revenge. Smoke and death filled his senses, until he was no longer sure if he was experiencing a memory or if he had shifted into a tribal war on the Steppes.

"It's over," Dvara said. "I killed them all." Tears streamed down her cheeks. "But it did no good. It didn't bring Qadan back." She clung to Rakan. "I can't lose you too. Promise me not to challenge a Kairök," she pleaded.

"I can't promise you that," said Rakan. "I can't let you be taken against your will."

"I'm not like you. I can't live alone." She turned away. "Just promise me not to challenge T'eng Sten, okay? He helped me when I needed it the most. When I wouldn't let Khotan help me, even though he tried." She faced Rakan. "I owe T'eng Sten my life."

Ingrid rattled Anna's doorknob. "Anna? Are you okay? Why did you lock your door?"

"Ugh," groaned Anna, rolling over. "What time is it?"

"It's 9:30. I brought you breakfast."

Anna got up and opened the door. "Thanks, Mom."

"I thought it would be nice to have breakfast together. It's been a long time."

Anna nodded and sat back on her bed. Her mom always used to bring her breakfast in bed when she worked a night shift on the weekend. Before Ulf.

"Where's Ulf?" asked Anna, pulling her bathrobe on.

"He went back to his apartment to get some work done. But I'm glad you guys are getting along better. He said you had a nice evening with Dawa and Pemba."

Anna nodded. She was sure he had enjoyed bringing Dawa home. Or wherever else he had taken her, since he hadn't come back to the apartment. How could Dawa flirt with Ulf when she knew he was dating her mom? It was disgusting.

"Ulf said that the two of you had a nice chat after dropping Pemba and Dawa off at the Tibetan House," continued Ingrid.

Anna choked on her coffee. The jerk. Ulf knew Anna wouldn't say Pemba had walked her home. But to have twisted her into his lie about Dawa… for once Anna wished Ulf was with them so that she could confront him about it.

"You okay?" asked her mom. "I'm going to go to bed for a while. Did you know that Ulf brought me flowers at the hospital this morning? He's so sweet. It was so nice, especially since we had such a crazy night at work."

Anna nodded, and her mom launched into a monologue about her night shift.

Rakan sat sullenly in science class, bored out of his mind. The sun was up from mid-morning to mid-afternoon now. Exactly when they were in school. But today was Wednesday, and they only had a half day. He looked at the fjord below in anticipation. The air shimmered in the crystal clear way it always did when it was just below zero. He needed out.

"Since no one has any ideas on how to make this hot air engine work, you will all partner up and figure it out," said the science teacher, Mr. Lund. "This afternoon."

A collective groan rose up from the class.

"I'll set the partners."

A second groan rose up.

"Silence," said Mr. Lund. "Or I'll assign a term project to go with this."

The class settled down sullenly as Mr. Lund called out the pairs. Rakan sank into his chair. He didn't want to have to work with anyone and pretend he didn't know how to build the engine. Not when the sun was calling him.

"Pemba, you'll work with June."

Rakan jerked up in surprise. "What?" She had ignored him completely since their last interaction, no matter what he tried. Or how well he behaved.

"But sir," June said. "I don't want—"

"June," said Mr. Lund, looking over his glasses "You surprise me. The answer is no. You'll work with Pemba. The day you have a job, you won't be able to choose your co-workers."

Mr. Lund pulled out a bunch of pre-packed kits. "These should take you about two hours to assemble if you work efficiently."

The bell rang. "Class dismissed."

June stalked out of the class and ran downstairs. Rakan picked up the kit and tossed it in his backpack. It wouldn't take him more than a few minutes to assemble it, and then he'd have the afternoon free to try to find where the void-trails lived. He had finally managed to trail them across the fjord in spite of the multitude of false tracks they created every day.

When he came out into the schoolyard, Anna was talking with June and Erling.

"What are you doing this afternoon?" she asked when he joined them. "For once I don't have any projects to work on."

"I'm supposed to work with June," Rakan said, smiling at Anna's hopeful expression. "But I think she has other plans."

"I'm sure you can do it on your own," said Erling.

"I believe it is within my capabilities," answered Rakan coldly.

"Why would you do that?" snapped June. "It's a group project which means we work together." She glared at Erling. "Why are you always interfering?"

"If you don't want her to be alone with me, why don't you come with us?"

Erling looked at him with an oddly detached look, as if he was seeing something else. "No. There won't be any problems today. My presence isn't necessary."

"Would you stop behaving like an oracle?" June snapped at Erling. "It drives me crazy." She turned to Rakan. "Let's just do what we have to do." She strode back into the school.

Rakan turned to follow, but Erling blocked his way. "I don't trust you," said Erling, so quietly that only a dragon's ears could hear it. "Even if I know you won't try anything today. I know you will eventually. And when you do, I'll be there. No matter what the consequences are."

Rakan glared at Erling. "I've never given you any reason not to trust me, have I?"

Erling's energy shimmered menacingly, and Rakan felt a responding flicker within. His body tensed, ready to fight. Eager to fight.

"Why are you all so uptight about a project? We do them all the time," Anna said, looking from one to the other. "What's really going on?"

"I'll call you as soon as we finish, okay?" Rakan said to Anna. He followed June's trail into the student lounge where other groups were already working on various projects, his senses on full alert. June's energy was crackling like an electrical storm.

"Here," Rakan said, tossing the kit on the table. "Do you want to do it, or shall I?"

"We're supposed to do it together."

"You want us to do it together? You've been ignoring me for the past week and now you want us to link?"

"What are you talking about? We just have to build it."

"Were you planning on doing it with your hands?"

"Of course."

"Why?"

"Well, how else would you do it?"

Rakan started to laugh but stopped when he felt her confusion. "You're serious?"

June's cobalt eyes searched his. "Yes."

Rakan stared back at her for a long time before answering. "Normally, I would do it with my mind. You feel the pieces and you assemble them. It's just a simple engine that uses the expansion and contraction of air to move a piston, generating energy. It's a basic example of thermodynamics."

June nodded, but didn't say anything.

"You've never done it before?" asked Rakan, laying out the pieces.

"No."

"Didn't your parents teach you anything?"

"Not like that. They don't have röks. I only started to learn to manipulate matter here."

Rakan sat back and examined June. "You expect me to believe that?"

"Yes. Because it's the truth." June held his eyes. "I'm a human with a rök."

Rakan sat still. It felt like she was telling the truth. "That's not possible."

June shrugged. "And yet here I am."

Rakan looked back at the one hundred and forty eight pieces. "Do you want to try?"

"Can you teach me?"

"You want me to teach you?"

"Why not? You don't think I can learn?"

"Erling will come flying in here to kill me as soon as my mind touches you."

"I've already put up a shield that blocks him out." June smiled. "He hates it when I do that."

Rakan searched with his mind-touch. "I don't feel it."

June smiled. "So what did your parents teach you?"

Rakan felt a shiver of doubt. "Not to trust you."

"But you do trust me, don't you?" June leaned forward, her eyes blazing a brilliantly bright cobalt blue.

"Yes," Rakan said, surprised to hear his own answer echo around him as if they were in a closed sphere. The idea reminded him of the twins. He jumped when he felt a ripple of energy run across him. But it was only June trying to link.

"Show me," she said, pointing to the pieces.

He let his mind-touch meld with hers and was surprised by both its power and its complexity. His rök thrashed in his chest, aching to fly free.

"Why is this hard for you?" asked June, helping him calm his rök.

"No. It's okay. I just…"

"Feel lonely," June finished for him.

Rakan forced himself to focus on the engine. When they had finished, he pulled his mind-touch back and looked at her.

She smiled. "You have a gentle mind, with hidden power. I'm letting the shield down." She packed up her stuff. "Don't forget to call Anna, you said you would."

Rakan watched as she disappeared, wondering if he had just made one of the biggest mistakes of his life letting her feel his mind-touch.

Chapter 14

Weighing the Facts

THE NARROW VALLEY TWISTED BELOW THEM ON THE MAINLAND. "THERE'S nothing here," Dvara said. "We're wasting our time. Let's go home."

"Their lair is hidden here," Rakan said without moving from his perch. "I saw something shimmer here last Wednesday." It corresponded to the light he had seen from Anna's porch. It had to be here, shrouded by one of their special shields. The island of Tromso twinkled in the distance. "It's almost sunrise." He sat stiffly, controlling his urge to face the Eastern sky and answer the Call to Rise. "We should wait."

"They'll never come out with us around," Dvara said, placing her hands on her hips and blocking his view. "In case you've forgotten, we can't hide our trails. There's no reason to stay. We can't morph here anyhow."

"Their shield will react to the coming light, even if only for a fraction of a second. And then we'll know where their lair is." Rakan stood and faced his half-sister. "I don't know why you decided to come with me, but you're not helping right now." He leaned forward. "Go home, Dvara."

Dvara tilted her chin up. "Not without you."

"Then stay out of my way." Rakan moved to the side and resumed his watch over the valley, pointedly ignoring his sister.

Dvara stood in front of him again, blocking his view.

A snarl escaped Rakan's throat before he could quell his desire to lash out and knock Dvara out of the way. "How can I figure out where they live if you keep standing in front of me?"

"We need to go home." Dvara grabbed his arm and tried to shift them both.

Rakan flung her away and froze the air around her. "Don't ever do that to me again." His voice shook with barely controlled rage. "I'm not a puppy. Go home if you want. But I'm staying here."

Dvara sank down on the crusty snow of late winter. "Why are you so stubborn?"

Rakan started to growl a reply, but the cold reflection of fear on Dvara's face froze the words in his throat. His eyes darted to where Dvara's gaze was fixed, but saw nothing. A fraction of a second later, Rakan felt two dragons approaching, and then Kairök Yttresken's bodyguards shifted into position twenty feet away.

"Why didn't you tell me?" snapped Rakan, transforming his human clothes into his black dragon pants. The guards stood like silent sentinels.

"Because you're as stiff and rigid as they are," hissed Dvara under her breath so that only Rakan would hear. "You'd never have accepted breaking the Code—"

"Try me next time," Rakan said, cutting her off with a freezing wave of energy. "If there is a next time," he added under his breath as the air shimmered in front of the guards. He squared his shoulders and braced himself to face the Old Dragon who had come for Dvara.

Kairök Yttresken materialized slowly, playing with his transformation so that he appeared to be both human and dragon at the same time. Rakan snorted. It was a vulgar display of the Kairök's talents as a transformer. When Yttresken solidified in his human form, he hit his right fist to his chest and held his left hand up in the sign of non-aggression. He opened his right hand and a single lotus took shape, floating in midair, its pale pink petals made of flickering flames.

"Greetings, Kairök Yttresken," Rakan said, pushing Dvara behind him. He eyed the fire flower suspiciously.

"Greetings young Rakan'dzor," replied Yttresken with a slight drawl. He scanned Rakan with his mind. "Although you are not as young as Yarlung would have you. You should have become a kai in one of the Cairns by now, unless I am mistaken."

Rakan bowed again. "I abide by my mother's will in all such matters."

Yttresken smiled, his lips making a thin line in his tight face. "That's good to hear." His caught Dvara's scent in the wind, and his pink eyes flared. "Indeed. Yarlung has spoken the truth. Come forward, Dvara Azura, and show yourself so that I may admire the beauty you are said to have blossomed into."

Rakan put his arm out to stop Dvara, but she froze his movement. "It is my will," she said coldly. She walked gracefully towards Yttresken, her vermillion gown glittering in the pre-dawn light that heralded the coming of the sun.

Rakan followed her with his eyes. The shape of her gown was different from usual. It was a backless turtleneck dress that revealed far more of her back and buttocks than usual. But it covered her chest in the front. And T'eng Sten's Firemark. Rakan seethed in anger. Their mother was asking Dvara to play a dangerous game.

Yttresken cupped the flickering flower in his hand. Dvara undulated as she approached the Kairök, only coming to a standstill when she was directly in front of him.

"Yarlung has spoken to me of your desire to join a Cairn," he said, his voice neutral despite of the evident arousal that Dvara's dance had stirred in him. "One where there are appropriate dragons able to mate with you. A function Khotan is too weak to assume, I gather."

A low growl escaped from Rakan before he could stifle his rök's desire to pound Yttresken to a pulp.

Yttresken arched an eyebrow and looked at Rakan, feigning surprise. "Did you not know there was a time differential between Earth and the Fragments? Through no fault of his own, Khotan has grown frail. Of course, he never was a real Kairök." Yttresken smiled maliciously. "And I doubt he was ever able to give you the pleasure you deserve." His voice dropped so low that Rakan had to strain to hear. "Your name suits you, Dwarf Jewel."

Rakan willed himself to stand still as Yttresken walked slowly around Dvara, examining her with his beady pink eyes. "You are a beauty that any dragon would prize as a mate," he said, his nostrils flaring. "Will you accept this humble fire flower as a token of my intention to claim you?"

Rakan's body crisped in apprehension. He had never seen a fire flower before, but his rök was yelling that it couldn't be a good thing. He felt the telltale tingling on his arms and braced himself for his mother's appearance in his mind.

"*Enough,*" she said. "*Dvara has agreed to accept him. You will not intervene.*"

The miniature dragons disappeared as quickly as they had come. Dvara bowed to the Kairök, and Rakan growled to himself. If Yttresken tried to take Dvara by force, he'd protect her, even if Dvara didn't fight back, even if it meant going against his mother's will.

Yttresken undid Dvara's hair and let it tumble down her back. He placed the fire flower above her head where it floated for a moment before bursting into thousands of miniature flames. They sparkled like glitter as they wove themselves into Dvara's hair. "What has Yarlung done to stop me from taking you now?" Yttresken closed his eyes and inhaled deeply. "You're so ripe."

"Only her wrath, should you take me without accepting me by your side," Dvara said sweetly. But Rakan could feel the loathing underneath.

Yttresken's laugh was sharp and dry. "Either you are naïve, or you play your part well. Either way, I must be reassured of a few things before offering you that honor." Yttresken's features hardened, taking on the solid aspect of armor. "Kairök T'eng Sten has let it be known that you wear his Firemark." Yttresken paused to watch Dvara's face. "If that is true, why hasn't he claimed you now that you are free?"

"He did. But I refused him," Dvara said, tilting up her chin. "It was a mistake of youth. I was lonely and he took advantage of my innocence."

Yttresken snorted. "Whether you refuse or not, he is strong enough to take you. And, unlike me, he would have no scruples in doing so. He is not the gentleman that I am."

Dvara bowed her head. "I did not understand the implications of my actions at the time. I have since asked him to release me."

"Be careful what you say, Dvara. If I do take your rök, I will know everything." He cupped a hand under Dvara's chin and she pulled back in a faint movement of revulsion. Yttresken's eyes narrowed. "I will not take having been lied to lightly."

Dvara stood perfectly still, neither turning away from Yttresken's piercing gaze nor rising to his challenge. But Rakan could feel the hatred that Dvara struggled to control. He crouched slightly, ready to spring to her defense should she burst forth in an uncontrolled attack on the Kairök. His only chance to save her would be to shift her home where T'eng Sten's shields would protect her. *If* he could shift her home without killing her. It wasn't a skill he had mastered yet.

Yttresken let go of Dvara and took out one of his three pronged dragon knives. He caressed the glistening black metal, turning it around in his hands. He smiled at Dvara and then inserted it into her dress, directly between her breasts. Slowly, he brought the knife up, smoothly slicing the metallic cloth and revealing T'eng Sten's Firemark. When he reached the top of her dress, he tilted her chin up with the tip of the blade. "You do know that there is only one way to release you from T'eng Sten's Firemark, don't you?"

Dvara gave a faint jerk of her head, her jaw muscles twitching.

"And what way is that?" he asked, leaning closer to her.

Dvara closed her eyes as his breath caressed her face, but she didn't respond.

"Tell me," he said, increasing the pressure of the knife and tilting her chin higher.

"Death," she hissed tersely.

Yttresken smiled malevolently. "Whose?" A trickle of blood ran down the knife.

Rakan growled and lunged for Yttresken, who quickly turned Dvara around so that her back was against his chest and his knife was on her jugular. "Don't even think about it, or she dies right now," said Yttresken as two more guards appeared.

Dvara shimmered as if she was trying to shift, but Yttresken gripped her tighter. "Why would you want to shift out of my arms, darling? Didn't you just accept my courtship?"

"Back off, Rakan," Dvara hissed. "This has nothing to do with you."

"Now that's much more reasonable, isn't it," said Yttresken, his free hand beginning to explore her stomach.

Rakan backed off, wondering if he could manage to shift Dvara back to their apartment. If Yttresken tried to kill her, he'd take the risk.

"So. Whose death, darling?" Yttresken asked again, his lips nuzzling her ear.

"The one who made the mark," Dvara hissed, jerking her head away.

"Indeed." Yttresken lowered his knife. "And since you have accepted my courtship, does that mean you renounce his?"

"I already said yes," she said, her voice a hiss of undisguised fury.

Yttresken nodded. "But words don't speak in quite the same way as actions. And right now, I need a little more reassurance. I like to know that my mates are mine. I don't share." Yttresken dropped his knife so that the point rested on T'eng Sten's Firemark. "So you will have to purify yourself of this before I will honor you by taking your rök."

Dvara paled.

"Of course," continued Yttresken, "as you have already said, only his death will release you. Which is a problem. Kairöks can't just go around killing each other in these troubled times."

Unexpected hope flickered on Dvara's face.

"Are you certain that you no longer care for him?" asked Yttresken, running his free hand over her hips. "Could it be that you might actually care for me? In time, perhaps?"

"My heart goes to those I respect," Dvara said, forcing herself not to pull away. "T'eng Sten said many things, but followed through on none." Her voice was bitter.

"He has never been known to be dependable," said Yttresken gently. "And unfortunately, you are not the first to have been deceived by his flamboyant good looks."

Dvara's face quivered and she looked away.

"Will you allow me to hope?" asked Yttresken. "Will you one day come to me freely?"

"Yes," she said, her head still turned away from Yttresken.

Yttresken's lips twisted into a sardonic smile. "Then I am confident you will find a way to cleanse yourself of T'eng Sten's Firemark since it is the only barrier to our union."

Dvara's face jerked up to look at Yttresken, her face momentarily vermillion. "I would have hoped that my word be held in higher esteem." She twisted violently out of his arms. "Especially by a Kairök as... upstanding... as yourself." Dvara trembled as she tried to control her revulsion, but she lost control and a shimmering wave of vermillion flashed around her, creating a shield of energy.

"If you can't find a way to free yourself," said Yttresken, "I will not be able to accept your rök." He dissolved the shield with a lecherously caressing hand that lingered over her breasts. "Although, since you have promised yourself to me, I will still have the pleasure of taking you." Yttresken ran the tip of his knife down Dvara's chest and over her hips. "The fiercer the battle, the sweeter the victory, my dear."

Yttresken waved his guards off, and they disappeared. "And since I care for what will be mine, my fire flower will allow me to track you." The Kairök shifted slowly, transforming his image into his pale pink air dragon form. "Should T'eng Sten come to see you, one of my guards will be summoned automatically."

"There's no reason to attack T'eng Sten," hissed Dvara. "I've already refused him."

"Tsk, tsk," said Yttresken. "Such concern for a dragon you've refused, especially when I have absolutely no intention of attacking him." Yttresken's ghostly pink illusion swiveled its neck to look Dvara in the eye. "So quick to ignite," he said, his dragon face nearly the size of Dvara's torso. "You truly are a fire dragon, aren't you? But I assure you, my dear, I was only thinking of your protection. We wouldn't want T'eng Sten to take you against your will, would we?" Yttresken's saccharine voice emanated from the unearthly pink glow of the fading illusion.

Dvara stood with her chin tilted regally until the Kairök finally disappeared. In a silent cry of fury, she erupted in a mass of vermillion sparks before morphing into her fire dragon form and slithering into the earth, leaving Rakan alone to face the rising sun.

Anna paced in front of the school lunchroom. Pemba still hadn't come down from class, even though June and Kristin had come down long ago. Anna looked at her watch again, but didn't see the time. She flung her bag over her shoulder and headed up the stairs. When she reached the second floor landing, she saw Pemba sitting alone in the middle of the stairwell.

"Hey, what's wrong?" she asked. She slowed down as she climbed the final stairs to reach him.

"Nothing." Pemba's voice was distant.

"Something happen in class?" She sat down and nudged him in the shoulder.

"No. Let's have lunch," Pemba said, standing up with a jerk.

Anna watched as Pemba walked down the stairs, oblivious to the fact that she wasn't following him.

Pemba stopped and turned around. "Anna?" He looked up the stairwell at her, then came back up to where she was sitting. He pulled her into his arms.

Anna stood stiffly, trapped between wanting to respond and her need to know what was bothering him. She felt his mind wrap around her and she wavered. She leaned into him. He was so warm, so deliciously spicy, that all she wanted was to melt into him. She buried her face in his neck and held him close. "Why can't you ever tell me what's going on?" she asked. Her lips lingered on his soft bronze skin as her body molded into his.

Pemba let go of her, and Anna gasped in pain as the connection between them ruptured with a sizzling flash.

"Let's have lunch," he said and went back down the stairs.

"Pemba…" Anna's voice trailed after him as she steadied herself against the railing, still reeling from the abruptness of the separation.

"What?" he said, turning around on the stair. His face a blank mask.

Anna started to say something but then closed her mouth. "Nothing," she mumbled. She rubbed her Firemark as she followed him downstairs. She didn't want lunch. She wanted Pemba.

"Why aren't you getting closer to her?" yelled Dvara from her bedroom doorway. "You spend hours with her at school. You've even had a project to do with her. Alone. And then all you do is come home and daydream in the window? What's wrong with you?"

"Building trust takes time," Rakan said, struggling to control his anger that was uncoiling like snake. June still wasn't talking to him, even after their project together. Although she watched him all the time.

"But we don't have time," retorted Dvara. "We need to know if Paaliaq is dead or not so that we know what to do with Jing Mei."

Rakan jumped out of his window seat. "I know that." He landed in front of his sister. If he could've forced June to listen to him, he would've done it already.

"Then why aren't you doing anything?"

"What do you think I'm doing when I'm sitting there?" He forced his
rök back into control. "I watch her trail all the time. Maybe you're the one
who needs to get out. You didn't even go to school this week."

The air around Dvara shimmered vermillion. She was dangerously close
to going wild. "You really are naïve, aren't you? What do you think Old
Pink Eyes gave me this for?" Dvara jerked a hand at her glittering hair. "To
watch me? Grow up, Rakan." She slammed the door in his face.

"Dvara?" Rakan reached out to open her door, but stopped when he felt
her shift elsewhere. "*Idiot*," he yelled and exploded her door with a back
kick.

He reconstructed Dvara's door and sank to the couch. The silence of
loneliness closed in on him, pressing into his chest. Everything was going
wrong. "*Anna,*" he yelled at the oppressive emptiness, as if his voice would
be enough to dispel it. "Anna," he repeated, quietly, gently opening his
clenched hands. "Where are you?" He let his mind run over the town and
found her in her apartment. He picked up his phone and called her.

"Hi, Pemba," she answered, but her voice was guarded.

"Can you come over?" his voice broke. He wasn't far from an uncontrolled morph himself.

Anna didn't reply, and Rakan felt his rök threaten to break free. "I need
to see you." He squeezed his eyes shut and painfully forced his rök into
submission. "Please."

"Okay," she said after a pause. "I'll be there as soon as I can."

Rakan heaved a sigh of relief and sank to the couch, his rök smoldering
in his chest.

Anna stared at her phone. She wanted more than anything to be with
Pemba. But she hated how he never told her what was going on. Snatched
hugs here and there weren't enough. She wanted to be close to him. But he
was always pulling back. It made her think he didn't really want to be with
her. And then he'd do things like this. Call her, desperate to see her. And
she couldn't say no. She shoved her phone in her pocket. Her mom would
never allow her to go over to Pemba's. Unless she lied.

"Was that Pemba?" asked her mom, as if on cue.

"Yeah. He asked if I could meet him for coffee." That was sort of true. Maybe.

"Oh, okay. Just be home for dinner. Ulf should be here around five."

"Sure," Anna said. She needed to get out and away from any further questions that would lead to more lies.

As soon as Anna arrived at the Tibetan House, Rakan jumped off the porch and hugged her close. She was here. He wasn't alone anymore. His mind-touch enveloped her and he groaned when she responded. He ran his mouth on her neck, his tongue finally tasting the sensitive skin that quivered under his touch. Rakan gripped her tighter. Her taste tingled on the tip of his tongue. The smell of her warm, wet skin filled his senses, blinding him with a passion that chipped away at all of his resolves not to mate with her. He pulled her hat off and ran his hand through her hair, moaning in pleasure as he felt it slide through his fingers.

"Pemba-la," said Ani-la from the porch, dousing his ardor with her flow of reprimands in Tibetan.

Anna wrenched herself away from Pemba and looked anxiously at the woman with the shaved head who had spoken. She was dressed in burgundy and yellow robes and seemed to be scolding Pemba. But she looked too young to be his mother.

Pemba nodded his head and took Anna's hand. "Ani-la is the nun who lives here. She says I shouldn't leave you outside." Ani-la continued speaking. "She says I should've gotten dressed this morning," Pemba said, translating what Ani-la was saying. "But I am dressed," he said to Ani-la before turning back to Anna. "Come inside, you're cold." Pemba touched her cheek. "She's right about that."

Pemba led Anna up the porch and into the house that was filled with the smell of incense. But it was more mineral than Pemba's. Anna stopped in the entryway; she could hear people chanting from the open doorway to the room off to the left.

Pemba turned and smiled. "It's just the local prayer group." He took her coat. "Leave your shoes here." He pointed to a dozen pairs neatly lined up along the wall.

Anna looked at Pemba's bare feet and realized that all he had on was a pair of pants that reminded her of those worn by the black belts at the ju-jitsu club. Except Pemba's looked like they were made of liquid metal and not stiff cotton. "Do you do martial arts?" Anna asked as Pemba led her to a sitting room that was next to the stairway at the end of the hall.

"No. I was just… letting off some steam." He walked over to the window that faced the tiny backyard. "We have a punching bag upstairs. In the apartment my father is renting."

Anna stood awkwardly in the middle of the room that was lined with ottoman-like wooden benches covered in futons, gawking at Pemba's back. It glowed like bronze in the sunlight from the window. Pemba faced her, his muscles rippling under the surface of his smooth skin. "You smell different," Anna said, pulling her eyes back up to meet his and nervously saying the first thing that came to mind.

Pemba gave her an inquiring look. "How do I smell different?"

"I didn't mean it in a bad way," Anna said, wishing she hadn't said anything. Again.

"I know." He came closer and touched her cheek. "Just tell me how it's different."

Anna closed her eyes and breathed in, aching to touch his skin. "You smell like a fire that's been put out. Usually you smell like incense. But not like the house." Anna looked cautiously at Pemba, unsure of how he would take it. "Is that weird?"

"No." He inched forward. It was the smell of his rök smoldering. And it wasn't a good sign. "I'm just surprised that you can smell it." His voice was barely a whisper.

Anna could feel the warmth radiating from his body as the distance between them closed ever so slowly. She trembled in anticipation, but he stopped before touching her. "It sometimes happens when I work out," he said quietly, his breath caressing her face. Anna stood with her eyes closed, silently pleading for him to take her in his arms, to feel the firmness of his lips on hers, to feel his braid wrap around her as she…

The rustling of Ani-la's thick cotton robes jolted Anna out of her reverie. Anna escaped to the window, her cheeks burning, while Pemba took the tray Ani-la was carrying, saying something that made them both laugh.

Anna turned to watch Pemba. He was different here with Ani-la. He was like a puppy, playfully getting in the way as Ani-la tried to pour the tea. But when they spoke it didn't sound anything like the guttural language that Pemba and Dawa spoke together. Or Haakon and Torsten for that matter. Ani-la said something to Anna and gestured at the table where she had placed two small bowls. Ani-la put her hands together and bowed before backing out of the room.

Pemba sat cross-legged on the ottoman in front of the table and beckoned for Anna to join him. She sat uneasily on the edge, her feet still on the ground. She looked around at the wall hangings depicting multicolored deities that didn't look anything like her idea of what Buddhist paintings should look like. One in particular caught her eye, with its dark blue figure that looked like a humanoid monster surrounded by flames. He had serpents around his neck and was dressed only in a tiger skin wrapped around his loins. He felt like raw power, ready to be unleashed in a violent wrath. Pemba picked up one of the silver-lined wooden bowls and offered it to her. Anna fumbled as she tried to take the bowl without touching him. She didn't want her cold hands to betray her nervousness.

"What language were you speaking?" she asked, making a face at the tea. It smelled like rancid butter.

"Tibetan."

"But what do you usually speak with Dawa then?"

Pemba's smile disappeared. "We speak Draagsil. The language of our ancestors."

"Oh. But weren't they Tibetan?"

"No." Pemba drank some tea. "Do you like it?"

Anna tasted it and choked. "It's awful. I mean—"

Pemba's laughter interrupted her. "It's made with yak butter. And it smells like the herds." Pemba inhaled deeply. "It's perfect."

Anna smelled it again, wondering if she could smell the herds. But it was just salty and pungent. And definitely rancid. "I don't know," she said, not wanting to disappoint Pemba. "I guess I prefer coffee." *Without butter.*

"We can get some later." He finished his bowl and took hers. "But this is better."

"If you say so." Anna tried not to grimace as he drank her tea. "Where's Dawa?"

"She's out."

"And your parents?"

"They don't stay here," Pemba said. He put her bowl down.

Anna stared at him blankly. "Where do they stay?"

Pemba took her hand. "You're cold and I said I'd teach you how to stay warm."

She understood from his crisp tone of voice that the subject of his parents was off limits. Confused, she looked at his Maii-a. It glinted like a treasure on his bronze-colored skin. His energy was like a coiled snake about to strike and it reminded her of the blue painting. He touched the Firemark and a searing heat flashed inside her. She didn't know if she should run away or throw Pemba on his back and tackle him. Anna closed her eyes and gripped his hands tighter, unable to tear herself away from his naked chest that was only inches away from her... begging her to dig her nails into the undulating muscles that lined his stomach, to sink her teeth into his neck and...

"Do you want to?" Pemba asked, his hands clutching hers.

Anna pulled back, startled, until she realized that he meant teaching her to stay warm, not ripping him apart. "Ah, okay," she mumbled, her blood still pounding in her tangled desires to possess him with a violence that made her distrust herself.

Pemba smiled and turned his hands so that their palms were touching. Anna felt a tingling at the base of her neck, just like when the void had been filled the other night at the snow screen. She looked questioningly at Pemba. But he was looking out the doorway at the stairs. Suddenly several voids were being filled in rapid succession. There was a crash at the top of the stairs followed by total silence. Only one filled void was left, and it was vibrating angrily.

"Dvara," Pemba said, his body as tense as a panther about to pounce on his prey.

"Dawa? I thought she was out?"

Pemba's attention snapped back to Anna. "She was. Stay here. I'll be right back." Pemba bounded up the stairs, his bare feet making no noise.

Anna stood, her whole body on edge as she watched Pemba turn out of sight at the top of the stairs. She heard him snarl something in Draagsil. There was a second crash and then Anna heard a door open and caught the sound of two people yelling at each other. And then emptiness.

Pemba was gone.

Anna panicked. She flew up the stairs, the wood creaking loudly under her feet. She turned and looked wildly around for any sign of Pemba. But all she saw was a shadowy figure lurking at the end of the dimly lit hallway. For a minute Anna wondered if she was seeing things. But she could clearly feel the pulsing energy that was sizzling with anger. The shadow figure, whatever it was, was real.

"Where's Pemba?" she yelled, but she knew without waiting for an answer that he had gone through the multi-colored door across from the shadow figure. She could feel Pemba, faintly, as if he was very far away. Or hurt. She rushed to the door, her eyes focused intently on the handle.

The shadow person lunged at her. Anna felt a horrible wrench of cold as the shadow passed through her. She stopped, gasping in pain. The door was only inches away. The thought of Pemba pulled her onward. She stumbled forward. The door flared with stinging sparks of energy. She grasped the handle and flung herself through the doorway.

Chapter 15

Sparks

AFTER ONE HORRENDOUS MOMENT OF SIZZLING PAIN THAT FELT LIKE BEING skinned alive, Anna stepped into the room and slammed the door behind her. There was a moment of stunned silence as three pairs of eyes fixed upon hers.

"Why didn't you tell her to stay where she was?" hissed Dawa.

"I did," snarled Pemba.

"It doesn't matter how she got here," said the last person Anna would have expected to encounter in Pemba and Dawa's rooms. "She's here."

Torsten's indigo eyes bore into hers, making her vision blur. But she didn't have to see him clearly to know it was the man she had met at the snow screen with June and Haakon. And for one mistaken moment thought was Pemba. "Torsten," Anna said, clutching the doorknob behind her back.

"Torsten? Who's Torsten?" said Dawa, spinning to face Anna in a flash of red.

"Let me see your arm," said Torsten. He moved towards Anna. "You're hurt."

"Don't touch her," hissed Dawa, blocking his way. "Let Pemba do it."

Anna felt Pemba's mind-touch wrap around her even before he had touched her, gently washing over the pain that gnawed her flesh like the embers of a fire. Anna sighed in relief as the pain receded, leaving only the pulsing memory of its passage.

"How do you do that?" she asked, seeking refuge in his arms.

He nuzzled her hair. "You should've stayed downstairs."

"You disappeared," she answered, choking on her own words. She buried her face in his neck. "You smell like you again." She breathed in his deliciously spicy smell that made her forget everything else. Almost. She pulled herself together and sought Pemba's eyes. "What is that shadow thing?"

"What shadow thing?"

"You saw Kariaksuq?" interrupted Torsten. "She should have been invisible to you."

Anna's attention snapped back to Torsten. "What are you doing here?"

"I think you've mistaken me for someone else," said Torsten calmly, his face unreadable. "We've never met."

Anna glared at Torsten. She'd recognize the intense fizzy pattern of his energy anywhere.

"This is my boyfriend, Tenzin," said Dawa, linking her arm through Torsten's, but the tension between them was anything but romantic. "He just showed up this morning." Dawa's voice was accusing as she glared at Torsten. "He's supposed to be in Tibet."

"Well, girlfriend," said Torsten, pulling Dawa against his chest with a determined grin. "I think you have some explaining to do."

"I'm still free to do what I want," retorted Dawa, struggling to get out of his arms.

Torsten held her tighter. "Are you?" he asked, his voice dark with barely controlled anger. "I'm not so sure."

"Uh, maybe we should go downstairs," Anna said, nudging Pemba.

"No, stay here," said Dawa. "We'll go to my room. Unless you have any objections, *Tenzin*?"

"It will be my pleasure to have you alone," said Torsten in a way that sent icy shivers down Anna's back.

Pemba called out to his sister in Draagsil as she stormed to her room. She turned and rolled her eyes. "Stop worrying, Pemba. I won't hurt him."

The silence that descended once the door was shut underscored the tension that had raged between Torsten and Dawa.

"Is she going to be okay?" asked Anna. She glanced at Dawa's door.

"I think so." Pemba cupped her face. "Are you?"

Anna nodded and held back the tears that welled up. Pemba pulled her in close and she lost it. "I couldn't feel you anymore," she barely managed to croak through her sobs.

"My feeling only faded," Pemba said gently. "There's a shield on our rooms."

"Because of Kariaksuq?" Anna stiffened at the thought.

"No. T'eng—, ah, Tenzin did it to protect Dawa from other… suitors."

"But… that's like living in a cage. Isn't she free to choose?"

"I don't know anymore." Pemba leaned his head on hers. "And I don't want to think about it right now." He wrapped his mind-touch around her and she floated in it until the cobalt blue light of the late afternoon brought her back down to Earth.

"I should probably go," she said, snuggling in closer to Pemba. "My mother is expecting me for dinner."

"Not until Kariaksuq leaves. I don't want her to know where you live."

"But then how am I going to go home?"

"She'll leave with Tenzin."

Anna felt her blood drop to her feet. Torsten already knew where she lived.

Pemba glanced at his sister's door. "They seem to have cooled off a bit. He'll probably leave soon."

Anna looked anxiously at Dawa's door and tried to hear what was going on. But all she could hear was her own shallow breathing.

"I can protect you," Pemba whispered. He put both hands on her face and searched her eyes. "If you'll let me."

Anna looked into Pemba's eyes that had taken on an orange hue in the fading light. "What is Kariaksuq?"

Pemba dropped his hands. He walked over to the window that had multicolored Tibetan prayer flags hanging across the top. "I can't tell you that, Anna." He turned to face her. "But I promise you that I will when this is over. If you still want me to."

"When what is over?" Anna asked, a sick feeling weighing in her gut.

"Anna," he said, coming back and taking her hands. "Can you just trust me enough to let me shield you, please?" He rubbed her Firemark. "Even if you don't know why? Kariaksuq is bad enough, but her master is worse. He'll do anything to get what he wants."

Anna wavered. She could feel the power rippling through Pemba's sculpted body and had a sudden feeling that he didn't just work out the way most guys did. He didn't practice a martial art, he trained to fight. She looked at his hands. They were soft and supple, and yet they could probably rip someone apart. And maybe already had. Anna looked back up into

Pemba's pleading eyes. His need to protect her was palpable. As was his need for her to trust him. And yet he still couldn't trust her enough to tell her what was going on.

Pemba nuzzled her neck and she felt a slow flame flicker deep within her. A moan escaped from her throat as Pemba's mind-touch embraced her. Her mind-touch flew forward of its own accord, throwing itself around Pemba as if she could take him inside her. Her arms wound their way around his neck as she stretched the length of his body, wanting to feel every part of him merge with her own.

"I trust you, Pemba," she said, her voice husky with a mix of passion and fear. "Protect me." She felt Pemba's relief followed by a wild fervor that erupted around her in a dizzying array of sparks. He held her tightly and wove a net of entwined lines of energy that she couldn't even begin to comprehend.

When he had finally completed the shield he pulled his mind-touch back and leaned his forehead against hers. "You'll be safe," he said in a voice thick with emotion. His lips were so close to hers that she could almost feel them.

Anna tingled in anticipation, her body alive with the contact. Her lips parted and she swayed in his arms, waiting for him to kiss her.

"Let me get changed," he said. "I'll walk you home."

Anna stumbled back as Pemba padded silently to his bedroom, the tip of his long black braid swishing across his lower back. Her face burned with shame. He wasn't attracted to her.

Ulf blew the whistle for the game to start again, tapping Dvara's butt at the same time. Rakan growled in the bleachers. Ever since Dvara and T'eng Sten had had their discussion last week, she had been recklessly out of control. She had even sought the twins out for lunch, dropping her tray on the table between theirs. It was as if she no longer cared if she lived or died.

Rakan felt the cool tingling of a void-trail appearing and turned to face it. Moments later Liv walked into the sport hall. Her pace was hurried as she approached Erling sitting on one of the lower bleachers. She stopped a few paces away and waited until Erling motioned for her to approach.

Rakan sat up. He focused his sight on Liv and strained his ears to hear what they were saying, but it was too far. Erling said something and Liv nodded faintly, the way someone would if they were bowing to their Kairök in front of humans. And then Rakan knew. Erling was the leader of the void-trails.

Abruptly, their attitudes changed and Liv sat down next to Erling, acting like they were just friends hanging out. Rakan looked around, wondering what had happened until he saw Haakon walk in with a big blond guy. He immediately recognized him as Red, Anna's cousin. Rakan let his mind-touch slip forward, sensing the energy around both Red and the slender brown-haired girl on his arm to confirm what he already knew. They were unarmed humans.

Rakan looked back at the court, his eyes going to Anna who was intently focused on the game. He wanted to wrap his mind around her and feel her as she ran across the court, giving her best shot at a first wave score. Rakan smiled. She wanted to win, and he liked that.

Dvara pretended to bump into Ulf, rubbing against him as she lunged across the court. What was wrong with her? In frustration he turned back to Erling and Liv. Erling was watching the game, but the others were talking animatedly, interrupting each other and laughing. Rakan wondered if Haakon knew what Liv was, or if she had hidden her true identity from him even though they were living together on the University campus. He had trailed them once, just out of curiosity, and all their trails indicated that Liv never shifted in and out. She always stayed with Haakon. Acting like a human.

Red turned to look around, running his eyes over the bleachers as if he was looking for someone. He caught Rakan's eye.

Rakan glanced back at the game. The score was 47-18 and most of the goals had been by Dvara. He watched as she made a fast break across the court, scoring yet another goal. She wished she would stop drawing attention to herself.

Red appeared in front of him, as big as an Old Dragon but as blond as Anna. "You must be Pemba."

Rakan stood. "You must be Red."

"I see Anna's spoken of me already. All bad, I'm sure."

"No. Actually, she was rather positive."

"That was a joke," said Red, narrowing his pale blue eyes. "But my warning to you isn't. If you hurt Anna, I'll kill you."

"I doubt that," Rakan said. No human could ever come close to killing him.

"Never underestimate your opponent."

"I never have," Rakan said coolly. "But if you're so keen to protect her, why didn't you teach her to fight?"

"What makes you think she can't?"

"She's never fought in her life. And you know it as well as I do."

Red laughed. "You're right." Red's voice dropped an octave. "But I don't lose very often. And believe me, if you hurt her, I won't lose."

Rakan smiled. He liked Red's straightforward manner and his desire to protect his own. "I have no intention of hurting her."

"I don't care about your intentions. I care about Anna." Red leaned forward and arched his eyebrows. "Got it?"

Rakan felt his rök respond with a fierceness that surprised him given that he was facing a human. He closed the remaining distance between them and said, his nose practically touching Red's, "You're not the only one who cares about her."

Red pulled back. "Good." He looked at the game where Dvara was making yet another spectacular goal, hanging in the air just a fraction of a second longer than any human could ever do. "Your sister likes attention, doesn't she?"

Rakan gave Red a hard look, trying to figure out what he meant. "Dawa's none of your business," he said finally, not taking his eyes from Red's.

"Not unless she hurts someone I care about."

"You care about Ulf?" asked Rakan incredulously.

Red exploded in laughter and tapped Rakan on the shoulder. "No. No. Not at all."

The game ended and Rakan felt Anna bound up the stairs, her deer-like movements once again triggering his increasingly volatile desires to chase her. His control was slipping.

"When did you get here? Why didn't you call me?" she said, flying into Red's arms.

Rakan stifled his urge to growl. Even though he knew Red was her cousin, he didn't like seeing Anna in his arms. He forced himself to unclench his fists.

"Be careful or you're going to get us into a fight," said Red, releasing her with a laugh.

"Don't be silly," Anna said. She let go of Red and wrapped her arms around Rakan.

Rakan held her close, not sure who she was telling not to be silly, but not really caring now that she was in his arms.

"Why are you guys here?" Anna asked her cousin. "Did you come for the Salsa Festival?"

Red gave Anna a look that clearly said, "Why else would we be here?"

"That's the big dance tonight, isn't it?" Rakan had overheard June and Kristin talking about going. He had meant to ask Anna to come with him, so he could get closer to June. "We should go," he said to Anna.

"What? You haven't planned it?" asked Red. "What's wrong with you, Anna? How can you miss something like that?" Red turned to Rakan. "Have you ever danced salsa before?"

Rakan shook his head. "No, but I'm sure I can pick it up." Dancing wasn't all that different from sparring.

Red burst out laughing. "I like your spirit. But I can show you a few steps before we get there. Anna still hasn't mastered it even though I've been trying to teach her for years."

Anna reached out and play-punched Red in the stomach, her fist uselessly loose. "That's not my fault. Every time you say you'll show me, you just dance with Ea instead."

"Well then, tonight's the night," said Red. "Ea can help you get ready while I show Pemba a few steps. And then we'll pick you up and go there together, okay?" Red smiled mischievously. "That way we can see who the better teacher is."

Rakan laughed as he watched Red bounce down the stairs. He had the playful competitive edge of a dragon. "I like your cousin," Rakan said. He could feel her blood throbbing through her still pumped up muscles and he pulled her in closer, sending jolts of electricity through his body. "But I think I'll like dancing with you even better."

Rakan wrestled with his need to posses her, even with everyone around. He closed his eyes and forced his rök back into control until he could release her. He leaned his forehead against hers, wondering if he would be able to control himself when they danced together.

Rakan let Red ring the doorbell before answering it, even though he had already felt him arrive. Humans got surprised by that kind of thing, and Rakan knew they didn't like it. Only Anna had ever reacted differently. But then again, she wasn't like other humans.

"You're not planning on going like that?" asked Red, eyeing Rakan's black jeans and body-hugging tee-shirt.

"What?" asked Rakan, his mind still on Anna. "Why not?"

Red shook his head. "There's more work to do than I thought," he said. He followed Rakan inside and took off his coat, revealing a dark red shirt that was only half buttoned over his muscular chest. "Don't you have a dress shirt?"

Rakan looked again at Red's shirt. It was a darker red than Dawa's and seemed somehow more solid. Like a brick rather than a gem. It felt oddly like Red himself. Rakan let his mind run over Red once again, intrigued by his dragon-like qualities even though he was human. Rakan felt a faint reaction and pulled back. Red had definitely felt him, just like Anna had the first day in the schoolyard. "You and Anna are a lot alike," Rakan said, wondering if it was something in their family. Or maybe humans had been changing and he hadn't noticed before.

Red burst out laughing. "Does she tell you to change your shirt, too? Go get changed while I set up the music."

Rakan walked up the stairs, wondering what he should do. He stopped on the landing and listened to Red start some music and begin to dance on his own. He looked at his black tee-shirt and transformed it into the same kind of button-down shirt as Red was wearing, but it didn't feel right. He transformed his shirt again, changing it from black to his orange. It felt good. He headed back downstairs with a light step.

"Much better," said Red when he saw Rakan. "Salsa's all about seduction, creating a give and take tension with your partner. But the basic step is this." He moved forward and back and back and forward. "Do you play any instruments? Can you hear the beat?"

Rakan laughed and mimicked Red's movements. "You don't need to play an instrument to be able to dance."

Red stopped, confused. "I thought you said you had never danced salsa before."

"I haven't. But it isn't that complicated."

Red didn't look convinced. "Most people don't pick it up so easily."

"Maybe the other steps are harder," Rakan said. He'd forgotten that humans couldn't feel movement with their bodies. "Go ahead. Show me what to do next." He'd force himself to mess up.

The doorbell rang and Anna pulled at the pale blue dress Ea had brought for her to wear. It exposed too much cleavage and she felt naked in the feathery chiffon gown, even though it was more conservative than Ea's amber-colored mini dress, with its psychedelic spirals of green, red and brown.

"Stop worrying," said Ea. Her light brown hair flowed around her shoulders in gentle waves. "You look beautiful."

"I still can't dance like you do."

"You will when Pemba's guiding you."

Anna heard her mother and the guys talking in the stairwell as they came up to join them in the living room. She turned away from the door, her hand hovering near her chest. Anna felt Pemba stop and turned slowly to face him. His face was blank and he stared at her. He didn't even reach out with his mind-touch the way he usually did. Her cheeks flamed. She should never have agreed to wear the dress or let Ea pin her hair up in an elaborate mass of twisted braids. Anna dropped her eyes.

Red waved his hand in front of Pemba's face. "She's not a museum piece. You're supposed to talk to her, not stare at her."

For a split second Anna saw Pemba snarl and she almost thought he was going to punch Red, but instead he smiled stiffly. He walked over to where Anna was standing without saying anything, his face emotionless.

"I can go get changed," she mumbled, unable to look him in the eyes.

"No." He took her hands in his. "You're beautiful."

Anna felt a flood of relief wash over her and she sank into him. "I'm not sure I want to go. I'm going to fall over in these shoes."

"Not if you stay in my arms," Pemba said, sliding his hands around her waist.

"Knock it off, guys," said Red, whacking Pemba on the shoulder. "Time to go. And you can't salsa like that – you're way too close."

"Maybe we'll just watch you guys," Anna said. "We'll never be able to salsa anyhow."

Red shook a finger at Anna. "Don't underestimate your partner. He's not too bad."

"What?" Pemba said, getting Red back with a thump on the arm. "I'll take you on any day."

"Boys," said Ea, shaking her head. But she looked amused. "Let's go."

"Have fun, honey," Ingrid said to Anna before turning to Red. "You promised me to bring her home." She gave him a meaningful look.

"Of course," he answered with a little bow.

Anna glared at her mom. "I don't need a chaperone."

As they shrugged into their winter coats, Red leaned forward. "I only promised to bring you home," he whispered, "not to watch you all night."

Rakan scanned the crowd at the dance hall where the band was already playing. The floor was filled with dancing couples. He tried to focus on June and Erling who were dancing on the opposite side of the room, but his mind kept slipping back to Anna. The pale blue dress that matched her eyes combined with her elaborate hairdo was reminiscent of how female dragons dressed. And it made him want to possess her. He groaned to himself. He wouldn't be able to control himself if they danced. Or maybe even if they didn't.

Anna slipped her arm through his and tilted her head just enough to the side to expose her throat. He bared his teeth and dipped his head in response, only catching himself as he was about to bite her. He clenched his jaw and pulled back, but his eyes lingered on the upward swell of her breasts. Rakan ached to touch her, to feel her soft curves, to pull her in and – maybe they shouldn't dance. He turned back to the dance floor only to be slammed by the rising passion of June and Erling, lost in their own world. Rakan's rök lurched. June was a dragon and Erling wasn't and it hadn't stopped them. He looked back at Anna. Maybe there wasn't any reason not to mate with her.

Except that Anna didn't know he was a dragon. She didn't even know his name. Rakan turned away again. Erling wasn't human. It was easier. Humans couldn't accept them for what they were. But he wouldn't live a lie, no matter how much he wanted her. His rök screeched in pain and Rakan pushed it back into submission.

Anna's mind-touch rubbed against him, jolting him with her gentle energy. "You okay?" she asked. "We don't have to dance, you know."

Slowly, he turned to face her, struggling to tame his desire. She was so close, so willing. His eyes followed her throat down to the graceful swell of her breasts. He felt her skin flush with heat, sending him nearly over the edge. She wanted him. Or thought she did. But if she knew what he was, would she fear him instead?

As Pemba's eyes slid down her throat, Anna spread her hands on his waist. The firm muscles under his silk shirt rippled under her touch. He leaned his forehead against hers, and his warmth spread through her. Her nails dug into him. He pulled back and turned away from her. Anna felt her cheeks burn and she looked away. What had she done wrong? Why didn't he ever kiss her?

Anna bit her lips and reached out to find June. "June and Erling are dancing." At least they were happy together.

"Be careful with your mind-touch."

"Even with June? She's my best friend."

Pemba threw his arms around her with a violence that forced the breath out of her.

"You're hurting me," she said, caught between a wild desire to give herself to him or to struggle out of his arms and run away.

His hand pressed against her lower back and molded her body into his. His raw passion ignited hers. She tore at his shirt until she could feel his burning flesh under her hands.

"Time to dance," said Red, punching Pemba in the arm. "Remember: make me proud."

Pemba jerked away from Anna. She stood awkwardly, fixing her dress and checking her hair. Red bowed with an elaborate flourish to Ea, inviting her to dance. Ea placed her hand in his and they stepped seamlessly out onto the dance floor.

"Maybe we should get a drink," Pemba said.

Anna glanced at his shirt where she had felt it rip, but it was impeccable. Had she imagined it?

"You okay?" he asked.

"Yeah, sure."

"Do you want to go home?"

"Isn't your shirt ripped?"

Pemba looked away. "Not any more."

"Okay. That's what I thought."

"Does it bother you?" he asked, his eyes challenging her.

"No." That he could fix it didn't bother her. But that she had ripped it in the first place did.

"Dance with me," he said. He took her hand in his and placed his other one firmly on her shoulder blade.

Anna placed her hand lightly on his shoulder, scared to touch him. He began to guide her out onto the dance floor, but she stumbled and fell against his chest.

"Push against me," he said, shaking her away from him.

"I don't know how to salsa." She dropped her hands and looked away. Red and Ea glided by, their bodies vibrating with an intensity that felt like a drum. She should never have agreed to come.

Pemba took her hand again and guided her back into his arms. "What's wrong?"

Anna shook her head, unable to answer.

"Keep this distance," he said, his arms taught. "That's all."

Anna felt his energy pulsing through her hands, rushing like a river. Her mind-touch slipped forward, mingling with his. And then she felt it. An invisible space, like a flexible ball, pulsed between them, uniting them through its center. Slowly, Pemba began to move forward and she answered, backing up, carefully maintaining the pulsing space. And then he moved away and it was her turn to come forward in a never ending game of give and take. Through the awareness of the space that separated them she could feel his body as if she was pressing against it. She was aware of his every movement as if it was her own. His hand squeezed hers. She felt his energy flare, urging her to come forward or to glide backward in an ever increasing rhythm that brought them together in a spinning vortex of unity. There was no room for any other thought than the pleasure of being together.

As Rakan guided Anna around the dance floor, he lost all awareness of anything else. There was only Anna. He felt his rök open up and glow with pleasure. Wrong or right, this was where he wanted to be. With Anna. For as long as her life lasted. He dropped her hand and pulled her in close.

A cold wave crashed through Rakan and he shuddered in shock. Dvara. She was in trouble. She was stuck, surrounded by scintillating sparks of vermillion. He was about to shift when he felt Anna stiffen in his arms.

"Pemba? What's wrong, are you alright?"

The panic in her voice calmed him. "Dawa's in trouble," he said. The cold intensified. He didn't have much time left to help her. "I have to go. You'll feel me disappear, but I'll be fine. Stay here with Red."

Anna nodded, her eyes a mass of unasked questions, but he knew she'd stay put. "I hope she's okay," he heard her say quietly as he ran to the empty entryway and shifted to the other side of the fjord.

Chapter 16

Shield of Light

RAKAN FOLLOWED DVARA'S TRAIL TO THE VALLEY WHERE THE VOID-TRAILS
lived. He materialized cautiously. Dvara was in mortal danger. She
must have gotten into a fight. He looked around expecting to see the void-
trails since he hadn't sensed another dragon, but she was alone. Frozen in
the mass of bright red sparks that he had sensed. Her face was distorted in
agony, her fingers spread like claws. He edged closer. The vermillion haze
crackled and snapped. Her panic washed over him. He fought the urge to
throw himself into the shield. He needed to protect himself or he'd be
caught too.

He broke off a branch and tossed it next to Dvara's frozen figure.
Nothing happened. He reached forward mentally. Nothing. He let his
mind run beyond the spot where Dvara was stuck. Still nothing. As he
suspected, the shield wasn't made of matter. He made an electromagnetic
shield like the one he had made when they first faced the twins. When the
shield was in place around him, he inched forward. As he advanced, the
shield began to register tiny pin pricks. Slowly, he continued forward. The
prickling sensation grew stronger. He could see orange sparks. His orange.
Rakan felt Dvara's consciousness slip away. He cursed and lunged forward,
but the orange haze grew brighter, stretching into a body-sized shield that
blocked him from getting any closer to Dvara. Rakan growled in frustration. The shield was using his energy as its source. If he got any closer, he'd
be stuck. The shield would drain him of his energy, like a spider sucking
its victim dry.

Rakan took a few steps back. His rök thrashed to get free. He forced
himself to calm down and think. The bright orange mass of energy had
disappeared when he moved back. He needed to pull Dvara out, but how?

T'eng Sten shifted into place next to Rakan. "Why the hell aren't you
doing anything?" he snarled and leaped towards Dvara.

"Don't do that," Rakan yelled. But it was too late. T'eng Sten flashed into a massive haze of indigo suspended in midair. Rakan averted his eyes, momentarily blinded. Now he'd have to save them both.

He looked at the two blazing dragons, wondering how their energy had been transformed into shrouds of light when the shield didn't react to matter. That was it. Rakan stripped a nearby tree of its bark, mentally twining the fibers into a long rope as fast as he could. He'd pull them out. He mentally maneuvered the rope forward and snaked it around Dvara. The energy crackling around her made it feel like trying to catch a fish with his hands. Finally, he got the rope positioned and pulled.

Nothing. It was like pulling on a huge suction cup. Dvara didn't budge.

Rakan cursed. The rope slithered to the ground as he dropped the contact. He guided his electromagnetic shield forward. If he could get his shield around Dvara, it would ease the flow of energy that was feeding the vermillion haze and draining her. She didn't have much time left. His shield wobbled as he battled with the flowing currents. Rakan closed his eyes and tried to visualize the pattern of energy flow. He needed to use the current, not fight it. If he could manage to see it.

Slowly, a pattern began to appear. An odd shape, like a squeezed cone, protruded behind Dvara. If he could get his shield in there, he might be able to place it around Dvara. Her energy was fading. It would have to work. He blocked everything and focused on the flow. He aligned his shield with the currents surrounding Dvara. As the shield got closer, Rakan had to struggle to maintain it in the whirling vortex of energy that surrounded her. He touched Dvara's back with the electromagnetic shield and flicked it into position around her. The vermillion sparks faded a notch.

Rakan repositioned his rope and dragged her back, inch by painful inch until the quicksand-like energy eased its hold on Dvara, and he was able to yank her out of its insatiable grip.

T'eng Sten's guards flashed into the valley, followed by a dozen or so other dragons of his Cairn. They crouched, preparing to spring into the shield to rescue their Kairök.

"Stop!" yelled Rakan, struggling to lay the unconscious Dvara on the ground. "I can save him, but I can't save all of you."

Kakivak ignored Rakan's warning and threw himself towards his Kairök. "No," yelled Angalaan. She froze Kakivak in midair. There was only the beginning of a violet haze in front of him. "Save T'eng Sten now," she snarled. "Or I'll kill you before I die."

"Care for Dvara," commanded Rakan to the crouching dragons. He turned to face T'eng Sten in spite of his exhaustion. Rakan worked the rope forward towards the still conscious Kairök. Hoping it would be enough. He wasn't sure he'd have the energy to work the electromagnetic shield again. T'eng Sten tried to grab the rope, even though he was stuck in place. But his efforts only quickened the flow of energy out of his body.

"Let me help you," said Angalaan. She put her hand on Rakan's shoulder. He felt an unexpected tingling as she merged with him. He could feel dozens of fainter sparks of energy through her. The other dragons of T'eng Sten's Cairn. He felt them. All of them.

She tried to yank T'eng Sten out. *"It's not working,"* hissed Angalaan through their mind-link.

"No. We need to place an electromagnetic shield around him first."

"What? Whatever, just do it. We have the rope."

As with Dvara, Rakan eased the shield into position. But this time it was easier. The other dragons had added their energy to his and allowed Rakan to guide it at will. The outward flow of T'eng Sten's energy eased off and he came flying out, like a feral tiger released from a cage.

"Dvara," he yelled. He threw himself on the ground and cradled her still unconscious body in his arms. "Dvara." It came out like a strangled sob.

Rakan sank to the ground, his head pounding and his rök spinning in a frenzy. It had felt so good, so right, to feel Angalaan and the other twenty-six dragons in T'eng Sten's Cairn. For the few seconds it had taken to get T'eng Sten out, he hadn't been alone.

"Well, well," said Kairök Yttresken, showing up with a dozen guards. "I'm not sure killing Dvara is going to make her any more willing to join you. And it certainly lowers her value as the only female able to breed on Earth at the moment."

"I would kill you right now if Dvara didn't need help," growled T'eng Sten.

"Tsk, tsk, always so dramatic," drawled Yttresken. "She'll be fine. In fact, a little suffering might be good for her. Teach her to temper her passions."

T'eng Sten threw himself at Yttresken. They tumbled over each other as their kais gathered around in a tight semi-circle. Rakan struggled to his feet and flung himself between the two Kairöks. "Enough. Kill each other if you will, but not here. Call off your kais. Both of you. Right now."

"How dare you tell me what to do, you little runt—" hissed Yttresken. His beady pink eyes narrowed as he lunged for Rakan.

"No. He's right," said T'eng Sten, pushing Rakan out of the way. "Earth is still their home until the Meet decides otherwise. And as Yarlung's offspring who still has his rök, he has every right to protect her domain."

"Since when do you abide by the Code?" sneered Yttresken.

T'eng Sten spat in Yttresken's face. "I always abide by the Code. The real Code."

Yttresken hissed, but didn't spit back.

"Dvara is mine," continued T'eng Sten. "You have infringed upon my territory in blatant disregard of the Code. I hereby challenge you to a duel to the death."

"You truly are a most disagreeable puppy, aren't you T'eng Sten?" said Yttresken with a wry smile. "You would never have been made a Kairök on the Red Planet."

T'eng Sten returned the smile. "Given your weakened state, I grant you the privilege of choosing the time and place. Unless you wish to renounce your own claim on Dvara Azura, in which case I would be willing to grant you clemency."

Yttresken turned to go. "If it amuses you, we can duel. But I would have thought you held your life in higher esteem than to throw it away on a bitch in heat. Who certainly wouldn't return the favor."

Rakan flashed in anger and was about to launch himself at Yttresken, but Angalaan blocked him. "It's not worth it," she hissed under her breath. "He's just trying to save face."

Rakan growled, but Yttresken and his guards were already gone.

As was Dvara.

ಬಂಧ

T'eng Sten stalked up to Rakan. "Go home. I'll join you there as soon as I can." His iron grip closed around Rakan's bicep. "Stay out of this – it isn't your fight. It's mine." T'eng Sten shifted elsewhere without letting go of Rakan's arm, leaving him the unpleasant feeling of having been touched by a ghost. Rakan was alone.

Rakan raised a fist to the star-filled sky. "It *is* my fight." If he hadn't been distracted by Anna, he would have felt Dvara's danger before it got out of control. He searched for Dvara's trail and cursed. The footprints of the dragons shimmered clearly in the moonlit snow, but their trails were so confused that he couldn't follow them. T'eng Sten had taken the time to scramble them – or one of his dragons had. Rakan verged on the brink of an uncontrolled morph, making the trails even harder to distinguish. But that wouldn't help Dvara. He took a deep breath. He needed to access his rök's full power. And to do that, he'd have to let his rök free. Something he had never dared to do before.

He sank to his knees and focused within himself. *Feel, my rök, feel.* His rök fluttered and then energy burst forth like the sun's first rays piercing the sky. Rakan stood, his rök's glowing energy humming around him in an orange mass.

The tortured trails stilled and the real ones solidified below the shimmering illusions.

He shifted.

"Rakan?" said Khotan, standing like a guard in front of the entrance to his lair. "What are you doing here?"

Rakan faced the three Old Dragons, unsteady on his feet. A wave of nausea welled up from exhaustion. He could sense Yttresken's and T'eng Sten's kais lurking in two separate groups on the wind swept plain that lay below Khotan's lair. "I need to see Dvara... it's my fault she's hurt."

"You said you were staying in Tromso," snapped T'eng Sten.

"He's an unruly whelp," Yttresken said derisively. "Just like his half-sister."

"How can it be your fault if she and T'eng Sten got into a fight?" asked Khotan, ignoring Yttresken's insulting comment.

"What?" Rakan said. Why had T'eng Sten lied? He hadn't fought with

Dvara. Dvara had jumped into the shield around the void-trails' lair on her own.

"Well, as touching as sibling affection is," said Yttresken with a denigrating drawl, "I must return to Yarlung's. I suppose your presence on this planet was because you intend to join us? Or are you spying on us for your cohorts?"

"I'm here to listen to what Yarlung has to offer," said T'eng Sten. "The only difference between us is that I admit the fact that I look out for my Cairn's best interest."

Yttresken raised his eyebrows. "Then we should be going. Dvara is safe with Khotan."

"She's in your hands now," said T'eng Sten with a polite nod to Khotan. In a near whisper he added, "Rakan should rest for a while. I believe the events of the evening were too much for him. I urged him to stay at home because he was a bit delirious."

"I'm not—" began Rakan before Khotan silenced him.

"I care for my own," said Khotan. "They'll both be out of harm's way."

Yttresken snorted. "They should have become kais before now. There's a reason for the Code we have always followed."

"Are you challenging Yarlung's decision?" T'eng Sten feigned surprise.

"Not at all. I leave that honor to you."

"Then we should be going." T'eng Sten bowed again to Khotan and shifted, followed directly by Yttresken.

"Where's Dvara? Is she okay?" asked Rakan. He was too tired to reach out with his mind-touch.

"She's in the nook." Khotan stepped to the side and let Rakan pass first into his lair.

Rakan crossed the vast stone hall and walked towards the dimly lit spiral stairs that led down to Dvara's favorite place in Khotan's lair. He stopped short on the top step. He turned to his father. "Why didn't you come when she was in trouble?" Khotan was the only one Dvara had a mind-link with. He would have felt her distress even more clearly than Rakan had with their partial link. Or than T'eng Sten had through the Firemark.

Khotan sat down in his massive arm chair, looking suddenly frail and worn. "She'll have to tell you that. I can't."

Rakan looked at his father, confused. "Why not?"

"Rakan'dzor, please. Not now."

Rakan turned and descended into the lower reaches of Khotan's lair, not sure if he'd find his sister in dragon or human form. He turned the final corner and stopped. She was curled around T'eng Sten, her dress reflecting the blazing fire.

"What are you doing here?" asked Rakan. "I thought you were at Yarlung's."

"I am," said T'eng Sten with a lift of his eyebrows. "Being a Master Transformer has its advantages. Once the meeting starts, I'll have to go. I can't maintain more than one real conversation at a time. For the moment no one knows if they can trust me or not, so they're ignoring me and I appear to be in a deep discussion with my seconds. Which means I can be here."

"Is that how you've managed to play both sides all the time? By creating illusions and pretending to be in two places at once?"

"I didn't come to argue with you Rakan'dzor," said T'eng Sten, standing up. "I came to thank you. And to tell you both to stop being so stupid."

"Does Khotan know you're here?" asked Rakan.

"No. And he can't. For his own sake. He's already done too much against Yarlung's will."

"Then why don't you leave?"

"Because you followed us here. No one can know what really happened to Dvara. Let them think I was so angry that I attacked her myself."

"Why?" asked Rakan, openly challenging the Kairök.

"Because you have no idea what you're doing or what the stakes are." T'eng Sten's voice shook with anger. "Just promise me to stay away from the valley and the shield."

"You're the one who threw yourself into it."

"I wasn't reacting rationally." T'eng Sten moved forward menacingly. "Whether you promise or not, I'll know if you go there."

"And then?"

"Oh, leave him alone," Dvara said, her voice faint. "He's not that stupid.

He wasn't the one who threw himself into the shield without thinking."

T'eng Sten shifted out of the room, leaving behind only a faint rippling in the air.

"He'll be back," Dvara said, more to herself than to Rakan.

"Do you want me to put up a shield?" Rakan asked, but Dvara didn't answer. He put a hand on her forehead. Her energy was dangerously low.

"You can't make a shield that Khotan wouldn't feel. Only T'eng Sten has managed to do that."

"So why don't you tell Khotan if you'd rather not see T'eng Sten?"

"I take back what I said earlier. You really are stupid, Rakan."

Rakan walked around the nook that was big enough for Dvara to curl up in even when she was in her dragon form. The smooth sandstone walls reflected the crackling fire, making them look like brushed gold. Finally, Rakan sat on the bench that had been shaped out of the rock near the fire. "Why didn't Khotan come when you were hurt?"

Dvara hesitated before answering. "T'eng Sten took away my tattoos."

"What? Why did he do that?" Rakan jumped to his feet. "How did he even know?"

"He felt the poison I was carrying," Dvara said, her voice so low that Rakan had to kneel in front of her to hear. "The day Anna came up into our rooms when Kariaksuq tried to catch me for Yttresken. She chased me into the earth where a couple of fire dragons were waiting for me. I was out numbered. I had nowhere else to go but home, even though I knew Anna was there."

Rakan bowed his head. He hadn't realized that she had tried to protect Anna. "But why did T'eng Sten remove the tattoos?"

Dvara didn't answer at first. "He said I should live as free as I was pretending to be."

"What do you mean, free? You have your rök. You are free. And so am I."

"No. The tattoos bind you to the marker. Your rök can't be taken. You're not free."

"What?" The burning sensation Rakan had felt several times recently flared in his veins. He stood with a groan and leaned his head against the wall. He needed to rest. He had pushed himself too far.

The air shimmered and T'eng Sten shifted back into the nook. He sat down and Dvara curled herself around him. "I can't live like this anymore," she said, burying her face in his lap. Her rök began to hum as if it was about to manifest. "Take it now, please."

"No. You're too weak. And even if you weren't you know why I can't."

Dvara curled away from T'eng Sten. "I hate you," she said viciously, her whole body shaking.

"Ask Khotan to take your rök," said T'eng Sten tenderly. "He's always been fair to you and he'd release you when the time came. We can trust him."

Dvara flipped around, her red eyes wild. "I can't ask Khotan. It would kill him."

"Then stay here until I can shift you back to the lair in Tromso." T'eng Sten leaned forward and kissed her softly. "I'll come as often as I can. I promise."

With a mournful wail, Dvara morphed into her dragon form. Her increased bulk snuffed out the fire and pushed T'eng Sten off the bed. Rakan jumped back, avoiding her black crested tail as it flicked angrily. Khotan rushed down the stairs, and T'eng Sten shifted out of the room.

"She's okay," Rakan said. He pressed a hand to his throbbing head. "I think." Her vermillion scales were dull and her crest drooped to the side. *I hope.*

Khotan's eyes flared. "No she isn't. And she hasn't been since I gave her back her rök." His voice softened. "It's not your fault. Go rest, you're tired. I'll take care of her."

Chapter 17

Secrets

A RE YOU SURE HE DIDN'T SLIP SOMETHING INTO HER DRINK?" ASKED INGRID quietly on the other side of Anna's bedroom door. "She didn't even want breakfast."

Anna rolled her eyes. Why was her mother so against Pemba?

"Yes, Ingrid, I'm sure," she heard Red answer. "We were with her the whole time. And, besides, Pemba wouldn't do something like that."

"Are you sure? You don't really know him…"

"Yes, I'm sure. He's really not that kind of guy. Trust me."

Anna pulled up her comforter. *Thanks, Red.*

"Alright, well, I hope you're right," she heard her mom say.

"I am. She promised to come with me to the Botanical Gardens today. I'll go shake her out of bed."

Anna's eyes flew open. *What?* After a long silence Anna heard her mother say, "Okay. Thanks."

The door opened and Red walked in. "Time to get up, sleepyhead."

"Humph."

"We're going for a walk."

"I never said I would."

"No," laughed Red. "But now your mother thinks you did, so you had better get up."

Anna smiled. "How do you always make me laugh even when I don't want to?"

Red sat down on the side of the bed. "He didn't call?"

"No."

"It's still early." Red glanced at the clock. "Sort of."

"He's gone."

"Just because he hasn't called you yet?"

Anna looked at Red. "No. I can feel when he's here. And he isn't."

Red met her eyes, his face uncharacteristically serious. "You're right. I can feel it too."

Anna shot up. "Really?"

"Easy, girl," said Red, moving out of the way. "Get dressed. We can talk about it in the Gardens, okay?"

Anna got out of the car in the Botanical Garden parking lot and tucked her chin into her scarf. She frowned at the dismal grey fog of late March. It was so thick she couldn't even see the fjord. "Why did you want to come here?"

Red faced the sky and spread his arms. "Because it's nicer to be outdoors where you can feel the sun."

Anna squinted at the blurry orange orb that hung miserably in the sky. "Maybe."

Red laughed and hooked his arm through hers. He guided her up a winding path covered in compact snow. It was still white, in spite of the many people who had trod there before. "How well do you know the Gardens?" he asked.

"Uh, like everyone else? Every year since kindergarten?"

"Have you ever felt anything here?"

"Like what?" she said, eyeing him.

Red smiled and pulled her forward.

"Like what?" she repeated. Curiosity quickened her stride.

"Like that." Red pointed to a huge black rock that contrasted starkly with the snow covered mountainside.

"The rock?" Anna went over and sat on it, not sure what to expect. A faint tingling in the back of her neck reminded her of how it felt when a new energy was about to appear. She looked at the rectangular rock again and then at Red.

"Touch it," he said quietly.

Anna took off her glove and placed her hand on the rock's surface. It felt warm, even though she knew it couldn't be. Curious, she let her mind-touch slip forward to the tips of her fingers. The rock almost felt like it should breathe. "It feels..."

Red sat down. "Alive. I don't know how or why. But it is."

Anna looked carefully at Red; she felt a sadness about him that she had never sensed before. Slowly, she let her mind-touch reach out to him.

Red nudged her in the shoulder. "Pemba teach you how to do that?"

Anna pulled back. "Sorry."

"It's okay, just…"

"Be careful."

"Yeah."

Anna felt the warmth of the sun on her face and looked up. The clouds were breaking. She could almost make out the long winding ridge of the Tinden peak on the other side of the fjord. "Why is your energy flat?"

Red didn't answer. Anna glanced at him, wondering if she had offended him. He gave her a terse smile. "It's not," he said finally. For a split second he shimmered. "I just hide it."

"How do you do that?" asked Anna, so amazed by her cousin's sudden transformation into a whirling mass of energy that she didn't even notice Liv come up.

"What are you doing?" snapped Liv, her eyes flaring like sparks. "You didn't even put up a shield."

Red jumped up to face Liv. "I trust Anna," he snarled.

"It's not a question of trust."

"Then what is it? I'm sick of creeping around and hiding."

Anna looked from one to the other. Red's energy was flat again, but Liv's shimmered like an electric blue shroud. Why did Red have to hide his energy when Liv didn't? and what did her own look like?

The air around Liv crackled with sparks of electricity. "Ea's Kairök will be in even more danger if your existence is suspected. Paaliaq needs more time than we have." Liv's voice was firm. "This isn't just about you. It's about all of us. My life is already on the line, Red. And so is yours." Liv gestured towards Anna. "Hers doesn't have to be."

Liv's blonde hair spread like a halo, making her look like an angel of wrath. Anna wondered if she should just get up and run.

Red sat down. "Did you erase my trails?"

The crackling disappeared. "Yes," said Liv as if they had never been arguing. "That's the first thing I did."

Red glanced at Anna before looking back at Liv. "Do we have to…?"

"I don't think so," said Liv, turning her attention to Anna. "Can you keep a secret?"

Anna stood up quickly, as if Liv had called her to attention. "Yes. But I have no idea what you're talking about." Her voice echoed and she looked around. "You put up a shield?"

"Yes," said Liv, her voice crystal clear. "But the echo that you hear is because of the light of Veritas, the light of truth." She cupped her hands, as if she was holding something but nothing was there. "No one can know that Red has the energy you just felt. No one. Will you keep his secret?"

"Why don't you hide yours?" asked Anna warily.

"I don't need to." Liv's eyes shone with an inner light that Anna found unsettling.

"But Red does?"

"Yes."

Anna shivered. "Because of the shadow thing?"

Liv looked distant – and then confused. "Is that why Pemba protected you?"

Anna felt her face burn. "Yes," she said before she was able to stop herself.

"Then you can understand why Red's identity needs to be hidden."

"Yes," Anna said quietly.

"Even from Pemba."

"No." She didn't want to hide anything from him.

"If you can't pledge to keep Red's secret, we can't let you walk away from here with your memory intact. It's your choice."

A cold, slithering feeling of freezing silt slipped around the nape of her neck and her knees wobbled.

"Will you keep Red's energy secret, from everyone?" asked Liv.

The cold started to snake inside the base of her skull. Anna stiffened. "Yes."

The air shimmered and the cold disappeared. "Your word is binding and can not be broken." Liv's eyes were so vividly blue that Anna couldn't even see the pupils.

"Or else?" asked Anna, feeling sick at the prospect of lying to Pemba.

"Your memory will be irrevocably erased before you have spoken."

ဆၵ

Rakan fidgeted in the hallway outside Anna's classroom, wishing he could make time move faster. But he couldn't. He stretched his hands on the wall. He could feel her on the other side. And she felt him. He pressed against the wall, as if it were Anna. Soon she'd come out and he'd take her in his arms. It had been too long since he had last seen her.

The bell rang and everyone flowed out of the room. Everyone except for Anna. She lingered behind, her energy a conflicting mass of emotions. He pushed past the stragglers and into the classroom. Anna turned nervously to face him.

"Hey," she said, her cheeks flushing bright red. "I missed you."

Rakan walked up to her slowly, trying to read what was wrong. "You okay?"

"Yeah, I'm fine. How's Dawa?"

Rakan gently touched her cheek. "I think she'll be okay."

Anna closed her eyes and leaned into his touch, her hands slipping around his waist. The smell of wild chrysanthemums greeted him and he leaned forward with a moan. He rubbed his cheek against her hair and ran a hand down her back, gently fingering her spine. Her energy was growing. It felt like a sail beginning to unfurl. "Your energy has changed," he mumbled into her neck. It felt good.

Anna stiffened in his arms. "It shouldn't have."

Rakan pulled back and examined her more closely. "What happened?" He brushed a strand of hair that had escaped from her ponytail out of her face.

Anna bit her lower lip and looked away. "Nothing." But her voice rang hollow.

"Anna, you have to tell me." He turned her around so that she was facing him again. Anger pulsed through him, making him want to stretch and thicken. Why wasn't he ever here when she needed his protection?

Anna dropped her eyes. "There's nothing to tell."

His hands convulsed around her upper arms. "That's not true," he growled. He had shielded her against any forced touch from a dragon, but he hadn't considered the void-trails. He felt her wince in pain and he released her, mortified by his lack of control. He walked to the window and looked out at the schoolyard. Students were playing in the snow that had been falling all morning, covering the town in a soft white shroud. She should be out there, too. But he was ruining her life and exposing her to dangers she couldn't even begin to imagine. A wave of nausea rolled up inside as it did every time he shifted now.

"Did you see the twins while I was gone?"

"What? No," Anna said, sounding honestly confused.

Rakan turned around slowly. "Liv," he said quietly, sure in his gut.

"Stop it, okay? I'm fine." She threw her books into her backpack.

Rakan reached out to touch her with his mind, but she recoiled from him. "You don't want me touch you," he said, his voice harsher than he intended.

"No. Yes. Oh, Pemba." Anna held her backpack stiffly.

Rakan's fists closed. He wanted to kill every single void-trail he had ever met. Starting with Liv. He hurled a chair across the room and then gripped the sides of a table, begging it to keep him grounded. To keep him from morphing in a wild rage and killing everyone in his path, destroying everything until there was nothing left. And no way of getting it back. He forced his rök to stop spinning and slowly let go of the table. He straightened. Anna stood, petrified. "I'm going home," he said without looking at her. He walked slowly to the empty hallway, hoping he'd make it back to Ngari before he morphed.

Anna closed her eyes and rolled over to face the wall in her bedroom. Her mother had insisted on taking her to three different doctors and having all kinds of blood tests. And Anna didn't feel like going to any more.

"Anna," said her mom, sitting on the bed. "You really have to eat."

"I don't want to."

Ingrid sighed. "Ulf said Dawa has been out sick too – do you know if the symptoms are the same?"

"No."

"What does Pemba think?"

Anna bit her lip and squeezed her eyes shut. She still couldn't talk about Pemba.

"Honey?" Her mother paused. "Is that what this is about? Did you guys break up?"

Anna didn't say anything and prayed that she wouldn't start sobbing until her mother left. The last thing she wanted was a pep talk from her mom.

Ingrid sighed. "Life can be difficult sometimes—" She tried to put a hand on Anna's shoulder, but Anna pulled away.

"Mom, it's okay. He's just out of town. He'll be back." *Maybe.*

"Okay." Ingrid hesitated but stood up. "You know I'm always here for you, honey. If ever you do want to talk about something."

"Yeah. I know. Thanks." As if she'd ever talk to her mom about anything like that. Anna rolled her eyes to the wall, hoping her mom would just leave.

"Hey, champion. How're you feeling?" asked Ulf, knocking at the door. "All the girls were asking about you. The team hasn't been the same with everyone out sick for so long."

"Oh, that's so sweet," Ingrid said. "Don't you think, Anna?"

As if he cared. Jerk.

The doorbell rang and Ingrid went to answer it.

"Uh, Anna?" said Ulf, lurking in the doorway. "Do you know how Dawa is? She's been out for a long time now."

"What? No. Why would I know?"

"Pemba didn't say anything?"

"No."

"Can you do me a favor? Can you just ask her to call me?"

"No." She turned out her lamp. "Get out." *Creep.*

In the silence that followed Anna heard her mom and Red coming up the stairs. *At this rate, I'd be better off at school.* She turned to glare at them all.

"She's tired," said Ulf. "We should let her rest."

"I'll just say goodnight and come down," said Red.

"Oh, okay." Ingrid poked her head into the room. "I love you, honey. I'll come back later."

"I'll get you a beer," said Ulf to Red on the way out. "And don't forget," he said to Anna with a wink, "I'm counting on you to pull through. For the team."

"What are you doing here?" snapped Anna when Ulf and Ingrid's voices had disappeared down the stairs.

"I wanted to apologize," said Red. "I didn't mean to drag you into this."

Anna glared at Red. "Well then maybe you can explain what 'this' is."

Red shook his head. "No. I can't. I—" but his sentence was chopped off by burst of energy that emanated from around Anna and flattened Red back against the wall, splintering the shelves and sending all of her things flying.

"Pemba?" Anna sat up. The energy had felt like Pemba. "Red?" She threw back the comforter and went over to her cousin who was squatting on the floor. "Are you okay?"

Ingrid came running in, breathless. "What was that?"

"Nothing," said Red. "I just had the bright idea of leaning against the shelves. I'll pick it all up. Sorry about the mess," he said, looking around the room. "It doesn't look like anything broke."

Anna narrowed her eyes. Nothing was broken anymore, but she was sure it had been. Her collection of glass animals would never have survived the fall.

"You scared us," Ingrid said.

Red laughed. "I scared me too. But at least it got Anna out of bed."

Ingrid laughed. "That's true. Here, I can help."

"Don't worry about it, Mom. I'll do it with Red." Anna glared in his direction.

Ingrid was about to protest, but Red nodded his head towards the door. "It's okay, Ingrid. We'll get it."

"I get the message. I'll leave you kids alone." She lifted her hands up. "I'm going."

Anna walked to the door and listened until she heard her mom chatting with Ulf. And then she turned to face Red. "What was—" but the words got caught in her throat. "Pemba?" She was hallucinating. There was no other explanation.

"What happened?" asked Pemba, looking around. "Who was in here?"

"My mom. And Ulf." *Could she even mention her cousin?*

"And someone else. But I can't tell who."

"How'd you get in?" she asked, desperate to avoid the subject of her cousin.

"The front door was open," Pemba said, coming closer. "I walked in, okay?"

Anna looked around her dimly lit room.

"Who are you looking for?" asked Pemba. "Who tried to hurt you?"

Anna shook her head. "No one. I was angry, that's all and then... my shelves fell down." Anna looked at her wall. "Everything is back in place."

"But who were you angry with?"

Anna began to tremble. "No one."

"Anna, I already know Liv did something to you. But she wasn't the one who triggered my shield. Who was it?"

"I can't tell you that." She threw herself into his arms. "If I tell you..." She screamed silently into his bare shoulder. Keeping secrets from him was killing her.

"What will happen?" he said, stroking her hair gently.

"My memory will be erased," she said in a whisper. "And I don't want that." Panic welled up inside. Had she already said too much?

Pemba's grip convulsed around her. "Don't say anything. I'll deal with it." His voice was hard.

"No. Don't. Please Pemba, I'm not hurt. I was just angry."

"Did you accept this situation of your own free will?" His voice as calm and emotionless as Liv's had been the other day.

Anna winced. "No. Yes. Sort of."

"No one has the right to place that kind of trigger on you, Anna. No one. And even if you accepted, it was probably because you had no choice."

"Promise me not to hurt anyone. Please," she said, searching his eyes. They had an orange hue in the dim light of her room.

Pemba leaned his forehead against hers. "I can't do that, Anna. I was brought up to protect my own. And I will."

"No. You can't hurt anyone because of me. I couldn't live with that." She wouldn't let Pemba fight Red. Or Liv, even if she hated Liv for forcing her to lie to Pemba.

"None of this would have happened if we had never met." Pemba walked to the window. "I shouldn't have gotten close to you." He pressed a hand to his temple. "I'm sorry."

"No. Don't say that," she said, joining him at the window. "I'm glad we met. I want to be with you." She wrapped her arms around him, but he disentangled himself and held her at arms length.

"No, Anna. You don't. Or you wouldn't if you knew."

"If I knew what?"

"I'll come if the shield is triggered," he said abruptly. He walked out and shut the door.

"No," Anna said, lunging for the doorknob. But he was already gone.

A week later, Rakan stood on the edge of the cliff overlooking the arid wasteland of western Tibet, his arms folded across his bare chest. "What else didn't Yarlung tell me about the poison?"

T'eng Sten didn't reply. His indigo overcoat snapped like a predator in the howling wind that had eroded the sandstone to the porous aspect of a giant natural sponge.

Rakan turned to face the Kairök, trying to suppress the anguish that he always felt when he saw the desolate ruins of what used to be the Guge Kingdom. They'd shift Dvara back to the safety of the Tromso lair soon. "Why did you remove her tattoos? Anyone can take her rök now." Rakan knew T'eng Sten well enough now to know that he wouldn't have exposed Dvara to a much greater danger than being bound to Khotan, if there wasn't a good reason. No matter what he thought of the Kairök, T'eng Sten's feelings for Dvara were real.

T'eng Sten held Rakan's unflinching gaze. "Kraal's neutralized poison can revert to its original state."

"That's not possible," Rakan said flatly. "It would mean death. A long and painful death. Yarlung would never take that risk."

"It only happens when you go against the binder's will, in equal measure to the transgression." T'eng Sten looked back at the plateau. "Ask Dvara if you don't believe me. Khotan warned her before marking her."

The wind whipped through the crumbling ruins, echoing the desperate cries of the slain, forever reminding Rakan of one of the bloodiest mistakes of his youth. He dug his fingers into his biceps and forced himself to maintain control. His control wavered. He clenched his jaw and fought to stand still.

"Stop blocking it," T'eng Sten said. "Morph."

Rakan threw himself off the cliff. He stretched and thickened in the late afternoon sun. His coral-colored wings glinted as they unfurled. His blood curdling howl reverberated through the ruins and shook the rock beneath T'eng Sten's feet. If Yarlung decided they should kill June, whether Rakan thought she was Paaliaq or not, he'd have no choice.

Or die of the poison that he carried around like a death trigger.

Chapter 18

Worlds Apart

R AKAN LOOKED OUT THE WINDOW FROM HIS FAVORITE PERCH. THE TOWN WAS still the same mass of interlocking trails. But his inner turmoil was no longer appeased by it.

"You should go to school," Dvara said. "I'll be fine."

Rakan watched the fluctuating trails without really seeing them. He needed to see June. He'd have to force a conversation with her even if she didn't trust him. The nausea that he now recognized as the poison had increased its hold on him. At first it had only been after a major exertion but now it was a constant ache in his gut. Whether Yarlung realized it or not, he was going further against her will every day.

Dvara nudged him. "You okay?"

Rakan nodded. He hadn't told T'eng Sten or Dvara about the poison that was being slowly released into his veins. "Do you know what T'eng Sten is planning?"

"No." She turned and blocked herself off, but Rakan could still feel her anger. "He won't tell me. He says the less I know the better."

Rakan nodded. T'eng Sten wouldn't involve her until she was free of Yarlung. He couldn't. But he wished he knew what the Kairök thought about June. Rakan followed the trails idly until he found himself about to touch Anna. He pulled back. He had already brought her into too much trouble. He wouldn't expose her to more.

Anna had woken up at 4:30 and hadn't been able to fall back asleep. From her bedroom window, she had watched the sky above the twinkling fjord change from black to the intense cobalt blue of the pre-sunrise arctic. Pemba had come back three days ago. And she still hadn't seen him. The sun hovered below the horizon, and the snow reflected the pale green light of pre-dawn.

The green-black water of the fjord flowed like a snake, quietly oblivious to everyone's problems. The sky went from green to pink, heralding the coming of the sun. Anna got dressed and wandered down to the docks. The gentle clanging of the sailboats made her feel less alone.

The town began to wake up and Anna headed up the hill. Students were buzzing expectantly around the schoolyard. "Hey," June said when Anna walked over to join her friends. "You okay?"

"Where are your skis?" asked Lysa. "Did you forget that it's our last ski day?"

Anna glanced at her watch. She'd just have time to run home, get changed and grab her stuff. How could she have forgotten?

"Sverd can drive you – it'll be quicker," said Erling.

"I can run." She didn't want to be alone with Sverd. He reminded her too much of a hitman. "Aren't you guys skiing today too?" Erling was dressed normally, as were the twins.

"No. The music majors have rehearsal today." He scowled in June's direction. "But I'd rather go skiing."

"I'll be fine," said June. She hooked her arm through Anna's and steered her towards the car. "He's so over-protective. It drives me nuts. I'll come with you."

"June—" Erling called after them.

"What? I'll be back in a few minutes. I need a little girl time." June tossed her long black hair over her shoulder and peered at Anna. "You don't look so good. What's up?"

"Nothing really… it's just…"

"Pemba?"

Anna nodded. "I haven't seen him since he came back. And his phone is off all the time. I haven't even talked to him." The words came tumbling out as they got in the back of Sverd's black 4X4. Anna felt the pressure that had been weighing on her lift.

"He's going through a lot right now," June said. "He seems pretty confused."

"But why won't he talk to me? Why doesn't he even call?"

"He just needs time."

They pulled up to Anna's house.

"You know what's wrong?" asked Anna.

June got out of the car, but didn't reply.

"Did he tell you?" Anna insisted, opening the door. She led June up the stairs.

"No," June said, shaking her head. "Not in so many words."

They took off their boots and walked into the kitchen. Ulf and Ingrid were having coffee. "I'll be right back," Anna said, running up the stairs two at a time. June chatted away with Ingrid, and Anna felt annoyed. How could June know more about what was going on with Pemba than she did? Had June seen him even though he hadn't come to school? She shook the thought away and changed into her ski clothes. Erling's jealousy was rubbing off on her. There was no reason to distrust June. She and Pemba were classmates. It wouldn't be unusual for her to have spoken with him.

Rakan got out of the school bus and breathed in the smell of the slightly damp snow that covered the mountain. It was just below freezing. The snow would clump and freeze instead of allowing the skis to glide. His mind-touch slipped into the mountain, feeling the earth's increasing impatience to quicken in response to the spring equinox that had just passed. Everywhere around them the Lyngen Alps were just beginning to open up. He ached to spread his wings and fly in magnificent arabesques, echoing the earth's slow awakening. June shimmered with excitement. He smiled to himself. He was sure he'd finally get her alone when they both sought freedom from the constraints of being with the humans.

Rakan stepped into his cross country skis. He skated over to the teacher who was explaining which trails they were supposed to follow. But first they were to do a warm-up circuit so he could match them up with a skiing partner. Rakan grumbled at the restrictions being imposed on them and skied up to the front.

The teacher stepped to the side. "Go ahead," he said.

Rakan took off. He tried not to go too fast. But his mind-touch instinctively smoothed the way, and he reveled in the feeling of the snow gliding under him.

He waited back at the bus until June finally glided in with the teacher. Her movements were fluid and elegant. She caught him watching her and skated over to him. He could feel her rök pounding like a gong. "Partner?" she asked. "At least we'll be able to ski that way."

June's rök vibrated with such intensity that he wondered how humans didn't feel it. He smiled. "Race?"

June laughed. "You bet. Once we get out far enough."

Rakan could feel her rök spinning in anticipation. She wanted to race, and win, as much as he did. And he couldn't wait.

June skated back to the teacher. "Can we start?" She waved at Rakan. "We'll go together."

"Sure, you seem well matched. Do you know the trail though?"

"No problem." June adjusted her backpack and turned to Rakan. "Let's go!" She hit an easy stride and Rakan followed, looking for a chance to take off. He let his mind enter the ground and run ahead. June joined him and motioned for him to follow her on an off-trail. When they came out of the valley, she stopped. "Race to the top?"

The peak towered above them and Rakan's rök expanded. "With or without skis?"

June considered. "Without." She kicked off her skis and stuck them in the snow. "Ready?" She dropped her backpack.

For a split second Rakan thought he saw June's eyes flash green. Paaliaq's green. She took off, but he hesitated. Was it a trap? But the urge to race was too strong. He transformed his human clothes back to his dragon pants and raced after her, feeling his way up the mountain that vibrated under his touch.

The closer he got to June, the faster she went, until they were nearly shifting up the mountain. The ground beneath them felt like a mass of viscous fluid, and it responded to their energy with its own. Rakan focused on the peak, willing himself to get their first. He reached out and felt June when he caught up to her. She didn't push him away. She laughed and took off faster, her energy shimmering with the thrill of the race. Rakan scrambled to keep up, blocking the mind-touch as a wave of nausea slowed him down. He focused on the mountain that urged him forward, until he could no longer tell where he ended and the mountain began. He glided up the rock and snow that melded to greet him. Just as he reached the top, June tackled him.

"No," she yelled, pushing him out of the way and jumping over him. "I'm first!"

Rakan didn't even think. He pounced on her and they tumbled to the snow in a wrestling match. June was stronger than Dvara, but not as strong as he was. And, like Dvara, she was more supple and twisted out of his grasp like a fish even with her stiff human clothes. She flipped him onto his back. Rakan lay still, his arms pinned above his head. Their röks hummed in pleasure and he gave up the fight.

"I won," she said, grinning.

"Are you sure?" he asked playfully. He flickered on the edge of a morph.

"Yes," she said, smelling his scent before letting go of his wrists. She sat up, her legs gripping his sides. "Because you've lost your contacts."

Rakan laughed and flipped her over. She twisted out of his grip and straddled his back, pulling one of his arms out from under him. She lay on top of him and Rakan stretched his neck. He ached to have her bite it and mark him. His rök condensed into a ball of fire, ready to manifest. His energy hummed and crackled, surrounding him with scintillating orange sparks. June pulled back. "Pemba, are you okay? What's happening?"

Rakan grunted in pain as he felt the black dragons attack his arms, burning him from within. *"What are you doing?"* screeched his mother. *"You're supposed to tempt her with your rök, not give it to her."*

"Pemba?" June put a hand on his face. "It's poison, isn't it? I recognize that pain."

Rakan couldn't respond. He clenched his jaws and wrapped his hands around his tattoos.

"Don't be a fool, she's not who you think she is," snarled Yarlung. *"Block her."*

"I'm trying," he yelled. Under no circumstances would he allow June to enter his body with her mind while his mother was still there.

"Stop moving," June said harshly. "I don't know how to destroy it, but I can put it in suspension the way I did for Erling."

"No." Rakan twisted out from under her and broke the contact. "I'll be fine."

Rakan felt June's mind-touch envelope him and even though he could feel her increasing irritation at not being allowed in, he maintained his shield until his mother's presence receded. Limp with exhaustion, he dropped his arms and let her in. It was only after she had put the active poison into a state of suspension that he realized just how much the burning sensation had been gnawing away at him.

"Thank you," he said, falling back, his arms spread eagle. He was giddy and light-headed. He was free of pain. Free of poison.

"Most of the poison is neutralized," she said, sounding confused as she pulled her mind out of his body. "I couldn't put it into suspension – it reacted... differently. Like it had a mind of its own."

Rakan glanced in her direction. He had thought Kraal was the only dragon who knew how to manipulate active poison. "Did you say Erling had been poisoned?"

"I shouldn't have said that," June said, turning to face him. "You have to keep that to yourself. Okay? Erling will kill me if he finds out that I told you."

"Who poisoned him?"

June looked away. "He's dead now."

Rakan felt her pain at the memory. The pain of having killed, not the pain of loss. "I know that pain." He sat up and wrapped her in a wave of warmth.

June leaned into him, their shoulders touching. "Thanks," she said. "It still hurts. Even if I would do it again."

"Was it your first?"

June nodded. "I... don't know what to think. I can't even kill animals. It hurts too much. And yet... I didn't hesitate when Fritjof..." June put her head in her hands, shaking at the memory. "I don't want to be a monster."

June's energy pounded around them both with a strength unlike anything he had ever felt. Her anguish thrashed at him so violently that the only thing he could think of doing was to let his energy slide forward, merge with hers and hope it would be enough to enable her to bring it under control again. It was like trying to stop an earthquake.

When her pain finally ebbed to a dull throb, they lay back in the snow, exhausted. "Thanks," she said. "I can't always control my emotions."

"They're intense."

"Yeah, I know. That's why Erling is always worried." June stared at the sky. "Sometimes he drives me crazy. So I block him out. Like I did today. But he hates it. He says that he wouldn't be able to help me if..."

Rakan felt her pain quicken and he sent her a wave of warmth, holding her until she calmed down again. She rolled back onto her back, her eyes closed. Rakan sat up, examining the smooth lines of her almond-shaped face that was the epitome of dragon beauty. But her black hair was spread wildly on the snow, making her look more feral than beautiful. Rakan let his mind-touch slip forward gently. Beneath her tranquil surface she was a writhing mess. He could feel her rök's energy, pulled now into a tight ball, but it didn't feel right. A part was dying. "You need to morph." *Soon.*

"No," June said, sitting up in a movement of panic. "No. I don't ever want to morph again. It scares me. I can't control it. So we... we're careful. We can't even make love."

"But he's your mate. How can you not possess each other?"

June flushed bright red and turned away. "I can't believe we're talking about this."

"I'm sorry," Rakan said, his rök spinning wildly. He wanted to help her, to meld with her and link through their röks. Rakan groaned in pain as part of the neutralized poison began to transform into active poison. Rakan's vision blurred and he wanted to lash out, destroy the mountain, take June's rök or let her take his.

"Hey, easy. It's okay, really," she said. She put her arm around him and nuzzled him with her mind at the same time.

Rakan flung himself onto June, sending them both back into the snow. "I hate being alone all the time," he managed to say through his clenched teeth. His arms jerked around her, holding her tighter than any human could have tolerated.

"I know," answered June gently, willing him to relax. "I know. But you don't have to be alone."

Rakan eased his grip. If only he could belong to a Cairn. Then he'd be okay.

"You could tell Anna," continued June. "You could be with her. She would accept you for who you are."

"I can't," he groaned. Even if he wanted to. Rakan began to shake as he forced himself not to morph, but his rök was beginning to take on a mind of its own.

"Start by telling her about your rök."

Rakan gritted his teeth. "She'll never understand—" Rakan threw himself back into June's arms. And even if she did, he'd be exposing her to too much danger.

"Pemba? June? Why are you guys rolling around in the snow? Are you... oh my god—" Anna's voice cracked.

"No," Rakan said, scrambling after her. Her pain stabbed him and he cried out in anguish. He exploded. He burst into his dragon form and thrashed at the mountain in wild fury. Blindly, he twirled around, his rök flying free. He saw Anna running away and the thrill of the chase overtook him. He needed to catch her. To possess her. He leaped into the air and stretched his wings, his body tingling in anticipation. In a desperate attempt to gain control, Rakan bellowed in rage and threw himself to the ground. But his rök was too wild. He flew back up and spotted Anna again. He torpedoed down towards her and then straightened, his claws stretched out for the final catch when a massive indigo dragon slammed into him. Howling in rage, Rakan turned on T'eng Sten. But the older dragon already had him by the throat and was digging his black claws into Rakan's hide. Rakan thrashed, but T'eng Sten only closed his jaws tighter, growling a low warning.

Suddenly, Rakan realized what he was doing and gave up the fight. His rök whimpered under the Kairök's guidance, but eventually it settled and returned under Rakan's control.

"Rough day, eh?" said T'eng Sten, releasing Rakan from his hold as they morphed back to human.

"What did I do to Anna? Is she okay?" he asked quietly, dreading the answer.

T'eng Sten didn't answer right away. "She will be," he said quietly. "Kakivak is tending to her. I was with Dvara when she felt you go wild. I was lucky to get here before you touched her. But it was hard to maintain the shield to keep your bellows from echoing out all over the mountain. So I think she heard at least part of our fight." T'eng Sten paused. "She might have seen you in your dragon form even if Angalaan tried to cover us both with a reflective shield that humans can't normally see through. The best thing to do would be to erase her memory."

"No," Rakan said, lunging for T'eng Sten. "Leave her alone."

T'eng Sten flipped Rakan onto his back. "Get a grip. She can't see Kakivak and he won't go into her mind unless I tell him to. He's just calming her down."

Rakan groaned and lay back in the snow. "I guess we're even now."

"Well, technically, no. I saved Anna's life. Not yours."

Rakan wished he could melt and disappear. He slid his mind into the mountain below, healing the gashes he had inflicted upon it. He felt June waiting for him not far from the bus where everyone was already gathered. She was trembling.

"I should shift back to June."

"No. I'm not cleaning up a second mess."

Rakan stood and faced the Kairök. "I'll be fine." A wave of nausea rolled up from the viscous poison. Without waiting for T'eng Sten's approval, he shifted to where June was waiting.

June gave a little jump of relief and hugged him. "I was so worried. Are you okay? Is Anna okay? Did you see her?"

Rakan shook his head and tried to speak, but a second wave of nausea rolled up and he groaned involuntarily. The poison was more viral this time.

June wrapped her mind around him. "Again? How does the neutralized poison change?" She slipped into him and put the newly active poison into suspension. "Is it when you have a bad morph?"

Rakan heaved a frustrated sigh of relief. How could he ever talk to her about what his mother was planning without killing himself? "No. Only when I do something that I'm not supposed to do."

June stared at him. "That's inhumane. Who would do such a thing?"

"My mother—" Rakan said, choking on the word.

"Hush. Stop talking or you're going to kill me too," June said, diving in once more. "I'm not strong enough to keep doing this. We need to find a way to get it out. What a bitch."

Rakan leaned his head briefly against June's. "Thanks." He transformed his clothes and stepped into his skis. If T'eng Sten's shields hadn't worked, Anna had just seen him morph and charge after her.

"I need to find Anna," he said, taking off. Nothing else mattered anymore.

Anna arrived late for handball. She didn't want to face June. Or Pemba. She shook with anger, wishing neither one had ever shown up in Tromso. But the image of Pemba and June lying in the snow together was burnt into her mind. They were here. And they were together. She leaned against the water fountain, trying to get herself enough under control to go join the rest of the team.

She felt Pemba approach her. "Go away," she said, without turning around.

"Can we talk, please?"

"No."

"I lost control. My... nature... took over."

Anna spun around, hatred flaring to new heights. "You just don't get it, do you? I don't care what you are." Anna gripped the water fountain behind her, "What matters to me is that you lied to me. You've both lied to me." Anna struggled to walk away calmly, holding back her tears until she was in the locker room.

"Anna," June said quietly, coming in a few minutes later. "Are you okay?"

Anna spun around to face June. "Am I okay? I see you rolling around with Pemba in the snow and you ask me if I'm okay?" Anna stood and threw her bag into her locker. "I thought you were my friend."

"No. I meant about seeing Pemba become..."

"Seeing Pemba become what?" A flicker of doubt crossed her mind. She wasn't sure what she had seen. It was fuzzy, half hidden. She pushed it away. It didn't matter. He didn't care about her anyway. And neither did June. "Leave me alone."

June came closer. "I was just trying to help him."

"By making out with him?"

"We didn't make out, Anna. Nothing is going on between us."

"Yeah, right." Anna slammed her locker shut. "I don't need people like you or Pemba in my life. And I bet Erling doesn't either."

"It's not what you think." June blocked Anna from going out. "Pemba and I—"

"Can get lost together." Anna pushed June out of the way and stormed out. But she didn't want to face the team. Or see Pemba in the bleachers. Watching June. Anna leaned against the wall. That was why he had never kissed her, because he had always been in love with June. She was such an idiot. The tears flowed freely.

Anna opened the door to the weight room and flicked on the light. Only to see Ulf making out with a black-haired girl in the middle of the room, his hand cupping her breast.

"What on Earth are you doing?" Anna hissed, trying to place who the girl was. There was something familiar about her erratic energy.

"Oh. Is this your girlfriend?" asked the girl, straightening her clothes. She looked like Dawa, but her face was more triangular and her eyes were a hypnotic honey yellow.

Anna stood perfectly still. She recognized the girl's energy. It was Kariaksuq. And there was nothing shadowy about her.

"You have no reason to be here," said Ulf, striding out of the room. "You're late for practice. Let's go."

Anna slammed the door behind him. "I don't know who you are or what you want," she hissed, "but you need to leave." Orange sparks flashed around Anna and she knew Pemba's shield was still in place. "Now." Because as much as she was glad to know the shield still worked, she didn't want to face Pemba again.

"I was just having some fun," said Kariaksuq, raising an eyebrow and beginning to fade in front of Anna's eyes. "There's nothing wrong with that, is there?"

Chapter 19

Trying to Fix It

R AKAN LEANED AGAINST THE PARKING METER THAT WAS ON THE STREET COR-
ner behind the library. Anna was inside. She had been avoiding him all
week. His eyes wandered down past the painted wooden buildings and out
across the fjord. He needed to talk to her. To make sure she was alright.
He looked back at the modern building that always reminded him of a
dragon in flight with its undulating roof supported only by walls of glass.
But would she listen to him? Rakan watched as the half-melted mound of
snow near the point of the roof that touched the ground slowly became
pink, and then fuchsia. The artificial light of the library spilled out into the
cobalt sky, as if urging the building to take flight.

Slowly, he pushed off the parking meter. He walked down the street to
the main entrance, hoping she wouldn't leave as soon as she felt him come
near the way she had been doing at school these past few days. Rakan
walked in and felt Anna stiffen, two floors above. But she didn't move.
He walked up the hanging metal staircase and paused on the first floor
landing. The sky had darkened, becoming nearly indigo, but he could still
make out the majestic form of the sleeping mountain they called Tinden.
It shimmered in the twilight, curled up on the other side of the fjord as
the city lights glittered playfully on the black water like puppies waiting
for their mother to awaken.

Rakan turned and walked up the second flight of stairs, each step
heavier than the one before. Had June been right when she said that Anna
would've been able to accept him for what he was? Was it still possible?
He glanced at her, curled up in a big red chair, her books stacked up on
the extra-large arm rest. She was facing Tinden, and stiffly aware of his
presence. Her blonde ponytail twitched nervously, like an animal judging
when to flee. Rakan felt a wave of nausea, but couldn't tell if it was the
poison or his emotions. Or both.

He approached slowly and sat in the armchair next to Anna, his hands folded on his lap. "Can we talk, Anna. Please?" His voice was barely a whisper and when she didn't answer, he wondered if she hadn't heard him.

"We have nothing to talk about," she finally said, her voice as hard and cold as it was quiet. "Everything you've ever told me was a lie."

Rakan cringed. More than she knew. "Not everything," he began, but the ice-cold hatred in Anna's eyes cut him short. Had she been a dragon, she would've blasted him out the window. Rakan dropped his eyes. "Can you just tell me why you're so angry?"

"What?" Her voice echoed through the library before she caught herself. She flung her legs to the ground and threw her books into her bag, her hands shaking.

"I can explain everything, if you'll let me." Rakan took a step towards her, unable to tell if she was angry because of June or because she had seen him morph.

Anna flung her bag over her shoulder, hitting him in the chest. "Anything you'd say would just be a lie covering another lie." She struggled to get her boots on, her bag thumping back to the ground.

"Anna," he said, reaching out to her. "What did you see?"

Anna recoiled from his touch as if he was poisonous. "Don't touch me. Don't ever touch me. And don't ever talk to me again." She half-ran down the stairs, fighting with her coat as she went.

He walked to the wall of glass and watched her take off down the street. His rök banged against his chest, urging him to go after her. To tell her everything whether or not she had actually seen him morph into a dragon. His eyes lingered on her trail that sparkled faintly. Her trail was changing. Becoming easier to see than that of other humans.

He fought the desire to punch the glass. His fists shook as his nails dug into his palms. Without even checking to make sure no one was watching him, he shifted home. He had lost the one thing in life he cared the most about, and he hadn't even been smart enough to know it before it was too late.

Anna sat with her back to the wall-sized photographs of the current exhibit at the Perspective Museum, glaring at her coffee. But even so, she could still feel the smiling faces of the Asian-Norwegian couples mocking her with their happiness. Had she known that the exhibit was about Asian women who had married Norwegian men she wouldn't have come. Even if the stark, modern café was probably the best place to be alone. None of her friends ever came here and her mom was still at work. And Ulf was screwing around with Kariaksuq in the weight room. Anna slammed the mug on the white table, splashing coffee all over its surface. She glanced quickly around the café that was filled with a group of tourists. No one had noticed.

She picked up her napkin and froze. The coffee looked like a flying dragon. She wiped the table quickly, her hand shaking.

"Can I join you?" asked Haakon.

Anna flew back, her metal chair clattering on the white tiles. The people at the next table looked up and Anna quickly picked up the chair. Haakon sat without waiting for an answer. Anna tried to act nonchalant. But she wanted to scream and run away. Haakon's dark brown eyes shimmered like bronze in the harsh light of the museum cafe.

"You saw him, didn't you?" asked Haakon without breaking the eye contact.

Anger uncoiled inside her. "Who?" she asked between clenched teeth. But she knew who he was talking about. Even though she didn't want to.

"Pemba," he answered. "When he morphed."

Anna's cheeks turned to ash. He knew. She glanced at the exit. Should she break for it before she had to swear not to say anything again? She let her mind reach out as far as she could, just in case Torsten or Liv were lurking nearby. But she couldn't feel them. He was alone. Or appeared to be. Her gaze narrowed. He was probably like Red, hiding his energy.

Haakon sat quietly, as if sensing her mistrust and letting her scrutinize him. He looked even more like a rock than usual. Quiet and solid. And implacable.

Anna sipped what was left of her now cold coffee. "What makes you think I saw something?"

"Because I felt him morph," he said as matter-of-factly as if he had been talking about snow conditions.

Anna put the cup down. She leaned forward. "But how can you know what that feels like?"

"Because I've felt others do it," he answered after a long pause.

Anna stifled a choke. Torsten. Kariaksuq. "Liv?"

Haakon gave a curt nod. "Liv is different. But, yes, she can morph too." His voice dropped to a confidential whisper. "I thought the world was about to end when I saw her do it for the first time." He glanced up at her. "I just wanted to see if you were okay."

Anna relaxed a little. Maybe he didn't want to bind her answer in some weird promise. "When did you first see her... morph?"

"Years ago." His eyes burned into hers. "But my situation was different from yours."

The image of Pemba rolling around in the snow with June flashed across her mind and she cringed involuntarily. Of course her situation was different. She wasn't even dating Pemba. She grabbed the daisy that was decorating the table and crushed it in her fist. How had she let herself think he cared?

"Anna," said Haakon, once again interrupting her thoughts. "Pemba is playing games with you." His voice was hard. "He's not worth your time."

"Neither is June," she responded in the same tone.

"June is none of your business," said Haakon so quietly that she almost couldn't hear him. But the metallic tone of his voice made it perfectly clear that she had trespassed on a subject better left alone.

Anna sat perfectly still, no longer daring to breathe. Haakon looked like a crouching tiger. And she was his prey.

"Frankly," he said, each syllable distinct, "the less you know, the better off you are." His eyes bore into hers. "For your own safety I should erase your memory of everything that happened the other day in the mountains."

Anna stood and her chair clattered again to the ground. "No. Never," she hissed. As much as she wished the day had never happened, she would never consent to go back to living a lie and believing that Pemba cared about her when he didn't.

Haakon's jaw twitched. "Then leave before I change my mind."

໒ୠ

Rakan sat half-perched on a stool in the Driv, the bar that was conveniently located just across the street from Ulf's studio apartment. The first band had finished playing and the second one was setting up, but Pemba didn't notice them anymore than he noticed the untouched glass of beer that was placed in front of him. Kariaksuq had been spending more and more time with Ulf. Rakan held his Maii-a in his hand that was hidden under the bar. He transformed it to feel like Anna. He knew without looking that it was a pale cornflower blue. He changed it into sphere. And then a pyramid. A cylinder. A cone. He flicked it through so many different shapes in quick-fire succession that it felt like a pulsing ball. The frenzied motion soothed him.

His mind roamed back up to Ulf's apartment. Kariaksuq had handcuffed a more than willing Ulf to his bed. Rakan snarled. He didn't care what Kariaksuq did to Ulf, but he knew that she wouldn't be playing with him repeatedly unless there was an ulterior motive. Dragons like Kariaksuq never used the same human twice. They possessed them and left them.

The only motive Rakan could see was to get somehow at Dvara through Anna. But he couldn't figure out how she planned to do it. Rakan changed his Maii-a back to his own orange and placed it on its black metal string. Ulf was a fool. He was completely under Kariaksuq's power. At this point, he'd do anything she told him to do. Including hurt Anna.

A drunken guy stumbled into the stool next to Rakan and started to babble about his problems. Rakan nodded every once in a while, deftly swapping his full glass with the guy's nearly empty one. He never drank alcohol. And couldn't understand why humans did. By the time he'd have to shift out of the bar in order to trail Kariaksuq, no one, not even the guy next to him, would notice it.

Rakan's mind slid back to Anna. She was alone in her room and still wouldn't speak to him or June. She had cut herself off from everyone. Pain had transformed her energy into a series of jagged spikes. He reached out to touch her, but she reacted with such anger that he pulled back.

Over the past week at school, he had manipulated the shield from afar so that it would trigger a warning in case a void-trail threatened her. Or so he hoped. He didn't really have any way of testing it. Rakan growled, earning himself a thump on the back from his bar mate. After he dealt with Kariaksuq, he'd deal with Liv.

Rakan disentangled himself from the incoherent ramblings of the drunken guy and left the Driv. Kariaksuq was getting tired of playing with Ulf. She'd shift out of the apartment soon and he needed to clear his thoughts before attacking her. But the intense cobalt blue light that greeted him stopped him in his tracks. It was the color of June's eyes. He ached to morph in a wild mass of coral-colored flames, merging his orange with her blue. But he couldn't. The poison he carried ensured his isolation. Even if tried, he wouldn't be able to give his rök to a Kairök.

Kariaksuq was leaving Ulf, who was too insanely thrilled to realize that he was still attached to his bed. Rakan gripped his three-pronged dragon knives. Finally. They'd fight. He transformed his human clothes into his black dragon pants. He was ready for her.

But instead of shifting, Kariaksuq walked slowly down the stairs. Rakan hissed. She was playing with him. She knew he was there, waiting for her. She walked out of the building in her honey-colored dragon dress, her hair half up and half down in the way that young female dragons did before their first mating. Her sweet scent of warm wood wafted gently in the near zero air. His blood throbbed in response and he snorted, trying to block her odor from filling him with blinding desire. But she was ripe, and he could take her. She glided over to where he was standing stiffly. She curtsied gracefully, leaning forward just enough so that he could see the fullness of her breasts as they pushed against her dress, jiggling playfully as if they wanted to be stroked. Rakan growled, forcing his eyes not to linger.

"Greetings, Rakan'dzor. I was wondering when you'd get the courage to show your face, instead of always trailing me like a puppy." Her eyes ran over his naked chest, appraising the size of his pectorals and lingering on his rippled abdomen. "Since you aren't really a puppy, are you?" She closed her eyes and tilted her head back. She inhaled deeply. "Hm. You have the most enticing smell. Spice and... something wild."

"What are you doing here?" Rakan said, ignoring his body's response to hers.

Kariaksuq opened her eyes and smiled. "Trying to get you alone. I thought that would be clear?" She moved closer and let her fingertips wander down his abdomen. "Yttresken is too old to give me what I need."

Rakan knocked her descending hand away from his pants. "Ulf seems happy enough to oblige."

"Are you jealous? Of a mere human?" She turned, exposing her bare back that looked even more enticingly like bronze because of the contrast with the honey colored dress that clung to her hips. Slowly, Kariaksuq reached up and undid the rest of her hair. She shook the blue-black mass and Rakan gave an involuntary growl as it slithered across her back. "Catch me. If you can." Her bare feet made no noise on the soft snow of mid April.

Rakan flew after her, his veins pumping with the excitement of the hunt. She shifted and popped back out on the glacier where Dvara had shown him the blue crevasse. They faced each other as her hair flickered in the night, reflecting the stars above.

"So, shall we fight first or after? Or don't you know yet?"

Rakan lunged for her, spinning her under him in a strangle hold. But her knives were already out and she slashed deftly into his ribs. In spite of the pain, Rakan didn't let go. He tightened his grip until she dropped her knives, and he kicked them away.

"Tell me what you're doing here, or I'll strangle you," he said.

"Is that what you want, Rakan? To take me while I'm unconscious? Because you know as well as I do that killing me without reason is against the Code."

"You're trespassing on our territory. That's reason enough." He tightened his grip on her throat. "What has Yttresken sent you to do?"

Kariaksuq laughed harshly. "You don't speak much with your mother do you? I'm officially here to protect Dvara for my Kairök." She struggled to face him. "And frankly I'd rather have a different kind of full body contact." Her hand slithered its way between his legs. "And so would you."

Rakan jumped up and threw her across the ice. "No," he hissed. Mentally, he fixed the bleeding gash in his side. If Yarlung had allowed her to come, he couldn't kill her. Unless she was lying.

Kariaksuq pushed herself back up to standing and re-did her hair. "That's a shame. Because your little human pet won't be thinking of you anymore once Syral'kaan comes and takes an interest in her. No human has ever resisted him for very long. Or should I say, no human *can* resist him very long. Whether they want to or not."

Rakan exploded into his dragon form and lunged for Kariaksuq. She morphed into her water dragon form and slithered into the ice. Her laughter echoed into the night. Rakan clawed at the ice, willing it to part. But he couldn't move the mass fast enough to catch up with a water dragon who swam through the ice as if it was water. In a raging fury, Rakan felt his rök explode. It engulfed him in a shimmering warmth that melted the ice around him. Kariaksuq snapped around to face him, her honey-colored eyes wide with a mix of surprise and fear. She spun around and headed to the edge of a fine crevasse in the ice, near the blue cathedral that Dvara had shown him. She positioned herself so that Rakan would pass through it, disturbing the delicate balance of the ice above. And ruin the work of the High Master.

Rakan howled in rage. How could she think that he wouldn't see the danger? He shifted through the shimmering crevasse, coming up below her. He sank his teeth into her tail. Deftly, he pulled her down through the ice as easily as if he were in the air. Knowing, instinctively that she wouldn't be able to twist around and fight him off until after he had poisoned her. Kariaksuq flailed wildly, caught completely off guard. She hissed and tried to yank her tail out of his grasp, her short back legs kicking uselessly in the ice. In a wave of panic she abandoned the fight and shifted back to Yttresken.

Rakan's jaws snapped shut on the emptiness where she had been, but he had felt his canines release a stream of poison into her blood. Not enough to kill her, but enough to make her think twice before coming back for more.

Rakan growled contentedly and twirled his long undulating body underneath him. And did a double-take. He shouldn't have a long undulating body. He spread his claws as if to catch himself, but the ice flowed through him. Or maybe he flowed through the ice. Either way, he wasn't tunneling. With a massive push of his tail he flung himself out of the glacier and into the air. Landing with an ungraceful thump on the glacier's surface.

He looked back at his body. His legs were too short, his wings were... nonexistent.

He morphed back to his human form and stood frozen, looking at the ice below. The ice that he had swum through as if he were a water dragon. When he wasn't. And yet he had seen the differences in the layers of ice as clearly as he could see the air currents when he was in the sky. But he wasn't a water dragon. He couldn't be. He had already morphed into an air dragon. And no dragon could take more than one form. It wasn't possible.

Rakan inched back to where he had clawed at the glacier, running his hands over the huge gashes that his claws had left, and feeling where he had parted the ice. There were no marks from when he had entered it.

Rakan fell to his knees, his heart resounding like a gong in the stillness of the night. No dragon could morph into two forms. Not even the High Masters.

Rakan clutched at the glacier, digging into its solidity as if it was his sanity. There had to be a reasonable explanation. He couldn't morph into two forms. It simply wasn't possible. He wasn't a water dragon.

But his mother was. She must have taken control of his body and charged after Kariaksuq. Rakan sank his finger tips into the ice as if they were claws.

Eventually, he rolled onto his back and looked up at the sky. He searched for what was left of the Red Planet but didn't find it. A bright green Northern Light rippled gently across the sky and he wished Anna was with him to watch it. But she wasn't. And she wasn't going to be. Rakan stood with a groan. The only thing that was sure was that he was going to have to find a way to remove the tattoos before his mother manipulated him again.

"Mom," Anna said, interrupting her mother's cheerful dinner babble. It was starting to grate on her nerves with its inanity. "Can we talk?"

Ingrid put her fork down, her monologue forgotten. "Of course, honey." Her hand floated midair before settling on the kitchen table near Anna's arm.

Anna looked away from her mom's expectant eyes, wondering how to start. "How would you feel if you discovered that someone you cared about was... lying to you?"

"Oh, honey, is that what happened with Pemba? I'm so sorry."

"No." Anna's voice was sharper than she had intended. "It's not about Pemba." Anna looked away again. It could've been. She swallowed back her pain. "It's about Ulf."

"We've been through this, Anna," Ingrid said, her voice like a brick wall. "I'm not even asking you to like him anymore. Just to accept him."

"I know." Anna played with the food on her plate. "And I know how much you care about him. But are you sure he feels the same way?"

Ingrid picked up her plate and put it on the counter with a clatter. She turned and crossed her arms, facing Anna. "Why do you dislike him so much?"

Anna took a deep breath. The list was too long. "He's dating other people."

Ingrid's face flushed with anger. "Ulf just needs a little more freedom than most people. But he isn't dating anyone else. They're short-term flirts. They don't mean anything."

"Flirting? I saw him making out with—"

"—I don't want to hear it." Her mom's voice was almost shrill. "And it isn't any of your business."

"It is when I see him making out with a girl before practice." Especially when that girl was Kariaksuq.

Ingrid gripped the countertop behind her. "A girl from the team?"

"No. I don't know the girl," Anna lied, wanting to reassure her mom.

Ingrid turned to the sink and began scrubbing one of the pots vigorously. When she had finished, she turned back to face Anna, her eyes brimming with tears. "Why can't you just let me be happy? Why are you trying to destroy the one relationship that has lasted since… since your father…"

"Mom," Anna said quietly. "I don't want you to get hurt. That's all."

"Ulf isn't hurting me. You are."

Anna stared back into her mother's pleading eyes, at a loss for words. She couldn't tell her about Kariaksuq, since she wasn't even sure what Kariaksuq was or why she was with Ulf. But in her gut she knew it had to be linked to Dawa and her 'fiancé'. And both Torsten and Kariaksuq would stop at nothing to get what they wanted, even if it meant hurting others.

And she wouldn't let her mom get hurt.

Chapter 20

Building Bridges

RAKAN SAT SULLENLY IN THE WINDOW, WATCHING THE FRESHLY FALLEN SNOW turn to slush as the early morning light went from cobalt to bright green to reddish yellow. The sun had come and he had had no problem resisting its call. There was nothing left to live for.

Dvara came into the living room and stretched lazily. "What are you doing up so early?" She gave him a piercing look. "Or did you never go to bed?"

Rakan didn't answer. All he wanted was to crawl deep into the earth and curl up in its warmth. But even if he decided to give everything up, he couldn't. He wasn't a fire dragon. For a second he was jealous of Dvara. She could slither down into the molten earth and feel its heat, but he'd never be able to.

"It's okay," Dvara said, gently placing an arm on his shoulders. "Everything will be alright."

But Rakan knew it wouldn't. How could anything be alright when he had gone wild, tried to take Anna against her will, morphed into a water dragon and let Kariaksuq get away?

"You should go to school today. You haven't been since the ski trip last week."

"You haven't been in even longer."

Dvara dropped her arm. "That's different. I'd go if I could. But I can't."

"You could if you wanted to," Rakan said, even though he knew it wasn't true.

Dvara's energy smoldered. "Sometimes you really are an idiot." She stormed back to her room and slammed the door.

Rakan leaned against the cold window pane. The street went from a heavy white to a glistening black as people began their daily routines. He should go to school. Dvara was right. But he didn't want to. The dark grey underbelly of the clouds hung low, and Rakan ached to throw himself into the sky. He wanted to pierce the clouds and feel the sun's rays.

"Uh, Dvara?" he said, not daring to open her door. "I'm going to school." He needed to warn June about his mother, even if it meant the poison would revert to its original state.

Dvara opened the door, her red dragon dress shimmering as if illuminated from within. "Then you should hurry up," she said. "You're late." She sent him a wave of warmth.

He returned the gesture of peace. "Thanks."

"Uh, Rakan?" she called out after him as he turned to go. "Don't forget to get changed."

Rakan turned and bowed playfully. "Don't get into any trouble."

She threw a pillow at him as he shifted out of their rooms and into the empty hallway in front of his classroom. Or rather the hallway that had been empty before the twins showed up, their arms crossed over their tattooed chests like two bodyguards flanking the classroom door. Rakan quickly created an electromagnetic shield, not wanting to know what Verje and Sverd intended to try.

"Interesting," Verje said, touching the shield mentally. "Although not entirely effective." Verje pried the shield open just enough to blast Rakan across the hall. "Be grateful that it came from me and not Sverd."

"What was that for?" Rakan stood and dusted himself off. He needed to figure out how to block them from prying open the shield again. Fast.

"We want you to leave." Sverd's purple eyes flashed as he closed the distance between them. "Now."

Rakan countered Sverd's advance with a spinning back kick but Sverd moved nimbly to the side. Rakan growled with frustration at not having the satisfaction of feeling his foot land in Sverd's gut. Even as they circled each other, Rakan kept the other twin in sight. It wouldn't be beneath the twins to set up an attack from behind.

The door to the classroom opened and June came out. She quickly shut the door behind her. The air warped as she put up a sound barrier.

"What are you doing?" she snapped at all three of them. "Are you crazy?"

Sverd and Verje bowed to June. "It is Erling's wish," Verje said.

"To attack Pemba at school?" asked June incredulously.

"He only seeks to protect you," answered Verje, still bent at the waist.

"I'm not a fragile doll that needs protection. I thought I made that clear the other day," June said sharply. "Leave. Now."

Sverd bowed and disappeared. But Verje hung back. "Your life is worth more than the impetuous whims of a child. I ask to be allowed to stay."

"It's not necessary," June snapped before adding more gently, "but thank you."

Verje bowed. "May it be as you desire, my Lady." He disappeared in a flash of purple light.

"I can't believe I'm fighting Erling over you," June said, throwing a hand in the air.

"I'm glad you did. I wasn't looking forward to fighting them both at the same time."

"Wimp."

Rakan lunged for her but she twirled out of the way, laughing. She held up her hand. "Another time. We're supposed to be in class." She shook her finger at him. "You've been skipping all week."

Rakan hung his head in mock guilt. "Sorry, my Lady." Before he had even finished his sentence, June had slapped him as hard as she could.

Rakan put a hand to his cheek. "What was that for?"

"Don't ever call me that." June's eyes sparkled with flecks of light, making Rakan recoil in revulsion.

"You didn't have to slap me," he said, doubt rippling through him. Not only were her eyes a bright blue-green, but they were halfway between a dragon's slits and a void-trail's nearly pupil-less orbs of light.

June looked away and shifted her weight from one foot to the other. "I didn't mean to. I just… reacted."

"What else do you 'just react' to? That way I'll know to avoid it."

"I said I'm sorry," June said defensively, her anger beginning to bubble again.

"It's okay." Rakan spread his hands in a gesture of truce. "Thanks for coming out," he added. "They weren't too happy to see me."

"No." June walked over to the window and Rakan felt her struggle to control her waves of emotion. "They say it would have been better if you and your sister had been killed by the shield." June turned and raised her chin, challenging Rakan to respond.

Rakan stiffened. "How do you know about that?"

"Why were you snooping around Erling's house?"

"Dvara was. I came when she was in trouble."

"Stop lying." June's anger flared, flicking Rakan like the tip of a whip. "You've been trailing him for weeks."

Rakan backed off. Of course she would know that. Neither he nor Dvara knew how to hide their trails. He looked back at June, determined to tell her about his mother's search for Paaliaq, but the words died in his throat. She was shimmering in a halo of light. Green light. Paaliaq's green. Panic washed over him. He wanted to lunge at her and rip her throat out.

June noticed his crazed look and turned her head. "Are my eyes green again?" Her voice was small, and scared.

"I don't know." He hadn't seen her eyes. "But your energy was. It's gone now." It wasn't even blue. It was... gone. "How do you hide it?"

"Hide what?" asked June, spreading her hands helplessly.

Rakan wavered. She felt too young to be Paaliaq. Her eyes were blue. "Why do your eyes change color?" If he had morphed into a water dragon because of his mother's presence via the tattoos, maybe June's eyes changed because Paaliaq had marked her in a different way and it came out through her eyes.

"I don't know. Usually they're blue. But sometimes they turn green." She looked back out the window at the dismally grey weather. "That's why I always wore sunglasses. The color freaks people out too much, even when they stay blue." Her voice cracked. "I used to lie. I told people I had colored contacts when I didn't."

Rakan wrestled with his conflicting desires to either protect her or kill her. He inched forward, bracing himself for an attack. "Why do the twins call you my Lady?"

June straightened. "Because I am Erling's Chosen and we have opened the first gate."

Rakan stopped. His rök quivered as if he had missed something crucial. But it remained just beyond his grasp. His fingers twitched. "What?"

"The seven gates. We have to open them to become united."

Rakan shook his head. There were no gates to open. "You can only be united with someone through your rök. Erling doesn't have one."

"No. And neither will I. It won't exist anymore. I'll be free." As she spoke, June's voice began to vibrate, becoming sweet and pure. Just like a void-trail's. And unlike anything a dragon or a human could produce.

Rakan felt sick. Was she becoming a void-trail by opening these gates? "Maybe that's not a good idea," he said slowly. "Your rök is a part of you."

"No. Not the real me."

"You'd die without your rök." Was that what Erling wanted? To kill her?

June looked at Rakan as if he was a puppy who didn't understand. "No. I won't. Or I couldn't do this." Two enormous green wings spread behind her as her clothes transformed into a draped white dress that crossed over her breasts. And then she disappeared in a flash of green and purple light. Rakan lunged at the air that shimmered momentarily where she had been. She was gone. He wanted to howl but knew he couldn't. The sound shield had gone with her. His heart pounded violently in his chest. His rök whirled even faster. The world was falling apart. It wasn't possible. He couldn't even sense where she had gone. She hadn't shifted through the matter that surrounded them. She had simply disappeared, leaving no trace. No scent. Nothing. And for the split second before she had gone, her rök had disappeared as if it had never existed.

Rakan stood staring at the spot where she had been standing, even when the students flowed into the hallway for lunch. He no longer wondered who she was. But what she was. Dragons moved through matter. Or not at all.

Anna had finally settled in a corner of the lunchroom. She picked at the sandwich that she'd throw out later anyway. For the first time in a week, she had felt Pemba at school. But he hadn't come down yet, even though she had already seen June head over to the music student lounge with Erling. It was where they went when they wanted to be alone. Not that she would've sat with them, even had they asked.

Pemba's slow throbbing energy resonated like a smooth deep bass. He was coming. Anna ripped her sandwich in half. He was no different than Ulf. And she hated herself for having thought otherwise. She turned away from the door, but her attention wouldn't leave Pemba alone. She tried to remember what he had looked like as a dragon, but it was blurry. She felt him come in. He was so close, so near. She ached to turn around, to see him morph... why was she being such a fool? He didn't care about her. He was looking for June. She glanced at him just to make sure. And their eyes met. His touch hovered over her like a tentative caress. She started to lean into it before she jerked back around and blocked herself from him. Her mind tingled and blurred with the effort. But he pulled his mind-touch back. Anna sat still, her forgotten sandwich trembling in her hands. He hesitated, almost coming to join her before sitting with some guys from his class.

Anna dropped the sandwich, bitter tears welling in her eyes. An acid wave of hatred rolled up from deep within. She wanted to lash into him and hurt him as much as he had hurt her. Whatever Pemba was, and whatever mess Dawa had gotten herself into, she needed to protect her mom. She stood and cleared off her table, pointedly ignoring Pemba's furtive glances. She needed to learn to fight.

T'eng Sten appeared in their rooms without warning, as always. Dvara jumped off the couch and pummeled his chest with her fists. "I hate you," she yelled.

"Greetings, Kairök," Rakan said, pausing briefly in his effort to pulverize their punching bag. Dvara had been getting steadily more withdrawn since the incident at the shield. Her rök was close to cracking and Rakan hardly dared to leave her at home alone.

"I see all is well," T'eng Sten said, holding Dvara by the wrists. He nodded to Rakan.

"Take my rök," Dvara said. She arched herself into T'eng Sten. He hissed and crushed her against his chest. "You want it as much as I do," she said, her voice was choked with desire.

"I do." His voice echoed hers. "But you know why I can't."

"Yarlung doesn't care what happens to us." Dvara pushed T'eng Sten away. "You know that."

"I think she does," T'eng Sten said. His emotions were back under control.

"Only because she wants to use us," Dvara said.

Rakan doubled his attack on the bag, fighting back a wave of nausea. Sweat streamed down his neck and over his abdomen.

"Whether she cares or not, I can't take your rök without starting an inter-Cairn conflict. She has publicly accepted Yttresken's claim. Not mine."

"And you're going to let her give me to him like a spineless snake?"

T'eng Sten growled. "You know it's not as simple as that. He can't touch you as long as you stay here. And if I can manipulate the situation correctly, my claim will be authenticated by the Meet, thus annulling hers with no honor lost. To anyone."

"Who cares about honor?" Dvara flung her hands to the ceiling. "I can't live like this anymore. It's like being in a cage. I hate it."

"You need a little patience." T'eng Sten reached out to take Dvara in his arms.

"No." Dvara pushed him away. "If you won't take my rök, you can't have me."

T'eng Sten's face hardened. "As you wish."

Dvara spat on the ground and shifted out of the room in a shimmering haze of red.

Rakan stopped pounding the bag. "Where did she go?" Her trail went straight down.

"In." T'eng Sten tilted his head. "But not too far. Yet."

Rakan remembered his own desire to tunnel down in despair. "Can she kill herself that way?"

"Yes. The day she stops hating me for refusing her rök is the day I'll need to take it or watch her die. But we're not there yet." His voice was matter-of-fact.

"How can you stand her suffering? I thought you cared." Rakan trembled with fury.

"I wouldn't be here risking my neck if I didn't care," T'eng Sten said, coming closer.

"You care, but is it about Dvara?" Rakan clenched his fists. It didn't really matter if he died attacking a Kairök or from the poison that was seeping into his every pore.

T'eng Sten laughed. "If only you knew how little your mother's idiotic politics mattered to me, you wouldn't ask that."

No longer able to control himself, Rakan threw a right hook at T'eng Sten's temple, concentrating all his pent up anger into that one blow. T'eng Sten blocked it and twisted his body weight into Rakan's gut with an uppercut. Rakan groaned as T'eng Sten's fist connected with a pocket of reactivated poison, splintering it into hundreds of flaming shards that pierced his organs.

T'eng Sten caught Rakan as he crumpled on his fist. "Idiot," the older dragon hissed. "You're in no shape to fight. Why didn't you tell me that the poison was transforming?"

Rakan struggled to stand back up, gripping onto T'eng Sten, but got no farther than onto one knee.

"I can help you, Rakan." T'eng Sten dug his hands into Rakan's biceps and forced him to look up. "But only if you want me to."

Rakan nodded, wondering how many dragons actually knew how to neutralize poison but kept it a secret. "Does Yttresken know?"

"What?"

"Can Yttresken neutralize poison?"

"I doubt it, but what difference can it possibly make? You want to ask him?"

"No." Rakan sank to the floor and hoped Kariaksuq was suffering as much as he was.

T'eng Sten raked through Rakan's body, dissolving the active poison but leaving the neutralized poison intact. Rakan groaned. T'eng Sten wasn't as gentle as June. "Can't you remove it all?" His head cleared as a rush of energy flowed through his veins.

T'eng Sten studied Rakan's face. "You know I can. I removed Dvara's. But you'd have to tell Yarlung first."

Rakan's anger flared back up and he scrambled to his feet unsteadily. T'eng Sten had the grace not to help. He stumbled to the window on his own. Rakan cursed under his breath. He was in a prison as much as Dvara was. Except that his sentence was death.

T'eng Sten sat on the couch. His long indigo overcoat slipped open, showing his chiseled bulk. A smile played on the corners of his mouth.

"If you tell her that I offered to do it, thinking that I could take you away from her, but that you intend to be a counter-spy instead, I think she'd agree."

Rakan's attention snapped back to T'eng Sten. "She'd expect information."

"I'd tell you what to tell her."

"What if I don't? What if I turn against you?"

T'eng Sten smiled. "You won't."

The Kairök's confidence unnerved Rakan. "How can you be so sure?"

"I can't. But you can't live without taking risks. And this is one I feel I can take."

Rakan tried to figure out what T'eng Sten hoped to gain from the situation. "Why?"

"Because sometimes taking a chance on someone in need can earn you a lifelong ally." T'eng Sten stood and faced Rakan. "But more importantly, you aren't like your mother anymore than Dvara is." He put a hand on Rakan's shoulder. "Think about it. But maybe not too long or she'll suspect something when she realizes that some of the poison has already been removed." The Kairök nodded with a self-satisfied smile and shifted out of their rooms.

Rakan sat on the low wooden table wondering if he could trust T'eng Sten. Because the idea was tempting. He'd be able to warn June without killing himself in the process. And maybe even protect her. But T'eng Sten probably had his own plans. And Rakan had no idea what they were.

T'eng Sten's trail shimmered on their couch. Why hadn't he ever noticed that the thin inner line wasn't indigo blue? It was brown. Sort of. Rakan zoomed in on the inner strand. It was a mix of all of T'eng Sten's kais wound together with his indigo, making it look brown. Rakan's nostrils flared. His mother's was pale turquoise. She didn't care about her kais any more than she cared about her offspring.

Rakan felt another wave of anger. And another wave of nausea.

Lysa leaned against the locker next to Anna's after lunch on Thursday. "Are you coming to practice tonight?"

Anna jerked back. She hadn't felt Lysa approach. But then again, she hadn't been thinking about what was going on around her, either. "Maybe," she said, eyeing Lysa cautiously. Pemba hadn't been at school for the past few days and his absence was almost worse than his presence.

"Good. We've missed you."

Anna snorted. She doubted anyone had noticed. Or if they did, they were probably just as glad she wasn't there.

Lysa smiled, her pale green eyes flecked with gold. "*I* missed you," she said. "And I know what it feels like to be manipulated... or to think you were."

Anna shut her locker, hugging the books she'd need for the afternoon. "What do you mean?"

"I didn't think I was being manipulated last year. I was blinded by what I thought I felt for my so-called boyfriend." Lysa paused, her voice oddly disembodied. "You tried to help me, when no one else did." Lysa's eyes were like orbs of light. "And now you think you've been manipulated when you haven't."

The bell to go back to class rang.

"Do you want to go?" Lysa asked with a nod to the classroom.

"No. Not really." Not anymore.

"Good." Lysa shimmered with excitement. "I've never skipped before."

Anna stared at her. "Really?" Everyone skipped sometimes. Or maybe it was only if you had a cousin like Red who couldn't stand being in school and dragged you out for a wild trip to the mountains. And somehow, Red and Haakon always got out of trouble as easily as they got into it.

Lysa linked her arm through Anna's, and they walked out through the schoolyard and down the hill. "Where should we go?" she asked.

"Anywhere but Helmersen's," said Anna, not wanting to be reminded of Pemba.

"Wherever." Lysa slowed down. "Erling is furious."

"How do you know that?"

"Because he's yelling at me. I..." Lysa stopped.

"We can go back," Anna said, looking at Lysa who stood still, her face blank.

"No. I just shut him out." Lysa's face was determined as she started to walk again. "I know it's the right thing to do even if Erling doesn't think so."

"But... I mean, don't get in trouble for this." Anna examined Lysa. Had she just been speaking telepathically with her brother?

"It's okay. I need to tell you what happened last year. So that you'll understand."

"Understand what? No, tell me that later. How can you shut Erling out?"

"With a mind shield."

"But do you actually hear him, or just feel him?"

"Both."

"But..." Anna said, stopping in the middle of the sidewalk. "How?"

"We're different, Anna. That's what I want to explain."

Anna considered her friend for a moment and then nodded. "Okay."

They walked on in silence. "Here," said Anna, leading Lysa up a flight of stairs to Hansen's café. It was the kind of place her mom would come with a friend. They wouldn't see anyone from school. The place was emptying out after lunch. They got coffee and heart-shaped waffles and sat at a table overlooking Tromso's main street.

Anna looked around the café, a mix of modern metal tables and dark wood counters, waiting for Lysa to start.

"I like the way they've decorated," said Lysa, nodding at a potted plant and a candle that were attached to the wall on long iron bars. "A perfect balance of light and matter."

Anna looked blankly at Lysa. "I don't know what you mean."

"Life is a matter of balance. We need both light and matter. But I forgot that."

"Oh." Lysa had gone off the deep end.

"Last year, I let myself be convinced that June was bad because she was different. Because she's a shapeshifter like Pemba."

Anna put down her coffee. "June's a shapeshifter?" She could morph too?

"I thought you knew," said Lysa, looking confused.

"No." Although she probably should have. She eyed Lysa. "Are you?"

"No," said Lysa. "Why would you think that?"

"Because you have a... shroud of energy. Like they do."

Lysa smiled. "I didn't know you could see that. But no, we aren't shape-shifters. Which is what I was trying to explain. Last year I listened to...

the one I thought was my boyfriend. I let myself believe that since June was a shapeshifter, she shouldn't be with my brother. But I was wrong. There's nothing wrong with their union if they love each other."

"Maybe Erling would change his mind if he saw June and Pemba together."

"They weren't together," said Lysa firmly.

"They were lying on top of each other," countered Anna. "I saw them."

"Shapeshifters are different from us. They need to live in groups, but both June and Pemba have grown up alone. Their reaction to each other is normal."

"Good for them. They can have each other," Anna said. "With Erling's blessing."

"No, Anna. It was intimate, not sexual."

Anna stared at Lysa. "What's the difference?"

"Have you ever watched a school of fish trying to avoid something? They react as one. Not as individuals. Shapeshifters are the same. They share in a different way than we do. They mind-link and become like one, but that doesn't mean that they want to sleep together."

"But they were together."

Lysa sighed. "No. Not that way."

"Then what were they doing?"

"Pemba wanted to link in a deeper way than they had done before and June didn't know what to do. That's all."

"You weren't there," Anna said defensively. "You went with the other group."

"I saw June's memory of it."

Anna leaned forward, not sure if she had heard properly. "What?"

"June was so upset by what happened that she showed me."

"How can you see someone's memory?"

"With a mind-touch."

Anna sat perfectly still. "Can you show me?"

"I can try."

"Now?" No one was left in their part of the café, although she could hear people in the back room.

"If you don't mind holding my hands."

Anna put her hands out. "What do I do?"

"Close your eyes and let your mind go blank. It might be more like emo-tions than images." Lysa's hands hovered over Anna's. "Shapeshifters feel things, they don't really see them."

Anna nodded and Lysa took her hands. At first nothing happened. She heard the clanking of dishes from the other room and felt the warmth of the sun on her face as the mountain rushed below. She was about to fly into the air and melt into the mountain all at once. "Whoa." Anna pulled back, surprised by the feeling of power and speed. "What was that?"

"June's memory. They were racing up the mountain. They go pretty fast. I should have warned you." Lysa looked apologetic. "Do you want to try again?"

Anna held out her hands and braced herself for the rush. The feeling came back, but this time she also felt June's thrill of racing, her happi-ness to be able to let go and be free. Pemba pulled in front in a blur of orange. He was there and not there at the same time. The vision changed. It became multiple, like a kaleidoscope, and she was tumbling over Pemba, victorious. Pemba shimmered as thousands of coral-colored sparks flashed around him. Anna felt June's panic. The vision shifted again and Anna saw Pemba twisting in agony. June tried to help, but he wouldn't let her. Anna felt June's anger and then her confusion as Pemba went limp, the pain gone. Suddenly, she saw herself and felt June's surprise and then anguish as she felt her own pain projected back at her through June's memory.

"Are you okay?" asked Lysa nervously, pulling Anna out of the memory.

"No. Maybe. I don't know." The images were still flashing around her mind, the rush of the mountain, the speed, the need to win, the feeling of helplessness as Pemba went wild. "Did you ask June if you could show me?" asked Anna, feeling a pang of guilt.

"Yes. She thought it would be better if you saw it."

Anna nodded. She felt even more confused than she had before.

"Most people can't accept others who are different from themselves," continued Lysa. "And so those who are, hide it." Lysa paused. "From what I understand, Pemba tried to show his true nature to humans before. And it went badly. Some of them became violent."

Anna felt sick. Had he killed them?

Lysa put a hand on Anna's arm. "I think he cared too much about you to take that risk. That's all."

Chapter 21

Intrigues

A NNA STOOD ALONE IN THE MIDDLE OF THE COURT AFTER PRACTICE, TOSSING A ball up and down.

"What are you doing?" Ulf asked, walking towards her. His hair was uncharacteristically slicked back. "Why hasn't anyone picked up the balls?"

"They did." Anna made a face at his overpowering aftershave.

Ulf stopped picking up the balls. "Are you trying to get me angry? Because it's working."

"No. I was just waiting for you."

Ulf walked around Anna, like a wolf sizing up its prey. "Well, here I am."

Anna waited for Ulf to finish his idiotic preening. "I wanted to warn you about Kariaksuq. She's not who she seems to be."

"Who?" said Ulf. "Don't know her. Maybe you should introduce me."

Anna threw the ball at Ulf's chest. "The girl I saw you with the other day. In the weight room."

"Oh, Kari. Don't worry. I haven't met a girl yet who could tame me. But I'm touched you care." He reached out to caress Anna's cheek.

"Don't even think about it," she said, slapping it away

Ulf caught her by the wrist and twisted her arm behind her, pulling her firmly against his chest. Anna struggled, but Ulf was stronger than she was. "Let go," she hissed.

"So much wasted passion," said Ulf, transferring both of her wrists to one hand so that his other hand was free to wander firmly down her buttocks. "It's such a shame that Kari is waiting for me or I'd show you a better way of using it than trying to hit me." Anna twisted furiously, but Ulf's grip just tightened. "Consider yourself lucky this time," said Ulf in her ear. "But don't ever do that again."

Panic exploded inside Anna. She felt a ripple of energy come up from deep within. She yanked one of her hands free and pushed the heel of her palm into his chest. It didn't knock him over but it surprised him enough for her to get free.

Ulf snickered and came closer. "You like it rough, don't you, little tiger? If that's what you want, I'm sure I can oblige." Ulf dangled the storage room key in front of her. "You can put the balls away, since you're the one who wanted this." He dropped the key on the ground and walked away. She picked up the balls with trembling hands. Maybe she was getting herself into more trouble than it was worth.

Saturday afternoon Anna sat on her bed, looking at the drawing Pemba had given her. She traced the dragon with a finger. "Is it you?" The doorbell rang and she jumped. She glanced at the clock. Two o'clock. Red was right on time.

"Ready?" he asked, gently punching her in the shoulder when she opened the door.

"Maybe," Anna answered, surprised to see Ea too. "I didn't realize you were both coming." Although she should have. They were always together. But she didn't want to learn to fight in front of Ea.

"She's a better teacher than I am," said Red, catching her look.

"You know how to fight?" Anna asked Ea as they took off their coats and boots in the entryway. "In a dress?" Ea always wore dresses, even in a snowstorm. She'd just put a pair of snow pants on underneath it.

"It's easier to kick someone in the head with a dress than with jeans," said Ea as if it should have been obvious.

Anna glanced back at Ea as she led them through the kitchen and to the living room. She had never thought about kicking anyone in the head. And she was surprised that Ea, with her perfectly styled hair and light brown eyes that reminded Anna of a doe, had. Ea was the kind of girl who always wore makeup and had a year-round tan.

"Looks can be deceptive," said Red in Anna's ear. He grinned at Ea. "She's always been a better hand-to-hand fighter than me."

"That's not true," Ea answered. "You've won. Once."

"That's only because you wanted me to," said Red, wrapping his arms around Ea's slender waist. "And I'm glad you did."

Anna sat down on the couch with a thump. "You guys aren't any better at teaching me to fight than you are at teaching me to salsa."

Red burst out laughing and released Ea. "Okay," he said, pulling Anna to her feet. "Let's fight. Come on, hit me with all you've got."

Anna smelled a familiar scent of autumn leaves and leaned closer to Red, inhaling deeply. Anna felt Ea looking at her and pulled away from her cousin. "Sorry," she mumbled.

"Can you smell him?" asked Ea. An eerie quietness settled around them that made Anna wish she hadn't.

"Uh, well, a little. But he smells normal. I mean, he's fine."

Red looked at her curiously. "What do you smell?"

"Leaves. Wet autumn leaves. Uh, do you guys want something to drink?"

"And me? Can you smell me?" Ea stood in front of Anna and arched her neck.

Anna backed up. "Look I'm sorry if I've offended you. I'll go make some coffee."

Red caught her by the arm. "Stop worrying. Just tell us if you can smell her."

Anna felt trapped. "Okay." She closed her eyes and leaned towards Ea. "You smell like..." Anna pulled away. "What does it matter?"

"I need to know," said Ea, her voice nearly a growl.

"Leave it," said Red to Ea, releasing Anna. "It doesn't matter."

"Yes, it does. We need to know if it's her or if..." Ea's voice trailed off as she and Red faced each other. The room suddenly felt small. Anna backed out towards the kitchen. Things were getting way out of proportion.

"No." Red's attention snapped back to Anna and she froze. "Tell us what you smell."

Anna felt her skin begin to tingle, like a warning of danger. "She smells like burnt rubber," she said quickly. "Alright? Can we change the subject now?"

Red burst out laughing.

"Knock it off." Ea punched Red so hard in the chest that Anna staggered in pain for him.

"Okay, okay," said Red, holding up a hand. "I just never thought of it like that."

"It's not funny. If she can smell us, maybe others can too."

"You're right," said Red, becoming suddenly serious. "Have you smelled either one of us before?"

"I don't think so. Maybe you, Red. Because it smells familiar." Anna looked from one to the other. "Can you tell me why that bothers you so much? Or is that another secret?"

"It's part of the same secret."

Anna felt a flicker of fear. Would they call Liv and get her to erase her memory?

"I think we should spar. Not talk." Ea's voice was as crisp as her fist.

"I'll go make coffee," said Anna, slipping into the kitchen. She stood by the coffee maker, listening to the reassuring sound of it percolating. But there was no sound coming from the living room. Curious, Anna peered out of the kitchen. They were arguing. Silently.

Ea turned, catching Anna watching them. "I have to go now," said Ea, striding towards the kitchen. "Red can take you through the basics." Anna scuttled out of Ea's way.

"Ea wants to go shopping," said Red.

"What? Oh, right. I forgot. I *love* to go shopping," said Ea, giving Red a chilling smile. "With Liv." She spun on her heel and twirled out of the kitchen. The air sparkled in her wake, and tension floated in the air like hundreds of charged particles.

The front door slammed downstairs. "Ready?" asked Red. He reached out and tapped Anna on the side of the head. "Block," he said. He reached out with the other hand. Anna blocked, but he pushed past her hand. "You have to mean it." He tapped her again. She swatted his arm away as hard as she could, venting her pent up anger.

"Better, except you have to keep your center of gravity lower down." He swept her off her feet. "You're too easy to knock over."

"Hey," she said, getting up. "That's not fair." And it hurt.

"Who said it had to be fair? How do you throw a ball when you need to score?"

"What?" Anna dropped her arms and Red pushed her in the shoulder. "Never drop your guard. Always be ready."

Anna bit back a sarcastic comment. This wasn't how she had imagined learning to fight would be. And she wasn't sure she wanted him to teach her anymore. Not after the scene with Ea.

"Think about the way you concentrate when you play handball. Fighting needs the same concentration. It's just a dance between two people instead of two teams. Try again. Just block for now. There, like that. No, not too fast – just respond to my movement. Better."

Anna searched for the same feeling of mental clarity as when she was in the mad rush of a game and pressure was on to score. To find that opening, to see where to attack. Red moved slowly, giving her time to block. She started to feel the dance. The give and take, the attack that needed a response. Red moved faster and at first she followed. But then she began blocking after the blow and he was touching her every time.

"You're too stiff. Stop thinking and feel it."

Anna dropped her arms and backed out of Red's reach. "I was."

"No, you weren't." He backed her up to the wall. "Hit me."

"No." She tried to turn away, but there was no where to go.

"Why not?"

"I don't want to hurt you."

Red exploded in laughter and Anna reached out to slap him, but he caught her wrist and twisted it painfully. "Ouch," she said. A rush of anger accompanied by sparks of tingling energy welled up inside her.

"Slapping won't do anything." Red dropped her hand. "Try punching me. No, hit with your first two knuckles. Harder. Here," he said, taking the pillow from the window nook. "Hit this instead."

She focused on the pillow and punched. She wanted him to feel it through the pillow. But he didn't react. So she tried again. And again.

"Keep going," he said whenever she slowed down. "Better, but use the floor."

"What?" she said dropping her arms and earning herself another tap on her cheek. "Would you stop that?" It was driving her crazy. But Red only laughed, annoying her even more.

"Keep your guard up," he said. "And put your weight behind it. Imagine the punch starting from the floor, twisting up through your hip and out your arm. Punch through to my back, not just the pillow."

Anna glowered at him. She had been trying to punch him through the pillow.

"You'll get it," he said, misunderstanding her reaction. "Keep trying."

She clenched her fist and slammed into him. This time the pillow flattened.

"Ah, finally." He dropped the pillow. "Now hit me."

"No."

"Why not? You can't hurt me."

Anger finally flared out of control and Anna threw a punch at her cousin, wanting to blast him out of the kitchen and wipe the knowing smile off his face. But the punch never connected. One moment he was there, and the next he wasn't. Her anger died as quickly as it had come. "Red?" Her skin prickled as the minute sparks of energy disappeared, leaving her feeling cold. And alone. "Red?"

"Behind you," he said in her ear, making her jump halfway across the kitchen.

"Don't ever do that again," she said, spinning around with her hand on her chest.

"Pemba's shield was about to blast me."

Anna gripped the back of a chair. "How do you know about the shield?"

"What do you think happened the other night? That I fell into your shelves?"

"But it doesn't do it every time." It hadn't worked on Ulf.

"It only works if the person has… the same kind of energy that I do."

"Oh," Anna said, examining Red more closely. Was he a shapeshifter too?

"I can't teach you to fight, Anna. You get too angry."

"I can control it."

"No. Ea was right. It's too much of a risk."

"Can't you change the shield so that it doesn't react to you?"

Red turned away. "If I did, he'd know I existed. And I can't take that risk. As it is, every time the shield is activated and I'm here—"

"What?" asked Anna, a sinking feeling in her gut.

"There's a risk that Pemba will show up and realize that I'm one of the ones he's looking for." Red faced her, his face dead serious. "And then I'd have to kill him."

Rakan crossed his arms over his oiled chest. Yarlung had placed him as a guard to her inner lair carved out of the rock beneath her lake. An honor he would rather have done without. Just like the oil that male dragons wore for formal occasions. He fingered the metal armbands that allowed him to mind-speak with Yuli, his mother's third in command. He had begun to fill out in the past few weeks and it felt good. Even if he wasn't as bulky as an Old Dragon, he was no longer as slender as a puppy.

The gentle hum of elegantly coifed females and seductively oiled males didn't hide the tension that gnawed under the surface. Rakan blocked it out. He didn't need to know what they were saying. Other dragons were taking care of that. All he needed to do was make sure that no weapons were brought into his mother's inner chamber. He had nearly shifted out of his mother's lair twice when he felt Anna's shield begin to react. But it had quieted down since.

Yuli, dressed in a simple lime-green sheath that matched her eyes, led Kairök Yttresken from one of the niches that surrounded the domed area. She motioned for Yttresken to stay a few feet behind and approached Rakan. "I see the Arctic agrees with you, Rakan'dzor."

Rakan bowed slightly, not sure what she meant. "Thank you."

"My pleasure." She ran her eyes over his chest. "We should fly together." Yuli turned slightly to the side, undulating just enough to be suggestive.

"I've always enjoyed flying with you," he answered slowly, confused by her behavior.

"My dear Rakan, when will you unleash the fire of your name?" A smile played on her lips. *"Yarlung would like you to distract Yttresken while she prepares for their meeting."* Her mental voice filled him with warmth, stirring a response that her flirting hadn't.

Rakan nodded curtly and broke the contact. "May her will be done," he said formally.

Yuli's lime green eyes danced with flecks of gold. "May your will be done," she whispered. She turned and motioned for Yttresken to come forward.

"Greetings, Rakan," said Yttresken.

"Yttresken," Rakan responded with the minimum of nods, returning the insult of familiarity in a formal setting.

"I see you've been brought back in order," said the Kairök, his beady pink eyes flicking to Rakan's thick metal armbands. "Although perhaps not far enough." Yttresken's voice oozed insult, but Rakan ignored it.

The bands were pre-molded to turn into daggers if needed. "My mother will see you shortly." He would be Yarlung's guard, but he wouldn't play her political games.

"Good," said Yttresken. He moved closer and spoke in a confidential tone. "I know that this... new... situation with T'eng Sten must be very trying for you."

Rakan's nostrils flared. Yttresken's cloying floral scent repulsed Rakan as much as the Kairök himself, but Rakan forced himself not to react. The Kairök couldn't possibly know about his agreement with T'eng Sten.

"His imprisonment of your poor sister is an abomination," continued Yttresken. "Such a dreadful situation. I trust she isn't suffering too much?"

"My mother has insight into these matters that I do not," Rakan said stiffly. No matter what he said about Dvara, it would be twisted against her: if he said she was unhappy it would be reason to attack T'eng Sten and if he said she was happy it would be reason to attack Dvara. Either way, it would make things worse.

Yttresken's pink eyes narrowed. "Indeed. Although you probably have some insight into Kariaksuq's current ailment, I believe?"

"I trust she is well."

Yttresken's thin lips curled into a vicious smile. "Apart from being a little delusional. She appears to believe you are a water dragon, and not an air dragon as Yarlung was so proud to proclaim." Yttresken leaned forward. "I can keep your little secret, Rakan. I'm always willing to help a *friend*. Yes?"

Rakan's anger flared. How could the Kairök think he could be black-mailed with something so stupid? Even if he wasn't an air dragon, all three forms were technically equal. Even if most Kairöks were air dragons. He squashed his reaction and bent his head. "You are too gracious," he said, letting Yttresken believe he was accepting his offer. Getting into the details of what had actually happened with Kariaksuq wouldn't help anyone.

"Good boy," said the Kairök, patting his shoulder. "I'm glad we understand each other so well."

It was all Rakan could do not to lash out at the Kairök. *"Can I send him in now?"* he snarled at his mother.

"What has he done to anger you?" she asked. She sounded amused.

"He thinks he can manipulate me to help him get Dvara."

Yarlung laughed derisively. *"And did you allow him to continue to think that?"*

Rakan hesitated. *"Yes."* He had just wanted to end the conversation.

"Good. Very good. You're learning, my son. You're learning. Send him in."

"My mother will see you now, if I may proceed?" Rakan said coolly.

"By all means, please do," said Yttresken with a self-satisfied smile. "But you won't find anything. I wouldn't need a weapon to kill someone."

Rakan continued in silence, trying not to snarl in repulsion as he searched the Kairök. Once finished, he dissolved the slab of rock that sealed off Yarlung's dimly lit inner chamber. Rakan deactivated the shields and the gentle sound of the gurgling mineral spring hushed the incessant chatter as everyone turned to see who was going in. Rakan stepped to the side and watched Yttresken saunter through.

He wouldn't need any weapons to kill Yttresken either.

Chapter 22

Schemes

ANNA PACED THE DINING ROOM, DEBATING WHETHER OR NOT TO CALL PEMBA. She reached out tentatively, trying to feel if he was somewhere in Tromso. But he wasn't. He had been gone for nearly a week now. Anna pressed her forehead against the cool window pane. But Dawa was home, she could feel her sharp energy behind the shields that surrounded the Tibetan House. She never even left their rooms anymore.

"Boyfriend give up?" Ulf dropped his gym bag on the living room floor and unbuttoned his shirt to reveal perfect abs that made him look like a male Barbie.

Anna glanced over Ulf's shoulder and into the kitchen, wondering if her mom had come home too.

"Don't get your hopes up." Ulf rubbed his hand over his chest. "I just want to take a shower before dinner."

"The shower is upstairs." She clenched her fists. She'd pummel him if he came too close.

"Tsk, tsk," he said, walking towards her nonchalantly. "So much frustration. Pemba doesn't know how to show you a good time, does he?" Ulf flashed his wolfish grin. "Or did he refuse to take you violently?" Anna tried to storm past Ulf but he sidestepped in front of her. "He never even kissed you, did he?" Ulf asked with a smirk.

"I thought you wanted to shower."

"You need to relax and enjoy life. You're too serious all the time. Even when you play handball. You'd play better and enjoy it more if you loosened up." He leaned forward. "You're too uptight."

Anna punched Ulf square in the chest and dodged to the side. But he grabbed her arm and yanked her close. "What was that for? I'm just trying to help." Ulf dropped her arm and walked away. "Dawa made me promise to give you this," he said, stopping in the doorway. He pulled out an envelope and let it flutter to the ground. "I don't know why I agreed."

"You have served me well," said Yarlung from the divan that rose like a throne in the middle of her bubbling mineral pool. Her dress shimmered alternately turquoise and white in the fine spray of the waterfall that rippled behind her back like an intricate tapestry.

Rakan nodded, unsure how to bring up the subject of his tattoos.

Yarlung walked down the gently curving steps and disappeared into the water. Rakan's nostrils flared. He wanted to feel the water rush around him, to move through it as if it was air. To feel himself as one with the movement of the currents. He snarled. He wasn't a water dragon. He shouldn't crave it. Undulating white coils flashed beneath the surface. She had morphed. He had missed his chance to speak with her alone.

Rakan bowed in her direction and turned to leave.

"I was happy to hear that Kariaksuq managed to get you to chase her. It is time you came into your full powers."

Rakan stopped. What else had Yttresken told her? He faced his mother and bowed again. "I thought my presence was no longer necessary."

"On the contrary," she said. She ran her mind-touch over him and dissolved the metal bands that circled his biceps. "Yttresken says it's a shame you aren't a water dragon or he'd offer her to you for your first mating as a dragon." Her eyes narrowed. "He seems to be taking quite an interest in you."

"He's not the only Kairök to have expressed an interest."

"I assume you speak of T'eng Sten?"

"He offered to remove the tattoos and in exchange requests that I offer to be your spy. He would then give me information to give you."

Yarlung's mouth twitched into a thin smile. "Did he not consider that you might tell me of his real intentions?"

"I don't know," Rakan said, lying for the first time. "But I do know that he believes I'm desperate, and as such will agree to anything to be free."

"And are you?" asked Yarlung mentally so that she could feel his reaction.

"No," answered Rakan calmly. Not anymore.

"Then you may tell him to proceed."

Rakan bowed, pleased that the discussion had gone easily.

"What do you think of Jing Mei?" asked Yarlung.

"I don't think she's Paaliaq," he said, bracing himself for her reaction.

"I see," said Yarlung. "And what does T'eng Sten think?"

"I don't know," Rakan said, surprised by her lack of reaction. "We haven't spoken of it." He wished they had.

Yarlung considered him for a moment, her mind-touch gauging his emotions. "Well, if she isn't Paaliaq then we shouldn't kill her. I'll take her rök. And her parents will answer for their transgression."

Rakan nodded. "I'll find out."

"However, if she is Paaliaq — are you ready to kill her? I fear I am too old."

Rakan's rök began to spin wildly. He forced it back into submission. June wasn't Paaliaq. He wasn't even sure she was a full-blooded dragon anymore. "Yes," he answered slowly.

Yarlung smiled. "Good. Then you can bind your answer to me in a blood pact."

Moments later, Yuli appeared. Her bright green dress a stark contrast to the turquoise tinted white of Yarlung's inner chamber. She knelt in front of Yarlung and held up a bowl made of kor, the sacred black metal of the Red Planet. A ceremonial knife flashed in Yarlung's hand. She slashed her palm and let the blood run into the bowl. Yuli wouldn't meet his eyes.

Silently, Yarlung turned the knife and offered it to Rakan, handle first.

Rakan stood still, his mother's attention focused on him like a honing missile. Finally, he took the knife. He balanced it in his hands, wondering what his mother would do if he said no. He studied her blank face. She had backed him into a corner and she knew it. He was tired of being manipulated. "Why isn't my word enough?"

"I thought you were sure she wasn't Paaliaq?"

"She isn't."

"Then you risk nothing."

Rakan stared into his mother's unseeing eyes, hating her for forcing him to make the pact. He slashed his hand savagely and let the blood flow into the bowl. The oozing mass coagulated and bubbled. The room filled with the smell of warm iron as the bowl frothed. The sizzling stopped and a small orange water dragon swam through the lingering vapor. Rakan tried not to convulse when he saw it. He knew the physical manifestation of a blood pact was always the color of the one swearing and the shape of the one asking. But he didn't want to see it.

Yarlung held out her hand and the miniature dragon settled on her palm. "You may go. I will place this in safe keeping until it dissolves upon fulfillment of the pact."

Or dies with me if I refuse to honor it, growled Rakan to himself as he stormed out of the inner chamber.

It wasn't until Rakan was already over the clay forests of his childhood that he realized where he was headed. He folded his wings and plummeted. He skimmed the nearly empty river bed and landed, morphing into his human shape at the same time. The teetering columns towered above him. He stood and listened to the wind, the constant companion of his youth. But instead of comforting him as it had before, it made him feel lonelier.

He shook his fists at the sky in rage, as if it could answer him. As if it could explain why his life was so complicated. Rakan watched the clouds follow their course, insensible to anything other than their own movement. Why couldn't he be like that? The mountains began to glow orange and purple in the late afternoon sun. He tilted his head. The warmth sank into him.

"You're hard to find," said Angalaan, shifting ten feet in front of him. She observed the clay forest and the mountains behind them. "They feel like you. You must have spent a lot of time here." She walked slowly in his direction.

Her indigo cape fluttered in the wind and caught his attention. He had rarely seen a dragon wear anything but their own color. And indigo was Kairök T'eng Sten's. Jealousy raced through his veins. Her loyalty to him went beyond the fact that he carried her rök. Would he ever know that feeling?

"You do know that you've been the center of every conversation, don't you?" she asked.

Rakan's attention snapped back up to Angalaan's fuchsia eyes. "No."

Angalaan smiled. "You've begun to fill out." She reached out to touch Rakan's chest with both hands, never dropping her eyes from his. "Everyone wonders who you chased."

He drew in his breath, her touch was warm. And kind. It had a gentleness to it that made his body want more. His rök began to throb, to thicken in a new way. He wanted to feel her softness, to explore the warmth of her body, to feel their necks twine around each other as they flew in the sky. "No," he said, putting his hands on hers. He squeezed her hands and held them to his chest. His body wanted her. And she wanted him. But he didn't love her. He dropped her hands and turned away. He should have realized that he loved Anna sooner.

"Are you concerned about T'eng Sten?" Angalaan asked quietly, coming behind him and placing her hands on his waist. The smell of cinnamon wrapped around him.

Rakan shook his head. His rök was pulling at him to morph. To chase Angalaan into the air and watch her fly away until he couldn't see her anymore. And then he'd chase her until he caught her and they… He clenched his fists. He wouldn't morph. He'd lose control.

"It's okay," said Angalaan, connecting mentally with him through their physical contact. "Maybe you aren't ready for your first mating flight, even if you appear to be."

He could feel the desire that pulsed through her body and the fact that she wasn't acting on it made him want her even more. Had she launched into the air, he wasn't sure that he wouldn't have an uncontrolled morph. No matter how hard he tried not to.

She released him. "I hope you'll come find me when you are."

Rakan turned and held her gaze, too confused to say anything. He had liked feeling connected to her. And a part of him wanted to feel it again.

"T'eng Sten wants to speak with you," she said, breaking the eye contact.

"Of course," he said. In his anger about the blood pact he had forgotten that T'eng Sten had requested to know the outcome of his discussion with his mother.

"Until we meet again," she said with a smile, her fuchsia eyes full of promise. Angalaan shifted back to Yarlung's and Rakan watched the spot where she had been. His rök spinning furiously.

T'eng Sten didn't appear right away, for which Rakan was thankful. By the time the Kairök shifted next to Rakan, he had calmed down and brought his rök back under control. "Greetings, Kairök," he said. "I should have come to you sooner." He bowed his head.

"Don't worry. I remember what it feels like." The Kairök glanced at Pemba's chest. "You've begun to fill out early, even by Earth cycles. Or maybe it was your frantic chase of Kariaksuq that triggered it."

"What?"

"A mating flight can sometimes be triggered," said T'eng Sten, looking amused. "Or didn't you know that? That was one of the reasons why all young dragons became kais by the time they were six cycles. It helped keep things in order."

Rakan's face burned. His filling out and his awakening desires were due to his unwanted reaction to Kariaksuq while he was chasing her? His nails dug into his palms. He'd track her down and kill her.

"Easy," said T'eng Sten, putting a hand on his shoulder. "You'd be better off flying Angalaan than killing Kariaksuq. And it would have the same effect."

"No," Rakan said vehemently.

"You've grown up too isolated, Rakan. Desires are natural. To love and to kill."

Rakan shook his head. He couldn't just fly her blindly. It wasn't right.

"As you wish," said T'eng Sten. "But it might help you to come into your full power. You keep your rök on too tight a leash. It's not good for you." He paused, a faint frown playing on his face. "If you make love with Anna now you could kill her by going wild. You know that, don't you? Humans are fragile. You'd be better prepared if you flew Angalaan first."

"Yarlung said you could remove the tattoos," Rakan answered.

T'eng Sten turned away. "I thought she would. She thinks you're betraying me?"

"Yes. She didn't seem to question it."

T'eng Sten examined Rakan. "She didn't bind you in another way?"

Rakan shook his head, too ashamed to mention how his mother had manipulated him into accepting the blood pact. He knew he shouldn't have accepted it even if he knew June wasn't Paaliaq. But he hadn't been able to find a way out.

T'eng Sten placed his hands on Rakan's shoulders. *"Ready? It won't take long."*

Rakan nodded, and the Kairök's mind-touch sank into him. His bones felt like they were being scrapped from the inside by thousands of miniature claws. Rakan would've punched the Kairök if he could have reacted, but the poison had tetanized his muscles. Rakan panicked. What if it was already too late?

"It'd be easier if you relaxed," said T'eng Sten. His voice was firm and Rakan clung to it. *"And it'll be easier for me."*

Rakan groaned as T'eng Sten dug in deeper.

Much later, once the sun had set and the chill of the evening began to settle around them, T'eng Sten finally pulled out of Rakan. "Yarlung's poison was much deeper than Khotan's." T'eng Sten sank to the ground. "I don't think she meant for it to be removed."

Rakan dropped next to him. "Thank you, Kairök." He felt like he had been flayed alive. He lay back and sank into the earth, letting its cold gelatinous mass surround him.

Anna sat in the window of Helmersen's cafe, watching the cars go by on the slick black street that made the slushy snow on the sidewalks look even uglier. The low lying clouds pressed in on her and she felt trapped. She glanced again at the envelope that Ulf had thrown at her two days ago, still unsure of what to do. It didn't smell like Pemba. Instead it had the heady, pungent aroma of musk. But it was sealed with a flying dragon stamped in orange wax. It looked just like the drawing Pemba had made for her.

A thick wet snow began to fall, leaving huge blobs on the window. Anna sighed. The letter couldn't have been handed to Ulf by Dawa – she hadn't even been to school in three weeks. And Pemba would never have asked Dawa to give it to Ulf anyway. She turned the envelope over, fingering the seal. The wax was the color of Pemba's Maii-a. It was Pemba. Anna peered closer, wishing she could zoom in to see the details. Wishing she hadn't run away on the mountain, assuming the worst. But she had been too angry, and then too scared to even consider slowing down.

The letter had to be from Kariaksuq. Of that she was sure. But she didn't know if opening it would have an effect on her or not. Or would Pemba's shield still protect her? Carefully, she began to pry the dragon off, making sure not to break it in case it was the thing that would trigger a reaction from Kariaksuq. She waited, but felt nothing. No shocks, no sparks. Thunder rumbled in the distance and Anna dropped the letter, looking up at the intense green-blue light of nightfall. She was being stupid. The seal wouldn't set off a thunderstorm. She calmed her nerves and picked up the letter. She slid the paper out of the envelope and opened it with trembling hands.

My dearest Anna,

I know you no longer wish to see me, but I must warn you about Kariaksuq. You can't trust her. We are at home where we are safe. No matter what happens, do not allow anyone to remove the shield I made for you or your life will be in danger. Destroy this as soon as you can or she will recognize it and attack you.

I miss your tender lips,

Pemba

PS: If you are getting this it is because Ulf can be trusted

Anna snorted. The letter was obviously a fake. Even if he was in Tromso, he would never have written Dearest Anna or that he missed her tender lips even if… even if he had kissed her. Anna looked back at the letter. The part of her that had hoped it was from Pemba was more disappointed than she wanted to acknowledge.

Anna put the envelope back in her bag and walked out into the slush, wondering what she should do with it as she walked home up the hill. Destroying it would probably alert Kariaksuq as to her whereabouts. Anna pulled up her collar. No. Kariaksuq obviously knew where she lived and how to find her. Maybe Kariaksuq had known that she wouldn't think it was Pemba, and what she really wanted was for Anna to keep it.

Anna stopped.

Dawa was home. She'd know.

Chapter 23

Confrontations

THE MOONLIGHT REFLECTED OFF T'ENG STEN'S OVERCOAT, AND RAKAN REAL-ized for the first time that each of the dragons embroidered into it was one of his kais. "You need to morph," said T'eng Sten, stretching out a hand. "And so do I."

Rakan groaned as he was pulled to his feet, but the Kairök was right. The moon was mid-sky. They had lain there for at least four hours. And he still didn't feel any better.

"*Ready?*" asked T'eng Sten. He put a hand on Rakan's shoulder, steady-ing him.

Rakan nodded and T'eng Sten morphed, his energy unfurling around them like an enormous gong. Rakan stumbled back, looking at the colos-sal indigo dragon who glittered like a jewel in the thin night air. T'eng Sten stretched his wings and sat back on his haunches, baring his vulner-able underbelly. It sparkled with the multicolored scales of his kais. The Kairök's power rippled out over the clay forest and Rakan bowed his head. The Kairök was magnificent.

Rakan's blood throbbed and thickened and then flickered. He didn't want to fly; he wanted to feel water flow through him. Like a water dragon. He yelled in indignation and burst into his air dragon form, standing on his haunches, his wings outstretched, fire billowing from his throat. Ready to fight.

T'eng Sten slammed him to the ground and bit his throat. "*Easy, Rakan. Relax.*"

A warm wave of healing surrounded Rakan and he went limp. Why did he crave an element that wasn't his? His mother was gone from his system, wasn't she? Another wave of anger ripped through him.

"*Fly with me. Now.*" It was a command and Rakan latched onto it, des-perate to bring his rök back under control. Rakan trailed the Kairök like a puppy on a training flight. T'eng Sten arched and turned, moving with the air currents, and Rakan followed blindly. And then the Kairök began setting Rakan up for unexpected turns that knocked him off the current until Rakan was flying next to T'eng Sten. They followed the currents together, trying to second guess the other's move in a flowing dance of equals.

T'eng Sten folded his wings and plummeted, stopping himself and morphing just as he was about to hit the ground. Rakan alighted in front of him but didn't morph. He wasn't ready to go back to his human form just yet. He put his head down on the ground between his two front legs, in a gesture of thanks.

T'eng Sten smiled and put his hands on Rakan's triangular head that was as big as he was, rubbing his palms lightly across the thin scales around his eyes. *"Be safe, Firebird,"* he said and shifted, leaving Rakan alone in the night.

Rakan eased himself into the ground, creating a smooth depression to curl up in. He knew that he should make a shield but wasn't sure if he had the energy. He reached his mind out and felt a shield. Rakan lifted his head. The Kairök had realized that he wouldn't be coming back to Yarlung's tonight and had shielded him. *"Thank you,"* he said, even though no one could hear him.

Rakan settled back down and examined their grey trails. They were geometric ghosts of what they looked like in the daylight. He liked analyzing their patterns without the distraction of color. But where there should have been the single strand of his rök, there was a twisted double strand. Rakan scrambled out of his nest and turned to stare at his trail, his nostrils quivering. It couldn't be. It wasn't possible. His claws sank into the ground. The Kairök's trail was normal. But his wasn't.

Anna scurried down the street. She was almost at the Tibet House. She reached out mentally to make sure Dawa was still there. She heaved a sigh of relief. She was. Anna shook her head. Had anyone told her she'd be running to see Dawa at 9 o'clock on a Saturday night, she would never have believed them.

She ran up the steps, two by two. And stopped. All the lights were out. The nun must be asleep. She searched to see if there were two doorbells, but there weren't. Anna groaned. She couldn't just wake up the nun.

Cursing to herself and wishing she had Dawa's phone number, she walked down the steps and looked up to the second floor. The lights were on. Dawa was awake. Anna glanced around for something to throw at the window, but there was nothing. Except some very wet snow. She cupped a handful and aimed for a window, but it disintegrated before getting that far. She pressed more snow together, making it as compact as possible. She aimed and threw it at the window. "Yes," she said as it hit with a satisfying splat. And then she waited. Nothing happened. No one came. She grabbed another fistful of snow and tried again. A couple walked down the street, leaning happily into each other. Anna held her next snowball in her now freezing hands, waiting for them to pass.

The front door cracked open and the nun poked her head out. Anna hurried back up the stairs. "Good evening," she said breathlessly. "I'm sorry to disturb you, but I was wondering if I could see Dawa?"

Ani-la smiled and said something in Tibetan and Anna thought she heard Pemba-la and Dawa-la, but wasn't sure about anything else. Anna pointed to her chest and pointed upstairs, "Can I go upstairs?"

The nun shook her head and made a sleeping gesture.

"Dawa. Can you go get Dawa?" asked Anna. She pointed at the nun and tried to show her going upstairs to get Dawa with her hands.

The nun answered, but Anna understood nothing. "Please?" Anna said, putting her hands together like a prayer.

The nun responded with the same gesture and shut the door. Anna leaned her forehead against the cold wood. Had the nun understood? Or had she just said goodnight? She waited without moving. Counting the interminable seconds and walking her mind down the hallway, up the stairs, waiting for Dawa to open her door, telling her to come downstairs... and still she heard no noise from inside the house.

Her fingers ached from the slush. Why hadn't Dawa heard her? Her head began to swim as an unexpected wave of nausea ran through her. Anna groaned and tried to will herself through the door. But it stood stiff and unyielding. It had been too long. No one was coming. Anna sank to her knees, one hand on her stomach and the other on the door. She wasn't going to make it home. She reached for the doorbell, but it was beyond her grasp. Her eyes welled in frustration. "Please," she croaked. "Please."

The door opened and Ani-la began speaking rapidly, but Anna barely heard her.

"Dawa?" Anna asked, looking around desperately.

Ani-la shook her head and tried to explain something again, gesturing at Anna and gesturing upstairs. Ani-la helped Anna to her feet and led her inside. Anna stumbled down the hallway, barely even aware that Ani-la had led her to the same room as she had been in with Pemba. "Dawa?" she asked again, hanging on to the nun. "Dawa?"

The nun answered and then left the room backwards, bowing as she went. Anna leaned back. Dawa. She needed to see Dawa.

She heard the nun and Dawa arguing and wished she could crawl up the stairs. She tried to stand but fell to her knees. "Dawa," she said. Her legs were like squids. She lay on the floor, tears flowing in frustration. Get a grip. She hoisted herself onto her elbows and began pulling herself forward. One inch at a time.

The nun came in and exclaimed frantically, calling out to Dawa. She tried to get Anna to her feet but couldn't. "Dawa-la," she yelled.

And then Dawa was there, helping her to her feet, getting her back onto the ottoman. The nun suddenly reappeared with a large thermos of tea, talking all the while to Dawa. She offered Anna a cup which Dawa took for her. The nun nodded and backed out of the room, her hands in prayer.

"Anna," said Dawa. "Can you hear me? I'm going to shift you upstairs, don't—"

Anna clung to Dawa, but her fingers closed around nothingness and she fell forward. And onto a bed. "Ughh," she groaned. Everything was spinning around her. She was hallucinating. A hand slapped her cheek and she snapped to attention. "Kariaksuq?"

"Good, you're not totally out of it. Always hard to know how much poison a human needs. But I want you to be awake. For *all* of it." Kariaksuq waved a hand over her and Anna felt cold.

"What?" Anna looked down. She was dressed in a short pink negligee. And nothing else. "Where are my clothes? Where are we?" Her words slurred.

"In Ulf's apartment. And you're my little going away present to him. He'll enjoy you so much." Kariaksuq yanked Anna's arms up over her head and lashed them to the bed.

"No," Anna gasped, squirming blindly.

"Enough," said Kariaksuq, slapping her so hard that her breath snagged. "Tell your little boyfriend about it. And tell him it's my payback."

Suddenly, Dawa was in the room, flying at Kariaksuq like a wild panther in full motion. Kariaksuq slammed into the large wooden dresser, scattering things everywhere. Kariaksuq howled and lunged. Dawa flipped her onto her back and straddled her. Anna could hear the sickening thump of fists meeting flesh as Dawa pummeled Kariaksuq. Anna pulled at her bindings, trying to undo the ropes that held her hands. But all she managed to do was to tighten them further. The cord bit into her wrists and her fingers went numb.

The room exploded in fireworks. They were gone. Anna's head swam. She no longer knew if she was standing or lying down. She tried to hang onto something, anything, but it slipped out of her grasp.

Everything slipped out of her grasp.

"Dvara," yelled Rakan into the dark of the now moonless night. He shifted to where he had felt her, in Ulf's apartment, dropping to his knees in exhaustion at the same time as T'eng Sten arrived with both knives drawn.

"Where's Dvara?" hissed T'eng Sten. He scanned the bedroom, sniffing the air. "Kariaksuq."

"Ulf?" Rakan struggled to stand when he saw Ulf bending over Anna. "Get away from her!" He sent Ulf flying across the room and into the walk-in closet behind the bed.

"Anna, what happened?" But she was unconscious.

"What was that for?" asked Ulf. He wobbled to his feet, holding a hand to his face. "I was just trying to help her. How did you get in here anyhow?"

"What did you give her?" yelled Rakan. He punched Ulf in the gut, sending him back into the closet.

"Enough," said T'eng Sten. He froze Ulf and grabbed Rakan. "You're a trailer. Tell me which one is real."

Rakan turned to the writhing mass of trails that covered the room. It was simplistic compared to how the Old Dragon in Tromso worked. He cleared his mind and looked for the trails with the mark of the rök. "There." He pointed to where Dvara had been pummeling Kariaksuq. "She was about to kill Kariaksuq when a dozen others came and shifted them to…" he saw a mountain, not far away. He put a hand on T'eng Sten. *"There."*

T'eng Sten disappeared, but even the fraction of a second that Rakan had touched him was enough to feel the pulsing anger of the Kairök's Cairn as they shifted with him. Ready to kill. Rakan jerked his hand back, even though T'eng Sten was already gone. He turned to the bed. Anna was lying on her back. Unconscious, but alive. Her hands were blue from the cords that were still wrapped around her wrists. Rakan dissolved the bindings and cursed. They were made from dragon gut. He'd have a hard time healing them completely. He put a hand on her head and touched his forehead to her cheek. He felt the poison inside her. Dragon poison. He tightened his grip.

"June!" he yelled. He reached out to find her, but she immediately blocked him. He cursed. She was downtown with Erling. Rakan stood, unwilling to leave Anna alone, but also sure that if he didn't get help quickly it would be too late.

Before he could decide, Red slammed into him and knocked him to the ground. "What have you done to her?" Red pulled Rakan back up, ready to punch him again.

"Nothing." Rakan blocked his aggressor. "I'm trying to help her." Rakan gripped Red's shoulders. "You just shifted in here," he said, feeling a rush of hope. He didn't care who or what Red was if he could help Anna. "Can you neutralize dragon poison?"

Red let go of Rakan and dropped to his knees near the bed. He put a hand on Anna's barely breathing form. "I feel a female and your sister," growled Red. "I'll save her first. And then I'll kill you."

Rakan sat next to Anna, his hand on her side. Red leaned his head on Anna's. His disheveled hair was exactly the same color as hers. Just like his pale-blue eyes. Even his smell was similar. And yet he had shifted. He had to be a dragon. Or could humans learn? He scanned Red while he worked.

Everything he was wearing, which was only a pair of jeans and white tee-shirt, was human made. He had no shoes, no weapons, no Maii-a. Rakan let his mind slip into Anna, and felt Red, gently but surely neutralizing and dissolving the orange coral poison. His poison. Rakan jerked up with a start.

"You lied," snarled Red. He turned and yanked Rakan off the bed.

"I didn't," hissed Rakan, blocking Red's hook to his temple.

"It's your poison."

"I saw that. But I didn't poison her."

"Stop it," wailed Anna. "I can't stand anymore fighting."

They turned to her in unison.

"Anna," Rakan said. He knelt in front of her and took her hand. "Are you alright?"

"Who did this to you?" asked Red. "No, don't try to sit up. You're not ready yet."

"I'm cold," she said, sinking back down.

Rakan pulled up a blanket, only then realizing that Anna was dressed in a flimsy pink cloth that barely covered the top of her thighs. He hissed. "Yttresken."

"What?" Anna said.

Red shrugged. "The clothing is from the female who brought her here." He glared at Rakan. "But the poison was yours."

"What poison?" mumbled Anna.

Rakan examined the caked blood on Anna's wrists. He ran a finger over them, healing the wound. But he couldn't take away the pain that pulsed under the surface. Or diminish the ugly pink welts. "What happened?" he asked. "How did you get here?"

Anna trembled, but whether in cold or fear, Rakan didn't know. "I went to see Dawa," she said, trying to remember what had happened. "I needed to show her... a letter. And then... I don't know. I couldn't move. Dawa was there. And then we were here. With Kariaksuq." Anna tried to look around. "Where are they? They were fighting."

"I don't know. But Dawa's still alive," Rakan said. "I feel her."

"What letter?" asked Red, interrupting Rakan.

"The one that Ulf gave me," Anna said. "It's still in my bag."

"Ulf?" growled Rakan. He looked behind Anna. "I'll make him pay."

"At the Tibetan House?" asked Red, ignoring Rakan's outburst. "Upstairs? Or downstairs?"

"Downstairs, I think."

Red nodded. "I'll get it." He stood to leave. "Don't you dare run off," he said to Rakan. "She can't be left alone yet. I'll deal with you when I get back."

"I wouldn't leave her now anyway."

"Good," said Red and disappeared.

Rakan leaned over Anna and wrapped his mind around her. "I'm sorry," he whispered. "This is all my fault."

"You didn't do anything," she said, her gentle mind-touch awakening to his.

"Yes, I did." He stroked her hands with his fingers. "Kariaksuq would never have bothered you if I hadn't wanted to get close to you."

"Your eyes are beautiful."

"Anna, listen to me. Please."

Anna smiled and touched his cheek. "Thank you."

"For what? Nearly getting you killed?"

"For coming. I thought you didn't care."

"I shouldn't have cared." Rakan stood up and walked over to the broken dresser. "We're trained to kill, Anna. To track and kill." He turned to look at her. "I was supposed to get close to you because you were close to June."

Anna didn't say anything, but the pain that filled the room stabbed through him more than anything she could have said. "No," he said, trembling as he tried to keep his rök in control. Her eyes reminded him of a rabbit backed into a corner. His rök lurched and the words came tumbling out. "That's why I never kissed you. I couldn't do it. You deserve someone better than me." His voice caught in his throat. "I love you too much to treat you that way. You don't even know how badly I've wanted to. But I never did." He clutched the pillow on either side of her head. He wouldn't smash through the apartment and fly off in a suicidal frenzy.

Anna touched his face, her fingers soothing his feral rage.

"No," he groaned. Her touch recalled Angalaan's. "Don't, Anna. Please. I'm not good for you." He sat back up and turned his head away from her.

Anna curled around him, her head on his thigh. She explored the gentle undulations of his chest. His skin was smooth and soft. And warm. He turned and looked at her, his orange eyes flecked with copper. "No," he said. He wrapped a hand around hers and held it to his pounding chest.

Anna moved enough to touch his lower back with her other hand, exploring the ridges on either side of his spine. Her hand brushed his braid. It was soft and supple, just as she had always imagined. The tip was undone. "You never wear it down," she said, gently undoing more of it and letting it run through her fingers. "You should." His hair was so long that it lay across her thigh.

Rakan leaned into her, his hand relaxing its hold on hers. She resumed her exploration of his chest and this time he didn't stop her. She rubbed her face against his leg, breathing in his smell of incense and wishing she could wrap herself in it. She was consumed by a sudden urge to bite him. She hesitated and then sank her teeth into his thigh. Rakan groaned and wrapped his fingers in her hair. "Anna, no," he said. His breath caressed her face.

Anna closed her eyes. Her mind-touch slipped forward and embraced him. His body was alive with desire and it made hers tremble in response. She gripped his arms. They were bigger than she had remembered. "You've been working out," she mumbled into his hair.

He pulled back. "No." He groaned without looking at her.

Anna outlined his face with her eyes, lingering on his full lips that beckoned her closer. She had waited too long for him to kiss her. She wasn't waiting anymore. She hoisted herself onto her elbow and then pushed up into a sitting position, her chest rubbing against his as she did so. He breathed in sharply and Anna closed her eyes. The only thing separating them was the flimsy bit of pink silk that she was wearing and the contact made her body tingle then rush with fire. She edged her way higher, pushing him back onto the bed, one arm on either side of his head as she lay half on top of him, her legs curled to the side.

Her heart raced against his as she leaned forward, her hair flowing around her face. His eyes were the same color as his Maii-a. She dropped her eyes to the perfect curves of his lips. Her lips parted in anticipation and she brushed them gently against his. His hands buried themselves in her hair. "Why did you do that?" he asked, his voice husky.

"Because you told me the truth." Her lips rubbed against his as she spoke.

"But didn't you understand what I was telling you?"

"Yes." She pushed up enough to look him in the eyes. "You said you love me."

Rakan spread her hair out with his hands and watched it slide through his fingers. "What have I gotten you into?"

"Nothing." Anna smiled. "I kissed you, remember?"

"Maybe," he said. "But I let you."

She pressed her lips against his, but more firmly this time. His lips parted and he responded, sending a jolt of energy through her center as his tongue wrapped around hers in smooth, gentle strokes. An inarticulate groan escaped from her. She arched her neck as his mouth followed the length of her jawbone. His teeth rubbed against the soft skin of her neck. "Bite me, please," she groaned.

"Anna," he said, swallowing hard. "We can't. I'm a dragon. I—"

"I don't care what you are," she mumbled, her lips finding his.

Red cleared his throat. "I see I haven't been missed."

Anna and Rakan pulled apart. Anna wrapped herself in the comforter, avoiding Red's eyes.

"I had a hard time getting your clothes," continued Red. He ignored their embarrassment and handed Anna her neatly folded things. "If you want to get changed."

"Uh, yeah. Thanks." Anna stifled a scream when she turned and saw Ulf half buried in the walk-in closet that was hidden by a wall behind the bed. "What happened to him?"

"He's frozen," Rakan said, flicking his re-braided hair back over his shoulder. "And that might be a problem." If T'eng Sten didn't come back.

"I can release him," said Red casually.

Rakan's attention snapped to Anna's cousin. *How?* Only the one who had frozen someone could undo it.

"Not until I get changed." Anna scrambled to her feet and then paused. "Can he hear us?"

Red approached Ulf and touched him. "Yes. And see. It's just a simple freeze, the least invasive physically. Although it can be traumatic mentally and emotionally." He turned back to Anna. "I'll decide what he can remember later."

Anna tugged the comforter closer around her and waddled out of the room, her cheeks nearly the same color as the pink negligee she was wearing. Rakan's eyes followed her out, his lips still feeling hers. He inhaled deeply, savoring the lingering smell of chrysanthemums that had begun to have the sweet smell of ripeness to them. He closed his eyes, losing himself again in the full firmness of her lips, the flowing magic of her hair. He hadn't gone wild. He hadn't lost control. He stood to follow her, to wrap his arms around her, to run his hands through her hair, to feel her lithe muscular body...

"You have a strange way of showing your interest in her," said Red, waving an envelope in front of Rakan's face.

Rakan growled and grabbed it. "What's that supposed to mean?" He had forgotten about Red.

"Look for yourself."

Rakan saw the orange seal and froze. It was impossible. But there it was. The seal was made out of his poison, solidified and turned into a miniature version of himself. But it smelled like Kariaksuq. "How did she get it?"

"You tell me."

Rakan touched the poison. It had been neutralized, probably by Red when he found it. "It's been mixed with Yttresken's." He sank to the bed. "That's why my shield didn't react. Anna was too sick to know what was going on."

Red's face softened. "When did you bite Kariaksuq?"

Rakan looked at Red in surprise. "Before I left. But I thought no one knew how to extract dragon poison." And yet everyone seemed to know. Except for him.

Red burst into laughter. "That's only so that puppies don't bite each other and try to extract it themselves before reaching a certain level of expertise. Otherwise it can cause permanent damage."

Rakan restrained the urge to crush the envelope. What had happened to Anna was his fault then. He should never have let Kariaksuq get away.

Red examined Rakan slowly, his eyes lingering on the increased bulk of his torso. "Were you trying to mate with her?" Red paused and asked quietly, "Were you wild?"

"No," hissed Rakan. He jumped to face Red, his fists clenched at the insult.

"What are you guys arguing about?" asked Anna, coming back dressed in her own clothes. She looked from one to the other as she pulled her hair into a ponytail. She avoided looking at Ulf. The sight of him frozen in mid-motion was freaky.

"I was trying to find out if Pemba had chased a female with intent to mate or not," said Red without taking his eyes from Pemba. "One I can forgive, the other not."

"Why do you think he did?" Anna felt a rush of doubt.

"Because the only way a shapeshifter can be stimulated into developing his mature mass is by responding to a female's challenge. And Pemba is filling out. Proof that he chased a female recently."

"Oh." Anna looked once again at Pemba's increased bulk.

"I chased Kariaksuq. We were fighting," Pemba said defensively.

Red growled and moved closer. "So who else did you chase?"

"No one."

"Then you weren't just fighting with Kariaksuq. And if it wasn't because you went wild and lost control, you were intentionally cheating on Anna."

The two men squared off, their faces only inches away from each other.

"No fighting." Anna pushed them apart. She glared at Red. "Don't even think about it. Is that clear?" She wouldn't let him kill Pemba. "And you," Anna said, turning to Pemba with a tremor in her voice. "Show me what happened."

"Maybe you should show me instead," said Red.

Pemba ignored him and pulled Anna into his chest. "It was a confusing fight. You may not understand it all," he said into her ear. "Because I don't."

Anna nodded and opened herself to the rush of feelings and emotions that she knew would flood her mind. But she still wasn't prepared for the intensity of Pemba's memory. She felt his anger, his frustration as he waited at the bar feeling Kariaksuq up in the apartment, this apartment, with Ulf. She also felt his loathing of the people in the bar and wondered if he hated all non-shapeshifting humans that much. She felt the crisp air, the tension as Kariaksuq walked down the stairs. And appeared dressed… to seduce. Anna clutched Pemba as the memory picked up speed, she was chasing Kariaksuq with him, hating her and yet strangely excited at the same time. Anna felt her body throb and thicken as if her blood had turned to lead and then she was a dragon, clawing at the glacier where Kariaksuq had disappeared. Suddenly the glacier enveloped her and she was swimming through it to kill Kariaksuq. She bit Kariaksuq's tail and felt the satisfaction of her teeth sinking into it as poison ejaculated from her canines with a bitterness that was almost sweet. And then it stopped.

Anna clung to Pemba, needing to feel him. She searched for his mouth, wanting to rekindle the closeness that he had just interrupted. Wanting to feel his power rush through her, herself both filled with hatred for Kariaksuq and a wild desire to possess Pemba. His desire echoed hers and he crushed her in his arms.

"Eh, oh," said Red, whacking them on the shoulder. "Can we move on?"

Anna rubbed her face in Pemba's neck. "Go away, Red."

"We need to decide what to do with Ulf."

Anna sized up her cousin. "And you need to promise me something."

Red shot her a questioning look and then his face went hard. "No."

"Yes." Anna pushed Pemba behind her. "You won't touch Pemba. Or erase his mind."

Red growled. "You have no idea what you're asking of me."

Pemba disentangled himself from Anna and walked over to face Red. "I don't know who or what you are, but I don't care. You saved Anna's life." Pemba hit his chest and raised a palm. "Your secret is mine."

Red stared at him, trying to judge his character. "Remember that," he said. "Or I'll regret letting Anna sway my resolve." Red gripped Pemba's arm. "I promised her father I would protect her," he said. "You're barely more than a puppy yourself and you have no idea what you're doing by awakening her." Red's grip tightened, pressing into Pemba's bone. "If you go wild on her, I'll skin you alive."

"Then why don't you offer to help me instead?"

Red dropped Pemba's arm but not his eyes.

Anna felt a horrendous ripping through the very fiber of her being. And then another. And another. She gripped Pemba, but the feeling was even worse feeling it with him. Each rip took part of her soul with it, leaving a gaping hole in its place. Anna cried out in pain. Pemba held her tightly, his fingers digging into her. Red dropped to his knees, his face twisted in anguish, shaking his head and muttering, "No, no. Let them go..."

And then it stopped.

Anna collapsed in Pemba's arms, crying uncontrollably. The world was emptier. Something was gone. Gone forever.

"Fourteen," said Red, standing up after the ripping had stopped. "Fourteen more dragons lost forever."

Anna shook in Pemba's arms, clinging to him, needing his warmth, his vibrancy. It had hurt too much to feel them die.

"Take her home," said Red. "I'll take care of this."

Chapter 24

Revelations

THE NEXT MORNING ANNA STUMBLED DOWN THE STAIRS. HER HEAD HURT from having cried herself to sleep and her eyes felt like huge puffballs. Pemba had disappeared right after seeing her home. He had gone to find Dawa. Hushed voices came from the kitchen and she slowed down. Ulf was speaking with her mom. She had forgotten about him. She turned to go back up the stairs, but her mom came out.

"Anna, wait," Ingrid said. She ran up the stairs and hugged Anna. "Ulf told me all about last night…" Ingrid trembled as she took one of Anna's hands and traced the pink welt with an icy finger. She looked at Anna and then turned to the kitchen. "Ulf? These are welts, not cuts. Oh, thank goodness." She started laughing and pulled Anna down the stairs. "You'll never believe what Ulf said. He was convinced you tried to commit suicide last night at some party because Pemba wasn't there. Isn't that just the silliest thing you've ever heard?"

Anna pulled her hand away. Had Red not been able to erase Ulf's memory and the events had come out scrambled in a weird way? "I'm fine, Mom. Really."

Ingrid hugged her. "I know you are, honey. Ulf's just not used to being in a parenting role." Ingrid went over to the counter and fussed over the coffee. "I can't believe you could mistake a few little scrapes for an open wound," Ingrid said to Ulf. "It's a good thing I'm a nurse. You had me completely panicked for a moment."

Ingrid came over and put a tray with three cups of coffee on the table. "There's nothing wrong with her, see? Right, honey?"

"Sure," said Anna. "Everything's fine." Other than being poisoned and shapeshifters killing each other. Anna choked back a sob.

Ulf stood up. "She's not alright, Ingrid. Look at her."

Ingrid shook her head. "She's fine. It's just hard to be separated from your boyfriend when you're so young. Or have you forgotten already?"

"But…" Ulf sank to his chair, his head in his hands. "I don't understand."

Ingrid patted Anna's hand. "Don't worry. I do." She turned to Ulf and caressed his hair. "You're so sweet, darling. It's touching how much you care. But really, it's nothing. It's just part of growing up."

Anna looked out the window, this was just what she needed. A clueless mom and a hovering Ulf. "I'm late for school."

"You can stay at home, if you want," Ulf said. "Right, Ingrid? You're not working. You could spend the day together…"

"Ulf, it's okay. I'm fine." There was no way she was spending the day with her mom. "Thanks for the coffee," she said and walked out of the room.

"See?" Ingrid said to Ulf. "She'd rather go to school. She's not depressed. Just love-sick."

"But, Ingrid. I'm sure of what I saw."

A coffee cup slammed on the table. Anna paused on the stairs. "That's enough," said Ingrid, her voice hard as rock. "She's my daughter and I know what's going on. She doesn't need to tell me for me to know she's okay."

"But she's a teenager. And no normal teenager will ever tell their mom how they are feeling. Especially if it's about a boy."

"Ulf, it's okay. She's not a normal teenager. Leave her alone. She doesn't need your help any more than she needs mine."

Anna gaped. Not normal? Why wasn't she normal?

"But you can't just let her—"

"Stop right now, Ulf." Her mom's voice was unlike anything she had ever heard. Cold and calm. And on the brink of imploding. "If you can't accept her as she is, you can leave."

"No, Ingrid, please. I just want to help. You're the only thing that is stable in my life."

Ingrid burst into tears. "Then help me," came the choked reply. "I feel so alone all the time. If only her father would come back…"

Anna heard movement and then muffled voices. Ulf must be comforting her mom. She gripped the rail and walked slowly upstairs. Her mom was hiding something. And so was Red.

ᛊᚲᛊ

Rakan watched over Dvara as she tossed and turned in her bed. The firelight flickered against the stone walls, giving the nook an incongruously cheery feel. Nineteen dragons had died. Fourteen of them in excruciating pain since Yttresken had refused to let go of their röks. The only reason more hadn't died was because T'eng Sten had managed to rip Yttresken's rök out of his chest before killing him. Otherwise all of Yttresken's kais would have died with him. Rakan shook with anger, wishing he had been the one to rip out Yttresken's rök.

Dvara moaned and Rakan moved to her side. "Dvara? Can you hear me?"

"Where's T'eng Sten?"

"He's alive."

"I know that." She opened her eyes. "Where is he?"

Rakan felt her try to reach out. "Don't," he said. "You won't find him. He's in the Hold." And nothing could reach through the shields around the Hold.

"What? Why? It's Yttresken's fault, not T'eng Sten's."

"Yarlung declared it wasn't an official duel."

Dvara hissed. Her skin flickered vermillion.

Khotan shifted into the room. He held a steaming bowl of yak meat stew. "Shh," he said, silencing Dvara's protests. "You can't help him unless you heal."

Dvara glared at Khotan. "How long will he be in the Hold?"

"They're starting the Meet as soon as the other Kairöks arrive from the Fragments. Today or tomorrow at the latest. His trial will be the first thing on the agenda."

"But he doesn't need to be tried." Dvara shimmered in anger.

"It'll be alright," Rakan said, trying to soothe her. "You should eat something."

"I don't want to eat," she yelled. She hurled the bowl across the room and exploded into her dragon form. She twirled wildly, scratching at the walls and blasting fire. Khotan morphed and flattened her, biting into her jugular. Rakan jumped into the spiral stairway. He cursed himself for not having morphed fast enough. Dvara went still and Khotan let her go. He morphed back into his human form. But Dvara didn't. She limped over to her dragon nest and curled up facing the wall.

"Come upstairs," said Khotan. He shifted out of the room with the remains of the bowl.

Rakan looked at his sister's drooping black crest. "I'll go see T'eng Sten."

Dvara didn't say anything and he didn't expect her to; she couldn't speak in dragon form. But she gave a low grunt and curled up tighter. Rakan bowed his head slightly. "I'll do what I can to help him. I promise."

June ran into the parking lot in front of Anna's apartment. "Oh, Anna, there you are," she said, throwing her arms around Anna. "I'm so sorry."

"No. Wait." Anna held June at arms length. "What do you think happened?"

June looked confused. "You were poisoned and Pemba tried to get me to come help you, but I blocked him out. Haakon said Red felt you." June paused. "How did he know what to do?"

"I have no idea. He just felt it?"

"Maybe. But he doesn't have a rök."

"A what?"

"A… dragon heart. A condensed ball of energy that allows you to manipulate matter."

"Oh." The source of energy he was hiding. And June didn't know. Anna hooked her arm through June's and headed towards school. "We're late." Better not to talk about it.

"It doesn't matter." June squeezed Anna's arm. "Are you okay?"

"I guess so." Anna let herself be wrapped in June's energy that felt so alive. "But it was awful. The feeling…" The numbing void of loss made Pemba's absence even harder.

"I felt them die too," June whispered, sensing what Anna was feeling. "It hurt. It hurt so much. I thought I was going to die with them." June began to shake. "I don't think I can go to school. Not today. The pain was like my nightmares. Except it was real. And they're all dead."

Anna steadied June. Pain worse than what she had felt the night before flashed through her. It felt like the planet was exploding around them. And everyone with it. She was consumed by hatred. She wanted to lash out and kill. To destroy. The girls stumbled. A soothing energy washed over them, easing the pain, the anger. She gasped and fell into Lysa as Erling took June. "What was that?" Anna asked, too stunned to think about how Erling and Lysa had shown up so suddenly.

"A memory," said Lysa. "But not a good one."

"Is she okay?"

"She will be," said Lysa. She looked at June and Erling. "It's a pain they share."

Lysa steered Anna towards school. "I think they need some time."

Anna leaned on Lysa and they walked down the hill in silence. Her energy was smooth and somehow tender. "You don't have that pain," Anna said.

"No." Lysa hesitated by the rock in front of the school. "We should talk about it."

"The pain?"

"No," said Lysa, her voice echoing slightly. "What caused it."

Anna sat across from Lysa, looking around Hansen's. They were becoming regulars at skipping school and hanging out here. Anna played with her floppy heart-shaped waffle. Lysa hadn't said anything and Anna was beginning to wonder if she would. "Did you feel it last night?" Anna asked, breaking the silence.

Lysa looked up. Her pale green eyes had an intensity that made them look supersaturated. "Yes. From afar. Like a reflection on the water."

Anna stopped playing with her waffle and put her hands in her lap. "It was awful."

"I didn't think anyone could be so cruel."

"What happened?" The pain had been too awful, too fresh, to talk about last night when Pemba had walked her home.

"Two Kairöks fought over Dawa."

"Two what?"

"Two clan leaders. One of them used you as a lure to get Dawa out of the protection of T'eng Sten's shields. But the deaths we felt were because one of the Kairöks didn't release the röks," Lysa paused. "Do you know what that is?" Anna nodded and Lysa continued. "A Kairök has to release the rök of their kai," Lysa paused, noticing Anna's confusion. "A kai is what

they call those who have given their rök to a Kairök. And the Kairök has
to release the rök when one of his or her kais is about to die. But Yttresken
didn't. So his kais died in agony."

Anna felt the pain of their deaths return. "Who won?" Her voice caught
in her throat, certain that it was Torsten, the one Pemba called Tenzin.

"I'll never understand the concept of winning when so many died," said
Lysa. "But to answer the question I think you're asking: Yttresken died.
T'eng Sten lives."

"Will Dawa have to go with him?" Anna felt sick to her stomach at the
thought of anyone being bantered around like nothing more than a piece
of cloth.

Lysa gave Anna a strange look. "T'eng Sten has been Dawa's choice from
the beginning. She wants to be with him. Why do you think otherwise?"

"Because she didn't seem to like him very much. And both Pemba and
Dawa were protecting me from Kariaksuq, who was doing what Torsten,
Tenzin, whatever his name is, was telling her to do."

"You mean the one who poisoned you with the letter? She was one of
Yttresken's kais, not T'eng Sten's. And Yttresken knew Dawa would come
out of their lair to protect you."

"But why did she protect me? I mean, I'm glad she did." The thought
of what would have happened otherwise made Anna shudder. "But we've
never been close." Far from it.

"She was doing it for Pemba. Because she's loyal to him. Not you."

"Oh." At least that was clear. She was beginning to understand what
Pemba meant when he said his family would never abandon him. "And
Kariaksuq was following Torsten, uh T'eng Sten, for the other Kairök. So
she was with Ulf to get to me?"

Lysa shrugged. "I don't know. I don't follow the pointless maneuverings
of the shapeshifters. Erling says I should, but I can't."

"It makes sense in a twisted way. Kariaksuq was with Ulf to give him
the letter to poison me, to lure Dawa out, to capture her..." Anna ripped
the waffle in half. It didn't make any sense. Not really. All the Draak had
accomplished was to kill 14 of their own. When Dawa should have been
free to choose who to be with anyway.

"I wanted to tell you about what happened." Lysa's voice had a detached quality that made Anna's attention snap back to her friend. "There was a war between the Draak and the Elythia—"

"—wait. Who are the Elythia?"

"People like me. June calls us angels, but the resemblance is rather far from the image most people have. We call ourselves Elythia, Beings of Light."

"But you don't have wings."

"I do," said Lysa with a faint smile. "But not when I'm in this form."

"But then you can change shape. You're a shapeshifter."

"I suppose so. I hadn't thought of it that way," Lysa said slowly. "But shapeshifters are Beings of Matter. They have a rök and can manipulate matter. We don't have a rök and we manipulate light and sound." Lysa laced her fingers. "As I was saying, there was a war. Before I was born. Thousands died. Since then we have had a tentative truce, but there are those on both sides whose hatred continues. And so we live in secret."

"Why are you telling me, if it's secret?" She didn't need any more secrets to be bound to her than she already had.

Lysa didn't answer right away. "Because Erling thinks Pemba is manipulating you. Dawa's father, Kraal, was the leader of the Draak against the Elythia when he was alive. And we believe Yarlung, their mother, has taken his place."

"But Pemba's father is alive." The story didn't fit.

"Yes. But Pemba's father is Khotan, one of Yarlung's bodyguards. Not Kraal."

Anna sat perfectly still. Was that why Pemba had said he wasn't sure his parents loved each other? Anna looked at her Firemark. Pemba had said they were trained to track and kill. But who? the Elythia? Was that the 'project' Pemba's parents were working on? "The trigger was for one of you?"

"No. The trigger was for June."

"But why do they want to find June? She hasn't done anything. And she has a rök, she's a shapeshifter."

"But she's with Erling. And most Draak and Elythia would rather see them dead, than together." Lysa paused. "Unfortunately, it's one of the few things both sides agree on."

"But you don't believe that. Do you?"

"No. Or only when Fritjof..." She looked down. "I'm sorry I ever let myself believe any of what he told me."

Things clicked into place. Fritjof, Lysa's now-dead boyfriend, had hated June. "He tried to kill June in the avalanche?"

"No. He used me to try to kill Erling."

"Why would he do that?" Anna felt lost.

"Because June is a Draak," said Lysa. "And if he had killed her it would've broken the truce and started a second war. Which even Fritjof wouldn't have wanted."

Anna tried to control her shaking. "Why did Pemba and Dawa want to find June?" she asked, dreading the answer.

Lysa leaned forward. "To kill her."

Yarlung crushed the letter in her hand. "How could you have been so careless?" she snarled.

"But the letter is proof that it wasn't just a wanton attack," replied Rakan. "Yttresken planned it. He knew T'eng Sten would come protect Dvara."

"Of course he did. I told him to. Why do you think my guards didn't intervene? But the idiot wasn't able to control his pride and he fought back." Yarlung waved her fist with the balled up letter in front of Rakan. "And this will look like proof that I sent you to bite Kariaksuq." Yarlung spat on the floor. "No one will believe that you spontaneously tried to mate with Kariaksuq – she's a water dragon. She's beneath you. You need to fly an air dragon. I would have given Yuli back her rök if you needed to mate with a dragon. At least she's worthy of your interest."

Rakan growled. "I wasn't trying to mate with Kariaksuq."

"Then you're a fool."

Rakan paced his mother's inner chamber, blocking out the gentle gurgling of the spring and the water that he could feel running under the rock. "Why are you calling for a trial?" he asked, keeping his voice level.

"Because T'eng Sten killed Yttresken by ripping his rök out of his chest." Yarlung touched Rakan with her mind. "You know it's against the Code."

"He was only trying to stop Yttresken from letting his kais die without their röks. Yttresken was the one who was wrong, not T'eng Sten."

"I find it interesting that you are defending T'eng Sten," said Yarlung coldly. "Why do you care what happens to him?"

Rakan held his mother's gaze. "I don't," he lied.

"Well then, if you don't care there's no reason to spare him." Yarlung paused. "Although we can give him one last chance." She smiled at Rakan. "Why don't you offer him the chance to give me his vote in exchange for annulling the trial?"

"But you don't need his vote," snapped Rakan, before he could control himself.

"No, I don't. I have the majority now that Yttresken is dead. But I wouldn't mind seeing T'eng Sten grovel for his life. Would you?"

Rakan bowed his head, wondering if he had just sealed T'eng Sten's fate.

Yarlung snapped her fingers and Yuli shifted into the chamber with a bow to her Kairök. "Bring Rakan'dzor to see T'eng Sten. He has a proposition to offer him."

Yuli bowed again and turned to Rakan. "I'll need to shift you into the Hold." She glanced at his chest. "If I may?"

Rakan nodded, not happy that Yuli would need to touch him.

"Oh, and Rakan," said Yarlung from her throne. "Tell him it was your idea."

Rakan stifled a growl. "Let's go," he said to Yuli.

"We can stop on the way," said Yuli, snaking her hands up his chest.

"No."

"As you wish," she murmured into his neck. She shifted him to the Hold.

The cold of the final wall of the Hold pierced Rakan and the deafening silence made his ears ring. His arms convulsed around Yuli, the only living thing he could feel anywhere. Even the rock didn't respond to his mind-touch.

Yuli responded, molding her body into his. Rakan pushed her away.

"Why not? No one can hear us here." She reached out for him again. "We're free."

"I need to see T'eng Sten." He tried to feel the Kairök. But there was only Yuli. And she was in no hurry to bring him to T'eng Sten.

Yuli came close, but didn't touch him. "You need to mate. You've been alone too long. Your energy is changing." Her lime green dress shimmered and transformed into her chest armor. "It doesn't even matter which dragon you choose. But if you don't free your rök it will start to die. And I'd rather not see that happen." She pointed to the wall between two torches. "He's in there. I'll fix the shield so that you can go through alone. Unless you want me to accompany you?"

"No. I'll be fine."

"As you wish." She touched the wall, but Rakan couldn't feel what she was doing until a rectangular space sprang alive. And through it he could feel T'eng Sten.

"Rakan," said Yuli, stopping him as he was about to penetrate the wall. "You have Yarlung's power and Khotan's mind. Don't waste it."

Rakan looked at Yuli, wondering what she meant. But she backed away, bowing at the waist, as if he was a Kairök.

"Kairök T'eng Sten," Rakan said, bowing as he entered the square Hold that was made of the same lifeless rock as the outer chamber. A wave of emotion filled him, T'eng Sten had saved Dvara. He put a fist to his hand in the sign of homage. "Thank you." But T'eng Sten didn't respond. Rakan straightened and came closer. T'eng Sten was seated on the slab of rock that was probably meant to be a bed. He looked like he was meditating with his eyes open. But when Rakan reached out with his mind-touch he could barely feel him. His body was there, but his being was elsewhere.

Rakan hissed. It wasn't normal. He grabbed T'eng Sten by the shoulders. And spilled out onto a white plain in his dragon form. Or rather forms. He flickered between an air dragon and a water dragon. The changing forms pulsed, blurring his view. His rök burned in his chest and he bellowed in pain. He lashed out at the barren whiteness of the oppressive hell he had fallen into. Cobalt mixed with emerald flashed in the distance. "June," he yelled. He could feel her. He tried to scramble forward, but couldn't move.

He had lost control of his body. And then the shimmering color that felt like June was gone. There was no trace, no pulsing trail left in the barren openness that threatened to burst his very being. The whiteness blinded him. Its brilliance flattened everything.

"How did you get here?" hissed T'eng Sten, pushing Rakan's head into the sand. Before Rakan could answer, he was back on the stone floor, T'eng Sten still straddling him. T'eng Sten stood up. "That wasn't supposed to happen."

Rakan didn't get up. He pressed into the floor. Even if it was dead to his touch, it was real. He felt Yuli move in the central chamber, ready to intervene if they began to fight. T'eng Sten's anger pounded through the room like a stampede of wild yaks. And Rakan had no intention of throwing himself in its path.

Finally, T'eng Sten's anger ebbed and he offered Rakan a hand.

"Where was that?" asked Rakan. The whiteness burned into his eyelids.

"I was in an alternate state. It's the only way to survive the Hold."

Rakan looked skeptically at the Kairök. "It seems worse." The wide open space had been the same glaring white in all directions. It was a place with no time, no change. And no smell.

"You don't know what it's like to be severed from all contact with other dragons."

Rakan snorted. "I've never had it. How can I know?" His rök vibrated angrily, but Rakan stilled it. He'd deal with it later. "But I don't create an alternative reality to escape."

"I wasn't escaping."

"Then what were you doing? And how did you create June's—"

T'eng Sten lunged for Rakan's throat. "That's none of your business."

Rakan blocked him and they tumbled to the ground. "But maybe it is Dvara's," Rakan said as he flipped T'eng Sten onto his back.

"When she knows the truth about her father and Paaliaq, she'll understand." T'eng Sten shoved Rakan off and slammed him into the wall.

"What truth?" Rakan said, suddenly more interested in what T'eng Sten was saying than in the fight. "Paaliaq tricked Kraal and killed him. Everyone knows that."

"And what if she didn't?" said T'eng Sten, his breath on Rakan's face. "What if Kraal tricked Paaliaq and she only killed him in self-defense? Have you ever even considered that?"

Rakan felt a rush of anger flow through him. He clenched his fists and forced his rök back into control. "No, I haven't. Why should I?"

"Because there are several theories about why they fought. And what happened when they did. You should at least know what they are before you decide to kill Paaliaq."

"But Yarlung felt Kraal die when they smashed to the earth."

"Yes. He did. Everyone agrees on that. But what happened to Paaliaq?"

"She went into hiding."

"That's Yarlung's theory. But I felt Paaliaq being frozen into a Fragment of the Red Planet by my Kairök at the time. I felt it and there was nothing I could do to stop it."

Rakan could feel T'eng Sten's memory. He was telling the truth. "But others must have felt it too," said Rakan. "Why did they grant Yarlung ten cycles to find Paaliaq here?"

"Because there were those who believed she could morph into more than one dragon form, which no dragon in the history of the Red Planet had ever been able to do. And it scared them so much that they even began to believe that she could split her being into three parts, one for each form — making her essentially invincible."

Rakan stood silently, his brain refusing to process what T'eng Sten had just said. No one could morph into more than one form. And yet he had. But from there to splitting his being into several parts? He sank onto the stone slab, unable to speak.

"I grew up in a time when Kraal was the Mighty, the Unbeatable," continued T'eng Sten. "He was pitch black, the color of purity, of perfection. Every acolyte came out of the Arena hoping to be taken into his Cairn. The biggest, the best, the strongest of all the Cairns. But Paaliaq refused his offer to join his Cairn. And after she became a Kairök in her own right, she challenged Kraal during the Games. And won. He vowed to kill her for it. And that was when I began to disagree with my Kairök. I realized that Kraal wasn't the hero I thought. But Paaliaq was. She never mentioned having beaten him at the games. But for Kraal it was enough that everyone knew. He told everyone she had tricked him to win, that all she wanted was to destroy the Kairök system so that she could rule the planet by herself."

Rakan stared at T'eng Sten. His version was so different from his mother's. And yet he could feel that T'eng Sten believed what he was saying.

"Neither Kraal nor Paaliaq are here. Their history is over. But we need to live again, to move on, to breed. We're dying on the Fragments, Rakan. We need to be able to come to Earth. No matter what happened in the past. It's time to start a new life."

Rakan felt a wave of warmth and returned it. "Khotan says the same thing."

"Khotan is a great scholar and his gifts are being wasted. He should be teaching but we have no puppies for him to teach. We need to free Earth. If we grant Yarlung more time, it will be too late for many of the Old Dragons to breed." Pain and anger erupted from the Kairök. "Or dead with Yarlung's stupid inter-Cairn machinations."

The cell was flooded with sorrow. He leaned into the Old Dragon, comforting him. "How many did you lose?" The pain of those who died without their röks had been so overwhelming that he hadn't felt who else had died.

"Five," said T'eng Sten, his voice flat. "Angalaan was one of them."

"No." A new wave of pain filled him. Not Angalaan. He put his head in his hands.

"She died courageously."

Rakan felt a flash of the fight and saw Angalaan throw herself between T'eng Sten and two of Yttresken's kais. She had given her life to save his. "No," Rakan moaned again.

"She was one of my best," said T'eng Sten. "And I would have given her the choice to become your kai the day you freed your rök."

Rakan stared at T'eng Sten.

"Your rök is meant to hold others, Rakan'dzor. But you need to free it first. Angalaan would've helped you realize your potential. And you hers." T'eng Sten's voice dropped. "I loved her. But as a Kairök. It's not the way I feel about Dvara. Dvara is different. And she must be going through hell right now."

Rakan felt a pang of guilt. "Yarlung wants to manipulate you," he blurted out.

"Of course. I wouldn't expect anything else." T'eng Sten nudged Rakan. "So what is it this time?"

"To stop the trial if you pledge your vote," Rakan said quietly. He didn't want to imagine the outcome of the trial. "It's supposed to be my idea."

T'eng Sten laughed. "She said that, did she?"

"Why is that funny?" Rakan said, looking at the Kairök.

T'eng Sten put a hand on Rakan's shoulder. "The outcome of the trial doesn't worry me."

"But the penalty is death."

"Only for me. And perhaps for Dvara," said T'eng Sten solemnly. "But if Yarlung keeps Earth much longer it will be the death of the Draak."

Chapter 25

Trials

RAKAN FINALLY CAME OUT OF T'ENG STEN'S HOLD. YULI'S LIME GREEN ARMOR changed back into her formal gown. "You okay?" she asked. He had been in there for several hours.

Rakan shrugged. He had accepted T'eng Sten's offer to stay with him in his cell if he needed some time alone. His mother's lair crawled with her spies. And there was too much that he needed to think through. He had debated whether or not to talk to T'eng Sten about what had happened when he had chased Kariaksuq and turned into a water dragon. But as much as he was beginning to trust the Kairök, he hadn't been able to bring it up. He wasn't even completely sure himself about what had happened.

"Don't feel guilty," said Yuli, misinterpreting his silence. "Yarlung didn't expect it to be otherwise. She knows T'eng Sten would rather die than give in to her. She just wanted him to choose his own death."

"Then why did she send me to try?" snapped Rakan, tired of the games.

"Why does Yarlung do anything? To keep you in her power by forcing you to make a choice and showing her where your allegiance lies." Yuli placed a hand on Rakan's chest. *"She knows you have the potential to be more powerful than she is if you can find the way to unlock it."*

Rakan forced down his fear of morphing into a water dragon. *"I thought you said if I flew someone it would unlock my rök."* Rakan put his fingers on her temple in order to feel her reaction more clearly. *"So why would she want me to fly you?"*

"Because you don't love me, and your rök wouldn't be freed. It would only have found a temporary relief."

"Why are you telling me this?"

"So that you stop holding yourself back and you go chase the one you are keeping yourself from." Yuli paused. *"I can't be free. But you can."*

Rakan took his fingers away from Yuli's face and bowed his head. "Thank you."

"Until you can set your rök free, you should flirt with me." She looked away. "It'll keep Yarlung from probing you too far for now."

"What do you mean until?" She was hinting at something but he wasn't getting it.

Yuli took a deep breath. "Some of Yttresken's kais didn't accept T'eng Sten's offer to become their Kairök."

Rakan looked at Yuli carefully. Yarlung had always said that when two Kairöks battle, the winner automatically takes the kais. Was it yet another of his mother's manipulations, or was it just T'eng Sten who had preferred to give them the choice, breaking once again with tradition?

Yuli touched his chest. *"Kariaksuq was one of those."* Before he could answer, Yuli shifted them back into Yarlung's reception room. It was teeming with dragons.

Rakan's arms jerked around Yuli, his heart pounding against hers. "Where is she?" he whispered into her neck, not daring to mind-speak lest his emotions come out too clearly. His need to kill Kariaksuq made his rök feel like a volcano about to explode.

Yuli twisted playfully out of his arms, her hair slipping gently around her shoulders. "Patience, little puppy, patience."

Rakan watched her fix her hair as she glided to a group of recently arrived dragons and begin her political dancing. Yuli knew where Kariaksuq was. He felt his mother's attention linger on him until he turned to face her. She turned away with a satisfied half smile on her face. Yuli was right. He needed to let his mother think he was chasing her.

"Anna?" Red sounded surprised over the phone. "Are you okay?"

"No." She stared at her bedroom wall. "I need to see you. Now." Some things she couldn't say on the phone.

"But I'm not in Tromso."

"That didn't stop you the other night."

Red was silent.

"I don't know how you do it and I don't care. Come. Now," she said and hung up. She sat on her bed and waited, wondering if he'd come or not. She reached out with her mind but felt nothing. She paced around her room until her special stone caught her eye. The trigger. She stopped and picked it up, her hands trembling. What if everything Lysa had told her was true? Her Firemark pulsed. It felt like Pemba and she felt sick. Was it all her fault? *Red, where are you?*

"What's wrong?" said Red behind her.

Anna flung herself into his arms, still gripping the now-dead stone. She wished life would go back to being simple. "Why did you make Ulf think I tried to kill myself?" she blurted out, instead of asking about Pemba. "He's constantly hovering all the time now. He doesn't even want to go out anymore."

"Because I thought he'd feel guilty. And he'd leave."

"It didn't work."

"Do you want me to change it?"

"What? Of course not. You'd have to change my mom's memories too." Anna scrutinized her cousin's face. "Don't you think it's wrong to manipulate people's minds?"

Red shrugged. "I don't know. People make themselves believe all kinds of things all the time. What's the difference?"

"Choice." Anna rubbed her Firemark. "And freedom." But maybe there wasn't always a lot of freedom in that choice. "Why did Pemba come to Tromso?"

Red didn't answer right away. "I think you know the answer to that."

"He can't want to kill June." Her voice caught. "He can't."

"It's not your fight, Anna. It's ours."

"But you're my cousin."

"Yes," he said, narrowing his eyes. "And?"

"So it's my fight as much as it's yours," she said, using the same logic that Pemba and Dawa had used.

"I won't let you get involved."

"It's too late for that, isn't it? I'm already involved." She had found the trigger and set it off by touching June with it. And now she'd have to find a way to stop it.

The reception hall carved into the sacred mountain crackled with tension and clanking armor. Rakan had never liked crowds, and this was worse. All the Kairöks were here. Some had elaborate, but impractical, body armor. Worn only for show. Others, like T'eng Sten, who had been let out of the Hold for the Meet, could throw themselves directly into a fight. But they all had the same vambraces on their forearms. They were intricately patterned with the Five Elements, symbolizing the five gifts of shielding, transforming, building triggers, strategic planning and trailing. It also allowed them to speak mentally to each other.

Yuli shimmied up to him. Rakan stiffened as she slid her hands up his chest. Even if he knew it was for the best that they pretend to be more involved than they were, he hated it. Her hands circled his biceps, and he felt armbands snap into place. *"We'll need these to speak,"* she said.

Rakan looked at the double strands of coral and lime green metal that Yuli had made for their armbands. They were twisted together like two long water dragons mating.

"I'm not a water dragon," he growled. And he'd just as soon not be one of Yarlung's bodyguards for the Meet either. It was an honor he could do without.

"No more than I am, but Yarlung is. Besides, they wrapped better this way."

"It is time," said Yarlung. Her voice echoed through the hall and she stamped her ceremonial lance five times.

"The Eld have not yet arrived," countered T'eng Sten. He looked more fierce than majestic. His indigo and platinum chest armor was by the far the most practical of any of the Kairöks. Even the ceremonial strip of indigo cloth that hung from his waist was made to rip off in a fight. "And they are our ultimate rulers."

"They've never come to our Meets here on Earth. We can decide these matters on our own. Enter," she said to the waiting Kairöks. "Let the Meet begin."

Around the edges of the rotunda five glowing tunnels appeared, one each for the five possible colors of dragon crests. They corresponded to the five sacred metals: gold for the shielders; platinum for the transformers; pure black kor for the triggerers; iron for the planners and copper for the trailers. They were each lined with a double row of Draak dressed in ceremonial breastplates the color of their Kairöks, holding a curved sword above their head, ready to strike. It looked like entering the mouth of a giant serpent.

Silently, the Kairöks entered the tunnels that corresponded to their gift, one by one. Rakan heard the clash of metal against metal from the platinum Tunnel of Transformers and stiffened. T'eng Sten. A guard, gripping his side, was shifted into the hall.

"Fool," spat the dark blue clad Kairök Tetherys. "He should have killed you. How could Kairök Japetus let you attack T'eng Sten here? Choose your time correctly." Two of Yarlung's kais came and shifted the bleeding guard elsewhere.

Rakan watched as Kairök Tetherys, limping from an old injury, hobbled up the steel grey tunnel of the Planners. Although she didn't look like much, her trail was clear and intense. She should have become a Master in a Training Arena, but there weren't any more. And even if there had been, there were no more young.

Rakan looked at the various trails. Each Kairök had a different way of 'holding' the röks of their kais. He looked back at Tetherys' trail. It was as if she had wrapped her rök around those of her kais, and Rakan wasn't sure if it would feel like being smothered or being kept safe.

"We can go in now," said Yuli, interrupting his thoughts. *"You'll be okay. I won't be far."*

"Don't worry," he answered, blocking her out. "I'll be fine."

"Probably. Keep alert anyhow." She turned and walked to the golden Tunnel of Shielders.

The hall had nearly emptied and Rakan glanced around the room. None of the other dragons were trailers. He was the last one. He entered the mouth of the copper Tunnel of Trailers. The heat increased as he walked up through the eight pairs of kais. It turned into near furnace-like heat as sparks of tension crackled up and down the tunnel. The tense immobility of the kais made Rakan slow down. He scanned each one before passing. One of T'eng Sten's new kais twitched and Rakan barely had time to react before the long curved sword came flying down, aimed at his leg. Rakan jumped lithely in the air and landed silently on the pulsing copper sand.

"You are neither Kairök nor kai," said the kai. "You have no right to pass." The kai stood in the middle of the tunnel, blocking the way. No one else had moved. The only sound in the tunnel was the kai's labored breathing as he struggled against Kairök T'eng Sten's wishes.

Rakan pulled the sword from the sand and examined its green patina. "Had it been up to either one of us, I wouldn't be here." Rakan handed the sword back, hilt first. "At least we have that in common." They locked eyes and Rakan wondered how far T'eng Sten had been able to integrate his new kais into his Cairn while he had been in the Hold. The kai melted back to his position, but his hatred clawed at Rakan's back as he passed.

The cool air of the upper rotunda made Rakan's hair stand on end. It was directly above the reception hall, and only slightly smaller. The sixteen Kairöks were seated in a circle on raised stone thrones. The seventeenth was empty. An arched passageway curved along the edge of the rotunda and gave access to seventeen alcoves that looked out from above. Most of the alcoves were filled with a dozen kais, grouped by Cairn. The swathes of colored cloth hanging from the carved balustrades corresponded to the Kairök below.

The last of the bodyguards were walking across the black sand made of the precious metal kor to join their Kairöks. Rakan clenched his jaw and headed towards his mother. She sat regally in her turquoise ceremonial armor with Yuli just behind her to the right. Yarlung's increasingly white hair, even covered in part by her crown-like headgear, was an anomaly amongst the black-haired Draak.

T'eng Sten sat like an indigo clad statue on the throne to Yarlung's left. Rakan took his place just behind his mother, next to the kai that had replaced Angalaan. He faced forward but his attention was riveted on Mnemozyne. She had been one of Yttresken's inner circle. Rakan's rök howled. Angalaan shouldn't have died. And she shouldn't have been replaced by the forest green water dragon.

Yarlung lifted her lance. The enormous gong that hung in midair resounded. The Meet had started. The middle of the rotunda shimmered in a mirage of gold, steel grey, black, platinum and copper. A murmur of surprise echoed around the rotunda as the billowing cloud of particles condensed into five sparkling pillars.

Rakan felt his mother's anger flash momentarily and then recede into nothingness as she suppressed it. The pillars morphed into the five Eld, the five Oldest Dragons who had veto power over the Kairöks – should they choose to use it. Each one faced a different direction, arms stretched to the side with their palms up, making a pentagon. The Eld were dressed in pure black and their identical body armor shimmered like hematite. Rakan felt a mix of fear and awe as they moved slowly forward, expanding the size of their pentagon. Their silver shoulder-length hair flowed freely – male and female alike. The only distinguishing element was the inner lining of their cloaks that flashed the color of their gift. Except some of the colors were wrong. The gold of the Shield Eld and the platinum of the Transformer Eld were as they should be. But the copper of the Trailer Eld and the iron grey of the Mind Eld shimmered between their natural and oxidized states: the Trailer Eld's inner lining was alternately copper and green and the Transformer Eld's was alternately iron and rust. But it was the Trigger Eld's cloak that made Rakan hiss. It was there and not there – and Rakan could alternately see through the cloak and not. It existed and didn't exist at the same time.

He felt the copper-eyed Trailer Eld examine him. Or rather his trail. And he knew that she could see the double twisted strand of his rök. *"You will come to me,"* she said, her voice echoing like a prophecy. *"Your place is with us. Not with the human."* Rakan stiffened. How did she know about Anna?

The Eld turned and faced each other. "The Meet will now begin," said all five voices in unison. They dissipated, filling the rotunda with a metallic light. Rakan stifled the urge to morph, they were there. He could feel them. But he couldn't see them.

The gong sounded again and a dark brown dragon with the copper crest of a trailer materialized. Haakaramanoth. Flames shot from his open mouth. His black claws were out-stretched to attack. T'eng Sten growled and morphed, lunging for Haakaramonth's throat.

"Enough," commanded the Eld in unison, freezing both dragons on the black sand.

There was a stunned silence as T'eng Sten morphed back to his human form and bowed to the circle of Eld that had re-materialized around the two dragons. "My apologies, your Eld. But he has no business being here."

"That is not for you to decide," said the Eld. "Return to your place."

T'eng Sten's energy shimmered in anger, but he bowed and returned to his throne. Everyone watched the dark brown dragon in an uneasy silence. He bowed his head and morphed to human within the ring of the Eld. Haakon. Rakan growled and tensed to attack, but Yuli froze him in place. "No," she hissed. "Let the Eld deal with this."

"By what right do you appear at this Meet, Haakaramanoth?" asked the Shield Eld, her gold-lined cape flashing.

"By the same right as all the other Kairöks here."

"And where is Paaliaq?" asked Yarlung, her voice piercing the silence.

Haakaramanoth turned to Yarlung with a slight bow. "She disappeared at the same time as Kairök Kraal."

Rakan could feel the truth of the Old Dragon's words, and yet something didn't ring right. Rakan examined Haakaramanoth's trail. It wasn't the trail of a Kairök. He didn't have his own rök even though it felt like he did. Rakan's rök flickered on the edge of an uncontrolled morph. It was an illusion.

The Trailer Eld entered his mind. "How interesting that you can see that," she said. Her voice froze his mind. "Either he tells some form of the truth or his need is great. We alone will decide. You will not speak of this." A cold slithering ran down the base of Rakan's skull and he knew that the Eld had set a trigger in his mind.

"There was no need," he hissed as soon as she released his mind. But she had blocked him out already. His rök throbbed. He wanted to throw himself at her rigid back and lash into her. She had no right to penetrate his mind like that.

"If that is true, then who is Jing Mei?" Yarlung's question caused a murmur to reverberate in the rotunda.

"Silence," commanded the Eld in unison. "Haakaramanoth will answer."

"She is a whelp of the Cairn," said Haakaramanoth. A vocal round of protests erupted.

Yarlung snorted. "You lie."

"Enough," said the Eld. "We will examine Haakaramanoth and determine the truth of his words. You will return to your own lairs until the Meet is reconvened." The Eld disappeared, taking Haakaramanoth with them. The Meet dissolved into mayhem as Kairöks jumped from their thrones, clamoring to make themselves heard.

Rakan stayed next to his mother's empty throne. The Eld's trails were unlike the other Draak even though they had one strand each. They shimmered like opals. The way June's did.

June sat alone in the cafeteria. "Hey, what's up?" asked Anna, as she and Lysa joined her. "Where's Erling?"

"Gone," June said dejectedly.

"What do you mean, gone?" Anna asked.

June picked at her lunch.

Anna looked at Lysa. "When did he leave?"

"This morning," she said. "Erling wasn't pleased at being summoned."

"Why can't he ever say no?" snapped June.

Lysa shrugged. "Could you?"

"Depends on what they asked me to do," she said quietly.

"Perhaps," said Lysa.

June perked up. "Verje is back."

Anna looked around. She hadn't felt anything. But a few moments later Verje came in and Lysa stood up. "Excuse me," she said and walked out of the lunchroom with Verje. June pushed back her chair and raced after them. Anna followed. Something was wrong.

June stopped in the empty hallway and Anna nearly ran into her. "Where did they go?" Anna looked around. She wished she could do that.

June flopped down in the stairway. "They went in the light."

"What's wrong?" Anna sat next to her. "Are you worried about Erling?"

"No. About Haakon."

"Why would you worry about Haakon?"

"Because he's gone to Pemba's."

"But Pemba's not here." Anna's cheeks tingled. "You mean wherever Pemba is, with Dawa?"

June nodded. "Pemba's mother imprisoned Torsten because he freed Dawa."

"Maybe it was because he killed someone."

"Thank god he did. Imagine how many more deaths there would have been if he hadn't." June trembled like she had the other day and Anna wished Lysa hadn't disappeared.

"It's over now," Anna said, wrapping an arm around June.

"No it's not." June leaned into her. "Haakon cut me off. I can't feel him anymore. He said he didn't want to risk them feeling me through him if he was attacked." June's pain washed over Anna.

"They won't attack him," Anna said, reassuring her friend. "There's no reason to."

June shook her head. "Pemba and Torsten are different. But the others... all they think about is revenge and power. And they'll do anything to get it. Like Yttresken and Kariaksuq."

"Is Kariaksuq still alive?" asked Anna, her heart sinking. She hadn't even thought about that yet.

"Yes. But Pemba's mother is worse," June said quietly.

Anna gripped June. "What if she attacks you?"

"Why would she?"

"Because you're a Draak and Erling is an Elythia." Pain ripped through Anna and she fell forward, gasping for air. "What was that?"

But June was gone.

Rakan paced around his mother's thermal spa. The gurgling baths made him want to morph into a water dragon.

"Would you relax?" said Yuli, not for the first time. "What'll Yarlung think if she sees your trail crisscrossing all over the room instead of lying on the bed next to me?"

"I don't care what she thinks."

"Well, you should," snapped Yuli. "I'm trying to help you but I can't if you won't play along."

Rakan stopped pacing. "You're right." She was risking her neck for him. "Why can't we even go outside?" He wanted to hunt for Kariaksuq.

"It'll only be a few more days until they reconvene the Meet."

Rakan groaned and sank to one of the beds.

"Lie down. I'll massage you. Okay?"

Rakan nodded and lay on his stomach. He was going crazy. Yuli's touch was firm as she kneaded his back, easing his aching muscles. Rakan groaned. They were sore from growing, not from having been used. It was a constant reminder of what had happened when he had chased Kariaksuq.

Yuli and Rakan tensed at the same time. Kariaksuq. She was nearby. He'd kill her now, injunction to stay in or not.

"She's on the other side of Mapam Yumco," said Yuli. It was the fresh water lake next to Yarlung's salty one. "Yarlung's coming," said Yuli, quickly lying next to Rakan.

Yuli stood when Yarlung shifted into the spa.

"I want you to capture Kariaksuq," Yarlung said to Rakan.

"We're supposed to wait here," Rakan said testily.

"You don't technically belong to my Cairn. You can move freely."

Rakan growled. He had been going crazy for no reason?

"Don't kill her. She'll be much more useful alive." Yarlung turned to Yuli. "Give Rakan'dzor access to the Hold so that he can bring her in quietly."

Yarlung disappeared. Rakan prepared to do the same but Yuli stopped him. *"I thought you wanted to mate with her, not kill her."*

Rakan pulled away so that Yuli wouldn't see the image of Anna that floated up to his mind when he thought of mating.

"But you chased her," she said.

Rakan clenched his fist and shifted out of the room. Kariaksuq was too close to ignore. He found her kneeling in the fresh water of lake Mapam Yumco, her amber colored dress billowing out like a medusa. She turned to look at him, her pitch-black hair stuck in clumps to her back and shoulders in abandon. "Have you come to take me or to kill me?" she snarled and staggered to her feet. "I hate you," she yelled. She lurched towards Rakan. But she never made it that far. She fell to her knees, blood oozing into the water. Her rök was spinning like crazy as she teetered on the edge of insanity. "Why don't you kill me?" she yelled. "Kill me, you fool." She reached out and tried to grab his ankles. "Please." She dropped into the water. "I can't kill myself anymore than I could join T'eng Sten. Not after everything I had done." She thrashed in the water, willing her rök to fly free, but it wouldn't.

Rakan felt a mix of pity and revulsion for Kariaksuq. He hesitated. It would be so easy to kill her. But he couldn't kill her in cold blood. It was wrong. His anger had disappeared. She had been used as a tool. Yarlung would only torture her. But his father might be able to help. He reached out to pick her up. "Let me help you."

She dug her nails into his arms, latching on like a leech. "If you want to help me, kill me."

"No."

"*Are you too weak?*" She wrapped herself around him. "*Or do you want something else first?*"

He tried to fling her away, but she wouldn't let go.

"*Get angry,*" she said. "*Remember what I did to Anna. And know I would do it again if I had to.*" Because she had had no choice. It had been the will of her Kairök. And she had never had the courage to die in rebellion. To die without her rök being released.

Rakan's anger died as quickly as it had flared back up again. He wrapped Kariaksuq in his arms and felt what she wasn't saying. He felt her pain and her anguish as her rök opened itself up to him. Her rök knew what it wanted: death, but not in the agonizing pain that Yttresken would have given her. T'eng Sten would've given her death, but she hadn't wanted to face the shame in front of him. As he held her, kneeling in the water with her legs straddling his, he felt her rök come out of her body and hum between them. And he knew what to do. His rök reached out and welcomed her inside and in that split second he knew everything she had ever felt, everything she had ever done. And he knew it was her time to die.

"*Swim free, Kariaksuq,*" he said. She went limp in his arms. He willed her rök to re-manifest and sent it into the center of the earth where it wanted to go. Where it would find the burning fire of peace. "You're free now," he said, as Kariaksuq's last breath shuddered through her body.

He sat there, rocking her stiffening body back and forth in the gentle waters of the lake until the sun sank below the horizon. He placed her lifeless body in the water and spread her hair out around her head. "May your body return to what it once was," he said, gently dissolving the molecules that had been joined to form her physical being. He sat by the lake until the last of the sun's rays slipped around the earth, staring at the grandeur of the world that made him feel small and insignificant in comparison.

He felt the stars dancing in the early spring sky. His eyes drifted to the remnants of the Red Planet that was now nothing more than a ball of gas surrounded by rings of ice and fragments of what it had once been. He felt the earth tilt and his rök expand.

When he had let Kariaksuq go, his rök had proclaimed itself. But it wasn't until now that he was able to hear it. His name. His dragon name.

Rakan'dzor Sa'aq, bearer of the line of Aq.

Not Lung, like his mother. Not Tan like his father.

But Aq like Paaliaq.

Chapter 26

Tribulations

RAKAN STOOD STIFFLY, HIS BODY COLDER THAN THE SANDS ON THE SHORE OF lake Mapam Yumco. He wanted to go home. To the lair he had grown up in. He shut his eyes and shifted to the mineral hot spring just outside Khotan's lair. He reached out and checked that his father was fine and then sank into the hot water, not yet ready to go in. The gentle gurgling of the spring soothed him, until he realized that he couldn't feel Dvara.

Rakan climbed out of the spring and walked the short distance to the entrance of his father's lair that couldn't be seen by the human eye. Rakan placed a hand on the external rock and shifted through it. Khotan looked up from his workbench and smiled.

"Welcome home."

Rakan nodded and turned away. "Is Dvara alright? I don't feel her."

Khotan lit a fire in the stone hearth. "It seemed better to send her back to Tromso than to keep her here." Khotan paused. "T'eng Sten's shields are stronger than mine."

Rakan turned to his father. His face was set in shadow.

"Is she alone?" Rakan asked. She'd go wild.

"No. One of T'eng Sten's old kais is with her." Khotan stood, his back to the fire, and Rakan noticed for the first time that he was starting to lose some of his mass. "You did the right thing," said Khotan after a long pause.

Rakan bowed his head. "Yes. I think so." He sat in his favorite chair and watched the play of light on the stone lattice work that he had helped his father carve long ago. It seemed like another world. "But Yarlung won't."

"Ultimately, it doesn't matter what anyone else thinks. It matters what you know in your own rök to be true."

"Maybe." But Yarlung would still make his life hell. Khotan's face flickered in the firelight, showing the passage of time. Even though Khotan was no longer in his prime, Rakan could feel his inner strength. He seemed, if anything, stronger than before. Rakan watched the crackling flames, zooming in on the wood as it was being consumed. Just as Kariaksuq's body had been consumed. Through her rök he had felt the Red Planet explode and hundreds of Draak die.

"You can't change the past," said Khotan, putting a hand on Rakan's shoulder. "But you can choose your future."

Rakan felt his father's suffering and knew that the longer he stayed, the more his father would suffer: Yarlung was punishing Khotan for sheltering him. A wave of anger rose in Rakan and he stood. "There are a few things I must take care of." He bowed to his father. "I must return to Yarlung's." And then he'd go find Anna.

"Yes," said Khotan. "I think you are ready."

Rakan shifted to Yarlung's lair but it was closed to him. He reached out with his mind and found Yuli, who immediately shifted to the entrance. "You shouldn't have come," she said.

Rakan scanned her. She was dressed in her lime-green armor and had an extra set of throwing knives. "I see my mother's wrath has been awakened."

Yuli's eyes lit up momentarily and she touched Rakan. "*Your rök is healing.*" The contact broke abruptly and Yuli doubled over in pain. "Yarlung will see you. Now." Yuli groaned and Rakan caught her. They shifted together into Yarlung's inner chamber.

"Don't touch her," commanded Yarlung. She flung Yuli against the wall with a flick of her hand.

"You have no right to make her suffer," said Rakan.

"Silence." Yarlung waved a hand to freeze Rakan, but he countered it with a shield. "How dare you..." she hissed. She walked up and slapped him. "I told you not to kill her."

"I did the right thing," Rakan said. He turned his face back to hers without raising his voice or retaliating.

Yarlung snorted and turned away. "Leave. I don't want to see you anymore. You're useless," she hissed, her rök sizzling in anger.

"As you wish," Rakan said, preparing to shift.

Yarlung spun around, grabbed his braid and yanked him to his knees.

"You will honor the blood pact," she said, spitting each word out. "And only then will you be my son again."

The only spot of color in her eyes was the black of her pupils.

Rakan stifled his anger. Getting back to Tromso was more important than fighting his mother. He couldn't change the blood pact, but he could protect Dvara and Anna. He shifted into the apartment and reached out to find Dvara. She was lying, comatose, in her bed. Amarualik was hovering by her side. Rakan threw open the bedroom door. "She needs help," he said, striding into the room. Dvara's vermillion had faded under Amarualik's suffocating loam-green presence.

Amarualik straightened abruptly and then looked oddly at Rakan. "Rakan? I felt a Kairök."

"What have you been doing?" hissed Rakan. He ignored her questioning look and put a hand on Dvara's forehead.

Dvara's eyes fluttered open. "Rakan?"

"You shouldn't be sleeping like that," Rakan said. Her rök was festering.

"It's best if she rests," said Amarualik. "Once Kairök can take her, she'll heal."

"I want to sleep until he comes," mumbled Dvara.

"No," Rakan said, shaking her. "Get up. Now." He sniffed her and then grabbed Amarualik by the throat, pushing her against the wall. "What have you given her?"

"Nothing." She quivered in Rakan's hold. "She wanted to sleep, that's all. Kairök said to help her." Amarualik's loam eyes reflected fear. But not betrayal. "So I help her sleep. That's all."

"She'll die if she cuts herself off from the world," hissed Rakan. "She needs to find the will to live. Don't you understand that?"

"She was… helping…" mumbled Dvara.

"I did what she asked," said Amarualik. "It's what Kairök said to do."

"Leave." Rakan flung her to the ground. She was incapable of understanding.

"Kairök said—"

"This is our lair. I don't care what T'eng Sten said. Leave."

"But…"

Rakan hissed. His rök expanded and he prepared to banish her from their lair. But Amarualik scrambled to her feet. She shifted before he needed to.

"Ama...?" Dvara struggled to sit up. "But... why?"

"Because you need to live," Rakan said. "Not let your rök shrivel up in a drugged-induced sleep."

Dvara sank back down onto her pillow. "The time goes by faster."

"You're being selfish. T'eng Sten has more than enough problems right now."

"If he loved me he'd be here." Dvara turned her back to Rakan.

Rakan snatched the pillow from under her head. "Get up."

"No," she said, glaring at him. "I don't want to."

He threw the pillow at her. "Then don't," Rakan said. "It's your choice. You can either wallow in pain until you die, or get up and live." He turned and walked out of the room. "I want to live."

Anna felt Pemba shift into the woods behind her apartment. She threw down the book she had been pretending to read and jumped off the couch. He was back. She ran down the stairs and reached out to touch him. He responded. She felt his mind-touch and it pulled her forward. "Pemba," she said, flinging the door open and running out onto the porch. Pink light reflected off the lingering patches of snow as the early May sun sank to the edge of the horizon. He was in the woods, calling her to him. The ground oozed cold and moist under her bare feet but she didn't care. He was back. She saw him, standing as still and majestic as if he was a nature god. She stopped. His black hair flowed down his back and his chest glistened in the last rays of the sun as if it had been oiled. His coral-colored eyes matched his Maii-a that flickered like a flame in the darkening woods. He was even more beautiful than before.

"Anna," he said. His voice rumbled around her.

"You're back." Her voice trembled. She had missed him so much.

He walked over and touched her face gently. She leaned into his hand. She could feel his warmth and his emotions. An inarticulate moan escaped from her lips. "Oh, Pemba."

"Rakan," he said, brushing through her hair with his other hand. "My name is Rakan."

Anna pulled back. "What?"

"Pemba isn't my real name."

Anna rubbed her bare arms, feeling suddenly cold. "Why didn't you tell me before?"

"When could I have told you?"

"Before I kissed you."

Rakan came closer. "I was trying to get you away from me, remember?"

"You still could have said something." She turned her head. He took her in his arms, but she squirmed away. "What else have you lied to me about?" she asked.

"Nothing."

Anna spun around. "Really? What about your parents' 'research project' to find June?"

Rakan's face closed. "Who told you about that?"

"See? You don't even deny it. You've lied to me about everything."

"No." He reached for her hands. She tried to pull them away, but he didn't let go. "Feel me, Anna," he said. "Reach inside as far as you can." He pressed her hands against his chest. "All you'll find is that I love you even though I shouldn't. I'm a dragon and you're a human. And I don't care."

Anna stopped struggling and slumped against him, breathing in his smell of incense.

His hold on her hands loosened and he wrapped her gently in his arms. "All I want is you, Anna. Nothing else."

"Pemba – Rakan, darn you." She pushed him away. "I can't just change your name like that." She had been calling him Pemba for the past four months.

"Then I don't care what you call me." He pulled her back in. "As long as I'm the one you're calling." He slipped his hands around her head and leaned forward. His lips burned against hers and his tongue found its way in with soft, insistent strokes.

Anna's tongue responded of its own accord and she melted into him. Literally. She couldn't tell where she ended and where he started. Their mixed desires pounded through her. She pulled back and broke the contact. "What happened?" She felt dizzy.

"Melding," he said. He ran his lips down her jaw line. She arched her neck and pressed into him as his teeth rubbed her skin, awakening a warmth deep within that made her forget her freezing feet. He bit her neck. His teeth sank into her and she groaned in pleasure. Anna felt a wave of power roll up inside Rakan and she clung to him as it exploded into her, gasping as it receded. An insatiable urge filled her and she bit his neck without warning. He gripped her so tightly that she nearly cried out in pain, but she didn't let go. Rakan dropped to his knees, pushing her legs apart so that she was straddling him. She arched back and held his head against her chest, squeezing him to her as hard as she could. Eventually she released him and leaned forward. Her fingers danced over his face and into his hair. Her mouth tasted of iron and she looked at his neck. "You're bleeding." Shame filled her. "I'm sorry."

"Don't be," he said, nuzzling her. "It's the only way you can mark me."

"And me?" Her hand went to her neck. There was no blood. "You didn't mark me?"

Rakan smiled. "Of course I did. But I'm a dragon. You're not."

She felt her neck again, it was smooth. "There's nothing."

"Yes, there is." He looked at her neck and ran his fingers gently over it. "Look." He put his hand on his neck and then withdrew it. Where she had bitten him was a small circle-like patch of slightly paler skin. A Firemark. Except it looked almost like a flower. A multi-petaled flower. She touched it. But all she felt was his smooth skin. She brushed her lips against his neck and felt an answering tingle. Her tongue explored the spot and it throbbed in response. She placed her mouth on it and knew it felt right. It was her mark. She bit him again. Rakan groaned and slipped his hands under her shirt. The feeling of his hands on her bare skin made her bite down even harder and he crushed her in his arms.

"You're cold," he said huskily, his hands firm on her hips.

"No, I'm fine." She pressed into him. "You're warm."

"We should go inside."

Anna groaned. "No. My mom will come home soon."

Rakan stood up, and she clung to him like a koala bear. "You'll freak her out," she said. She could barely see his eyes in the darkening woods even though the sky was a dramatic green-blue laced with steel grey clouds. But she knew they were orange.

"Here." Rakan set her down. "Better?" His eyes were brown and he was dressed in normal clothes.

"No." Anna unzipped his coat and pulled up his tee-shirt. She needed to feel his skin again.

"Firecat," he said. He picked her up and carried her across the parking lot.

"Look." She pointed behind him. "Northern Lights. In May." She wriggled out of his arms and turned him, holding his waist. "You never see them at this time of year."

Emerald green and cobalt blue streamed across the sky. The Northern Lights coalesced and then shot across the visible part of the sky in a shimmering array of colors that lasted no more than a split second, leaving only the lingering clouds. Anna searched the barren sky. They were gone. But they had felt alive. "June," she said, nodding her head. "June and Erling." She was sure. She knew their feeling.

"What?"

"It was June and Erling," Anna said, turning to Rakan.

"How can light be a person?"

Anna shrugged. "Because they aren't people? And Erling is an Elythia. Maybe he taught June how to do that?"

Rakan stood dead still.

"What? Why is that so strange? You're teaching me to do things humans can't usually do." Anna looked back up at the sky. There were only the scattered clouds, but no lights. "So why can't Erling teach June things that a Draak can't usually do?"

"What did you call Erling?"

Anna looked back at Rakan. "Uh, did I say something wrong?" He still hadn't moved. "Are you okay?"

Rakan gripped her shoulders. His hands were cold. "He's an Elythia? They're not all dead?"

"Isn't that why you were looking for June? Because she's dating an Elythia?"

"No. We were looking for Paaliaq. The dragon who killed Dvara's father. We thought June was Paaliaq, but she isn't…" Rakan's voice cracked. "Is she?"

"Dvara? Who's Dvara? Your sister? Dawa?" Anna searched Rakan's eyes in the artificial light of the parking lot. They were orange again. "You didn't know what Erling was?" What had she done now?

"No." Rakan sank to his knees. "I need to see Dvara," he said. And disappeared.

Chapter 27

Paaliaq

R AKAN BURST INTO HIS SISTER'S ROOM AND FOUND IT EMPTY. "DVARA," HE shouted.

"Hey, hey," Dvara said, coming in from the living room. "Easy. What's wrong now?"

"Erling. He's an Elythia."

She looked at him as if he had grown two heads. "None of them survived."

"Well apparently, they did." Rakan slammed his fist into the wall. "How could I have been so stupid?" He hadn't taken the time to analyze Kariaksuq's memories. He hadn't *had* the time. And now they were gone. All he had left was the flash impression from when he had held her rök. But as soon as Anna said Elythia it had linked to one of Kariaksuq's memories. "Erling means the Inheritor."

"And Paaliaq seduced the Inheritor." Dvara sank to the couch. "But Yarlung said Paaliaq made it up to scare the other Cairns into submission."

"No," Rakan said. "Kraal said Paaliaq wanted to use the Elythia to overthrow the other Cairns. That's why they attacked her."

"Where did you hear that?"

"I didn't. It's one of Kariaksuq's memories. They aren't all clear. But she was scared of the Elythia and the thought of Paaliaq allying with them terrified her."

"You mated with her and read her mind when you wouldn't read Anna's?" Dvara's anger lashed out at him like a whip.

"No. I took her rök. She wanted to die."

"Why did you do that?" Dvara jumped up to face him. "She didn't deserve to die in peace."

"She did what Yttresken told her to do," Rakan said coldly. "She had no choice." His hatred for Yttresken had multiplied after taking Kariaksuq's rök. "She never chose to be in his Cairn." Yttresken had grabbed her rök when her Kairök had died during the war.

"Anna," he said. He felt her running down the street. He bolted out of their rooms and down the stairs. He opened the door before she could ring. "What are you doing here? It's late. Come upstairs before Ani-la hears you."

"You can't stay," said Dvara to Anna when they came back up. "I need to talk with Rakan."

"She probably knows more than we do," Rakan said. "How do you think I learned about the Elythia?"

"From Kariaksuq," Dvara said.

"You saw her?" asked Anna.

"He killed her," snapped Dvara. "Why didn't you tell her that?"

"Stop bickering," yelled Rakan. "It doesn't help," he added more calmly. He faced the two girls who were staring at him. "June can't be Paaliaq. Not if she can go in the light. Only Elythia can go in the light."

"But June has a rök," Dvara said. "How do you explain that?"

"I don't know. Maybe she's a half-breed." Rakan glanced at Dvara. "You said Khotan had children with humans. Why couldn't a Draak and an Elythia have had offspring?"

"Amarualik might have known," Dvara said. She glared at Rakan.

Rakan walked back to his perch in the window and studied the street. It was dark even though the sky was still faintly greenish-blue. The only Elythia trail that was recent was Lysa's. The others were gone. He cursed.

"You can't kill her," Anna said quietly.

"We have to kill her," snapped Dvara.

Anna glared at Dvara. "You'll have to kill me first."

"No one is killing anyone, okay?" Rakan changed his dragon pants back to human clothes for the second time that evening. "I'll walk you home. Ingrid is worried." Rakan turned to Dvara as Anna walked down the stairs. "The sun will come back up soon. Meet me for the Call to Rise." He flashed her an image of a craggy peak in the Lyngen Alps.

Dvara didn't answer but he knew she'd be there. She needed to morph even more than he did. And she wasn't ready to do it alone.

෨෬

The dusk turned to dawn as the sun began to edge back up after having disappeared for a few hours. The thin veil of obscurity that had marked the night slipped around the edge of the earth. Rakan knelt on the mountain, facing the Eastern sky, his hands on his thighs. He waited for the earth around him to wake. He had needed some time alone. And now he was ready.

The flat greenish blue sky had only just begun to have a hint of purplish pink when Dvara arrived.

"They say Paaliaq could morph into all dragon forms," Rakan said.

"Yeah, right. And I can turn into light like an Elythia."

"I want to test that theory," continued Rakan.

"Don't be stupid." Dvara stood in front of him, her hands on her hips. "You'll kill yourself."

The last of the greens receded, giving way to the intense fuchsia that heralded the Call to Rise. "Something happened when I chased Kariaksuq."

Dvara snorted. "I noticed."

Rakan stood slowly and towered over his sister. "I need your help."

"To do what?" she asked warily.

"To answer the Call as a fire dragon."

"No," she hissed. She clenched her fists.

Rakan closed his eyes and opened his arms to the coming day. It was almost upon them. Every muscle of his body tensed in anticipation of the first electrifying kiss of light, and his fingers began to curl into claws. The first rays raced across the ground and touched him, igniting every fiber of his being with fire. His blood thickened and burned through his veins like molten lava.

"Rakan, stop. Don't do this. I can't lose you. I—"

Coral-colored fire burst forth from Rakan's mouth as his claws sank into the mountain. He could feel the heat that pulsed below, calling him in. He opened his eyes and rocked his head towards Dvara. She was crouched down in front of him, her back to the sun, her vermillion eyes wild.

"Idiot," she said, standing and dusting herself off. "Watch where you throw your fire." She walked around him, still ignoring the sun. "You had better be able to morph back."

Rakan snorted, sending small coral flames from his twitching nostrils. He stopped resisting and sank into the ground. The stone enveloped him and he felt like he was swimming through cold, wet sand. He dove towards the heat that radiated from below, gliding through the different layers of rock, testing each one as he descended. Suddenly, he felt Dvara next to him. He faced her, seeing her form in heat. She glistened and sparkled with an inner fire that made her look like a gemstone. She lunged towards him and then twisted back on herself in an undulating fluidity that made everything he had seen on Earth look clunky and heavy by comparison. Rakan stopped. Were all fire dragons so beautiful? He turned to try to see his body but only caught a glimpse of his tail before a ripple of movement reverberated through him. Caught off guard by the unexpected seism, he nearly morphed into his air dragon form but Dvara slammed into him, pushing him lower and deeper into the earth. The layers of brittle outer crust gave way to a semi-solid state and Rakan slowed down, enjoying the feeling of being one with the earth's mantle. A tantalizing smell of iron filled his senses and his skin itched. He dove towards the smell and launched himself into the liquid rock.

He groaned in pleasure as warmth enveloped him, wrapping him in its undulating movement. Carried by the current of the viscous lava, his scales tingled with pleasure as the thickly grained magma massaged every inch of his being. He stretched his stubby wings that had always seemed useless when he had looked at fire dragons and realized that they were perfectly adapted to maneuvering in lava. He glided on the currents in a movement that felt halfway between flying and swimming. His massive air wings would only get in the way here. And a streamlined water body with no wings at all wouldn't allow him to use the existing currents. Rakan floated in perfection.

He hit a warm spot and curled up. Sleep would be so peaceful, so complete. Dvara slammed into him from below and he turned to snap at her, but she was already swimming away. He growled and chased her. A deep chill racked his body as they shot back up to the surface. He felt his blood thin as they penetrated the surface layer of earth. He felt a moment of panic until he realized that his body was simply adapting to a different set of physical conditions. Dvara stopped and watched until he popped out onto the ground and morphed back to human without even bothering to stand up. He was exhausted. But at peace. He'd forever crave the heat and fluidity of the fire bed he had just discovered.

"Fire is the best," he muttered into the ridiculously immobile dirt.

Dvara curled up beside him, still in her dragon form. He felt her put up a shield as he slipped into an unconscious sleep.

Anna ran to school, her heart aching to feel Rakan again. But she slowed down and scowled when she saw Red leaning against the low stone wall at the intersection at the bottom of the hill where they had met every day last year to walk to school.

"School gotten that much better since I left?" asked Red, standing up as she arrived.

"Why are you here?"

"Just wanted to make sure you were okay."

"Why wouldn't I be?"

Red's forehead creased slightly. "Because I felt Pemba here last night."

"And you think he would hurt me?" Anna trembled with anger.

"I just don't want anything to happen to you. That's all."

"Why are you all convinced that Rakan—" Anna stopped abruptly. But it was too late.

"Rakan? His dragon name is Rakan? Why would he be called that?"

"What's wrong with the name Rakan?" asked Anna quietly, wishing she didn't always blurt things out.

Red sat back on the wall. "It means Fire. But he's not a fire dragon."

Anna sat next to him, a small smile tugging at her lips. "It suits him." She glanced at her cousin. "What's your dragon name?"

Red didn't answer right away. He just sat there fiddling with a rock he had picked up. "I don't use it anymore," he said finally. "I'm an outcast. By choice."

Anna felt Red's sadness and his pain. She scooted closer and nudged his shoulder. "Is that why you hide your energy? So that the others can't find you?"

Red examined the rock and nodded.

"But June... she's not an outcast, is she?"

"No," said Red slowly.

"Do you think she's Paaliaq?"

Red glanced quickly at Anna and then looked away. "I don't know anymore," he said. "I used to think she was because her energy feels like Paaliaq. And she looks like her. But she doesn't act anything like her. And yet she can mind-speak with Haakon."

Anna felt a flicker of excitement. "They can speak mentally? Like the Elythia?"

Red shot her a look. "How do you know that? No. Don't tell me. I don't want to know. But the Elythia are different. They can all speak to each other if they want, but only the higher ranking Elythia can initiate it. Whereas for the Draak, it has to do with being linked through their röks. Everyone in the same Cairn has a mind-link with all the others. So they can mind-speak anytime they want. But Ea is in the same Cairn as Haakon and she can't mind-speak with June." Red paused. "If June isn't Paaliaq, why can she mind-speak with Haakon? And if she is Paaliaq, why can't she mind-speak with Ea? In fact, June doesn't even realize Ea's a Draak, let alone one of her kais."

"Wait. June has kais? So she's the Kairök of Ea and Haakon's Cairn?" asked Anna, trying to understand.

"No. Not June, Paaliaq. But Paaliaq disappeared after a fight years ago. And they all keep looking for her. They thought – and Haakon still thinks – that June is Paaliaq. But I don't know. She ignores Ea completely. And Ea has been suffering because of it."

"So maybe Paaliaq's dead," Anna said hopefully.

"No. She can't be." Red tossed the rock back onto a patch of dirt. "She didn't let go of the röks she was holding and if she had died with them, her kais would've died too. And they didn't."

"But June isn't Paaliaq. She's never killed anyone. She doesn't even eat meat."

"Not as June, no. But Draak live in cycles, not years. From a human perspective Draak would seem immortal."

"You reincarnate?"

"No. We just try to look the same as other humans. But we aren't."

Anna sat thoughtfully. "Do your parents know?"

"Yes. And your father…" Red took Anna's hand in his, like he used to do when they were little. "I promised him to protect you. But I should've protected him too." Red traced her fingers with his other hand. "He didn't just die, Anna. He was killed. By a Draak." Red squeezed her hand tightly. "And I won't let that happen to you too."

Anna's hand trembled in his. "Who killed him?"

"Yarlung," said Red. "Rakan's mother."

Rakan leaned against the boulder at the top of the hill, feeling less calm than he appeared. He had felt Anna running down, but she had stopped to speak with Red. And hadn't come yet even though the bell had rung. He felt June coming up and turned. All the Elythia except for Lysa were gone. And Haakon was still with the Eld. June waved and ran up the hill to join him.

"Welcome back," she said, giving him a hug. "You've been gone a long time." She was radiating so much happiness that she almost seemed to shimmer in her own light. "You've changed," she said. "You're more… complete."

He looked at the halo that surrounded her. "You've changed too." It was brighter.

June turned toward the school. "Aren't you going in? Or are you waiting for Anna? It's okay, don't say anything, I felt the answer." June looked up the other hill that continued beyond the school where Anna was, even though she couldn't be seen. "She'll come."

Rakan knew that, but he didn't feel like waiting to see her. "Where's Erling?"

"His parents asked him to stay after we opened the second gate," June said, annoyed.

"What gates? You mentioned them before too." As well as not having her rök anymore after it. His fists clenched.

June's gaze shifted to the sky. "The gates that mark our union. We have to open all seven before we can become a true Pair."

"But there are no gates."

June smiled at Rakan. "To join Erling as his Chosen there are." She looked back up at the sky. "I can't even begin to tell you how good it feels.

It's like... being free of everything. You just let go and... the sky dances around you in a symphony of light and sound."

"It's not possible." He could feel her rök. "You're a Draak."

Anger exploded around him. June flipped Rakan over her shoulder before he even had time to react. "Never say that," she hissed. Her eyes flickered alternately blue and green. That, more than her violence, scared him. Eye color never changed.

"Easy," he said, lying still in the mud. "I'm not fighting you."

June knelt and helped him up "I'm sorry. I get so..."

"Emotional?" It wasn't the first time.

June looked away. "I really hate that about myself. I just can't talk about certain things... and I don't know why. It's as if something snaps in my mind."

"Maybe it does." Rakan let his mind slip forward gently, wondering what he could say and what would trigger another reaction. "I mean, maybe there are things you no longer are." He felt a flicker of fear run through June, but it stayed manageable. "Or maybe there are things you just don't want to remember," he said softly.

"Like my dreams? The pain? The planet exploding? You think they're real?" she asked, searching his eyes. "You think they're memories that I've repressed?"

"I don't know. The planet exploded before I was born."

"That's why you don't have that pain. That's why we can talk." She trembled. "I don't want to feel it anymore." She spoke, but Rakan wasn't sure she even registered his presence. "When we're in the sky, I don't feel anything."

He felt her begin to fade in his arms. Her opalescent trail of three twisted strands dissolved. A new trail, almost like an Elythia's, took its place. Shining a bright emerald green. He gripped her arms tighter. "No," he said. "Don't do that." His own trail caught his eyes. Running through the middle was a triple twisted strand. Just like June's. "June, snap out of it." He shook her.

She looked blankly at him, her eyes shimmering orbs of emerald light. "Sverd and Verje will appear shortly."

"Did they just tell you that?" asked Rakan, trying to meet her eyes. Trying to get her attention back on him, back on the world around them. Her rök was fading.

"No, I can see it," she said, her voice echoing slightly. "And just before they appear, you will attack me."

"But I don't want to attack you. I want to help you be yourself."

"But this is me," June said with a sad smile. "This is what I want to be. And when you see what that is, you'll attack me."

"No," Rakan said. "I won't. June, stop."

The air shimmered around her and she stood before him in a white gown. But it wasn't a dragon gown. It was made of particles of light. And she had two enormous wings of green feathers. Her face radiated peace, but in the split second before her rök disappeared, he had felt dozens of röks throbbing below the surface. He panicked. They'd die if she turned into an Elythia. He lunged for her. A flash of purple and green light erupted around him and he was flung against the rock.

She was gone.

Rakan howled in rage and shook his fists at the green and purple lights that played in the sky as if nothing was wrong. June was Paaliaq. Or she used to be. She was changing, becoming an Elythia. But at what price? He wouldn't just stand by and let Paaliaq's kais die.

Chapter 28

Choices

Lysa and Dvara shifted simultaneously in front of Rakan. "What happened?" hissed Dvara, pushing Lysa out of the way, ready to fight.

"Why did you attack her?" asked Lysa. "You said you wouldn't."

"I saw her kais."

"What?" said Dvara. "Why didn't you kill her?"

Lysa threw a punch at Dvara's face, but Dvara blocked and counter attacked. Lysa dodged her attack so quickly he almost thought she had shifted, except she hadn't. Dvara snarled and the two lunged for each other.

"Would you knock it off?" Rakan pushed them apart and received a double hook for his trouble.

Red appeared. "What's going on? Where's June?"

"The twins were sent to get her," said Lysa.

"What do they want now?" asked Red, his fists clenched.

"She needs to pass the Test of Refusal," said Lysa calmly, her eyes only half focused on Red.

"What?" Red threw himself at Lysa but she flashed out of his way, leaving him stumbling where she had been standing. He growled and spun around to face her again. "Where are they?"

"What's the Test of Refusal?" asked Anna, breathing hard from her run. "And why are you all fighting?"

"Liv refused to pair with Erling, even though she was born to be his Chosen," said Lysa as if reciting a lesson. "My brother chose Paaliaq and Liv chose Haakon."

"So what's the problem?" asked Anna.

"Elythia can only pair once," said Lysa. "It's a lifelong bond."

"What?" Dvara said. "And if you make a mistake?"

"You can't," said Lysa. "Only beings whose energy match can merge."

"But what if they don't love each other?" asked Anna.

Lysa looked down. "Love is a fleeting emotion that blinds."

"What happens during the Test of Refusal?" asked Rakan.

"I don't know," said Lysa. "Liv and Erling never bonded. But they were supposed to. No Pair has ever refused their match before. This will be the first in our history. I hope a test of strength will suffice."

"Between who?" asked Red, his voice barely more than a growl. "Liv and Erling?"

"No. I don't think so. Liv is the one who officially refused, since Erling is the Inheritor. So I assume it will be between Liv, the Refuser, and June, the new Chosen."

Red lunged again for Lysa. But she wasn't there. He spun around and hissed.

"I'm not responsible," said Lysa from where Red had been standing.

"But you know where they are," he said. He strode over to her. "Take us there."

"I've been told not to." Her face went distant. "It just started. Oh, no. Not like that."

"Like what?" asked Dvara.

Lysa's eyes glowed pale green. "June and Haakon are to fight the twins. Liv and Erling are watching. They've joined their energy. I don't under-stand. June's not fighting. She's watching Erling and Liv. The twins have attacked Haakon. This is wrong."

"Haakon is fighting the twins?" asked Anna. "They'll kill him."

Red grabbed Lysa. "Show me where they are. I'll go on my own."

"No. They have to fight. And then June and Erling can become the Inheritors."

"No," hissed Rakan. "Her kais will die. I saw them. They're suffering."

"You saw them?" said Red, spinning to face Rakan. "You're sure?"

"Yes."

"Damn it," said Red. He took a deep breath. "Lysa, you have to help us stop this. June can't become Erling's Chosen. She doesn't even know she has her kais anymore. Even if she survives giving up her rök, her kais won't. Ea will die. They'll all die."

"I know that," said Lysa, clenching her fists. "But we can't intervene. My brother has chosen June." Lysa groaned. "Why won't she fight? They're crippling Haakon." Lysa punched Red in the chest. "Why won't she free her kais? Why didn't you get Haakon to do it for her?"

Red took the punch without reacting. "Because he can't. We've tried."

"Why do you even have Kairöks? It's a ridiculous system." Lysa shimmered. Pale green light emanated from her. "This is wrong. They'll kill Haakon. It's gone too far." A blaze of light burst through Rakan. He lost all sense of where anything was. The material world had vanished. He couldn't even morph.

Suddenly, they were on a dune in a desert and Anna stumbled into Lysa. They scuttled out of the way of the three dragons snorting and stomping beside them. She recognized Rakan's coral-colored orange. He stood on his hind legs, wings outstretched. He howled in rage and Anna ducked to the ground holding her ears. The larger, brick-red dragon next to him felt like her cousin. The shorter, more compact one was Dvara. Anna took a few more steps back. They were huge. And Dvara's pitch black crest instilled a fear in Anna that she couldn't control.

An opaque dome shimmered like a mirage on the desert below. But before she could ask Lysa what it was, Lysa disappeared in a flash of pale green light that merged into the dome. The dome flickered and the sounds of the fight burst in her ears. Lysa was undoing the shield. The dome paled and she could see them. The twins were pulverizing Haakon.

It was as Lysa had said. June was staring at Erling and Liv. They stood, their wings outstretched in two different shades of blue, on a dais. A circle of blue light surrounded them all. Anna did a double-take. The light was coming from Liv and Erling. Why weren't they stopping it instead of standing there as if they were about to open a ball? Haakon fell to the ground. He stood back up and lunged for one of the twins, only to be sent flying once again. They were killing him. Anna screamed and ran towards the barely visible dome. Rakan morphed back to human and ran after her.

"Don't touch it," he yelled. Coral-colored sparks flickered in front of him as he approached the dome.

Anna ignored him and ran through it. After a split second which felt like being skinned alive, she was inside the circle. The smell of blood and anger throbbed everywhere, choking her.

"Do something," she yelled at June. She pushed her friend fiercely. "Stop the twins before they kill Haakon. Why doesn't Liv do something? Doesn't she care about her boyfriend?"

June's eyes snapped to Anna and she came to life, roaring in rage. Anna stumbled backwards as June morphed into an enormous emerald green dragon with a magnificent gold crest. She bellowed and the ground trembled as if a gong was ringing deep within the earth. The circle fell suddenly silent. All eyes turned to June. She twisted in rage and flew at Liv, her black claws outstretched and her jaws ready to snap.

"No," yelled Anna. "Don't kill her!" She lunged toward the dais, desperate to stop the fighting, but a flash of opalescent light blinded her and she fell to the ground.

When she looked up again they were gone. Rakan scooped her up in his arms and squeezed her to his bare chest, his Maii-a flashing wildly. Dvara tore at the ground where the dais had been, snorting and bellowing in rage. Out of nowhere an indigo blue dragon with a flashing platinum crest slammed into Dvara, his jaws on her neck.

Anna screamed.

"Let T'eng Sten deal with Dvara," Rakan said, holding her tighter. "She's gone wild."

"But he's killing her," she yelled. She thrashed in his arms.

"Anna, listen to me. Sh. Calm down." He surrounded her in a warm mind-touch. "You're going wild too."

"What?" Anna felt sick as the tension washed out from her body. She leaned into Rakan and held onto him. "Where are they? Are they still fighting?"

"No. It's over," he said into her hair. "I thought you were going to kill yourself running through the shield like that." He held her tighter. "Don't ever do that again."

Dvara stopped struggling. The ground was covered in blood. Anna pushed out of Rakan's arms and went over to her. "Is she okay?" Anna asked, reaching out to touch Dvara's vermillion dragon face. It was nearly as big as Anna's torso. "Did you kill her?" she yelled at the indigo dragon. She recognized him as Torsten even before he morphed back to human.

Dvara's eyes flashed open. She melted into the ground. "Dvara!" Anna
yelled.

Anna's pain pierced through Rakan. "She'll be okay," he said. He
wrapped her in his arms and she trembled against him.

"She needs time," said T'eng Sten.

"I thought you were in the Hold," Rakan said without letting go of
Anna.

"The Eld ruled to set me free once the Meet started again."

"But then how did Haakon get here? The Eld would never have stopped
the Meet for this."

"I don't know. They stopped the Meet just before the Ascended called
for Haakon."

"They know about the Elythia, but don't say anything?"

"Do they ever say anything?" T'eng Sten came closer. "Do you?"

"He won't say anything," Anna interrupted.

"I heard about your blood pact, Rakan'dzor." T'eng Sten's nostrils flared.
"How could you have been so stupid?"

"I didn't think she was Paaliaq." Rakan held his ground. "You should
have told me."

T'eng Sten snorted. "Telling you at the time would've been equivalent
to telling Yarlung. Or have you forgotten? You're the one who should've
told me about the blood pact when it was made. I might have been able to
deactivate it. It's too late now."

"Wait," Anna said. "What blood pact?"

"Rakan swore with his own blood to kill Paaliaq. And if he doesn't, any
dragon anywhere can kill him." T'eng Sten stiffened. "Damn her," he said
and disappeared.

Rakan pushed Anna behind him and faced the east just as Khotan and
Yarlung appeared with Yuli and Nima'kor right behind them. He searched
quickly with his mind-touch, wondering if Dvara had gone and told
them. But he neither smelled nor felt her trail on them. *Damn Yarlung*, he
thought, echoing T'eng Sten.

"Where is she?" hissed Yarlung, scanning the desert.

"I don't know." Rakan cursed himself for not having shifted Anna elsewhere.

"I felt the poison react when she morphed," said Yarlung. Her dress sparkled a blindingly pure white. "She was here."

"What poison?" asked Rakan.

"The one you so kindly gave her when she neutralized yours," said Yarlung, her voice silky sweet. "I made it especially for her. I knew she'd get close to you."

Rakan's fists clenched of their own accord but he bit down his anger. He needed to protect Anna.

Yarlung smelled the air. "I'd know her smell anywhere, even after all these years." She twirled to face Khotan. "How could we have missed her? I thought you said the trigger would be immediate."

"The shield slowed it down," said Khotan, pointing to where the Elythia ring had been. "Or we would have been here when she was most vulnerable."

"I can't even see where she went," hissed Yarlung, walking around the circle. Her eyes fell on Anna. "Is this the little human?" Yarlung's mind-touch flicked out like a snake and smashed through Rakan's protective shield. Anna cried out in fear and clung to Rakan. An indigo flash sent Yarlung flying backwards. Nima'kor launched into the air, morphing into a bright yellow dragon, turquoise claws outstretched.

"Trust me," hissed Rakan, shifting Anna to their lair without waiting for an answer.

It took Anna a few moments to realize that they were standing in Rakan's living room in the Tibetan House. Alone. Unharmed. Rakan was brushing her hair with his hands and murmuring something, but she was too panicked to understand what he was saying.

"Where are they?" she asked, clinging to Rakan.

"They can't come through T'eng Sten's shields. You're safe."

"Yes, but..." she began, but Rakan's lips found hers. They were so warm, so soft, so full of life... she responded, needing to feel his energy. Fire burned through her. Rakan's fire. His hand slid to her lower back, angling her into him as the fire continued to spread. "Fire," she said into his neck. "Rakan. What does dzor mean?"

Rakan pulled back surprised. "Dzor? It means bird. Why?"

"So you're a firebird?" Her hands wandered up his chest and over his face.

"My full name is Rakan'dzor Sa'aq. The Flowing Firebird of Aq." Rakan leaned his head against hers, his hair enveloping them both. "I've never told anyone that before. You're the first." His lips brushed slowly against hers. He took the time to explore them before gently going deeper, stoking the already burning fire that threatened to explode from her aching body. *"Let go,"* she felt him say and she did. She dissolved into him. They melded and she had no idea where her body ended or his started. And she didn't care. She let herself flow into his burning passion that throbbed like lava. Until a freezing cold drip oozed down the back of her skull and she gasped in pain and shock.

"I'll kill Liv," hissed Rakan. Anna's head swam and Rakan steadied her. "I'm so sorry, Anna," he said, holding her close. "How can you ever forgive me for everything that has been done to you?"

"It's not your fault."

"Yes, it is. I shouldn't have gotten close to you."

"I shouldn't have set off the trigger."

Rakan kissed her hair. "Maybe you should never have kissed me either."

"Probably not," she said, finding his lips. "Should I stop?"

"No," he mumbled into her lips. "Never."

"Good," she said, wrapping her hands around his head and pulling him in. But he didn't meld with her. "What's wrong?"

"Even though I don't like it, I knew about Liv's shield. Although I didn't realize it would stop us from melding completely. Still, I knew it was there."

"But?"

"I didn't know about T'eng Sten's."

"T'eng Sten? When? He never touched me."

"But it was his shield that protected you from my mother's mental attack. Not mine."

Anna's knees almost gave way. "That was your mother?" *Her father's murderer?*

"Yes." Rakan closed his eyes. "Can I look into your mind to see when he placed it?"

"Will you see everything?" She wasn't ready for that.

"No. Only the memory and when he placed it." Rakan paused. "And I'd like to check if there are any other shields, if you'll let me."

Anna hugged him. His warmth spread through her and she wished they could just meld again. "Will it hurt?"

"It shouldn't. But if I feel any pain, I'll pull out. Okay?"

She nodded and felt him surround her. She tried to let go but couldn't.

"You're too tense," he said, tilting her chin up to his. "Relax." He nuzzled her face and the knot that had gripped her insides eased away. She reached for his lips. Suddenly, she saw the second floor corridor at school, Rakan shifting in front of her, T'eng Sten and two other shapeshifters between him and Dvara. She dug her nails into Rakan and screamed.

"It's okay, it's over," Rakan said. "It happened the day of the first sun rise."

Anna trembled uncontrollably. She had felt herself transported into the hallway, not into a memory. She leaned against Rakan. "He erased my mind, didn't he? Just like Red did to Ulf. And I would never have known." She put a hand on Rakan's face. "Promise me never, ever to do anything like that. To me. Or to anyone else."

"I don't have to promise. I don't know how."

"Good." She paused. "But then you don't know how to remove it?"

"I might. But I'd rather T'eng Sten did it. Just in case there's a trigger I didn't feel."

Anna nodded. She'd have to ask Liv to remove the one she had placed as well. After the events of the past few days, everyone seemed to know everything. She walked over to the window. "Did you feel anything else?"

"No. Just T'eng Sten's repression of that one memory and his shield to protect you from any dragon's unwanted mental probing. His shield reacted first to my mother because it was set to be triggered when the intent was felt." Rakan's voice was full of respect.

Anna looked back at Rakan. She still had an uncontrollable loathing of T'eng Sten. No matter what anyone told her about him. "Could he have made it so I hate him?"

"Maybe. He didn't actually delete the memory. He just transformed part of it and suppressed the other with a shield. He's much more respectful than I ever gave him credit for." Rakan paused. "But maybe that's because I've only ever known my mother's way of doing things."

"What are you going to do about the blood pact?"

"There's nothing I can do."

"Will you kill her?"

Rakan came and stood in front of Anna. He took her hand in his and turned it over so he could see the Firemark. He traced it with his fingers and it blazed coral. "No."

Anna threw herself into his arms. "You can learn to hide like Red has. We could hide together somewhere."

Rakan held her gently. "I can't live my life hiding, Anna. And I'd never ask you to live that way either." He cradled her face in his hands and brushed the tears away from her cheeks with his thumbs. "I won't kill her and I'll face the consequences."

Anna nodded and gripped him tighter. "I love you," she whispered. Her mind slipped into his and she felt herself expand in an undulating wave of warmth.

"I love you, my firecat," he answered in her mind.

Rakan pulled back slowly, carefully extracting his mind from Anna's. Yarlung and Khotan had left. And he needed to confront them. Anna resisted, and he smiled. "I'd rather stay here, too. But if I don't stop Yarlung, she'll kill June herself."

Anna dropped her hands. "What are you going to do?"

"Try to convince my parents not to kill June."

"Will they listen?"

"Probably not. Maybe T'eng Sten can help. Or the Eld. If I can speak with them." Rakan stood next to her by the window. "But what I do know is that if they kill June now, they'll kill her kais too."

"But is she really Paaliaq?"

"Yes. No. Or maybe a fragment of Paaliaq. I don't know. But I saw her kais."

"Would you kill her if there weren't any kais?"

"No," Rakan said. "Not June. But I don't know what she was like before." He held up a hand to keep Anna from interrupting him. "June isn't like any of the stories I heard about Paaliaq. She isn't the Destroyer." He looked out the window. "But no one with a rök can go in the light. So she's changed in ways that shouldn't be possible. Whoever or whatever June is now, she isn't Paaliaq anymore."

Anna slid her hands around Rakan's waist. "Will I see you again?"

He took her face in his hands and kissed her. *"I don't know."*

Rakan shifted onto the ledge outside his father's lair. He needed to gather his thoughts before he could face Khotan and Dvara. They were inside, tense with excitement. He looked at the empty plateau and breathed in deeply. The air was moist and the earth was stirring. Life, as meager as it was, was everywhere. He stretched his arms and embraced it. His mind sank into the land he had grown up with. The land he had loved. He dropped his arms. The land he would join all too soon. He turned and entered Khotan's lair.

"Rakan," said his father. "I wasn't sure you'd come. Are you alright?"

Rakan nodded. He didn't want to talk about their last encounter. "I take it the Meet started again?" Otherwise Yarlung would have come as soon as he arrived. And he was glad she hadn't.

"Yes. Did you find Paaliaq?" he asked. "We can't locate her."

"I don't know where June is. But even if I did, I wouldn't tell you."

"Why not?" snapped Dvara. "How can you doubt who she is anymore? You saw her."

"Yes. But I've also seen her morph into an Elythia. And no Draak can do that."

"Yeah, well, no Elythia can turn into an emerald green dragon either."

"So she's neither a Draak nor an Elythia. She isn't Paaliaq."

Dvara threw her hands up. "You drive me crazy. Why'd you come here?"

"Did you know the Elythia had survived?" he asked his father.

"No. No one knew. And Yarlung wishes to keep it a secret."

Rakan nodded. For once he agreed with his mother. The hatred for the Elythia hadn't diminished even with their presumed extinction. "Could a Draak and an Elythia have offspring?"

Khotan stroked his chin thoughtfully. "Theoretically, yes, since humans and Draak can. But I doubt it'll ever happen. There has been too much hatred. And even if it did, the children probably wouldn't survive very long anyway." Khotan paused and added quietly. "Just as with the human-Draak children."

"Well, if June isn't a mix of the two, then she's changed so deeply that she's no longer Paaliaq. Either way, we shouldn't kill her."

Dvara snorted. "It doesn't matter who she is. If we kill her we can start a new life. We'll all be free."

"But her kais will die."

"She'll free them."

"No, she won't." Rakan sank into his favorite chair. "She doesn't even know they're there. I don't know how to explain what I saw. It's like they're in suspension. They're suffering."

"It's not our problem," Dvara said.

"Yes, it is. I can't just let them die. There are over a hundred of them. Father, can't you make Yarlung understand that?"

Khotan shook his head. "No."

"Can't you even try?"

"There are some things you can't change, Rakan. Yarlung was my Kairök. She won't listen to me."

"But she isn't anymore—"

Khotan held up a hand, silencing Rakan. "Even when she gave me back my rök, I knew I'd have to choose my battles. I was willing to give up almost everything. But there was one thing I couldn't," said Khotan. "And that was you. I fought her to have you here with me and Dvara. And I'll never regret what she made me accept in order to have that."

"What did she make you accept?" Rakan asked warily.

Khotan growled and turned his back. But Rakan could feel his father's pain.

"He can't talk about it, okay?" snapped Dvara. She squared her shoulders and crossed her arms. "But I can, since I'm no longer connected to him."

She looked defiantly at Khotan and then back at Rakan. "Why haven't you ever wondered how he and Yarlung can speak? He has his rök."

Rakan felt his pulse slow down. "Kraal's poison." He had never questioned that they could mind-link. They always had.

"No. Her own. And she made it so that no one, not even her, can remove it without killing Khotan."

Khotan walked towards the fire that flickered in the stone hearth. "It's okay." His voice was choked. He leaned against the stone mantle. "I have chosen my final battle." He faced Rakan. "I will give my life so that you and Dvara can live yours. Remember that, when the time comes," he said. "It is my choice."

Rakan stared at his father's outline, wondering how to protect June from a suicide attack without anyone getting hurt. Including his father.

Chapter 29

The Ultimate Sacrifice

RAKAN PACED HIS FATHER'S LAIR. HE WANTED TO GO BACK TO ANNA, BUT IF the Meet adjourned he wouldn't feel it in Tromso. Especially not if he was with Anna... he shut his eyes, imagining her lips press against his, her energy that felt like a shielder's mingle with his. Warmth filled his body and he realized a second too late that he was being shifted by one of the Eld.

"You disappoint me," said the disembodied voice of the Trailer Eld before dropping him into a free fall.

Rakan flipped in midair and landed on his feet, both knives drawn, ready to fight. The rotunda had been restructured so that the Eld were clearly in charge. They were seated behind a stone podium facing a semi-circle of Kairöks on their thrones. The alcoves behind the Eld were empty. Rakan straightened and put his knives away. They'd be useless anyway. He faced the Eld.

"Show us your memory of Paaliaq," they said in unison.

"No," Rakan answered. A murmur of surprise rippled behind him.

"It was not a request." The Mind Eld stood. The rust and iron lining of her cloak flashed brightly. She spread her hands. An image appeared of June launching herself at Liv and Erling. Their wings and fair hair left no doubt as to their identity as Elythia. The rotunda broke into cries of anger and hatred that intensified as June morphed into an emerald green dragon with a gold crest, her black claws stretched to attack Liv. Fury exploded within Rakan and the image shattered. But it was too late. Everyone had seen June as Paaliaq. And they had seen the Elythia.

"Well," said T'eng Sten coolly, his voice carrying above the mayhem. "I suppose that disproves Haakaramanoth's claim to having taken Paaliaq's place as Kairök after she died. Perhaps he should leave now."

A gong sounded. "Kairök Haakaramanoth's position is not subject to discussion. He remains," said the Eld. "The question at hand is Kairök Yarlung's claim to have found Kairök Paaliaq."

"But the Elythia are alive. Who cares about Paaliaq?" cried Kairök Japetus.

"Silence. Kairök Yarlung's claim is legitimate. A duel between Kairök Yarlung and Kairök Paaliaq will be held at the next Call to Rise. The Elythia will be left alone as per our truce."

"What truce? We thought they were dead."

"We signed a truce with the Ascended after the war." The mention of the Elythian rulers brought a communal hiss of anger from the assembly. "Enough. The Draak and the Elythia will forever remain apart. The truce remains." The Eld's statements caused an uproar.

"A duel can't be set without both parties being present," stated Kairök Tetherys, once silence had been restored.

"Kairök Paaliaq is being summoned." Another ripple of anger travelled around the rotunda. Rakan clenched his fists, ready to protect June.

A tense silence filled the hall as the Eld shimmered, searching for June. Rakan hoped that she was in the light. Even if her kais were suffering, it would be better than being called into the Meet. Time dragged on and Rakan glanced at Haakon. His face was immobile and he seemed unconcerned until Rakan noticed the tension in his jaw.

The flickering light of the huge torches that had been installed for the trial made the rotunda look like the inside of a dead dragon's ribcage. Rakan looked closer. The torches were made of the black metal known as kor. The only metal not found on Earth. And the only metal that could slice through a dragon's hide. But they didn't feel like the metal of his knives. They felt cold to his mind-touch. And strangely empty. The flames that licked up the sides of the vault gave no light. Instead they absorbed it, making the dark markings that looked like ribs. It was a shield, disguised as light. Or rather, a shield against light. A shield against the Elythia. Maybe the Eld weren't as sure of the Elythian adherence to the truce as they tried to appear.

The enforced silence began to weigh on Rakan. All but the Kairöks were shifting their weight uneasily. Rakan hadn't noticed before, but Haakon didn't have the standard two bodyguards with him. Rakan felt Haakon's awareness turn to him, even though he didn't move. Rakan resisted the urge to look away. He focused on Haakon's trail. It wasn't a Kairök's, but it wasn't exactly a kai's either. And it occasionally shimmered oxidized green.

Rakan felt a strange sense of calm wrap around him. A wave of warmth filled him and he floated in limbo. Rakan forced himself to resist, but it was too strong. The Eld were altering his perception of time, and there was nothing he could do.

When he came back to himself everything was as it had been. Except that June was curled up on a stone throne that had been added next to Haakon's. Rakan cursed himself for not having been able to resist the Eld's manipulation of his center of gravity. He hadn't seen her arrive and had no idea how long she had been there. The Kairöks were fully awake, but most of the kais were unnaturally still. The Eld were speaking but he couldn't catch what they were saying. He focused on June. She looked out of place in jeans and a plain black turtleneck, her hair in a ponytail.

"The Meet can now be adjourned."

Rakan forced himself into motion and staggered forward. The air was as thick and cloying as mud. "June isn't Paaliaq," he said. Angry cries greeted his words. "Could Paaliaq go in the light?" asked Rakan, raising his voice to be heard.

"Of course not," said Kairök Tetherys. "No Draak can."

"June can. She isn't Paaliaq. There's no fight."

"Rakan, that's enough. How dare you interrupt?" snapped Yarlung.

Rakan walked towards June. But she didn't react to his presence. The throne was nearly as high as he was and she was curled up in a corner. He put a hand on her leg. Her head jerked up like a rabid animal's and Rakan cursed his mother's poison. June's eyes were a wild mix of blue and green and he wasn't even sure if she could hear him. "June? Are you okay?"

"Pemba?" she said, her eyes not quite focusing on him. "What are you doing here?"

"You need to go in the light."

"Why?"

"Because even if you are Paaliaq, you've changed. And you can prove it."

"I have nothing to prove."

"You can stop the fight."

June gave him a sad smile. "Maybe I don't want to."

The Eld stood in unison. "Enough. There will be no discussion. How she has evolved is of no concern to us. Her trail is that of Kairök Paaliaq. The Code applies."

Rakan tried to protest, but the Eld silenced him.

Haakon strode over to the Eld. "She's in no shape to fight."

"It's just a show," hissed Yarlung. "Smell her. She's made herself seem even younger than she was when she killed Kraal. How can you believe anything in her appearance? She's always manipulated everyone—" Yarlung's voice was drowned in the uproar that greeted her words.

"Then I will fight Paaliaq," Rakan said, facing the Eld. "I will uphold the Code. There was a stunned silence.

"How can you uphold the Code when you prefer a human mate over a dragon?" said the Eld, speaking as one.

The uproar re-ignited and Rakan wondered if the Eld were doing it on purpose. He waited for the snorting and hollering to calm down. "My private life has nothing to do with this," he said calmly. He knew what he had to do.

"It does, when you put the survival of the human race in peril by exposing our existence. They are incapable of understanding." The Trailer Eld put up a hand for silence. "The humans belong here. Their extinction is not desirable." The copper eyed Eld leaned forward. "Why did you refuse to mate with Kariaksuq, Angalaan or Yuli? Even if you wanted to take the human—" A murmur of displeasure rose and the Trailer Eld once again lifted her hand. "Silence. The only Kairök who hasn't taken a human here is T'eng Sten." She turned back to Rakan. "There was still no reason to turn from your own kind."

Rakan bowed his head. He needed to get the conversation off of Anna. "I was not yet one with my rök. But now I am." He stood on the black sand in the middle of the rotunda and hit a fist to his chest. "I request the right to uphold my blood pact—" Rakan let the noise die down. "The blood pact that I entered upon with Kairök Yarlung."

The Eld turned to Yarlung. "Show us."

Yarlung snarled, but she extended her hands and the coral-colored water dragon appeared. The rotunda fell silent as the miniature dragon swam to the Eld.

The Trigger Eld held out his hand and the dragon alighted. "The blood pact is real," he said, holding his hand high. "But you can't replace her. You aren't a Kairök."

"I am a Kairök. I have held another dragon's rök." He morphed into his air dragon form and spread his black claws. He felt the Eld search him and he pushed them out in a wild rage, spraying them with his fire. No one had the right to do that.

A tumultuous uproar exploded.

"Indeed," said the Trigger Eld, eyeing him carefully. "So you have."

Rakan morphed back to human.

"Although your motivation is still unclear. But even if it were, you have no second since Kariaksuq, your only kai, is dead. You are not technically a Kairök right now."

"That can be remedied," Rakan said, his anger flowing towards the Eld. "I refused to take Yuli because she belongs to my mother. Let me have her rök and I will fight."

"I will offer a kai to Rakan," said T'eng Sten. He jumped off his throne in a flash of indigo and platinum. He joined Rakan in front of the podium.

"That won't be necessary," said Yarlung. "I can offer Rakan'dzor Nima'kor, a much stronger second than Yuli or any of Kairök T'eng Sten's kais."

Rakan clenched his fists. If there was any kai of his mother's he didn't want, it was Nima'kor. He should never have tried to save Yuli instead of asking T'eng Sten for a kai.

The Eld shimmered in silent discussion. A gong sounded. "Kairök Paaliaq will face Kairök Rakan'dzor. They will be seconded by Haakaramanoth and Yuli."

Yarlung started to hiss, but was silenced by a flash of platinum as the Transformer Eld spread his fingers and drew a circle in the air. Yuli's sparkling lime-green rök appeared, floating between the Eld's brilliantly shimmering fingers that reflected Yuli's fire in a crackling display of sparks.

The Transformer Eld turned to Rakan, his platinum eyes reflecting Rakan's coral. "We are willing to grant you the care of Yuli's rök if you agree to the terms of the fight."

As disturbing as it was to see his own eyes reflected back at him, Rakan held the Eld's stare. "If the outcome of this duel is final, no matter what that outcome is, then I do. I will fight Paaliaq and I will fight to the death." He allowed his hatred of the Eld to project out, hoping his motives wouldn't be questioned further.

Next to him, he could feel T'eng Sten's anger. Behind him, his mother crooned in pleasure. The Kairöks, at least, believed he would fight to kill.

The Eld's eyes narrowed. But he said nothing. He simply spread his hands and Rakan instinctively reached out and took Yuli's rök before she had time to feel the panic of being alone. She burst into his consciousness with a flood of terror and relief all mixed together.

"Hold back," he snapped and she disappeared to the back of his mind.

"Then so be it," said the Eld. The gong sounded.

He would fight. And he would die. And he'd have to find a new home for Yuli. He'd never give her back to Yarlung.

"No," said Khotan from under the arch where he had been standing. "Circumstances may have made Rakan'dzor a Kairök before his time, but nothing changes the fact that he is barely more than an acolyte. He hasn't even filled out completely, as anyone here can see."

The rotunda fell silent as all eyes turned to see how the Eld would react.

Khotan walked forward, his head held high. "I request a parent's right to replace his offspring in a duel to the death, as permitted by the Code. The fight is not his. It is ours."

"It is time that Rakan'dzor prove himself," they answered.

"He has nothing to prove. His rök is free."

"Then he is ready to die."

Khotan trembled in rage. "You're supposed to protect us, not destroy us."

"It's alright, Father," Rakan said. "It's my choice."

"I should be the one to fight Paaliaq," Dvara said, coming forward. T'eng Sten turned to block her, but was stopped by the Eld. Dvara tilted her chin. "Kraal was my father."

"Go home," snapped Khotan. "You're in no state to fight anyone."

Dvara launched herself at Khotan, morphing in a streak of vermillion in midair. Rakan lunged and slammed Khotan out of her path. He morphed to neutralize her, but the Trigger Eld had morphed into a nearly transparent fire dragon and held her to the ground. Rakan stared. His crest, his eyes, his claws and his hide were all the same translucent grey. He could make out a shadowy version of Dvara's vermillion through the Eld's body.

Once again, the platinum eyed Transformer Eld spread his fingers and Dvara's jewel-like vermillion rök appeared. The Eld turned to T'eng Sten. "Do you accept the care of Dvara Azura's rök?"

"No!" yelled Dvara, twisting in agony. "He won't let me kill Paaliaq."

T'eng Sten bowed his head. "I'll wait until she's ready to give it to me."

"You may refuse," said the Eld. "But her rök can't wait." He spread his hands. The rök flew in the air and a mad scramble ensued, pierced only by Dvara's screeching agony.

T'eng Sten emerged from the scuffle with Dvara's rök, seething with rage. "How can you treat someone's rök like that? Have you no respect for anyone or anything?" He spit on the ground. "You force us to your will in a barbaric distortion of the Code."

"What Dvara desired was irrelevant," said the Transformer Eld sharply. "As you will see when you take her to your lair and unblock the walls she has erected within her rök. She can no longer be alone, and you knew that. But instead of taking her you let her suffer in a misguided desire to let her choose, because of your own pride in wanting her to come to you. You have failed as a Kairök. We will reconvene for the Call to Rise tomorrow."

"Wait," said Haakon, his voice booming throughout the rotunda.

"Speak," said the Eld, once again in unison.

"Given the animosity between Yarlung and Paaliaq, I request that the fight take place on neutral ground in the open."

"Oh, Haakon," June said, speaking for the first time. "Who cares? It makes no difference. Let's go."

"Request granted," said the Eld as one and disappeared.

The pent up tension exploded and the rotunda became a squabbling mass. Rakan ignored it and mind-touched Yuli. She sprang to life inside him. He'd have to figure out how to block her a bit. *"We'll go to my father's,"* he said, not sure he wanted someone else in his rök right now.

"I can block myself," she said, dimming her presence. *"I saw more of you than you intended right there,"* she added sheepishly. *"Thank you, Rakan'dzor Sa'aq."*

Rakan met Yuli's eyes and nodded, but before they could shift, Yarlung came up. "You have grown since taking Kariaksuq's rök," she said. She touched his cheek with her fingertips. "You have come into your power."

Rakan bowed, breaking the contact. "I must prepare."

"Paaliaq's greatest weakness is her pride. Pretend to be weaker than you are and let her think she is dominating you." Yarlung leaned closer and the smell of cold salt filled his nostrils. "Her rök is unlike any other: it has multiple parts and is ungraspable except for the split second before she goes for the kill. It's the only moment she is vulnerable." Yarlung cupped his chin. "Remember that." She dropped her hand and shifted out of the rotunda, taking her kais with her.

The black torches flickered and he suddenly realized that had June gone in the light, the torches would have absorbed the energy of her being, just as the shield around Erling's house absorbed the energy of their röks. She would have died.

"I don't know what you think you're doing," said T'eng Sten, sinking an uppercut into Rakan's gut. "But this isn't a game."

"No, it's okay," Rakan said to Yuli who was ready to attack.

"You're a liar and a manipulator," continued T'eng Sten. "Just like your mother."

Rakan bowed his head. "There's more truth in what you say than you'll ever know." He held T'eng Sten's accusing gaze, even though it hurt to see the hatred that blazed there. "Take care of Dvara," he said and shifted to his father's, Yuli in tow.

"What in Kor's name has gotten into you?" his father yelled, greeting him with a hook to his jaw. Rakan's head flew to the side but he didn't retaliate.

"No," he yelled at Yuli as she flew forward. "It's okay. He has the right to be angry." Yuli growled but backed off. Rakan rubbed his jaw and stopped the bruise from forming. "I didn't expect that."

"It's not your fight," said Khotan, his voice wavering uncharacteristically. "They've hated each other since they day Paaliaq was born."

"What do you mean – since she was born?"

"They're sisters, Rakan. It's their fight. Not yours."

"What?" Rakan felt the floor move under him. Sisters? "Why didn't you ever tell me that before?"

"Because Yarlung didn't want to be reminded of it."

"Why do you always do what she says, she's not your Kairök," exploded Rakan.

"You know why."

Rakan sank to his favorite chair. How many lives had Yarlung managed to destroy with her poison? He looked at Yuli. "Why can't I see it in your memories?" Even though he had only seen Kariaksuq's mind briefly, he knew Yuli's wasn't as it should be.

"Because Yarlung blocked my mind from you. But when the Transformer Eld took my rök he felt it and removed it. And then he put it back. I don't know why."

Rakan growled and a wave of hatred for the Eld washed over him. "Because they thought that if I knew, I'd refuse to kill family and the fight would be cancelled." *At least it means they didn't realize that I have no intention of killing her.*

"I won't let you kill yourself," said Yuli. He could feel her anger flood the room.

Rakan's attention snapped to Yuli. He wasn't used to being heard. *"It's the right decision. And it's not up for discussion."* Outloud he said, "Can you tell me what happened, even if I can't see it?"

Yuli's face paled. She shook her head and then clutched the back of a chair to steady herself. Rakan growled in anger at the pain he felt ripping through Yuli. *"Don't. It's okay,"* he said. *"How can they let my mother do things like this to her own kai?"* He sent a wave of warmth to Yuli but she barely responded. *"To my kai,"* he corrected himself.

Yuli relaxed and responded with a wave of warmth.

Khotan sat wearily. "I'll tell you. Briefly. Kraal didn't take Yarlung's rök when he found out that she was related to Paaliaq. He wanted Paaliaq instead. But she refused him. And Yarlung never forgave her sister for being Kraal's first choice."

Rakan felt the poison oozing into Khotan's veins. "Stop. You're killing yourself. It doesn't matter anymore. The past is gone."

"No, Rakan'dzor. It's not. Let them finish what they started. It's not too late."

"No." June could kill Yarlung easily if she wanted to, but she wouldn't. She'd just let Yarlung kill her. "I can't. I need to do this. It's what's right, Father. I'm sure."

"But you don't have to." Khotan banged his fist on the table. "Too many lives have been wasted as it is."

"I know. And that's why I'll finish it."

"But you have no idea what she's like when she fights. You can't win. No single dragon can beat her. She can morph into all three forms at will."

Rakan walked over to the fireplace and then turned to face his father. "So can I."

"What?" Khotan gripped the arms of his chair. "How long have you known?"

"Since I took Kariaksuq's rök and felt my true name."

Khotan's face radiated hope and Rakan wondered if he shouldn't have said anything.

"Then maybe you do have a chance, especially now that you've finally accepted your rök," Khotan said. "Does anyone else know?"

"No. Only Dvara. And T'eng Sten now." Yuli nudged him mentally. "And Yuli."

"Good. Don't let anyone else know and keep it secret in the fight until the right moment. You'll only have one chance to surprise her. And then, when she wavers, you'll be able to rip her rök out and kill her." Khotan stood and hugged Rakan. He held him at arm's length. "You're thinking of the human."

"Anna. Her name is Anna."

Khotan smiled. "It sounds like Hana. Flower. She almost has a dragon name." Khotan gave Rakan a last hug. "Go to her. The Eld will call you when it is time." Khotan turned to Yuli. "And I'll try to undo the blocks Yarlung has embedded in your mind."

"Thank you, Father." Rakan turned to Yuli, "Is there anything you can do for his poison?"

"No. Yarlung made it so that it couldn't be undone without killing him." She looked at Khotan thoughtfully. "Although I might be able to put a shield around the active poison."

"That would already be better," Rakan said. *"Thank you."*

She sent him a wave of warmth. *"I'll block you out when you're with Anna."* He felt her fear of being alone. *"You'll have to want to reach me to feel me again,"* she said, disappearing from his mind.

Rakan hesitated. He could feel her tremble even without the mind-link.

"Don't worry," said Khotan. "I'll take care of her."

"I know," Rakan said, placing a hand on his father's shoulder. "Thank you." His father would have to take care of her much longer than he expected. But they would be happier together.

Anna sat on her bed and hugged her pillow. She stared out her window at the incongruously sunny sky. She hadn't gone to school since Rakan had left the week before. There was no way she could go to class. Not when Rakan might never come back. The only people she had seen were Red and Liv when they came to remove the trigger Liv had placed in her mind. And Anna had had to insist before Red agreed to remove T'eng Sten's shield. He would rather have left her with more protection than less. But in the end, they hadn't stayed long. They had left right after she told them about Yarlung and how she had poisoned June.

The back of her neck tingled. *Rakan.* She felt him. As soon as he appeared, she jumped up and threw herself into his arms, sending her pillow and comforter flying. He gripped her so tightly she could hardly breathe, but she didn't care. She'd stay like that forever if she could.

"I've missed you," he said, nuzzling her neck that she stretched for him to bite. She groaned in a wave of pleasure when she felt his teeth sink into her. And then his mouth was on hers, crushing her lips. Her mouth filled with his tongue and the taste of blood and she clawed into him, wanting him to explode into her, aching to feel him burn through her. She resisted as he pulled back, biting down on his lips to keep them next to hers. He smiled, pulling his lips away. "Firecat," he said. "You'll make me take you like a dragon."

"Is that so bad?" she asked, searching his eyes. Her smile faded. "What is it? What did they say?"

Rakan's hair braided itself. "We fight tomorrow."

"What do you mean, we?"

"June and I."

"What? Why?"

Rakan picked up the pillow and sat on the bed. "They wouldn't listen. And June didn't want to prove she had changed." He tossed the pillow to the head of the bed. "I asked to replace Yarlung. June won't fight back tomorrow. She's like... a shell. I've never seen anyone like that."

Anna sat next to him. "But... you won't fight her, will you?"

Rakan took Anna's hand and traced the Firemark. "You know the answer to that."

Anna nodded and leaned against his shoulder, her hair mingling with his. She screwed her eyes shut. She'd die with him.

"Anna." He placed his hand on her cheek. "I need you." His voice was husky and his hair slid over his shoulders, reaching for her. Anna turned to him, her lips finding his as the tears streamed down her cheeks, giving their kiss an edge of salt. His tongue explored the contours of her mouth, gently filling her with warmth until she could respond, her tears momentarily forgotten. He eased her onto her back and his hips angled into hers. His hand slid under her shirt as he continued to kiss her. She stiffened. He pulled back and looked at her. "You don't want this?"

"Yes. No. I... I never have... I..."

Rakan leaned on top of her, elbows on either side of her head. "Neither have I. But I want to." Their eyes locked. "I love you, Anna."

"I don't want you to... to..." She couldn't say it. It was too awful.

Rakan cradled her face. "Neither do I. But I don't think there'll be any other way."

"Why not? Why does it have to be you?"

"Because if I die there's only me. I'll give my kai to my father."

"What?"

"The Draak who's linked to me."

Anna pushed Rakan up. "I know what a kai is. I just didn't know you had one. Can he feel everything you feel?"

"She. Her name is Yuli. Yes."

Anna scrambled out from under Rakan. "You're connected to a female? Since when?"

"Since a few hours ago."

"And where is she?" Anna looked around, remembering Kariaksuq's shadow figure.

"At my father's. She's my second for the fight."

Anna sank back down on her bed. "Can she feel when we…"

"No," he said, running his hands through her slightly damp hair.

His hand touched the spot on her neck where he had marked her and she felt the flame-shaped scar come alive. An inarticulate moan escaped from her throat, and she bent her head to the side. "Why don't they look the same?" she asked, seeing the round mark she had left on him. It wasn't nearly as pretty as the one he had given her.

Rakan smiled. "Because we're not the same. Mine is a flame. And yours is a flower."

"But why a flower?" It seemed so plain and worthless compared to his fire.

"Because it makes life worth living." Rakan paused. "Your name sounds like the word for flower in Draagsil. And it suits you. You smell like wild chrysanthemums. Like these." His hands filled with dozens of small blue flowers. He lifted them up and smelled them. He sprinkled them on the bed and pulled her up to standing. "I wanted to make a bed for you out of them." He held her close. "And I wanted to make love with you for our first time on them." Rakan's arms tightened around her. "You'll be the last thing I let go of when I die."

Anna shook in his arms. "I don't want you to die."

"We'll all die one day."

"But why do you have to die tomorrow?"

"If I could change the world, I would. But I can't. All I can do is to try to do what's right."

"Why can't we hide?"

"We've been through this." Rakan dropped his arms and walked over to her shelves. He picked up the sketch he had made and passed his hand over it. "At least that way it looks like me," he said, putting it back.

Anna peered around him. Where the simple sketch had been was a nearly photo perfect drawing of a coral-colored dragon hurling flames of fire in the sky as the sun rose. And in the lower corner was a sketch of Rakan's human face, hair pulled back in a braid. "Can't you make it with your hair down?" she asked, running her hand through his hair.

"No. You're the only one who's ever seen me with it down. And you're the only one who ever will. I'll never be intimate with anyone else."

Anna choked on a sob and buried her face in his hair. "You can't die."

"I'll tell Yuli to come see you." He took another piece of paper and drew a lime-green dragon with coral claws. He paused and changed them to burgundy. "I'll give her rök to my father. They both know about you." He sketched her human form.

Anna picked up the drawing and touched it. Yuli looked about her mother's age. "She looks like you could feel safe with her."

"She's a shielder – you can see it by her golden crest. Just like June."

"And what are you?" asked Anna, looking at the drawing of his copper crest.

"A trailer. Dvara's is black – she's a triggerer. They explode things."

"You don't?"

"Of course I do. But I'm better at seeing trails and tracking."

"If I were a dragon I'd want to have a golden crest. And then I'd save you both tomorrow." Anna sank into his arms. "But I'm not." Her hands explored his naked chest and ran over his shoulders. "Can you make a bed of blue flowers?"

"Are you sure?" he asked. His coral-colored eyes flashed in the early evening sun.

"Yes," she said, reaching for his lips. "I am."

Chapter 30

Dragon Fire

Rakan let his hands slide down Anna's sides, gently transforming her oversized tee-shirt and shorts into a pale blue dress that crossed over her breasts and flowed out like gauze to the floor. He placed a hand on her lower back and groaned in pleasure as she pressed against him. "Anna," he said, smelling her neck. He slid his hand even lower. "My Anna."

Rakan felt her body temperature rise in answer to his own. She ran her hands up his chest and over his shoulders. Her breathing grew shallower and she fell into him, her hands sliding into his hair. She tilted her head and he caught her lips that were cool from having been open. The unexpected change in temperature sent a flash of desire searing through his body and he wondered if he'd be able to take her gently enough not to hurt her.

Rakan slowly untied the knot of material at her lower back that gave shape to the translucent sheath that glittered with flecks of gold underneath. He stepped back to watch as the cloth uncrossed from over her hips to her back and then her breasts. He gently eased the blue strands over her shoulders so that it hung like a train, leaving her breasts free under the thin layer of shimmering gauze.

Anna looked down. "When did you change my clothes?" she asked. Her hands flew to her chest in a gesture of surprised innocence that excited Rakan even more. "And all the flowers." She scooped a handful and let them flutter from above in a gentle rain of blue chrysanthemums. Rakan kissed her cheek and followed her jawline down, lingering on her neck before running his teeth on her shoulder. She arched into him. "Don't stop."

He rubbed his face against her neck and inhaled deeply as she ran her hands through his hair. She sank to the ground and pulled him with her, her hair billowing out over the flowers. "You're so beautiful," he said. His eyes traced the lines of her lips, the gentle curve of her neck, the exotically pale hair that he'd never tire of seeing as it rippled through his fingers. She ran her hands up his arms and he shuddered in pleasure. He leaned forward slowly, feeling every inch of his chest make contact with hers as his lips approached her mouth, their eyes never leaving each other's as he bore down on her. Her lips parted, moist and beckoning and he answered their call with soft, gentle strokes. He closed his eyes and followed the outline of her lips with his tongue until he felt her twitching with the same wild desire as his own. "Meld with me," he said, kissing her. She answered, opening herself up to him and they melded, their bodies responding as one in an ever rising inferno.

"You're free," he said. His surprised pleasure at being able to meld so deeply overflowed into her. He kissed her more deeply, aching with her to feel their bodies even closer. His hand slid down her side and over her hip. Her body was ready for a child.

He stopped. He hadn't considered that possibility.

"What?" She pulled him back down, her lips calling him closer.

"No," he said, gently sliding off of her. He ran a hand over her stomach. His mind-touch went deeper and confirmed what he had sensed. She was in the middle of her cycle. "You'd get pregnant."

He felt an unexpected joy wash over her and it confused him.

"I'll keep the baby," she said. "I'll still have a part of you."

"You can't have a baby like that by yourself."

"Why not?"

"Because… what if it's like me? Then what'll you do?"

Anna propped herself up on one arm. "You don't think I can take care of your baby without you?"

"No. That's not what I meant. It's just that having a baby isn't something you should do alone." Especially not if it was part Draak.

Anna turned her back to him.

"I'm sorry, Anna." He reached over to touch her, but she pulled away. Her pain wrenched through him. "I love you," he said quietly.

"No, you don't. Or you'd let me have a baby to hold on to."

"A baby won't replace me."

Anna didn't answer. Instead, she threw herself into his arms.

Rakan smoothed her hair. "I can't do something I know I wouldn't do if I were to live. We aren't ready to have a baby yet. We'd do that later. Not now." He cradled her in his arms, trying to calm her choking sobs. "I need to be able to free my rök tomorrow," he said quietly. "June won't know how and I don't want to suffer the pain that Yttresken's kais had if I don't free my rök myself. And I'll only be able to do that if I can face myself. If I leave you with a child when you're not ready for it, I won't be able to."

"I don't want you to die."

He held her close and rocked her back and forth, crushing the flowers underneath them until she had cried herself to sleep. He lay next to her until the sky turned the various shades of green that marked the setting sun of late May, stroking her hair and telling her a thousand times how much he loved her.

He felt the Eld gathering nearby. He lifted Anna to her bed, being careful not to wake her. He kissed her softly and inhaled one last time. He took some of the flowers and put them on the shelf in front of the drawing. The others he compacted into a small statue of a pale blue air dragon with a golden crest and placed it next to her bed.

"I'll always love you," he said and shifted to meet the Eld.

"Indeed," said the Trailer Eld, her cape flashing its oxidized green and copper lining. They were in a silvery black in-between that had no horizon and no mountains. It continued on as far as the eye could see. *"Most interesting that you have been able to join us here."*

"Where are we?" asked Rakan, surprised to feel himself morphing smoothly in and out of his three dragon forms. The place had a profound calmness to it, as if they were at the center of the world.

"We are in Kor," said the Trailer Eld, morphing into a magnificent oxidized copper air dragon. *"You have promise. As your unwillingness to father a child with the human shows."*

"That's private."

"Private is a matter of debate when your actions could have an incidence for the survival of both the Draak and human races." The Trailer Eld rose

on her hind legs and spread her wings, blinding Rakan with her polished copper underbelly. *"As will the outcome of the duel today."*

"All that is affected are our own lives." And those of June's kais.

"No. That is were you are wrong." The Trailer Eld launched herself into the warm blackness that was both horizon and ground. *"I will show you the Rift."*

Rakan threw himself into the air, sure that no matter what his form he would be able to navigate through Kor. But nothing prepared him for what he saw when he looked down. There was a blinding streak of white nothingness that pulled at his rök like a black hole that had been stretched and deformed until it appeared straight. His bones ached with a cold he had never felt before. The Rift was a void. And there was nothing. Absolutely nothing.

The Trailer Eld caught him with her wings as he plummeted toward the Rift, petrified by the nothingness that was a hundred times worse than death. *"The Rift was first opened by Paaliaq. We managed to close it, but the one you call June has re-opened it."*

"But how could she?"

"By crossing boundaries that should not be crossed. As you said yourself, she has learned to go in the light. And every time she does, the Rift widens, ripping the röks of her kais. It is their pain you feel reflected in her trail."

Rakan sank his claws into the Trailer Eld. *"Show her the Rift."* She had to be stopped from making it worse.

"We have," said the Trailer Eld. She motioned towards the edge of the Rift where Rakan could just barely make out June's human figure.

"Why is she in her human form?" She should have been in her true form as a dragon.

"Because Jing Mei doesn't exist separately from the other parts of Paaliaq. And until she accepts that she is a fragment, she will appear as June." The Trailer Eld moved forward, gliding over the smooth black surface until they were so close to the edge of the Rift that Rakan wasn't sure he would survive the pain of emptiness that sucked at the fiber of his being. *"The Rift will cease with Paaliaq's death,"* said the Trailer Eld. *"And for Paaliaq to finish dying, June must die."* The Trailer Eld stopped a few yards away from June. *"She understands this."*

"*No,*" Rakan said. "*She just has to stop becoming an Elythia and accept being a Draak.*"

"*She has chosen death over being a Draak.*" The Trailer Eld motioned towards June. "*Ask her yourself.*" The Eld disappeared. Rakan stood, unable to go any closer to the Rift. White tentacles of cold nothingness reached up and leached the energy from the pure black ground of Kor that radiated life. A tentacle slithered across June's knees, turning them the color of ash, but she didn't react. Rakan lunged and yanked her away from the Rift.

June hissed and threw him back. "Leave me alone."

"*You can't let yourself die or all the others will die too.*"

"What others? There aren't any others." June looked around. "Who else do you see? There's only me." She sank to the ground. "Let me die and everything will be over."

"*No,*" Rakan said. "*All you have to do is accept who you are.*"

"Everyone thinks I'm someone I'm not." June stood. "Look at me. I'm human. I'm not even a dragon. How can I be Paaliaq?"

"*You have a rök.*"

"Not when I'm in the light." June motioned towards the Rift. "Can't you feel how pure, how beautiful, it is?" She dropped her arms. "But none of that matters anymore. Erling only loves me because I remind him of Paaliaq." Her voice wavered. "Someone I don't think I'd even like." She looked down at the blinding emptiness that wormed its way up her legs. "I could pretend I was her and be with Erling. No one would stop me. But it would be a lie. Everything would be a lie. I have no reason to live anymore." She turned to face Rakan. "But you do. You have Anna, and you love each other for who you are. And that's worth living for." She spread her arms and breathed in deeply. "I have nothing," she said and let herself drop into the void.

"*No,*" yelled Rakan, "*I won't let you kill them all.*" He flew after her and whacked her as hard as he could with his tail, sending her spinning back up out of the void in a blood-curdling yell. A dull thud confirmed that she had landed on the edge of the rift as he himself plummeted, his claws outstretched in petrified terror.

৪৩৫৪

Anna's eyes flew open. She was in her bed. Alone. "Rakan," she yelled. He was about to die. She threw off her comforter and jumped up to run... where? To Lysa. Anna flew down the stairs, flipped her phone open and called Lysa while she struggled to tie her dress and get her boots on. There was no answer. Anna cursed and threw the phone down.

"Anna," said a golden voice. A hand touched her shoulder.

Anna screamed and then threw herself into Lysa's arms. "You're here," she said, nearly hysterical with fear for Rakan. She held onto Lysa's shoulders. "Where are they?"

"I'm not quite sure," said Lysa, her eyes bloodshot. "Erling went ballistic. But I think I found his trail even though Verje was blocking me."

"Where are they?" Anna's nails dug into Lysa. "I need to find Rakan."

"Things don't feel right. I might not be able to bring you home."

"I don't care. I need to know what's happening to Rakan."

The light around Lysa shimmered a pale, peaceful green. She put her hands on Anna's shoulders. "I shouldn't do this," she said with a mischievous smile. "But it won't be the first time we've ignored the rules. Ready?"

Anna didn't even have time to say yes before she felt herself being ripped apart and then reassembled again in a pain so deep she didn't know where to begin to hurt. She clung to Lysa, suffocating in the heat that made her feel like they were in an oven. Lysa gripped Anna's shoulders and whispered, "No. This is wrong. All wrong."

Anna looked up and saw Erling struggling like a wild animal to get beyond the twins. She turned to see where he was trying to go and saw a glass-like dome in the desert. And inside, there were two battling dragons. One emerald green with a golden crest. And one coral orange with a copper crest. June and Rakan.

Anna lunged and ran down the sandy dune. She hit an invisible shield. She pounded on it as she watched in horror. "No!" Around the dome were hundreds of black-haired people in various forms of armor, all watching in tense silence as the dragons tried to kill at each other. "Stop them," she yelled.

"They can't hear you," said Lysa.

"Why are they fighting?" she wailed.

"I don't know."

"I won't let you kill yourself," snarled June. She slammed Rakan to the sand they had smashed into when the Eld had intercepted their fall in the Rift after June had morphed and followed him in an attempt to save his life.

"You need to live," answered Rakan in Draagsil, the very sound of which seemed to stoke June's anger. She finally lost the last of her self-control. Her rök exploded and she no longer felt like June. She felt like Paaliaq, the Destroyer. She snarled and attacked him with intent to kill. Rakan stopped fighting and stretched his throat. The green dragon lunged and sank her teeth into him. If she wouldn't let him kill himself when she was June, he'd let her kill him as Paaliaq.

She bit through his hide, but as soon as her poison began to ejaculate, she stopped. She lifted her head, his blood dribbling from her mouth. Slowly, she took in the scene around them. And then she roared in rage. Her head swiveled to face the Eld who sat on their thrones, watching the fight with unblinking eyes. A brilliant white flame burst from her jaws and her hide shimmered gold. For that brief moment, she looked like a Shield Eld. A ripple of anger and fear rose from the crowd. June morphed back to human, dressed in a flowing gold gown, her black hair billowing out like snakes ready to strike. She stretched her hands and white light crackled forth. She was creating a shield like the Elythia had around their home. The Draak stumbled back in chaos, a few unlucky ones crackling as their energy was sucked from their bodies. June thrust her hand out and a white tentacle flew forward. The tentacle split into five and latched onto the throats of the unresisting Elds.

Rakan morphed back to human and tackled June, breaking her concentration.

"Stop it," she snarled. "They're the ones who are making us fight. But they're the ones who need to die." June flung him to the side and resumed her attack on the Eld, channeling their energy back against them.

The Shield Eld deviated the attack from the other four Eld to herself, protecting them as her own energy waned. Rakan tackled June again. Her shield faltered as she flung him across the ring, freeing those who had been caught. Khotan suddenly appeared out of nowhere, his burgundy wings tucked in close as he dove for the kill.

"No!" Rakan yelled, struggling back to his feet.

June spun around but it was too late. Rakan's gut wrenched as his father exploded his rök in a suicide attack. A brilliant purple light blinded Rakan. It was the color of the twins. "June," he yelled. He staggered through the sand in the silence that ensued the explosion. She was alive, he could feel her. He fell to the ground next to where she lay sprawled under a motionless Verje.

Anna clawed at the burning sand. She gagged on the acrid smell of burnt dragon that made her eyes water. She couldn't see anything with all the sand that was still suspended in the air. "Rakan," she yelled. Someone grabbed her arm and everything disappeared. She was in the tundra to the east of Tromso, her nose and throat still burning. "No," she howled, ripping herself free from Red. "Where's Rakan?" She glared at Red, she hadn't even realized he had been there. "Why did you bring me here? Take me back there."

"Calm down," said Red. "He'll come."

"What if he doesn't?" she demanded.

But Red didn't answer. He lunged forward and caught Ea as she shifted into being, falling over in pain. As Anna helped him lay Ea on the ground, June appeared supporting a staggering Verje. Erling and Lysa arrived next, in a flash of blue and pale green light. Their wings angled for flight. She felt a dragon approaching and her heart raced. Liv appeared, alone. Her energy crackled with electricity.

"Where's Haakon?" asked Anna with a sinking heart. *And Rakan?*

Liv folded back her electric blue wings. "He's trying to bring Rakan." Her voice was disapproving.

Anna's eyes narrowed. She still didn't know what Liv really thought about Rakan. Or anything else. Liv stood still, in a half-trance, and Anna examined her. Her gown was pure white. Her wings were the same color as her eyes and her long hair spilled over her shoulders. She looked like an angel. But something underneath was hard and cold. Emotionless. If Liv thought the world would be better off without Rakan, Anna wasn't sure she wouldn't eliminate him. For the good of everyone else.

The back of Anna's neck began to throb. They were close. They had to be. Finally, Haakon and another dragon who Anna immediately recognized as Yuli, appeared, holding a struggling Rakan between them.

"Rakan." She rushed over to him. "Are you alright?"

"Anna," he said. "How'd you get here?" He shrugged off the two other dragons. "You can let go now." Yuli backed off right away, but Haakon hesitated.

"He's dead," said Haakon. "You can't help him. And going back there will only get you killed."

"I know that," snarled Rakan. He pushed Haakon away. "Leave me alone." Rakan crushed Anna against his sand-covered chest. The pain that pulsed around him like fire overwhelmed her. His mind touched hers and she saw flashes of the burgundy dragon in both human and dragon forms. And then she understood. It was his father. Pain engulfed her. She clutched Rakan. He grabbed her head with both hands and kissed her brutally. Anna tried to pull away but his hold was too strong. For a split second, she felt another dragon in Rakan's consciousness. He snarled and it disappeared. He eased his hold on her. "I'm sorry," he said hoarsely, his body still as tense as a coiled snake. "Yuli was right, I was hurting you. And you're cold." A pale blue cloak appeared out of nowhere, covering her. "Although I prefer the dress by itself," he added in her ear.

Anna slumped against him, feeling his warmth that she thought she'd never feel again. "Why did you fight?"

"Because neither of us would let the other die. But it would've been better if we had."

"No. Don't say that. Don't ever say that..." her voice trailed off as Rakan's pain resurfaced.

"My father killed Sverd," Rakan said, his voice barely audible. "He unintentionally killed an Elythia because Verje shielded June. And Sverd took the attack to protect his Pair. And died. The truce is broken. The Draak and the Elythia will fight again."

Anna glanced at Ea. She was still unconscious in Red's arms. "Did an Elythia attack her?"

"Yes. She was protecting Erling, but I guess not all the Elythia realized it."

Red snorted. "It's more likely she was attacked by an Elythia who did. And wanted to kill her because of it. Very few of them are happy that their future ruler chose a Draak to pair with."

"Red's right," said Haakon. "When Paaliaq and Erling tried to unite the two groups before, it didn't work. Most would rather exterminate the other group." He took Liv's hands in his. "And now that you're no longer banished, they'll try to kill you for having refused to pair with Erling."

The clear sky of late May made the tundra look like a pastel postcard. But all Anna could smell was death.

June looked up at Rakan, still cradling Verje's head in her lap. His purple eyes were wild with pain. "The Eld wanted us to fight. But I didn't realize that when they showed me the Rift. But they were wrong," she said, her voice harsh. "The Rift isn't destroying the world. It's uniting it. It's bringing the Draak and the Elythia together."

"From their point of view," said Liv, her voice flat and clinical, "it is destroying their world. They want to keep the Draak and the Elythia apart. As do the Ascended."

Erling's cobalt blue wings stretched menacingly. "If June and I finish opening the seven gates and become the Ascended, we can stop this war."

June shook her head. "It doesn't matter what the Ascended want. The Eld will still make the Draak fight and the Elythia won't have any choice but to defend themselves."

"You can't become an Ascended until you free the röks that are linked to yours," Rakan said. "As it is, they suffer every time you go in the light."

"But I don't even know who they are," June said, panic creeping into her voice. "Or why they're linked to me."

"But are you Paaliaq or not?" asked Anna confused.

"I don't know," answered June, meeting Anna's eyes. "But I'm no longer sure it matters. If I can do something to stop their suffering and end this fight, I will."

Verje struggled to his feet. "It's the only reason I didn't follow my Pair in his death. I will finish the work we were meant to do. I will bring Erling to the throne of the Ascended. And only then will I allow myself to go beyond and join Sverd."

"But I don't know what to do," June said. She looked so fragile and unsure sitting on the tundra, her head tilted down, her hands in her lap. It was hard to imagine she was the same person who had faced the Eld and tried to kill them.

Erling knelt in front of June and placed his hands on her shoulders. "Access Paaliaq's memories. And maybe you'll see how to free her kais." Erling stood and pulled June into his arms. "We can't let Earth be torn apart like the Red Planet. And I can't lose you again."

Anna clutched Rakan as a wave of pain rippled out from Erling and June.

"But I don't know how to access her memories," June said. Her voice wavered. "What if I can't?"

Haakon snorted. "What makes you think you'd be doing it alone?"

June looked at Haakon and Anna could feel the mental connection that flared between the two.

"I know where the memories are," said Lysa, her eyes only half-focused on their mixed group.

The sudden silence of an Elythian shield slipped over Anna and she looked at Liv whose eyes were brilliant orbs of light. It was her shield.

"Why didn't you say so before?" Liv's voice echoed in the shield. "We've wasted too much time as it is. Your duty would have been to help us." Liv's crystal calm voice felt like a cold knife slicing through her flesh. Anna tightened her grip on Rakan.

Lysa answered, apparently unconcerned by Liv's disapproval. "Because I didn't know to look for it." She smiled shyly. "I think that's my skill. I can't see in the past or in the future like the Ascended. I see what needs to be found. No matter where or when it is."

"Where are they?" asked Anna. She dreaded the answer. Wherever it was, her gut knew it was far away.

"On a Fragment. Where part of Paaliaq is... frozen." Lysa paused, her eyes unfocused. "Interesting. It's as if she's neither dead nor alive. Maybe that's why no one ever found it."

"Then we'll start by going there," said Erling, standing up. He offered June his hand as if they were about to open a ball. "Will you do this with me, June?"

June put her hand on his. "Yes." She looked at Rakan. "Will you join us?"

Rakan looked around the ring of Elythia and Draak that surrounded them. Liv and Haakon, June and Erling, Red and Ea, Verje, Lysa and Yuli. They weren't numerous enough to stop the war. Even if Erling and June became the next Ascended, there would still be the problem of the Draak, urged on by the Eld. But maybe if they could free Paaliaq's kais they could find a way to protect Earth. And Anna. He held her as tightly as he dared.

"Yes," Rakan said. "I will join you. And no matter what happens, we need to find a way to protect Earth." His rök resonated in his chest. It was the right thing to do. He no longer belonged to the Draak. "How long will it take to unblock the memories?"

June leaned against Erling. "I don't know. I think it depends on how much pain I can take."

Haakon cleared his throat. "How much *we* can take." He looked at the group. "We'll all have to do this with her. It's too dangerous on her own."

Anna felt a shiver run down her spine. She had felt what Haakon hadn't said: June was willing to try to see the memories, but what she needed to do was accept them. As hers. And Haakon believed she was in denial of her true self. Anna looked back at June. She didn't feel in denial to her. And the glimpse of the green dragon they called Paaliaq didn't feel like June.

"Can I come with you?" she asked. June was going to need a friend who had no stakes in her identity. Haakon and Ea wanted to find their Kairök. Erling his Pair. She caught Lysa's eye. Maybe Lysa could help.

"No," Rakan said. "The atmosphere on the Fragments isn't suited for the human form. That's why the Draak haven't been able to breed there. We can only stay human for a few days before we have to morph back to our dragon forms." He pressed his lips against hers. "But I'll come back." He couldn't live without her. She was his mate. And would always be.

June turned to Erling. "I need to take care of a few things first. I can't just leave my host family without letting them know I'm going."

"I can protect you," said Verje. "Our shields are still in place. But you don't have much time. Fritjof's supporters are probably already planning an attack on the Draak."

Erling turned to the rest of the group. "We'll join you on the Fragment as soon as we can. But you should go and shield it now." He turned to Haakon and Liv. "You know what to do."

Haakon nodded and Liv bowed to Erling. Blue and green light flared, laced with purple, and Erling, June and Verje were gone.

Haakon turned to Red. "Ea needs to be cared for," he said. "You should stay with her."

"I wouldn't have come anyway," said Red. "Earth is my home. I belong here."

Haakon bowed. "I know." He turned to Rakan. "We should go."

"Yuli will go with you. I'll join you once I've said goodbye."

Haakon looked around the tundra. "The shield won't last very long without me. And yours won't stand up to the skill of the Old Dragons. You'll both be easy prey."

"I know," Rakan said. Normally, the shield would disappear with Haakon, but he was stretching it so that they could say goodbye. Rakan bowed. "Thank you, Haakaramanoth."

Haakon shifted and Yuli followed. *"Be careful,"* she said. *"Even a High Master can't keep the shield for very long from that far away."*

"Stop worrying," Rakan said. *"I won't risk anyone's life."*

"Not on purpose, no. But—"

Rakan shut her out for the moment. He wanted Anna for life. Not just a few more minutes. He wouldn't take any risks. With her life or with Yuli's.

Red stood, Ea's unconscious form in his arms. "Ea needs more help than I can give her here," he said. "I'll feel the shield go down, and I'll protect Anna when it does." He turned to Anna. "I'll put a trigger in the shield so that you can call me when you want me to come get you."

Rakan growled. "I'll kill you if anything happens to her."

Red smiled. "And I'll kill you if you don't come back." He nodded briefly and disappeared with Ea in his arms.

"I'd rather come with you," Anna said.

He stroked her cheek. "Your place is on Earth."

"My place is with you."

"Once this is over, our place will be here, together." Rakan felt Yuli rematerialize on the Fragment. "The shield will fade soon."

Anna's arms jerked around Rakan. He brushed her hair back and kissed her gently. But she responded with a savage passion that ignited his own. His rök throbbed in pleasure and he ran his lips down her neck until he felt his mark warm under his teeth. A guttural groan escaped from her throat as she arched her neck for him to bite her. But it wasn't enough. He needed to take her, to possess every inch of her supple body that molded into his. He gripped her hips and pressed into her. "Will you accept my fire?" he asked, his lips moving against hers.

Anna nodded and he felt her mind slip forward and meld with his. His rök expanded and shimmered. He arched back. His fire gathered within until it could be contained no longer. It exploded out, enveloping them both in his coral-colored blaze. Rakan kissed her as the fire flared around them. He felt a twinge as the shield began to waver. Reluctantly, he pulled back. He reached out and caught a flame, cupping it in his hand. "This is my fire," he said. He passed his other hand over it, encapsulating the flame in a Maii-a shaped crystal drop. He attached it to her gold chain. "I'll be able to feel you through it."

Anna wrapped her hand around the little coral flame that danced within the crystal. "I can feel you," she said, closing her eyes. The flame was the same color as his Maii-a, the color of his eyes. The color of her stone. "It is you."

"As long as the flame is alive, you'll know that I live." Rakan leaned forward and kissed her as the shield disappeared. "And as long as I'm alive, I'll always love you."

Rakan dissolved in her arms and she grabbed at the air, but there was nothing there. She sank to her knees and held the flame that was all she had left of Rakan.

"I love you," she said. Her words dissipated across the sea of open tundra that stretched to the horizon. The flame pulsed in her hand and she held it to her heart. *Come back to me.*

She sat like that until the evening grew cold, watching the tundra that had seemed lifeless until she had felt it through Rakan. She stood and called Red in her mind. She'd make him teach her how to manipulate matter and how to fight. If there was going to be a war, she wasn't going to stand still and do nothing. She'd find a way to help. It was her world too.

THE END

About the author

Born in the US, Dina von Lowenkraft has lived on four continents, worked as a graphic artist for television and as a consultant in the fashion industry. Somewhere between New York and Paris she picked up an MBA and a black belt. Dina is currently the Regional Advisor for SCBWI Belgium, where she lives with her husband, two children and three horses.

Dina loves to create intricate worlds filled with conflict and passion. She builds her own myths while exploring issues of belonging, racism and the search for truth... after all, how can you find true love if you don't know who you are and what you believe in? Dina's key to developing characters is to figure out what they would be willing to die for. And then pushing them to that limit.

If you enjoyed this book, please post a review
at your favorite online bookstore.

Twilight Times Books
P O Box 3340
Kingsport, TN 37664
Phone/Fax: 423-323-0183
www.twilighttimesbooks.com/